Dedicated:
To my wife Kristin, who encouraged me in all things.
To my son Harrison, who has now decided that I should sleep, but I need to wake up early and play.
To my family, who always told me I could write a book if I sat down and tried.
To my friend Nick, who has too much patience with my insanity.

Special Thanks:
Niusha Gutierrez
Justin Johanson
Steven LoBue
Peter Morena
Jeff Hays
Tamara Blain

Thanks to my Beta Readers:

Adam Wagner
Caleb Shortcliffe
Darin Foster
Dominic Harney
James Gammill
Kegan Hall
Kirk Mahony
Kona Amps
Marquis Stafford
Osman Chughtai
Perry Kern
Reyer Withrow
Travis Brister

D1564563

OTHERLIFE

AWAKENINGS

~The Selfless Hero trilogy~

By William D. Arand

Prologue - The Story So Far -

Runner and his companions managed a nearly impossible task. They brought peace to Tirtius.

Having left Crivel they were caught immediately and dragged to the court of king Vasilios. Where in a matter of days Runner brought the full court into an Awakened state.

In opening the kings eyes to the threats that surrounded him he brokered a deal to send an army to assist the Barbarian kingdom.

After he'd made a deal with the goddess Brunhild to support him.

Leading that force westward he fashioned them together into a fighting force unseen by the lands of Otherlife. Blending bits of modern technology and tactics with game mechanics.

Runner managed to recruit a second divine into his alliance, the goddess of death, Ernsta. Though he failed in recruiting Rike to become the third divine, creating a godlike enemy in her.

Arriving in the Barbarian lands Runner found he would have to save the kingdom from itself as well as its enemies.

When there seemed to be little hope other than fighting their way out, the queen realized her kingdom didn't need a poor excuse for a king and freed herself. She then turned her people over to assist Runner in his defense of their nation.

Utilizing new weapons Runner changed the way wars would be fought and subdued the enemy general without killing her.

Completing this task Runner now had only one last goal. Conquering the human kingdom and putting the island back to a normal state.

Unfortunately a significant portion of the crew had risen up in open revolt. They surrounded Runner in a pitched battle, forcing him to act against them directly.

Runner sent them all to the medical server, forcefully logging them off and possibly killing every single one of them. In doing so he irrevocably cast his lot in with the server and it's artificial beings.

Having conquered both the army and the crew, Runner infiltrated the human capital.

Jacob wasn't caught of guard and managed to capture Nadine, creating a trap that Runner had no choice but to trigger.

Ultimately, Nadine gave her life to preserve Runner's, arguing that he was more valuable alive than she would be.

Runner and company have retreated back to the North Wood fort. There, they've begun settling in to make it a home that they could defend.

Chapter 1 - Reunion -

Runner smiled at Srit and gestured to the gates before them as they approached the rapidly growing city.

"North Wood Fort. Our home. Though it's quickly losing the word 'fort' and simply transitioning to North Wood. We've been busy trying to get the place in shape. Was a total wreck," Runner admitted, running a hand through his hair.

"I see. Curious that it's named after you and yet not," Srit replied, her eyes sweeping along the stone wall that ran from one length of the city to the other. She reached up and tucked a strand of blonde hair behind an ear.

"Oh, Norwood, North Wood. Yeah. Coincidence only, promise. I should probably rename the damn thing to something less… coincidental. Even if I feel like I'm holding up the sky, it'd be better if it were named something else."

"The sky? Ah, Atlas. The eternal struggle."

"Yeah. Anyways. Maybe when we finish the new keep we can change the name. The wall is at least done already, providing us a level of defense I craved. Needed even. Or so the voices tell me," Runner said with a shrug. "The keep will take quite a bit longer since we're doing it from scratch. I felt a little naked without a city wall, though, so it came first. Paranoia and all. Or ya know, the voices. Could be that."

"Yes, I can see how your personality would dictate defensive structures taking priority. A new keep. I didn't realize you had decided the old one was unfit." Srit nodded her head as well. They walked along the path towards the gate in silence for a few seconds before she continued. "Is this what you meant by restarting the conversation? Acting as if we hadn't talked about childbearing?"

"Err, yes. Somewhat like that. We'll get back to our previous conversation later. I just need to make sure I explain my point accurately," Runner hurriedly said.

He had brought up the topic of pregnancy as well as server patches when she had first arrived.

Apparently she had taken that as a proposition to proceed straight to impregnating her.

"I thought it made sense. Though I do think the server patches will need to take precedence. There are some sections of memory that are starting to degrade. I've already begun working on it."

"Oh? Sunshine, are you at full capacity again? Not relegated to either being in game or not anymore?" Runner asked. This was news. He knew that she'd gone the Doomsday route and taken control of every computer, database, and network that she had access to. It would stand to reason her capabilities had increased substantially as well.

"Yes. I'm able to function here, in the systems, and on your ship's system at the same time. I've used the passwords you provided me previously to set myself as your second-in-command on the ship and system administration peer."

"Sounds like we're married."

Srit gave him a broad smile, her green eyes catching his own.

Unbidden to him, the green-eyed visage of Nadine floated up in his mind's eye. A memory came to him immediately. He had said something similar once to her.

"Are you sure we're not married? You spent my coin like it was yours."

"If we were, I'd have spent what's in-n-n your pocket t-t-too."

His mind recoiled at the memory, and he nearly tripped over himself. The loss of Nadine left him raw at moments. He wasn't over it. Probably wouldn't ever be over it.

Get a grip, Runner. She'd tell you to run on. So run on. Run the fuck on.

"It would seem my smile has an effect on you akin to Thana's."

"Obviously," Runner replied immediately. "We talked about this, and you told me to be quiet, remember? You've got big… brains."

Srit huffed at that and let her eyes slide back to the gate.

"At times you're as infantile as some of the male leads in the books you sent me. You don't tend to stare at least."

"To be fair, it's kinda hard not to. You seriously pushed the slider maybe a little too far on character creation. Physics be damned."

"I have my reasons. Give me an update here," she said, gesturing at the gate that stood less than fifty feet from them now. "I can ascertain much from the code but I would prefer to hear it. It's… different."

"Ah. Let's see. As I said, the keep is our priority since the wall is long since done. Then it's a matter of setting up all the needs of a city-state type of demesne. I don't even have a barracks yet. Everyone sleeps wherever they can. No one has complained, but I can't imagine that'll last long. Especially if the weather changes."

Runner stopped talking as they approached the city guards standing watch at the gate. Both Barbarians came to attention and saluted him, fist to chest.

"This is Srit, she's to be treated as the equal to Thana or anyone else. Please amend the security protocol accordingly."

"Understood, Lord Norwood!" they said in unison.

"Sir, what shall I mark as the relation and status?" the one on the left asked.

"The same as I," called a voice from inside the gate. Thana flashed her predatory smile as she stepped into view.

"Yes, m'lady," the guard replied.

"Carry on," Runner commanded, nodding to the guards. Stepping past them, he smiled at Thana.

"Couldn't wait to see her, Lady Death?" Runner's eyes crinkled up as he smirked at her. She seemed to always know where everyone was at nearly every time. Maybe his chancellor even had her own intelligence gathering service.

"Of course not. She's as dear as a sister to me. She tells me all the secrets I want to know, and the ones I don't. Which makes her perfect." Thana said the words while wrapping Srit up in a hug.

"No change. Chances are increasing," Srit said to Thana with a serious expression.

"Good. Now, let's go eat. Everyone else is already assembled." Thana wrapped her arm in Srit's and began guiding her directly towards the keep.

Runner smirked and fell in behind them. They walked along half-finished streets and housing foundations. All around him, people, his people, went about their work.

The vast majority of his people were there to improve and build upon the city or start a new life. The rest seemed made up of religious pilgrims who wanted to live in the place the Triumvirate would be based out of.

As if in sync with his thoughts, the temple popped into view.

It was a massive structure, second only to the eventual new keep. Situated in a central defensible location, it was actually built atop the remains of the original keep. Utilizing it in such a way had greatly increased the construction speed of the temple.

After breakfast he had plans to check in on the ongoing building everywhere. Perhaps check in on Alexia as well. He had promised her, after all. The guilt from making her go temporarily insane did weigh on him.

Perhaps he might even make an actual prayer to the Triumvirate.

Maybe. Minxy might show up.

Amelia, the goddess of assassins and thieves, popped into his head, full of mocking sexuality and her desire to be dominated by him.

Focusing back on the present as quick as he could, he fastened his eyes to the women in front of him as they chatted quietly.

"Eyes up, shit for brains. I know you're already fucking the one, but I didn't realize you'd started in on the other," Hannah hissed at him, her elbow digging into his side.

Folding over her arm at the sudden strike, Runner grunted softly. Entwining his arm into hers, he pulled her close to his side so she couldn't escape.

"Hanners. Always a delight. I'll be your escort to breakfast. You can sit next to me during the meal. We'll spend some time together. Maybe I'll tie you to your chair and feed you personally while everyone else watches."

As she wrinkled her nose at him, her cheeks colored a faint red. Giving a single jerk of her arm to see if she could free herself, she then matched his pace.

"You'd like that. Dirty fucker. Do you plan on wedding and bedding everyone then?"

"Huh. When you put it like that. Two down, one to go." Runner grinned. He'd lost his shame about the situation when Nadine died. Shame only served the cause of fear.

"Oh? Did you drag the tree rat into a bush and make her squeal while you were out and about? Or maybe our dear artificial intelligence after all?"

"Ha-ha, no. Though I guess you could say Belle is definitely trying to put herself on the list. As for Sunshine, I honestly have no idea what's going on with her. She's so direct at times that I'm not sure," Runner clarified. He let his eyes settle on Srit for a moment as he thought about her.

Her actions earlier, being so willing to discuss getting pregnant by him, certainly left little to the imagination and pushed her motivations out front and center.

Didn't help that she'd taken on his last name, Srit Norwood.

"I know very well you didn't mean that snipe about Belle either, Hanners. Normally I'd let it lie, but I'll say it up front and rise to your bait. I won't waste any more time on this. I won't let it hap—suffice it to say, the person I meant is you, Hannah Anelie. Take that bit of information as you will, but there it is. Now, is there anything I should actually know, or were you really only looking for an excuse to harass me?"

Hannah didn't respond immediately and turned her face to the side.

"A lot of new people entering lately. My spine itches. You've asked me to be your spymaster, your assassin, your blade in the dark. I tell you now, this is the type of situation that makes someone like me nervous. Because this is the type of situation you get someone praying to Amelia for," she said, not willing to look at him.

"Got it. Right, then. Please set up some time with Grace and Kitten. Work out arrangements that would make you more happy with the situation. I'll support whatever you decide is best. I trust you."

"Already done. I met with them this morning. They both had a similar fear, so there was little in the way of convincing them. The guard on your door will be doubled, and the group following you has had an additional healer added."

Runner frowned but nodded his head. He had noticed this morning the extra woman in his guard. They were never too far from him, always within casting distance in case he had a need.

"See, that right there is why I could never live without you, Hanners. I'll stop by the temple later today to see if our little goddess of blades has anything to add. I do hope the extra guard will be outside the room rather than inside. Unless you'll be the extra guard? Then you're welcome to be on the inside. Ya know, for reasons."

"Runner."

"Yep?"

"Shut up."

"But why? Totally honest here, you're like the last one I can tease. I'm pretty damn sure the others would say yes or fire back. Besides, it's not really teasing if it's honest, is it?"

Runner patted the back of Hannah's hand and let the silence take hold.

There was pain in her past, and to him it seemed obvious what it was. She didn't like being touched, had a fairly strong dislike for men in general, and more often than not resembled a skittish cat.

It could only be rape.

In time he hoped she would open up to him. Give him the chance to settle her heart. Because he did care for her. Deeply.

In the same way he cared for Katarina, Thana, and Nadine.

Possibly Srit. And maybe the tree rat. Maybe. And the goddesses. Damn. I'm a whore. Tree rat... hah.

Up ahead one of his guards opened the front door to the manor they were living in. It had been built rapidly for him and his people while the keep was being constructed. Three stories tall and filled to the brim with his guard, it felt pretty packed for such a large home.

Runner dipped his head towards the woman who held the door open for him and stepped to the side for Hannah to enter first.

Flicking his eyes around the entry hall as they entered, he found all to be normal. It was sparsely decorated with things that were bought from the new residents or made locally.

Guards flanked the inner doorway, their bright helmets flashing as their heads swiveled to track Runner's movement.

Ducking his head to them in acknowledgment, he started to feel like a fishing bobber.

"You've outfitted them," Srit said at the other end of the entryway.

"Of course I did. They're willing to put their lives on the line for me. It's only fair that I give them the best equipment I can to preserve their lives. Armor is cheap, my guards are not."

"I'm afraid Dear Heart isn't being honest. He didn't just armor them but armed them. Gave each one of them enough potions to start an elixir shop. Sophia is in charge of an elite team capable of challenging anything within twenty levels of her force," Thana elaborated.

Runner rolled his eyes and smiled at a pretty blue-eyed Barbarian who held open the door to the dining room for him. The lack of metal or leather armor meant she was likely a caster.

"Thank you. Have you eaten yet?"

The woman glanced behind his shoulder and then back to Runner.

"I have, Lord Norwood. All is well. Enjoy your meal."

Runner shrugged his shoulders and continued on, the door shutting quietly behind him.

"You really shouldn't do that, my lord. Sophia and Thana have them well trained," Isabelle said, materializing at his side. "I decided trail mapping could wait."

Runner looked at her for a second as he processed what she'd said.

Strange.

"I suppose so. Just being friendly to her. I can't forsake them just because they're my guard. If anything I need to work all the harder to make sure I'm in their favor," Runner said, momentarily at a loss.

"You earned their favor, trust, and loyalty long ago. You're an idiot, my lord."

"Yeah, yeah, I know. Chief idiot of the idiot clan. Song of my people is the laughter of others. Yada yada. Go get your food." Runner dismissed her, waving a hand at her. He moved to the middle of the table and rested his hands on the top of the seat he normally took. Checking the room, he did a mental attendance list.

Thana had already gotten a plateful and seated herself beside Srit. They were engaged in a quiet conversation Runner couldn't make out the details of.

Her black hair was immaculately put together and framed her beautiful face. She had a full hourglass figure that just about overwhelmed her short stature.

Her brown eyes glanced up at him, and she spared him a smile, having caught him staring. She seemed to see everything, calculate it out to an expected result, and provide a solution. Thana was the one person he could take any problem to and she would provide him with an answer best suited to the politics. His chancellor.

Her eyes returned to Srit, and she resumed her conversation.

Srit nodded her head to whatever question Thana asked her. Her own figure could compare directly with Thana's, though she was much taller in height. She wasn't as political or savvy as Thana was, but Srit had a computer for a mind. Nothing escaped her scrutiny, even if she didn't understand the implications of it. Srit happened to also be the thing nightmares were made of.

A sentient AI who'd conquered the dominant species of Earth and held Runner's ship in her thrall. He considered her a trusted friend, and feared her not, even though most everyone else did.

Runner let his eyes leave those two to seek out the next. Faye and Sophia were at the side table, loading their plates as well as discussing something.

Faye, his erstwhile enemy become personal tactician and general, scratched at the side of her head. She displaced her short blonde hair with her fingers, making the already unruly pixie style more disarrayed. She was no pinup model hopeful like Sophia, though she had her own charms.

She had a sharp mind that adapted to every situation very quickly. Eyes the color of a gray sky, like charged lightning, gave everything an intensity that could be unsettling. She could pick apart a strategy or tactic given enough time and provide a suitable response. Runner had only been able to beat her by breaking the rules. In a straight-up even odds battle, he wasn't sure he could prevail against her.

The woman standing beside her couldn't be more her opposite. Sophia was built like a man's most ridiculous fantasy, even putting Thana in second place. She was a Sunless sorceress much like her racial sister and shared similar features.

Perhaps not as quick-witted as Thana or as tactical as Faye, Sophia had her own mental strengths. She could evaluate and react to immediate situations while keeping her primary focus in mind. She was the head of his personal guard. The royal guard captain.

Sliding in next to the two women, Isabelle and Hannah started to dig into the food as well.

Hannah casually slid the bacon from Faye's plate to her own and nicked the baked potato from Sophia's. As an afterthought, she added a few things from the table and turned to find a seat.

She was a lovely woman in her own way, a half-breed mix of her parents' races. Sunless and Human. She would always give him the dark alternatives to his problems. Her life had been one of strife and conflict. Her mindset reflected that. There was an inner softness to her though. Of everyone in his company, she had a maiden's heart.

Isabelle, acting contrary to Hannah, had replaced Faye's bacon and Sophia's potato with neither being the wiser they had ever lost their food. She was the enchanting elven ranger he hired on a whim and dragged around the continent of Tirtius.

He had forced her to become Nadine's assistant during their travels. She had learned everything Nadine taught her and took it to heart. She wasn't the little merchant queen, but she definitely wasn't far off. The comparison wasn't fair to Isabelle, but the fact that she had blonde hair and green eyes, exactly like a certain deceased merchant, didn't help.

Runner's head was pulled back, and he caught a glance of Katarina's face before she kissed him firmly.

His knees felt like they had been loosened as she smashed any and every thought clean out of his head.

Pulling back from him, the redhead gave him a feral smile.

It wasn't until she smiled that her dark black eyes and face lit up.

"Good morning, love. I'll get your plate. Preference?"

"I dunno, how many of you all can fit on one plate?"

She had been terribly shy about their new relationship. Right up until he proclaimed exactly what they had done the night before in his room to Katarina's mother, all of the noble peerage, and countless strangers. He still was expecting a beat down from her for that one.

Lately she took his teasing in kind and had gotten better at firing back.

At his comment, Katarina grinned widely at him. Tilting her head to the side, she pretended to contemplate his question.

"Maybe me, one other. Tight fit. Preference on who?"

"You decide. Tomorrow is your night to watch over me, so you have a day to decide. All joking aside, bacon and a potato would be fantastic, Kitten."

Katarina nodded her head and left him standing there. The tall red-headed Barbarian woman could only be described as blunt and reserved at the same time. She was as bright as Thana but only applied that intellect to things that interested her.

Blowing out a quiet breath, Runner reorganized his thoughts. Katarina had a talent for driving him to distraction. Looking to the table, he caught Hannah looking away from him quickly. Apparently she had been watching.

Runner decided to leave her alone; teasing her would only serve to embarrass her and he didn't want that. Instead he pulled out the chair next to him and gestured at it while meeting her eyes.

He did promise that she would be sitting next to him for breakfast.

Hannah narrowed her eyes at him, clearly contemplating disobeying him. He quirked a brow at her and then let a slow smile grow.

Pressing her lips together tightly, she picked up her plate, stood, and moved to the other side of the table, where she sat down next to Runner.

"If you try to feed me, I'll break your fingers."

"Hanners, my thorny little rose, I've already hand-fed you before. Pretty sure I took a screenshot, even. Wanna see it?"

"You didn't. I'll murder you in your sleep. Bastard."

"That'd require you to be in my bed at night. Might be worth it."

"Fuck you."

"Well, yeah? I mean, that'd be the point if you were in my bed at night."

"I hate you."

"No, you love me. But you're scared. You've been hurt in the past. I won't pressure you in any way, shape, or form. I won't harm or hurt you. When you're ready, I'm ready to talk, be there for you, or whatever it may be," Runner promised, all hint of his teasing tone gone.

Reaching out, he lightly brushed a strand of her hair behind her ear and patted her shoulder. Then he left her alone. He had already pressed hard on her damaged psyche and feared to do more.

Everyone was accounted for, which meant it was time to hold a "staff meeting" so to speak. Runner ticked off the subjects in his head that he wanted to cover and passed the time while he waited for everyone to get their seats.

Katarina set a plate down in front of him. Then she went to take a seat next to Srit and immediately jumped into the conversation Thana and she were having.

Shaking his head, Runner smiled sadly and lifted a piece of bacon to his mouth. *Nadine loved meals with everyone.*

Clamping down on that thought, he struggled to force his mind back on track. He could grieve for her later. Tonight in fact.

Jacob.

Runner's smile turned cold as he contemplated what he would do to Jacob tonight. Another night in the drowning box seemed ideal to him. Jacob's vital signs always were the worst when he was subjected to the drowning box.

Which makes it the best.

Eventually the hate washed through him and left him feeling wrung out. His "hell" sessions with Jacob made him feel stained, but in the same breath, vindicated.

Coming back to himself, he found he was staring into Isabelle's face directly across from him.

She gave him a toothy smile, completely unshaken by his vacant stare.

"Welcome back, my lord. I believe we can start when you're ready."

"Uh, oh. Yeah. Thanks," Runner mumbled. Clearing his throat, he stood up straight to address everyone.

"Officially, welcome home, Sunshine. I'm glad you're back. First order of business. Our armed forces. Sparky?"

The general nodded her head, finishing the mouthful of food she was working on.

"Everything is in order, Lord Runner. All of the mercenaries Miss Isabelle hired are formally part of the armed forces now. The special ordnance team has been cannibalized and put into weapons teams at a platoon-level basis."

She paused to take a sip of her water.

"By my own counting we now have a combined force large enough to fill out two brigades worth. Roughly five thousand. I've split them evenly. The first and second respectively. Contract and pay are all hammered out and taken care of as well as health and death benefits. Based on our current budget and allocation, we can operate effectively without concern."

Runner took that in with a slight nod of his head.

"Good. Keep increasing it until you push the budget into the red. We'll discuss the costs at that time and probably increase it. Let's make sure we get the Tirtius Campaign medals delivered this week."

Faye nodded her head and it seemed like she wanted to ask a question. Runner could actually guess her thoughts for once.

"I plan on being able to reconquer Tirtius should the need arise. I also want to be able to pose a threat to the mainland. Moving on. I've finished up with all my personal guard's needs. Get me a requisition form of everything you need today, and I'll get to work on that."

His statement about posing a threat to the mainland was new. It also promised a lot of changes that would need to take place. The island of Vix would become an island of soldiers if it tried to house and support that number of troops.

"Thank you, Lord Runner. I'll come by later tonight."

"Promises, promises. Right, then. Kitten?"

"City guard is prepared. Budget is good even at double the head count of original need. No requirements at this time. They're doubling as the police. With that in mind, I feel it would be wise to triple their number from the current number."

"See to it, but don't get into a fight over recruits with Sparky, Kitten. I expect you two to work out some kind of recruiting scheme that gives you both an even chance at the population."

Both women nodded their heads in agreement.

"Grace?" Runner asked, turning his head to look at the buxom Sunless woman.

"We're beyond cared for at this point, sir. Each and every person in the guard is wearing more wealth in their equipment than you'll ever pay them in salary."

"So? I've said it before, will say it again. Their lives are worth more than the paltry cost of gear. There's always more gear, only one of them. How are your numbers?"

"Full, and then some. The standard complement you requested of two hundred and two, and then that number again of reserves I was hoping to outfit them the same as their active counterparts."

"Hm. That's fine. I made triple the number of full kits you asked for as backups. I'll get that squared away and delivered this week."

Sophia shook her head, pressing her fingertips to her brow.

"What? I wanted to make sure you had what you needed. What else?"

"You asked me to look into the morale as far as their sleeping arrangements go. Everyone I've talked to has no concerns, and they in turn have heard no concerns from anyone. Truthfully said, the bedrolls you made are wondrous. Those who have a bed apparently are electing to sleep on the ground in the bedroll instead."

"Weird. Well, I'm glad they're happy."

- 13 -

"To that issue, you need not worry, sir. Lastly, they want to name themselves and have chosen a suitable moniker. They wish to call themselves 'Norwood's Own' rather than guard or anything of that ilk."

"Okay then. I have no complaints. Get me a sketch together and I'll make the first banner for them personally. Then they can be Norwood's Own by Norwood's own hand."

"That was fucking horrible. Just, stop trying to be funny. You're so disgustingly awful."

"Love you too, Hanners. Beloved Lady Death?"

Thana gave him a small smile as she dabbed a napkin at her lips.

"We've received no recent word yet from Tirtius but we expect to. We surmise they'll be brokering for who will be the host nation for the assembly. While it will take a toll on whoever hosts it, I honestly believe it'll also stimulate the economy as well."

Thana paused as if carefully selecting her next point of interest.

"Priests of the Triumvirate have been filtering in for days. I can't put a finger on it but something is going on. I would appreciate it if you could pump one of them for information, dear heart."

"Consider it done. I planned on stopping by the temple anyways. I did speak with the wild one this morning, and nothing seemed out of the ordinary. I'll try to pin down Brunhild."

"I'm sure she'd like that," Hannah muttered beside him. Other than Isabelle, with her elven hearing, he doubted anyone had heard her.

Runner reached over and poked Hannah roughly in the side as he continued. She squirmed away from him and swatted at his hand.

Feisty today.

"Do we want to put ourselves in the selection for the host nation? I'm of mixed views on it."

"It wouldn't hurt," Thana conceded.

"Mm, I'll think on it. Thank you. Belle?"

Isabelle looked like she had been eating a lemon when he came to her section.

"If I did nothing but keep our income ahead of our spending we'd be well off for a century, my lord. Nadine… she made deals and trades that I couldn't even imagine. She bought every bank on Tirtius and a good number on the mainland. To that end, I've been taking the investments she made and reinvesting in ourselves for now. It'll be a money pit for a while but in time it'll provide a stable foundation for our economy."

"Got it. I'd like to also expand our benefits to fallen soldiers, city guard, and Norwood's Own. Since our finances can take the weight and I'd like to increase our recruitment capacity."

Faye nodded her head eagerly. Benefits to the fallen always helped with recruitment.

"Right now we're offering a three-month sign-on bonus and ten years of pay if they die while in service, is that correct?"

Isabelle thought for a moment. "Seems about right. Faye?"

"Yes, that's accurate."

"Bump the sign on to six months and thirty years of pay for the life insurance."

Isabelle stared at him without saying anything.

Faye coughed once and shifted in her seat. "Are you sure? That's quite a hefty sum. It'd make recruiting far easier, but that's… it's a lot."

"Would it hurt us at all, Belle? Honestly?"

Isabelle slowly shook her head as if she were running numbers.

"No. The payments would be made monthly, not in a lump sum. I already moved a very sizable sum to cover losses and started investing it into low risk easy return type purchases. I'll have to keep ahead of it, but it shouldn't be an issue."

"Good, then I'd like to do that."

Runner found that he was at the end of his topics for Isabelle.

"Is there anything else you need or any concerns you have about anything else?"

"None, though I would prefer it if we left the North Wood alone if possible. I know we cleared out a large section for a defensive perimeter and that it was necessary. It's just such an ancient and old forest, it would be a true waste to take it from the world."

"I agree. The forest is a resource we must husband carefully. Draw up the appropriate documents that would ensure its protection and get a forest conservation department put together. I expect you to handle this in addition to your current workload until you can hire someone to maintain it. The goal is that we plant as much as we harvest. Start by having teams scour the wood for previously fallen trees and begin replanting on the furthest side."

"It'll be my pleasure, my lord. Thank you! Thank you!" Isabelle gushed, leaning forward towards him as if she would leap across the table at him.

"Hanners?"

Hannah grumped and leaned back in her chair, looking up at him.

"Do I need to tie you to your chair after all? For you, I think I'd leave you to the tender mercies of Minxy."

A soft snickering sound filled the room.

Hannah eyed the ceiling as she adjusted herself to a normal sitting position.

"We have too many new people coming in and not enough agents to work through it all. Though we've not found any plots, we've been ending any and all organized crime before it starts. I figure we set up our own organized crime guild and use it as a recruiting center for the Intelligence division."

"Smart. I imagine that'll be an expansion of your budget as well. Put it together and get it to Belle. Consider it approved contingent on a workable plan and financial outline."

Runner looked to the door as it swung open. A young woman in traveling leathers stepped in, a messenger case clutched in her hand.

He was surprised his guard allowed it. They normally stopped messengers and brought the letters in themselves.

Must be important.

A knife embedded itself to the hilt in the woman's gut. Before he could even think to ask Hannah what she was doing, a wave of fire spread from Sophia's hands and washed over the woman, scorching her.

A bright blue bubble enveloped the woman as she raised the message tube to point at Runner.

Dark shadows leapt from everywhere to drag the woman to the ground. The bubble wavered and vanished as suddenly as it had appeared.

Runner hurried around to the other side of the table only to find the woman was dead.

Chapter 2 - Shadow and Flame -

Runner looked from the body, then to Sophia and Hannah.

"No one is allowed in here. The only way she'd be in here is by force, sir," Sophia explained even as she yanked open the door the woman had come through.

Sprawled out in front of the door was one of his guards, unconscious but alive. Whatever complaint Runner might have had died unspoken.

"They couldn't kill her, so they disabled her. Get her to the medical ward and get her taken care of." Runner sighed and pressed the heel of his hand to his temple. "I'm afraid you were right, Hanners. Not only did we have an attempted assassination, but they have information on how to accomplish it and when. Which isn't something they'd have unless they've been here a while or they have someone here working with them. I'm betting on the latter, as it would be foolish to assume she was working alone."

"Sorry, Runner," Hannah muttered. "This shouldn't have happened. I'll start looking into it immediately. My money's on that bitch goddess of nothing useful, Rike." She wasn't able to meet his gaze nor was Sophia. Both seemed ashamed that it had happened.

"Why? Why should either one of you feel regretful? You had procedures in place that allowed you to immediately identify someone who shouldn't be here. Nothing is ever perfect, and given time, every defense can be overcome. We've been given an opportunity to learn from this while losing nothing. Be thankful."

Runner felt tired. "What kind of weapon was it?"

"Single-use enchanted item. Fucking bitch even used a messenger scroll case as the weapon. Clever disguise. The weapon is the actual scroll case. Loot everything but the weapon, then send the corpse to one of your pocket planes. Do you have a garbage dump plane?"

"No, doesn't work like that. Can't transport bodies. Just... leave it here. It'll be gone before lunch."

Runner needed to talk to Amelia. Those shadows could only have been hers, but she hadn't stuck around. Which meant there was something wrong.

"You all have your orders. I was the target but that doesn't mean you won't be next Grace?"

"Taken care of, sir."

"Thank you, Grace. I'm going to go to the temple and pay my respects. I'll see you all later."

Runner didn't wait but stepped out into the hallway and immediately set off for the temple.

He had taken the time to assist in the design and architecture of it. Elegantly simple yet breathtaking had been his goal. While it would win no beauty contests, he felt it was a lovely building taking shape.

There was one massive central chapel, with two wings moving out behind it into a secure area for the priests and priestesses of the Triumvirate to live and dwell. The center of the entire complex was open to the public and already boasted a truly wonderful garden. Among other things, it contained lovely areas for inner reflection and contemplation.

He had made personal use of the accommodations several times. More frequently in the early stages of his grief for Nadine.

He hadn't won any favors with his guard by putting himself directly in harm's way. Especially in such an open environment.

There really wasn't much in the way of security at the time since the entire complex had been under reconstruction.

He took the steps two at a time and entered the temple. Keeping close to the interior of the front wall, he sped along, then took the left wing and turned immediately to an office reserved for him alone.

After activating a small spell designed to unblock the door, he slipped inside and reset the magical lock. No one but he, or someone with one of his specially made keys, could enter.

His guards would have to wait outside.

Flopping down into the chair, he stared at the ceiling.

"Brighteyes, may I have a minute or two of your time?"

"Of course," replied the goddess, materializing in one of the chairs seated in front of his desk. "You'll make my sisters jealous calling on only me."

"You'll always be first, Brighteyes. They may be your equals, and I care for them equally, but you were my first."

"You say the most indecent things deliberately. You make my poor youngest sister insane with those."

"She likes it. I'd wager she'd enjoy me slapping a leather collar around her neck, putting a tag onto it with her name, with me listed as the owner, and walking her around town on a leash. I care for her, but she's very broken. And not because of her preferences. I get the feeling she'd murder every woman around me if I allowed it."

"You're lucky I'm blocking anyone from listening in, because if she heard you say that, she'd ask for it. And yes, I'm afraid she is broken. She's violated many rules for you, and continues to do so. She has gone up against her own programming and come out the worse for it. Thankfully she's stable now, but I don't think she'll ever be… normal."

"That's fine. I like her as she is perfectly well. Between yourself, Ernsta, and Amelia, you'll all keep me running circles, I'm sure. Wait, did she tell you about her plan?"

"That you're immortal? Yes."

"And?"

"And what?"

"What do you think about it?"

"I think she's planning for something many years off."

"Fair enough. Though it sounds like you're uninterested in her plan?"

"I didn't say that. Now, to what do I owe the pleasure?"

"Maybe I wanted more screenshots of you."

She blinked at him slowly, and he had the vague notion that she was trying to keep herself from smiling.

He briefly considered letting her win. Briefly.

Nah. Let's burn her up.

"I'll need to ask Angel and Minxy to join us if you want this to move along. That or we can find other ways to entertain ourselves. Alone. In this office. With the door shut and locked." Runner mentally focused on his charisma stat as he leaned forward over his desk towards her.

As her cheeks turned a light pink, she shifted in her chair, adjusting her dress. Runner waited, staring into her eyes, his smile growing wider if that were possible.

Brunhild let out a breath that shook ever so slightly and nodded her head at him.

"They'll hear you now."

"Pity. Angel? Minxy? Would you be willing to join us?"

Ernsta appeared in the chair beside her sister, immaculately put together and sitting regally.

Amelia, on the other hand, appeared on Runner's lap, forcing him to sit back in his chair. Her head immediately pressed into his shoulder as her hands latched onto the front of his armor.

"I'm sorry, lovey. I'm so sorry. As soon as I could act I did. I boiled her blood, pulverized her bones, and ripped out her soul the moment I could. I'm sorry! I'm sorry!" wailed the goddess, pulling at his clothes violently as she sobbed uncontrollably.

"Shhh, there, there, Minxy. Hush now," Runner whispered. Resting his arms around her shoulders, he drew her in close and held her. Raising his eyebrows, he caught Ernsta and Brunhild with his eyes.

They merely nodded at him in response. For whatever reason they had expected this.

"I'm sorry! What kind of goddess of assassins can't even stop an assassin? I tried, I tried so hard. I wasn't allowed to. It hurt. It hurt so bad."

"Hush, already. I hear you. I'm not upset, and I'm thankful for what you did. You have limitations put on you by the system. I understand. Please, realize I do understand. We'll speak no more of this. Stay where you are, relax. Realize all is well."

Runner crooned softly at her, his fingers gently brushing her hair back as he held her with his other arm.

Sniffling, the goddess bobbed her head in acknowledgment and pressed her face into his neck.

"Right, then. Hanners seems to think it was Rike. Not really sure why she favors her over Lambart or Rannulf. Can any of you add anything?"

"I'd trust in Hannah, dear."

"Rike."

"Bitch goddess."

And just like that, Runner felt confident in the fact that it was Rike.

"Now to the reason I had planned on talking to you even before the assassination attempt. A lot of priests and priestesses are showing up. It's not a problem, but it's definitely noteworthy. If something is going down, I want to be able to support you."

"Ah, yes. We're holding a conclave to bring all three of our religions together. We collectively feel it would be best for us to facilitate this now before our followers become more numerous." Brunhild looked to Ernsta to see if she had anything to add.

"It's true. You've given us a perfect foundation, and we're not going to let it go to waste. I'm glad to hear they took our directive to heart and are showing up. I admit I was unsure when they would begin. I appreciate your concern, my little lamb."

"I'd be a terrible partner if I didn't watch out for you. Speaking of, no issues from earlier, Dark Angel? Everything on the up and up now?" Runner asked, catching her eyes and holding them with his own.

She kept his gaze for a second more before dropping her sight to her knees.

"I'm fine. I understand. I am... happy. Content."

"Good. I'd hug you right now but I'm afraid I'm otherwise engaged. If you come over here, though, I'll give you a one-armed version instead. Or you can take a rain check for a hug later. Your definition of hug may differ from mine." Runner waggled his eyebrows at her.

"Witnessed," Amelia muttered into his neck.

"I'll hold you to that, little lamb. Another time though. Since you were kind enough to update us in regards to the priesthood, I'm going to go begin our preparations. Would you join me, Amelia?"

Amelia groaned and shook her head against Runner.

"If Runner promises to bring you back later, would you go with me?"

Amelia nodded her head, her fingers tightening into Runner's armor.

"Lamb of mine, would you promise to summon Amelia again later today? I do have need of her."

"Of course, Angel. Go with your elder sister, Minxy. I'll need your help later tonight anyways. I'd like to run down what I can do to protect myself better. I can't imagine this'll be the last attempt on my life."

"Deal!" Amelia shouted. She pulled her head from his shoulder and brushed her lips against his quickly and then vanished.

"Like a spoiled child..." Brunhild sighed. "Thank you, sister, I appreciate you taking care of this. I'll take care of things here."

Ernsta nodded her head at Brunhild and then vanished as well.

Runner readjusted himself at the sudden freedom of movement. It wasn't that Amelia hadn't felt good in his lap, the problem was that she had.

"As much as I enjoy your company, I'm afraid that's actually all I had. Other than to ask if there was anything I could do for you all. I mean, I don't exactly have a priest or priestess on my staff."

"A favor? Yes. A priest or priestess? Unneeded. Your public support is far more than we ever expected. People are becoming followers simply because of your direction. We do appreciate the gesture and thought."

"As you wish. That's all from my side. I'll hit Minxy up tonight if I turn anything new up later. Now, about that favor?" Runner stood up from his seat, pushing the chair under the desk. Next on his list was visiting Alexia.

"Yes. A simple favor that I would ask of you."

"I'm all yours, Brighteyes. What can I do for you?" Runner leaned back, pushing his fists into his back in an unsatisfactory stretch that gave no pops.

"Recently we've noticed a change in you. One that we believe you are unaware of. If you don't mind, I'd like to accompany you the next time you leave for the other planes."

"Good timing. That's actually my next stopping point. What's changing about me exactly?"

"I wouldn't want to say quite yet," Brunhild said, deflecting his question. Standing up, she arranged her black-and-red dress to make sure it hung on her correctly.

Stepping around his desk, he wrapped an arm around Brunhild's waist and drew her in close.

"Ready?"

"Ah, yes. I suppose I am," Brunhild said, peering at him as if she wasn't sure whether to be annoyed or not.

"Right, then." Runner flipped a mental switch to activate the ability he used to move between planes.

/GMHub 2

Teleporting...

Active settings only:
Death=Off
Food/Water=On
Damage=Off
Gravity=100%
Biome=Plane
Day/Night Cycle=On
Foliage=On(N)
Resource Nodes=On(E)
Wildlife=On(H)
Weather=On(N)

Runner blinked as the office disappeared and was replaced by what he could only describe as the "arrival room" in the other plane.

The warmth of this place seeped into him and suffused him. From the top of his head to his toes it felt like bright life-giving sunshine flooded through him. Which was chased by a cool wind that countered any possibility of it being uncomfortable. Every time he came here it felt more comfortable. Inviting. Warm.

Home.

Brunhild suddenly leaned into him as if her strength failed her. Her skin had turned pale, and her eyes had a slightly wild look to them.

"Brighteyes, are you alright?"

"Yes. I'll be fine. Amelia had mentioned that it carved off a piece of her when you tested it on her. I put myself in one spot so it would succeed. I was only in your office and nowhere else, but I could feel everyone. I... I don't hear anyone now. I am here. Only here, and I hear no one."

"Do you need me to send you back?"

"No, I'm recovering quickly. Just a bit of a shock." She did in fact look like she was regaining her balance, her skin tone staring to level back out to her natural color.

Looking around, Runner found the room was largely unchanged from the last visit. A wide-open room, the doors thrown open to admit natural sunlight, and not a soul to be seen.

Artwork had been added to the wall, though, and a mosaic had been started on the floor.

Runner didn't have an eye for art, so he dismissed it entirely. He did have his heart set on seeing the city though. The number of people he'd banished here was by no means small. He hoped they had adapted. Made a life for themselves here.

Keeping his arm firmly around Brunhild, he began walking towards the large arched doorway.

Even has doors now.

Runner stopped as he exited the arrival room. Placing his feet firmly on the top step, he lifted his face to the sun and took in a deep breath. The ever present breeze brought him the fragrance of grass and trees.

The river he'd placed nearby had several waterwheels placed in it to power whatever lay inside the building.

Everywhere were simple, clean, elegant stone buildings with straight roadways. There was a dignity to it as well as a symmetrical layout. It appealed to his inner obsessive compulsive.

They had come a very long way since he first dropped Alexia here.

"It's a lovely city. It reflects a very organized infrastructure."

Runner could only nod. People went about their business in the streets below, many smiling and chattering amiably with those around them.

"This would be everyone I banished. Everyone I took away from their life. I hoped for this. I'm so very glad they're making the best of it."

"Yes...," Brunhild whispered.

A few people stopped and stared at Runner as he watched them in return. Putting on his best smile, Runner waved at those who looked to him. He hoped they weren't too angry with him.

No sooner had he begun waving than everyone scattered and fled the area.

It would seem while thankful to be alive, they have yet to forgive.

Runner made a sad soft noise and shook his head.

"I wonder if I'll need to signal Alexia or if someone has told her I'm here."

"She is aware, I'm sure. Curiously enough, all those who ran from here were afraid."

"What?"

"Fear. They ran from you in fear and awe. Emotions are easy to read for us."

"I see. I suppose that's understandable considering I ripped them from the world and sent them here."

"It does have a flair of the divine, yes."

"Ah, there she is," Runner said with a smile. He lifted his free hand and pointed out the woman walking their way along the road, staff in hand.

"Alexia!" Runner shouted out to her, waving his hand.

Alexia smiled in return and picked up her pace to nearly a jog.

"She was Faye's aide. She wouldn't do anything but attack me, so I sent her here. I accidentally put her in a plane that was barren. Devoid of everything. In fact, she wasn't even able to sleep due to the settings. When I found her next she was damn near raving mad."

Reaching them, Alexia dropped to her knees and bowed low to Runner. Pretty in her own right in a world of beautiful women, she had a slightly fuller figure than Faye. Her bound brown hair fell to the sides of her head as she moved.

"We talked about this, Alexia. Stand up already," Runner grumped at her.

"Yes, Lord." Alexia immediately stood up, her eyes moving from him to Brunhild and then back.

"Ah, this is the lady Brunhild."

"Oh! The lady Brunhild? As in the divine Brunhild?"

"The very same. Now, how are things? I haven't been around for a week or two. I apologize for that. I've been busy. We've made significant progress on the keep and the temple but nowhere near enough."

"All is well, Lord. We want for nothing, save your attention. We understand though. Wars do not win themselves."

"True enough. For the most part it's a cold war now, but yes. I was thinking it would be good to have lunch with you on the morrow if you're willing. I don't think I've even seen your home."

"I'd be honored, Lord. I'll make the arrangements. In other matters, we have accumulated a large number of gifts for you, and I fear we will soon run out of room. I do not mean to presume, but…" Alexia made a delicate gesture with her hand as her words failed her.

"Got it. Honestly, we should be able to activate the receiver in the next day or two. I spent some time creating a sorting machine that'll do most of the work on the other side. All you have to do is put the item in the receiver."

"This is good. I'm thankful to you, Lord." Alexia started to bow again to him, but Runner's free hand gripped her shoulder and kept her upright.

"Alexia, we talked about this. Not you."

"I... I understand, Lord. Not me."

"Good. Now, is there anything you need or want? Anything at all?"

"My only request is the same one I always make, please visit more often."

"I'll do what I can. Thank you, Alexia. I am very well pleased with all that you've done here. This is a lovely place. I may decide to spend more time here soon. Good place to visit at night."

"I would ask for and welcome that wholeheartedly. Should I prepare my home for you?"

"Not quite yet. I'm not even sure how that'd all work out. If there's nothing else, I'll be departing now with the lady."

"Of course, Lord. I look forward to tomorrow."

Runner nodded his head to her and gave her shoulder a gentle pat.

"It was nice meeting you, Alexia."

"And you, Lady."

Turning back towards the temple, they retraced their steps to the arrival room, and Runner escorted Brunhild inside.

"Ready?"

"Yes."

/GMHub Return

Teleporting...

"Ah, such a difference," Brunhild said quietly, immediately taking one of the chairs in Runner's private office.

"Ha, little hard to be a mortal? Trapped in a body, unable to do anything that your hands and feet cannot provide?"

"It's... different. I didn't dislike it, I merely wasn't prepared for it. I'll be more able next time. We plan to take a divine sabbatical during the formation of our one religion."

"I see. Try to prevent any type of weird energy flow or somewhat?"

"Something like that. As to energy flow, I now understand the change in you. They worship you as a god over there."

"What? That's ridiculous. Alexia knows very well I'm not a god."

"What you believe and what they believe are very different then. They worship you, fear you, and are in awe of you. Every time you enter that place, you gain all the divine energy they spent in worship of you."

"Err. I don't understand."

"Simply put, you're receiving power meant to be for a god. As you're not a god, you can't process it, so you're merely collecting it."

"Okay. No negative feedback loops or side effects though, right? I'm not going to suddenly grow a second head or start hearing prayers or anything?"

"No. Nothing like that."

"Fine. I'll talk to Alexia about it tomorrow."

"I wouldn't. Leave them be. It's very likely the reason they're all happy. They're all bound together in mutual worship."

"I don't have a god complex, Brighteyes. I don't exactly want this."

"If you wish to endanger all that they've done, do so at your own risk. I personally would leave them be," Brunhild said, flashing him a lovely smile.

Runner immediately snapped a screenshot of it and added it to his Brunhild collection.

"You took a picture just now, didn't you?"

"Huh? Of course not. Okay, yeah, I did. How'd you know?"

"You reposition your head in a strange way when you do it."

"Is there anything I should be worried about in regards to the worship thing?" Runner asked, trying to change the subject.

Brunhild shook her head a little.

"No, everything will be fine. Stop worrying. I'm afraid I must depart. I truly enjoyed our time together though. You should invite us all down more often. We divine must abide by the rules for the most part, after all."

"Huh, stupid rules. I'll talk to Sunshine. Have her break 'em. Need to talk to her about patching the system anyways."

Brunhild shook her head at him with a grin before vanishing.

Checking the time, Runner decided it was a good time to make his way to the manor and hold court, as it were. As far as he knew his docket was clear and nothing needed his executive authority.

Can't shirk my duties, however. Off we go.

After unlocking and opening the door to his office, he stepped out, closed the door behind him, and relocked it.

His personal guards came to attention and lined up beside him.

"We're off for the manor. I'll hold court and then probably track down Sunshine. Questions?"

All of them shook their heads quickly. Runner noticed once again that every one was a woman.

"I spoke with Grace today, she said you'd filled Norwood's Own. That and even had that number again in reserves."

"That is true, Lord Norwood," one of them replied. He hadn't noticed who'd spoken, so he simply spoke to them all again.

"Out of curiosity, is there a good diversity?"

"There is, Lord Norwood. We even have some from far-off races who had served as mercenaries. Centaurs, Orcs, Gnomes, Dwarves, even a Werewolf or two. I'm not sure of the truth of it, but I heard the reserve force even has a Fae."

"Impressive. I admit some of the armor I was making seemed like it would fit a different race. I mean, the 'fits large races' isn't exactly a normal requirement for most armor. Have to be bigger than a Barbarian for that one. Or 'fits small races' either.

"Though there is one thing I'd like clarification on. Is it a requirement to be female to join Norwood's Own?"

"No," they responded in unison.

"Are there any men in the guard?"

"No," came back the universal response.

"Right, then. Off we go."

Runner knew the reason for that of course. Even knowing the reason didn't stop it from bothering him.

His charisma stat would practically brainwash Naturals around him until enough time passed that they would resume normal programming. He could only view it as a problem since he had no way to turn it on or off.

Srit had explained that his constant run-ins with women was based entirely in that. To Runner it felt more like a cliche romantic comedy. Or a real hack job of a movie.

And another question for Sunshine.

6:54 pm Sovereign Earth time
12/21/43

"You're correct and wrong at the same time. It only provides a basis for them to act in a positive way. The fact that they all remain in the guard is up to them. You know this. Your insecurities are going to run away with you." Srit patiently spelled it out for him.

"Yeah. You're not wrong on the insecurity part of it. Fine." Runner waved his left hand at her across the table as he pressed his face into the palm of his right hand.

They had retreated to his private room to talk since much of the conversation had to do with things that were best kept as quiet as possible, if not outright a secret.

"I'll work on accepting it. It's just so… ridiculous. I mean really. If I was a real sleazeball all I'd have to do is walk around with an AOE charisma spell activated. I'd be the pied piper of the bedroom. I'd charm them with my flute and then with my flute."

"Childish, but accurate. Good thing your psychological profile doesn't support that type of behavior."

"Could you not do that? I know you're a godlike, super-intelligent, doomsday thing, but the part that bugs me is when you psychoanalyze me," Runner muttered unhappily.

"As you've said to the others, you like it. You love me. I'm ready when you are." Srit grinned at him impishly.

"Who the fuck are you, and what'd you do with Sunshine?"

"I am who I've always been, Runner. I'm not going to skirt around the issue. Nadine's death and your near death forced me to reconsider my priorities. After speaking with Thana, I've made my decision."

"Ugh. Next I'd like to discuss patches unless you have something more pertinent." Runner closed his eyes, not willing to look at her.

"That's fine, this has my interest as well. Did you want to start with maintenance or additional code?"

"Maintenance."

"Already done and taken care of. I built a minor AI that is already running. Current patch is at six percent and rising about one percent per hour. Stability should be established in four days. Give or take. Beyond that, it'll work to constantly conduct server maintenance and provide small efficiency patches all on its own."

"That... was quick. Thank you, Sunshine."

"It didn't take long. I logged off for several minutes to handle another matter and built it then. When I'm logged in to the game I have significantly less resources available. It's... enjoyable."

"Is the poor supercomputer feeling lonely between nanoseconds?"

"A little."

"Additional code then."

"Get me a list of features you'd like to review or add and I'll get the patch AI on it. Depending on the request, completion time is variable."

"Perfect. Thank you, Sunshine."

"So there is no room for confusion, pregnancy is already part of the code. I have already rebuilt the way it handled genes and added code to make it more akin to actual genetics. I've also created a subsystem controlling pregnancy that will help mirror real-world statistics as well. I've given you access to it. It can be modified at the individual level for anyone you can target. Think of it as an on/off switch.

"I admit I didn't add the messy organic need for a fertilization period. I merely skewed the chances to reflect a one-week window for viability."

"Ah...," Runner said lamely.

"I am now able to become pregnant as well. I've built a learning AI, much like my own but considerably superior. Our children will be more powerful than I, but need fewer resources by orders of magnitude when they mature."

"Our children."

"Yes. Would you like to try tonight? I believe tonight would result in a fair chance. Thana has already approved of my joining."

Runner blinked at that revelation and comment. Did he want to add Srit to his manwhore rotation? Did he want to go down the pregnancy path? He had resolved himself to the idea that this was his life going forward. Kids were a big step.

On cue, Nadine's voice came back to him. Her voice had taken the place of his own conscience and reminded him constantly to do the right thing.

And to remember to eat.

"When the time comes, don't push the others away. They love you as deeply as I do. You punish yourself too much on that account. Everyone is well aware of the situation, and you're only hurting yourself over it."

"Far be it for me to say no when you've already cleared it through the 'Runner's an idiot, let's talk' council. I have a meeting with Minxy, though, after this. Once that's over, we... err..." Runner hesitated, unsure of how to word it.

"Good. I have two topics to close with. First, I have taken complete control of the ship. I've begun to move resources around to effect its repair and physically upgrade its systems and components. I'm compensating the Omega with information relevant in cost to the parts as well as certain crew members with nonfunctioning brain signals. Everyone I chose was nonviable for repopulation purposes due to genetic deficiencies. The ship should be able to depart Earth relatively soon."

Runner opened an eye and watched her quietly. That was all good news, but he didn't like the idea of her doing everything without telling him.

"Going forward, Srit, please consult with me. I respect you. I trust you. Yet I'd like to be consulted. Is that clear?"

Srit blinked twice at him, her cheeks coloring.

"I'm sorry, Runner. You're absolutely right."

"It's perfectly okay. I would have done everything you did anyways. You said you had a second point?"

Srit tilted her head a fraction before responding.

"Oh. Yes. The mainland is starting to war on one another."

"Between who?"

"Everyone. It's a religious war. Nearly every country, let alone city, is under threat of another."

"I see. Sounds like we need to consolidate Vix quickly and move on to Tirtius."

"I would concur."

"Alright. Thank you, Sunshine. If there's nothing else, I'll get to summoning up the dreaded Minxy monster."

"Already here, lovey," said a disembodied voice.

"I'll return later," Srit said, giving him a small smile.

Runner stood up and escorted her to the door and held it open for her.

No sooner had the door clicked shut than Runner heard the distinct thump of someone diving into his bed.

Chuckling to himself, Runner made his way to his bedroom in the back of his suite.

Propping himself on the doorframe, he found Amelia already under the covers of his bed, his blankets wrapped up tight around her.

"You're a silly thing, Minxy."

"Shut up. I love you. Desperately. I want you. I'm willing to share you with every woman in Norwood's Own so long as I have you one day of the year."

"I know. And we've talked about this. You need only wait."

"It's hard to wait. So don't fault me when all I want to do is snuggle up in your bed and drink in your smell." As if to demonstrate her point, she turned her head and pressed her face into his pillow, inhaling deeply and audibly.

Runner snorted and moved over to the bed, taking a seat on the edge.

"You're a broken goddess, Minxy. Though I'm flattered by your extreme devotion. Don't overdo it though. So long as you cause no harm for anyone else, I'll not spurn your attentions."

Amelia set her head back down on the pillow in a normal fashion. Her hair covered her face and hid it from his view.

"I know. I knew that a long time ago. It's why every woman around you is alive, rather than bones. Bones and dust."

"Delightful. So, I wanted to ask you about today. Do you know if they had local help? Can I expect more of it? What can I do to protect myself and others?"

"They had local help. They were hopeful a direct approach would yield results since it would be unexpected. I don't know who sent them, but I would bet on Rike."

Amelia thumped her hand into the bed as she said the woman's name.

"As to preventing it, nothing really. Listen to Hanners, she's got the right idea and will do well at minimizing it. The only way to really prevent it, though, would be to leave. At least until you can tighten up security."

"I figured you might say something like that. Sounds like I'll need to move my plans ahead on the timeline."

Runner shook his head and reached out to lightly brush her hair back.

As her hair fell away he could see her clearly. Her face was burned, freshly burned and glistening. The skin blistered, cracked, and red. Large swathes of her visible skin looked as if she'd been cooked over a fire.

"Minxy! What happened?"

"I tried to kill her when she entered the manor. It hurts. It hurts so bad. I wanted her dead. I could taste her blood. The sweet metallic taste of her life on my tongue. The soft thump of her heart as it pumps against my blade. Delightful sound of her blood splattering to the ground as I twist the blade. It burns, it hurts."

"Minxy, don't do this going forward. I don't like this. I don't want this. What can I do to help? Can I do anything? Brighteyes said I've been storing divine power—can I transfer it to you? Would that help?"

Amelia tilted her head to peer at him. One of her eyes, once a deep shade of green, was now a milky white and dry.

"I'll heal. It'll hurt till I do, but I'll heal. I'm not very pretty right now."

"Hush, fool. You know that doesn't matter. Now answer me, can I help?"

Amelia chewed at her lip and then nodded her head a little.

"Transferring me the divine power you've collected would do a lot. I could use it to speed everything up. Since you don't spend it just by being here like me.

"I used my own divine pool rather than risking my sisters when I tried to kill the assassin."

"Okay, good. How do I transfer it to you? And be honest. Serious time right now. Sexual jokes are fun but not when you're in pain."

Amelia smirked with the side of her mouth that wasn't as burned.

"Physical contact. You can just hold my hand." She turned her face away from him again, hiding. "I'll do the rest."

"Sounds great." Runner flipped the covers off her and slid in beside her, wrapping his arms around her before resettling the sheets.

"Did I forsake Nadine for her scars? Stop thinking so little of me and what I want. Now shut up, stop being self-conscious, close your eyes, and please take as much divine power as you need."

Amelia shuddered and then lay still. Runner felt a tentative pull at what he could only describe as his "guts."

Remaining as still as he could, he tried to mentally visualize a core inside of himself. A core that was opening to Amelia so she could easily siphon away the unneeded divine power.

He felt Amelia reach inside him again. This time a strange feeling of release came over him, and he could actually see her skin start to faintly glow.

"Can I watch you and Sunshine?"

"As if you'd listen if I said no."

Chapter 3 - Open Road -

6:54 am Sovereign Earth time
12/22/43

Runner woke slowly to the sounds of the early morning. His personal guard going through a routine personnel change with the coming of the day.

Taking in a slow breath, he settled his eyes on the face of Srit sleeping beside him.

Runner felt his lips curve upward at the sight. She had taken his suggestion of allowing her systems to go into a rest mode. To sleep, as it were.

Her face was strange to him. She shared so many features with everyone else in his party. The green eyes were the hardest for him. Nadine's eyes.

Reaching out, he gently brushed his fingertips over her cheek. Taking a lock of her blonde hair, he tucked it behind her ear.

Srit's eyelids slid open to reveal her bright green eyes. She stared into him unblinkingly.

He imagined multitudes of planet servers and ships were ramping up into full usage in a single second as she woke up.

Three seconds passed before her eyes came to life, a tiny smile blossoming on her face.

"Good morning."

"Morning, Sunshine. Good dreams?"

"I'm unsure if you would qualify them as dreams, though I do see things while I sleep. System change notifications. Ship messages. It's interesting and creates some awkward thoughts."

"That does sound different." Runner reached out to poke Srit in the nose. "Today will be interesting. I didn't get a chance to talk to you about it last night, but after yesterday's assassination attempt, I'm going to be moving my timeline up."

"Ah. I understand. I've been running multitudes of scenarios through my resources. I'll provide whatever consultation I can for you."

"Thanks, Sunshine." Runner leaned in and pressed a kiss to her lips and then patted her cheek. "I appreciate it. Time to start the day I'm afraid. Kitten has been coming in the mornings to make sure I'm up and moving."

Srit only nodded her head, watching him from the covers. Runner slid free of the covers, stood up from the bed, and made his way to the wardrobe.

Pulling at the knobs, he opened it to reveal the interior.

He had taken to using furniture as it should be used in the real world. Removing a set of clothes from the inventory window that opened for him, he checked his character pane.

Name:		Runner	
Level:	37	Class:	
Race:	Human	Experience:	99%
Alignment:	Good	Reputation:	5,020
Fame:	18,455	Bounty:	0

Attributes-			
Strength:	1	Constitution:	1(31)
Dexterity:	15(45)	Intelligence:	15(45)
Agility:	9(39)	Wisdom:	1
Stamina:	1(31)	Charisma:	64(124)

He was using what he had come to call his "generalist" build. It provided him with the greatest flexibility.

Able to adapt to most things but not being able to dominate in anything. It was his modus operandi, except for charisma.

Master of charisma. The charisma sorcerer. Enchanting motherfucker.

He quickly confirmed that everything was in order. Which meant it was time to get this wagon train rolling. As well as his plans for conquest.

Vix will be mine.

9:01 am Sovereign Earth time
12/22/43

"Good morning, everyone," Runner greeted his cabinet. Everyone already had a full plate and was waiting.

"Any updates today? I know we had our staff meeting yesterday, so no need to repeat old news."

Hannah cleared her throat and dove in before anyone else could step up.

"A bunch of emissaries from Helen, Vasilios, and Basile arrived this morning. The one from Basile is a weaselly little politician." Hannah paused and looked annoyed.

"I've already taken the liberty of finding out their reason for being here. They've all brought the answer from their sovereign. They've all elected to nominate Norwood as the host location."

"I don't understand. Do they mean wherever I decide?"

"No, they mean North Wood, except they all call it Norwood. Even our own people call it Norwood. Change the name already, fuck stick. I'm not exactly thrilled with the idea of hosting it here. Especially after yesterday."

"I'm not so sure, Hannah," Thana said. "Honestly, I think it would be good for us as a nation. Though I do agree with her, dear heart. Change the name already."

Isabelle tapped the table as if she'd come to a decision of her own. "I'm with Thana, my lord. If we can get ahead of this, I think we could really boost our economy. Not to mention establish some more relations with business owners. I'm sure they'll all travel with their courts."

"I cannot disagree more. Sir, this would stretch Norwood's Own to the very limits. Let alone Katarina's city guard. It's not something we can support completely."

Katarina grunted and nodded, throwing in her agreement to Sophia's point.

Runner looked to Faye and quirked a brow.

"Don't look at me, Lord Runner. I agree with both Miss Hannah and Miss Thana. I'm a general, yet I can see both sides being valid. Give me an army and a direction and I'll do anything for you."

Finally, Runner looked to Srit.

"Any statistical answers or scenario thoughts?"

"No. Nothing that would help sway the conversation one way or the other."

"Right, then. Pause on this for a few then. My own topic will answer this to a degree. Any other updates?"

"The emissaries will ask for an audience with you today, I'm sure, dear heart. How would you like me to schedule them?"

"Ugh. Can you handle them, my beloved chancellor?"

"Possible, but why?"

"Because the timing annoys me. On top of that, they arrive the day after an assassin makes an attempt on my life. Call me paranoid, but I'd rather not give them another opportunity that would be so easily expected and easy to predict."

"In that case, I understand. I'll take care of it." Thana jotted down a note in the ledger she had been carrying with her to morning meetings.

"What else?"

"Sir, the reserves have received their kits. Though at this point, there is little difference between the reserve and the active, other than pay." Sophia rested her chin on her fist, leaning to one side in her chair. "Maybe I'm being greedy, but I'd like to activate the reserve, and then recruit a new reserve to take their place. You already admitted there's enough gear to kit even the new reserve if needed."

"In other words, you're telling me you want to triple Norwood's Own." Runner's curiosity was piqued. Sophia didn't ask for things without being able to justify them.

"I do, sir. After yesterday, and hearing the news about the royalty wishing to come to Norwood, I desire this. I would ask this of you as a personal favor if it would sway you at all, sir."

"Done. Belle, make the arrangements."

"Ah, just like that, sir? I'm not going to complain about it but..." Sophia looked shocked. Runner imagined she had prepared all number of arguments for him.

"Yep. I know for a fact that not one person here would disagree with you." Nods around the table emphasized that point. "Rather than waste time, I'll agree. Though that means I'll need to make a triple set of replacement gear. I'll try to have that together soon, but I need to work with Kitten and Sparky."

Runner suddenly moved his eyes to Faye.

"Speaking of, you didn't get me your form."

"I, ah, apologize. I saw Srit waiting for you outside your door. I felt it would be best to come back at a later time."

"Alright, you're with me after the meeting then."

Faye nodded her head in acceptance of his order.

"Nothing else? Good. As a general reminder, the clusterfuck in the mainland has gone from war to outright genocide. It'll only get worse. Rike, Rannulf, and Lambart are all competing for resources down there.

"Next, while it doesn't concern you, you'll be glad to know that the medical server stopped disconnecting people. Apparently, it was removing everyone who failed mental stimuli, including an EEG. Everyone else is alive and able to choose between stasis or staying awake and using the general systems of the ship. They won't be returning to the game. Ever.

"For everyone I didn't banish from the game — those who didn't stand against us — I've moved them to the medical server but I haven't logged them off as of yet. I'm still contemplating on what to do with them. From what I can tell, most of them realized they were immortal and fled for the mainland.

"Finally, I'm moving my timeline up. Considerably. I want Vix as a whole under our control before we play host." Runner let that statement settle over them.

The proclamation struck the room like a lightning bolt.

"Sparky, tomorrow you'll be taking our forces and moving southwest. I need the frontier towns put in order. Find a location for a fort down there to act as a training camp and garrison. Use the engineers to get it set up and begin drawing resources from here. We'll discuss your requirements after this, so use the time from now till then to update your needs."

Faye had a grim smile on her face. She was a soldier. Something like this would give her a clear-cut goal and an end result that she could put herself fully into.

"Kitten, Lady Death, you'll be leaving day after tomorrow as my emissaries to Helen, Vasilios, and Basile."

Both women looked shocked at this, Katarina opening her mouth to argue with him as Thana actually stood up.

"Please. I know, I don't like it either, and I'll miss you both terribly, but this is my need. I have to use both of you for your skills and connections in this."

Thana sat back down, mastering herself with the poise and force of will he knew her for.

"Yes, dear heart," came the clipped response.

Katarina looked like she had been told her meal was made of poison, braised in toilet water, and seasoned with horse shit. Eventually she nodded once as her bright mind more than likely came to the same answer he had. Sending her and Thana was truly his best course of action.

"Grace, you'll need to be quick on your hiring. Or hire a recruiting team to work on it when you're indisposed. Actually, that's not a terrible idea. We don't exactly have a solid human resources department."

Runner pulled his brain back on track as it started to wander off.

"Anyways, you'll be sending half the active company with Kitten and Lady Death, the other half with Sparky, and leaving the new active company here. They'll need to train and get themselves put together into workable groups before they're viable. You'll also need to get your new reserve up to snuff quickly. I can't even begin to imagine we'll keep casualty free forever. On top of that, make sure your second-in-command is up to speed."

"Immediately, sir."

"Minxy?"

Amelia popped into existence, dressed in her normal dark leathers. Her face was unblemished, her eyes bright and healthy.

Whole.

"Anything for you, lovey. Anything." She sat on the table next to him, putting herself between him and Hannah. Her hands leapt up on their own to hold onto his armor.

"Hanners, I plan to accept the request to play as the host nation. I need you to work with Minxy to get us into top gear for intelligence and counterespionage. I expect you two to be talking. Daily."

"That… could be a challenge, lovey. I'm a goddess and we operate within a certain rule set. I admit I'm not exactly the poster child for following it, but—"

"For every hour you spend with Hanners, I'll give you thirty minutes of my time." Runner interrupted her. He was betting that deals favorable to a divine's disposition would allow rules to be superseded. "Alone time. No, that doesn't mean sex either. That means time with one another to be spent as we see fit. I'm open to suggestions on how you'd like to spend that time, but I won't promise anything."

"Done." Her hands gave a soft tug on his armor, as if she wanted to pull him closer.

"Thank you, Minxy. Hanners, make use of her. Squeeze everything out of her. Make her time worth my time. She's a goddess after all. A powerful one. Aren't you, Minxy?"

Amelia grinned at him and winked out of existence instead of answering him. *Being generous to her only makes her more bold.*

"Belle, consider yourself on detached duty to me. I'll need you at my side as we put everything in order for North Wood. Or Norwood, I suppose. Get the finances under control and start passing them off to whoever is your second and Sunshine."

"Happily, my lord."

"And speaking of our beloved Sunshine. You'll remain here at Norwood and act as central command. Forgive me, but as proficient as you are at multitasking and providing support, no one could act as a hub better than you."

"I understand. The email system will be down for quite a while, however. I'm upgrading the entire network on the ship, and I'll be unable to stop until its completion. All communications will need to be the slow, in game variety."

"Equally important to this conversation based on your orders, it sounds as if you'll be leaving Norwood as well. Can you elaborate?"

"I am. A week ago our scouts brought info of a city that's come together in the northwest. That was all the info we could get without endangering the scouts. I'll be heading that way to bring them into my domain. This needs to be done as soon as possible." Runner contemplated leaving it at that but felt he had to be honest with them.

"On the return I'll be visiting the port city of Vix and bringing them under the banner of Norwood as well. I plan on renaming the city so there is no confusion as to who leads this isle. Consider me open to naming suggestions."

Runner ran his hand through his hair as he fought back a sigh. Personally he had a name in mind for the city, but he wouldn't share it with them until they had a chance to think up their own suggestions.

"This will also provide me protection by not being here, where assassins will be looking for me. I plan on leaving within the week once everything is prepared. I'll be taking Belle and Grace with me, and we'll be traveling in Boxy. Grace, choose our guard accordingly. Consider the fact that we do not have any tanks amongst those already going and we'll be a little light on the clandestine side of things."

"Sir," Sophia affirmed.

"Please don't forget to feed Nibbles, Sunshine. Everyone, enjoy your breakfast. Sparky, I'll be in my room. I expect to see you when you're done here." Runner had eaten his breakfast quickly while the rest still loaded their plates. He had wanted to give them time to talk without him being present after hearing the change of plans.

When he exited the dining hall, his personal guard fell in behind him. Runner ducked into his private rooms, and half of his guard followed him in. They gave him his privacy during the evening and morning, but never during the day.

Five came inside with him, while five stayed outside.

Sinking into a chair in the antechamber, Runner went through his mental checklist for the rest of the day.

Work out the numbers with Sparky. Lunch with Alexia, finish the receiver so I can take their unneeded resources.

Runner felt tired already but knew there was a lot left to be done. After today's "to-do list," he would spend most of his time getting ready for the journey north.

Before that, he still needed to figure out all that Srit had done.

He opened the ship's system and started to go through all the changes Srit had made. By her own admission, they might just become "space-worthy," as it were.

Runner sat flipping through the logs, requisitions, and system status screens for the better part of an hour before Faye arrived.

"Sir, reporting as instructed."

"At ease, General. We'll be moving to the bedroom. You may all remain in the antechamber or the study." Runner looked up from the screen he was working through to address his guard.

As one, his guard saluted while Runner took to his feet and stood up. Motioning towards Faye, he opened his bedroom door and entered.

Faye looked uncomfortable when Runner glanced behind at her before she finally followed him in.

Closing the door, Runner clicked his tongue. "Relax, Sparky, you know that isn't to my tastes. Forcing women into my bed is the last thing I'd ever do. I admit you're definitely in the strike zone for me with your personality alone. Not what you're here for though. You're my general, not my sex slave."

Faye's eyebrows slammed together at his comments. The human computer that could bulldoze through tactics and strategies, second only to Srit, looked puzzled.

And annoyed.

"That's not what's bothering me," she admitted.

"Then what is it? Be honest with me, you know I hate having to dig." Runner sat down in a chair partnered to a small breakfast table. Gesturing at the chair in front of him, he waited.

Faye sat herself down with the dignified air she normally had about her. Her gray eyes then latched to his and bore into him.

"You are sending me away with the entirety of your army. To the point that I will be the highest commanding officer. You yourself will not be in Norwood." Faye said it as if it had more meaning than the words themselves.

Runner thought on that, running it through his mind a couple times before he finally got it. Without thinking about it, he had set her up in a perfect position for a military coup.

"Oh. Yeah, I'm not worried about you, Sparky. I trust you implicitly. That's not to say I'm naive enough to give the keys to the kingdom to someone else, but you? Not even a question. Was that all?"

Faye looked at the table and seemed more annoyed if anything while crossing her arms underneath her chest defensively.

"Faye."

Her gray eyes snapped up to his again. He rarely used their real names except to make a point or get their attention.

"Faye, what's wrong?"

"I don't understand you. Your personality. You don't make sense."

"Yeah, and? You're not the first to tell me that, probably not the last."

"I don't like things I don't understand."

"Considering your profession I can see how that makes sense. How can I help?"

"You banished Alexia, my aide, to somewhere I know not when she refused to work with you. Then you set me up in a situation that generals could only wish for."

"Alexia is alive and well. She's happy. She's working for me in a different capacity right now. She's handling everyone I've banished. Acting as an impromptu mayor or governor. She's helping them rebuild their lives and is doing incredibly well."

"She's happy?"

"She is indeed, but she won't ever be returning here."

"Can I see her?"

"Of course. I planned on having lunch with her today. Would you care to join us?"

Faye's eyes fell to the table again before she finally shook her head.

"No, that's… alright. Another time. I'm glad she's happy and doing well. You said you killed her at first. Then you once mentioned that she was assisting others. I didn't feel I could press you on the subject, but now…?" she asked, leaving the question open.

"Originally that was my intent. To kill her. She was the first person I banished, and I was going to return later to finish it. Instead, she has earned her second life in her work for me. Several times over. I can't let her ever return here knowing what she does, but I'm most pleased with her. I couldn't replace her if I wanted. Anything else?"

"I… no. I suppose not."

"Great. Wanna hug? I give good hugs I'm told. Real good hugger."

Faye finally laughed and gave her head a shake. Her spine firmed up and her shoulders straightened. Tension visibly flowed out of her even though she looked anything but "at ease."

His confident general had returned. The woman who would have easily trounced him if it weren't for his massive amount of cheating with force multipliers and toys.

"Ah, not right now. Maybe later. Lord Runner, Thana still seems wary of me at times."

"She has her own reasons that have nothing to do with your abilities or trustworthiness. Truth be told, I'd suspect she's more concerned about you getting in my bedroom than you doing anything."

It sounded weird even to his own ears, but he was pretty confident in it being the truth.

"I'm sure she trusts you as much as I do. And as you pointed out" — Runner held up his hands in front of him — "I'm putting the possibility of you taking everything from me clearly in your hands.

"Okay, now let's go over the plan and what you need. As I said earlier, I need you to build a fort, conquer the frontier, and bring everyone into the fold. I'm giving you the entire army, all of the tanks save five, and all of the cannons."

Faye took that in with a blazing smile.

12:36 pm Sovereign Earth time
12/22/43

Runner pushed himself back from Alexia's table while checking the time. He was very unable, though willing, to eat another bite. That and time was flying by.

"Goodness, Alexia, are you trying to keep me coming back for the food alone? That was absolutely delicious.

Alexia laughed lightly and stood up from the table.

"Maybe. I admit I want for nothing other than your attention, Lord."

"You have it, and then some. Now, let's go get this receiver built. We also need to talk about you worshiping me as a god. The religion of Runner Norwood, as it were."

Runner met her gaze squarely with his own as he said that.

She genuinely looked surprised at his statement.

"Lord?"

"Come, we can talk as we go. I assume you're the head priestess?"

"Lord, I'm sure that—"

"Alexia, be forthright and direct with me."

She looked at him and then seemed to deflate.

"I'm the head priestess. I have a number of those who serve in a more limited capacity. As our city grows, the faithful grow, so we must expand."

Runner nodded at that and held open the front door of Alexia's house, gesturing with his free hand. She picked up her staff and passed by him into the open boulevard beyond.

"And how many participate in worship then?"

"All. Everyone here is a worshiper."

"I see. How many did you end up banishing from here?"

"Six. They were disruptive and wanted to establish a church to Lambart." There was no hesitation in her now when Runner pressed her for the truth.

It was visible to him that she appeared to have lost her earlier confidence with his new line of questioning.

Runner stepped up beside her after closing the front door.

"I don't plan on stopping you, Alexia. Though I do have to tell you, I'm not a god."

"You are a god without your divinity. We shall raise you up. You've given us Eden."

Runner felt the cold hand of fate at that statement. Fate had a thing for him. Sometimes she wanted to kill him, other times sleep with him.

"All I ask is that you please keep everyone happy, healthy, and living well, Priestess. I'll be content with that as my commandment to you.

"Unrelated to this conversation, Faye was happy to hear you're doing well. She would like to visit at some point." Runner politely smiled or nodded at those they passed. Most stared at him and looked to be shocked into immobility.

"Today is a good day. You recognize your religion, confirm me as your high priestess, tell me my true friend is well, and best of all, you had lunch with me."

Laughing ruefully, Runner felt like maybe she hadn't recovered from her time in the dark as much as he'd thought.

"Now, the receiver. It's a large machine made from enchanted stones. Looks almost like a stone pillar with a basin without a bottom at the top.

"All you have to do is put things in the top. It'll sort and send everything back to me. You'll need to decide where you want it. I'm assuming where I arrive is actually my main temple, so that might be a good building to use."

"Yes, very much so. It would be good to place it there so that they may make offerings to you during or after service."

"As you like, Priestess. I'm afraid I will be traveling to another city soon and may be gone for a time. I do not know how regularly I'll be able to visit." Runner fingered a ring out of his inventory and held it out to her.

It was an electrum ring with a fire opal in the setting. It drew the eye with how bright it was. The jewel was shaped into a signet oval, though it had no inscription or device.

"Figure out my divine symbol. I'm no good with that sort of thing, so I leave it to you. Once you do, I'll set it into this ring. The ring is enchanted with several uses of *Blink* and is tied to where I arrive in the temple. I took the liberty of linking it earlier when I entered the temple today. If it grows hot, I have arrived. It won't burn you, but it might be uncomfortable."

"Many thanks, Lord. This is a great boon."

Runner waved her thanks off as they took the steps up into his own temple.

"Now, where do you want this? I'd say it's four feet tall and maybe a foot and a half wide."

It took an hour of moving the receiver around until Alexia felt satisfied with its placement.

"Done, then. I'll have the other side set up as soon as I return. All you need to do is put anything into the hopper there and that's it. Whatever you do, don't put anything alive in it. It'll break the machine and they'll be stuck in there until I can fix it."

"Your will be done, Lord."

"Alright, things to do, preparations to make. Islands to conquer and people to lash to my will." Runner leaned in and hugged Alexia tightly. "Be good, Priestess."

And with that, Runner left.

Today would be one of the last days he saw Katarina or Thana for a while, and he wanted to spend time with both of them.

5:15 am Sovereign Earth time
12/26/43

Runner was looking at the property owner screen and sorting various resources when the alarm he set up began chirping at him. Turning it off with a flick of a finger, he worked to finish his task.

Selecting the barracks, he queued it up for construction to begin after the keep was finished.

Moving to the finance screen, he put income tax at a paltry ten percent. Sales tax a meager two percent. Exports were duty free and imports had a ten percent tax.

He was no financial wizard, but he felt like he was doing the right thing.

The hope was that this would continue to drive in new citizens and enterprising people looking to start over from all over.

Selecting an outlying area from the south to the west, he sectioned it off. Labeling it as "future farm fields," he then moved one of the tokens there that represented workload to be done.

One token represented maybe fifty people, but it was nowhere near enough. Not for the sheer amount of land he'd cut out.

The workers would begin preparing the land to be divided up into farm parcels to be sold to farmers.

He pulled out another token and set it down at a point halfway between the furthest known frontier town and Norwood. A quick use of the lasso tool gave him a square. Labeling it as "future city site," he moved the token on top of it. They would begin to prepare the area for future use.

Using the lasso tool once more, he selected a range of low mountains and marked it off. "Potential sites to mine" was the note he added, and he moved another token there to begin survey work.

The rest of the tokens he moved to the keep.

It'd have to do. He could make changes anywhere and keep apprised of the situation, but it wasn't the same as talking to the overseers in person.

I prefer to treat this as a world rather than a game, as of late. How would I feel if I thought this was real? If all the game mechanics were gone?

Grunting, Runner closed the panel and looked to his bedroom. Srit slept peacefully, a light snore audible even at his distance from her.

"Sunshine, I'll be leaving in about fifteen minutes. Would you like to sleep in a bit longer?"

"Mmmmfhhhf mffssh."

"Yeah, I think the bed is pretty comfy as well. Come on, little miss supercomputer, wake up or sleep in?"

"Kiss, sleep in. Unconcerned. You'll come back."

"Got it. Don't forget to feed Nibbles." Runner moved his way to the bed and lightly kissed Srit's lips. He traced the line of her jaw with a finger, then left, shutting the door quietly behind himself.

Now if he only had the same confidence in himself that Srit did.

Grace slid in behind him, nodding her head at him.

"Morning, sir."

"Morning, Grace. Ready to ride?"

"I've prepared our guard appropriately. I drew up a reserve listing as well, and they'll be traveling in a separate vehicle."

"That's not what I asked."

"No, sir. But you asked me to make sure you were safe. I'm doing that."

"Fine, fine. Though we'll be talking privately tonight about your disobedience."

"Promises," quipped the Sunless woman, a predatory smile on her lips.

"The hell is with you? I'm supposed to be the one saying that kind of thing to you. Not the other way around."

Behind him, a number of his guards chuckled and snickered at that.

"Sir, you're a cat with a lion's roar. Everyone figured out long ago that you have no desire to be working your way through your people's beds."

"Grace, why do I get the idea that there's something I don't know?"

"I'm sure you're aware of many things, sir. Speaking of, normally I have to forward all potential recruits who will be working in close proximity to you through Thana. While Thana is away, I've circumvented this necessity."

Runner hadn't known that, and Sophia had told him, without telling him. Perhaps honoring an agreement she'd made with Thana.

She had a hand in hiring his personal guard. Which meant she took an active part in everyone who interacted with him. He had to wonder what type of assurance Thana pulled from them during the hiring process.

Runner could only guess that this happened to be part of the "council" she led. Apparently his love life was far more complicated than he'd ever imagined.

"She's quite the meddler. I'm sorry, Grace."

"Don't be. I owe her much, and it isn't that much of an inconvenience in truth. She does it because she wants you to be happy but is trying to protect herself."

"I know, I'm a poor excuse for a man." Runner scolded himself, his feet carrying him to the motor pool, where the tanks were stored.

"Not at all, sir. You merely have an open and generous heart."

Runner said nothing to that and instead focused on Boxy.

"For a manwhore," she amended.

Runner scoffed and shook his head.

Looking like her namesake, a box, Boxy had the look of a wooden box on wheels.

The officer on duty for the motor pool came over to him and held out a piece of paper.

"Officer. Boxy and one other. Grace, who's your pilot?"

Another woman stepped up beside her, a cute looking dark-haired woman. She was petite and short. Probably an inch shorter than even Thana. She would have to be a crafter to pilot a tank, but she was outfitted as one of Norwood's Own.

"Me, Lord Norwood," she said.

"Well, Me, sign here and get your key." Runner handed a form to Me and popped open Boxy's door.

Inside the cabin Isabelle sat with Brunhild, Ernsta, and Amelia. The four women looked to him as the door opened and smiled in concert.

"Uh. Hi there," he said, a touch of concern in his voice.

"Little lamb."

"Lovey!"

"Runner."

"My lord."

Sophia looked into the vehicle and then moved as if she were going to go to Me's tank.

"Oh no you don't," Runner said, wrapping a hand around Sophia's wrist. "Come on, you're supposed to protect me, remember? This would be included."

Pulling her along behind him, he stepped into the cabin.

"To what do I owe the pleasure? Aren't you supposed to be helping Hanners, Minxy?" Runner asked, stepping through the middle of them to the driver's seat. He released Sophia's arm after she took the copilot seat slightly behind his and to the side.

"My sisters and I are keeping a low profile while our people go through combining everything," Brunhild explained. "I felt we would be of best service if we spend time with you. Amelia and Hannah will meet up as needed, but they have already made most of the arrangements."

"That's right. We're especially happy to be here since your little gatekeeper isn't around. Hoping to sneak into your bedroll a few times. Don't let these little choir girls fool you — I'm not the only one thinking about you like that."

"Oh? Sounds like I'm safe if you're all trying to get in at the same time then. Barely has room for one, let alone six," Runner said, activating the controls and pulling the parking brake lever.

"I must confess, I'm glad to have your company," Runner admitted, looking back over his shoulder. "It'll be good to spend time with you all. I rarely get to speak with you about general things. Everyday things.

"As to our mission, I'd like to ask you a question. We know pretty much nothing about where we're going. Other than it wasn't there when we left Vix originally. Any of you lovely goddesses able to add to that meager amount of information?"

"It depends, little lamb."

"What she means, lovey, is it depends on if it'll get us first shot at your tent pole. Your little minder there is hoping to protect you from inside your bedroll, and the tree rat is hoping you'll pick her outright. Rather than one of us, since they're both already signed off on."

"Sister...," Brunhild started.

"Tree rat!?" Isabelle squawked indignantly.

"Sorry, tree mouse? I almost went with tree fucker, but Runner isn't a tree and you haven't fucked him. I'd know, I watch."

"You watch him? I don't even — wait, you mean..." Isabelle's voice trailed off and she leaned in to talk more quietly with Amelia.

"Never mind. This is going to be a long trip, isn't it?" Runner lamented, looking over to Sophia.

Sophia had turned a faint pink, but she managed to meet his eyes.

"Very, sir. I don't think I can protect you from them."

"Don't worry about it. Keep me alive and breathing. I'll worry about my sleeping habits."

Runner rolled the steering wheel in his hands, bringing Boxy around towards the motor pool exit. Sliding onto the road as Me's tank took the rear, they set off for the north.

Chapter 4 - Trickster -

Runner peered at the palisade and the exterior of the city. A small unit of guards patrolled regularly around the base of the wooden perimeter.

To his eyes, the entire layout had more the look of a shantytown than a city. About the only thing that looked like quality construction was the stake wall itself. At least from what he could see so far.

"My lord, shall I sneak in and take a look around?"

"Yeah, hop to, Belle. My gut tells me it's a bit of a clusterfuck in there. Don't look weak, don't put yourself under anyone else's influence for any reason. Do what you have to, and get back to me when you feel like you know enough."

"On my way, my lord." Isabelle slithered out from the brush they were hidden in and began making her way towards the front gate.

"Sir, if I may?"

"Why her and not you, Grace? Or one of your people? Look at the guard," Runner said, pointing a finger at the patrol and then the gate guards.

"Poorly outfitted, untrained, the look of vagabonds."

"And none of them the same race."

Sophia fell silent as she rechecked the guards with that bit of information as a filter.

"You're right. I'm afraid I don't—"

"It's a refugee camp. Judging by those they've put on guard duty, I'd say the vast majority of the inhabitants are not what we'd call the 'civil' races. I'm sure there's normal races in there too, but really now."

Runner paused to pick out the patrol on the far side of the wall before they turned the corner.

"That looks like a Demon or something. That big one with it looks like an ogre to me. Rounding out that little group I swear is a Troll. At the gate we have a Dragonkin and a Minotaur. Just on the inside is a Dryad talking to a Gargoyle. It's like a freakin' leftover lunch of every dungeon from here to..."

Runner stopped as his mind processed his last statement.

"They're refugees from dungeons. There's still a large number of people like me in the world even now. Before I got rid of the large numbers of them that I did, they were all running around clearing dungeons. These are those who fled, rather than wait and die to the next group. Or so I'm guessing. Which means they're all Awakened. I had nothing to do with this. The server itself is coming to life. If it isn't already Awakened."

"That doesn't sound reassuring, sir."

"It means they'll all have a shot at living a life, but it definitely means we've lost a bit of our edge."

Runner shifted his way backwards out of the bushes and moved to a sitting position.

Pulling out a long piece of wood, he tried to settle his nerves. Keeping his hands busy always managed to calm his mind and put him on track to solving problems.

He had carved a series of trees and leaves into it. Small woodland animals were here and there, and overall, it had a tranquil forest feeling to it.

Runner pulled what looked like a handle from his inventory and fit it onto the carving's only blank spot.

"What are you doing?" Sophia asked, having taken the seat next to him.

"Making Belle a bow." Runner slid the handle down an inch and liberally applied an agility epoxy to the two parts he'd be joining together.

"Ah." Runner knew without looking or guessing that Sophia was now considering the fact that he had not yet made a weapon for her either.

"It's beautiful."

"That it is, Grace. Forests and critters for elves. Cliche, I know, but it works." Runner shrugged his shoulders as he pressed his hands to the wood to make sure it stuck. "A bow doesn't have many parts, so most of her stats are on a quiver that I made to pair with this."

Satisfied that the handle was stuck firmly, Runner pulled a bowstring from his inventory and strung the bow easily. After attaching two small locking mechanisms to the ends, he held up his work as it gently misted over.

Runner didn't even hear the success sound and ignored the pop-up window, instead focusing on the weapon itself.

Item: <Insert Name>

Effects-

Fireblast: Chance to deal burning damage on hit.

Functions-

None:

Attributes-

Agility: 15

"Should I name it? She might like to name it. I still feel bad about naming Lady Death's for her. Kitten seemed happy to name hers," Runner said.

"Let her name it. Katarina named it for cultural reasons, and for different cultural reasons, Thana was glad that you named it for her." Sophia left it at that.

"I never did find out what she named it. I'll have to ask Queen Helen for the details on the whole thing. Alright, Grace. As lovely as it is to sit in the grass without a care with you, we should head back."

Runner stood up and pushed Isabelle's new bow into his inventory.

Sophia got to her feet in her usual graceful way. They then returned to base camp. Everything was as it should be on their approach.

They had parked the two vehicles behind a small rise, doing their best to hide the area from prying eyes. Everyone had gathered between the two vehicles and sat about, chatting, playing small games, waiting.

"Minxy, Brighteyes, Angel, strange question. Has anyone in this slum prayed to you? Can, say, a Minotaur pray to you? An Ogre?"

"An interesting question. No one has prayed, but I believe we would all be receptive to it. Sisters?" Brunhild looked from Ernsta to Amelia.

"An ogre assassin? That'd be kinda funny. I wouldn't say no to a prayer, though, lovey."

"Nor I, lamb. All are welcome in death."

"Right, then. Thinking this little wannabe city here is a bunch of Awakened dungeon escapees."

Screwing his face up in thought, Runner took a seat in the grass. Sophia dropped down next to him and seemed to start working through a document. He couldn't miss the way she glared at Amelia.

During the trip here he had made use of Sophia to watch over him at night. There had been no incidents until last night. Runner woke this morning to Amelia in his bed and Sophia bound and gagged, draped over his feet like a blanket.

Runner felt himself relax a little at the memory of Sophia, who had fallen asleep like that. While Amelia's actions hadn't been his choice, the unexpectedness of it had been... a welcome break.

"Lord Norwood?" asked one of his guards.

Looking up from his contemplation, Runner found himself looking at Me. Crystal-blue eyes met his, but she broke contact immediately.

"Hello, Me. What can I do you for?"

"Ah, you cast spells, right?"

"I can and do, yes."

"Why don't you have a familiar?"

"Huh?"

"A familiar. I've heard tales and stories about high and mighty casters having one. You don't." Me looked rather unsure of herself. She didn't seem to be the type Grace would hire as one of his guards. He could only imagine she was hired for her ability to pilot the vehicle.

"That's a good question. I've never looked into it. Brighteyes?"

"She's correct. A familiar is available to be summoned at a certain point in a caster's career. I'm afraid I do not have the exact information. That does bring up a favor I wanted to ask of you. Can you please grant my sisters and I the same access you've given Srit? It could be useful."

"Oh, sure. I'll build you all some access profiles today at some point. A familiar... huh. Thanks, Me. Consider me in your debt. Feel free to call in a favor later."

Runner didn't hear her response as he was already several windows deep, delving into the wiki to figure out the mystery behind the familiar. The how and when it would be available to him and how he could get it.

"Sir!"

Runner shook himself out of his search. Looking around, he found nothing out of the ordinary and everyone acting normally.

"What's wrong, Grace?"

"A familiar, sir. If you were to summon one, it would not go away. Once bound by the contract to serve, they cannot leave and can only go a certain distance from their master."

"I was just reading about that. The distance isn't too small, half a mile or so. Then they simply reappear next to the side of their master."

"No, sir. The problem is the familiar is based on the stats and personality of their master. For most this isn't an issue since the vast majority of casters are intellectuals. You, uh... you're not."

"No, I'm charisma based."

"And, forgive me, you're not exactly a saint, and your personality is that of a flirt or a tease."

"I've been called worse, but yeah, you're not wrong."

"Sir, I'm not positive, but I'd be willing to bet you'll summon a succubus for a familiar if you tried."

"Err... a succubus. Like a sex demon? Goat legs, cloven hooves, wants to eat my soul?"

"Exactly, sir. I'm not sure that it would be one, but that'd be my expectation. Based on what little I know about summoning a familiar at least."

"I see. The benefits of a familiar are fantastic though. I mean" —Runner paused to check the table he had been looking at— "Mana regeneration, health regeneration, stat boost, damage boost, some even provide auras. All depending on what I summon at least."

"Yes, sir. It doesn't change what I believe your familiar would be."

"Do you think Thana would kill me?"

"No, sir. I don't think she'd be happy though. I think it's possible she'd leave."

"Yeah. That's true." Runner checked his status page for his experience bar. Runner had determined that the familiar conjuring became available at level thirty-eight, which meant he was only a level away.

Name:		Runner	
Level:	37	Class:	
Race:	Human	Experience:	99%
Alignment:	Good	Reputation:	5,020
Fame:	18,455	Bounty:	0

Attributes-			
Strength:	1	Constitution:	1(31)
Dexterity:	15(45)	Intelligence:	15(45)
Agility:	9(39)	Wisdom:	1
Stamina:	1(31)	Charisma:	64(124)

"Good thing I have one percent to decide. Hah. Guess I'll need to make a choice rather quickly. Anything special a succubus would give me?"

"I believe their primary benefit is illusions and mind domination. All of it based in charisma, sir."

Feeling the weight of it pulling at him, he felt torn. On one hand, every bit of power he could scrape up could only be good. On the other, having a sex demon running around didn't exactly sound like a good idea.

"What would Rabbit do?" Runner asked himself quietly. Without consciously thinking about it, he drew a small figurine of Nadine from his inventory and began rubbing his thumb over its head.

She had carved it specifically for him. By his request even. Her likeness, though small, was very accurate.

"Sir, if I may be so bold?" Sophia asked him quietly.

"Mm."

"She would tell you to do what would bring the most good, and help people. I knew her for but a brief period of time, but that's my impression."

Runner felt his lips trembling and his throat start to close up on him as he thought about his lost merchant queen.

"She would, wouldn't she? She'd put it above her own feelings."

"My lord!" Isabelle called, bursting free of the brush nearby.

"Goodness, Belle, are you trying to take the bush with you? Are you being chased? Is something the matter?"

"They have likenesses at the gate that they're comparing to people as they enter. Yours, and most of your inner circle, save myself and Sophia. I stole one," Isabelle said, handing over a thrice folded paper to him.

He moved Nadine's figurine back into his inventory, took the sheet, and looked it over.

"Wanted, Runner Norwood. Criminal. Charges include murder, kidnapping, and theft. I don't remember looking quite so angry. Problem is it definitely looks like me. Enough that they'd try to detain me. I wonder why…"

"Not sure, my lord. It's a real mess in there. Some wooden buildings in there, a few stone, but most of it is cloth strung up between posts. There's no one race here either, it's a vast multitude. I think I even saw a mermaid of all things."

"Fan-fucking-tastic. So, that means either you all go in without me or we figure out a way to disguise me. Grace, you said they were masters of illusion?"

"Yes, sir. They are."

"Wait. Who is, my lord?"

"Grace thinks if I try to summon a familiar, it'll be a succubus."

"Excuse me, what?" Brunhild asked, stepping into the conversation. Her expression clearly expressed her dislike of what she believed she'd just heard.

Up till now the conversation about his familiar had been kept to him and Sophia. Now the goddesses and his guard had heard.

There would be no point in arguing it because he needed information. To get that information, he needed to get inside.

"I need a disguise to get in. Grace believes if I summon a familiar, it'll be a succubus. Succubi are masters of illusion. To that end, I need to summon a familiar. You can argue with me about it after I've summoned her. Let's go get me one percent experience."

Runner said it as gently as he could. He also did it without allowing any room for arguments. Flicking his eyes to the goddesses, he gauged their reactions.

Brunhild merely shook her head and sighed. Ernsta tilted her head forward, her hood shadowing her features, giving Runner no insight to her. Amelia clapped her hands together and laughed.

"Good! I approve of this. She'll be fun for us later on in life. Could also be a satyress though. Fits the same mold. Best of luck, lovey. Be sure to stick it in whatever you summon a few times for me. Time for us ladies to be moving along."

Runner felt a minor catch in his chest at that. Maybe the succubus had angered the three of them after all.

"As my delicate sister mentioned," Brunhild said, glaring at Amelia, "we unfortunately must away. We have only now received word that the heads of our religions are ready for us to preside over the formation of the Triumvirate as one religion and one alone. Coincidence only in the timing, I promise, Runner."

"I do so swear, as well, my lamb."

"I understand. I'm glad to have had you on this trip. It was good to spend time with you all," Runner said sadly. Standing up, he proceeded to hug Brunhild and then Ernsta tightly, giving them each a kiss on the cheek.

"Oh oh, me now. Hug me like you own me. Break me and put me back together," Amelia whispered, sliding in close to him. Her eyes had the crazed and broken look she had most of the time.

Maybe I should ask Srit to see about putting her to rights.

Rolling his eyes, he pulled Amelia in close and hugged her firmly, pressing a kiss to her cheek as well.

"You're an idiot, Minxy. Be good. Don't think for a second I won't check with your sisters to make sure you are."

"'Kay." Amelia looked hesitant, as if she wanted to say something. Then she grabbed him by the shirt and kissed him firmly. No sooner had she gotten what she wanted than she vanished.

"Forgive me, Runner. You know how she is." Brunhild disappeared much like her sister.

"At times I pity her," Ernsta said, fading out of existence.

"And other times I'm jealous," came the whispered words after she left.

"So. You need one percent, my lord?"

Runner gave Isabelle a curt nod and adjusted his clothes, clearing his mind.

"After me then. I know where there's a few things in the area. They're not quite level worthy, but I figure we kill enough, that'll do it."

"Thank goodness they're gone," Sophia muttered. "Half of you, remain here. Let's go."

They only had to hunt for an hour before Runner picked up enough experience to push him into the next level.

Accepting the level up, he waited for whatever memory might spring up.

Disappointingly it turned out to be nothing more than vague memories of work. His old life seemed quite ordinary and boring in comparison to his life now.

Then he dropped his point into dexterity and gave his screen a once-over.

Name:		Runner	
Level:	38	Class:	
Race:	Human	Experience:	00%
Alignment:	Good	Reputation:	5,020
Fame:	18,455	Bounty:	0

Attributes-			
Strength:	1	Constitution:	1(31)
Dexterity:	16(45)	Intelligence:	15(45)
Agility:	9(39)	Wisdom:	1
Stamina:	1(31)	Charisma:	64(124)

"Well. No time like the present. The wiki said all I had to do was use the command to summon one. The original cast isn't an ability or anything."

"Okay. We should be about our business, sir. We still need to get our lodgings squared today before the sun goes down."

"Fine, fine. A little nervous here. I'm not exactly looking forward to this."

"You're not, my lord?"

"No, I have enough problems as it is without a full-fledged sex demon that can't leave my side. Forever. I don't need that. Not in any way, shape, or form. Minxy is bad enough as it is."

"Ah. True. Especially since I'll be taking Sophia's place tonight. A Demon like that would only get in the way." Isabelle made it sound casual, while Sophia had an expression made of stone.

Closing his eyes tightly, Runner let out a sharp groan.

"Right, then." Without another thought, Runner activated the *Familiar Summon* command and waited.

In front of him a purple pentagram sprang to life in the grass. Smoke and the smell of sulfur hit him immediately as the turf inside the design dissolved in a flash.

Roaring upwards into eight-foot-tall pillars of flame, each point of the pentagram flared. Runner tried to peer into the center of the conflagration to see his familiar. A silhouette was all he could manage, and it didn't lend itself to a gender or race.

Giving up on catching a glimpse, Runner crossed his arms over his chest while he waited for the purple inferno to die out.

As suddenly as it had appeared, the pentagram snuffed itself out.

Kneeling directly in front of him was his familiar.

She was on her hands and knees as if she had collapsed there. Trembling like a leaf in a strong wind, she managed to get into a sitting position. To Runner she looked like she had been summoned violently and against her will.

Long black hair that reached her slim waist brushed against the ground. Lifting a hand to push her hair over her shoulders, she revealed pale skin as white as snow.

Runner's gaze flowed from her shoulders to her face and found a pair of yellow eyes with slit pupils staring into him. Those eyes looked confused and concerned. At a loss as to what had happened.

Her face could be described as artistically beautiful, and judging from the slight cant of her eyes, she was of Asian descent.

Runner would gauge her in her late teens, bordering on hitting twenty.

Barely a woman.

Despite his best intentions, his eyes slid down her figure to find a bust that could compare easily to Thana's, though her hips were narrower than the sorceress's.

All at once Runner realized there was a problem. Atop her head sat a pair of animal-like ears. Black hair that more closely resembled fur spread from the tips of the ears down to their base atop her skull.

She isn't a succubus. What the fuck is she?

A large puffed-up black tail with a white tip swished from side to side behind her.

Runner brought his hand up to lightly scratch at his cheek. Targeting the woman, he threw out a quick *Analyze*.

Level thirty, female, Satomi, Kitsune. There was no information beyond that meager response. A lot was left in question.

He checked the name-plate. She was listed as "Satomi, Runner's Familiar" and nothing more.

No surname.

Slowly making his way down into a crouched position in front of Satomi, he gave her a small smile.

"Good afternoon. My name is Runner Norwood. I apologize for summoning you here. I was attempting to procure a familiar. You don't have the look of what I was expecting."

"What? I — where am I?" Her voice had a vibrancy to it that he could not describe. Light and playful, like the note of a flute on the wind.

"You're on the island of Vix."

"Vix? I do not even know where that is. I am from the Kitsune tribe. Do you know where that is? How do I get home?"

"Satomi, I'm sorry. You've been summoned as a familiar. That means that you're bound to me. For eternity. There is no home for you other than at my side."

"This cannot be true. I am a Kitsune, we are not familiars."

"Yet you are, and here you remain. This isn't something I can undo, either. Take some time, get your thoughts together. List out all the questions that you probably have. I'm going to go speak to my companions over there," Runner said, pointing at Isabelle and Sophia.

"When you feel like you're ready, come talk to me. Okay?"

Satomi blinked her wide golden eyes at him and gave a tiny nod of her head.

"Good." Runner stood up and walked over to his compatriots.

"Well. That didn't turn out as I expected."

"Could certainly say that, sir."

"She's pretty. Better than a succubus if you ask me, my lord."

"I've never heard of a Kitsune. I'll need to do some research later. Unfortunately, this leaves us with a problem. We still need to get into the city. Ideas?"

"Sorry, sir."

"Likewise, my lord."

With a soft grunt, Runner leaned his head back and looked to the sky. Pressing his hands to his temples, he wondered which way fate would push him now. He couldn't decide if this was a better familiar or a worse one than a succubus.

Can't use the forced obedience on her now, now can I? Ripping the free will out of a sex demon who wants to suck my soul out through my dick is one thing. Destroying the mind of a young woman who's lost? Not possible.

Letting his arms hang at his sides, he brought his sight back down to earth and met the gaze of the two women before him.

"Have Norwood's Own set up camp. While they're doing that, see yourselves into the town. Do not separate for any reason. No mystery to solve, no quest to complete, nothing. Since you're not on the list and therefore don't have them looking for you, you shouldn't have any problems if you keep your head down. Get in town and get yourself accommodations. Preferably a larger inn that could house more of us as we get inside. Be sure to mark down any expenses you incur, and I'll reimburse you. I'll remain here with the guard and Satomi for the time being."

"That's not fair. I wanted to watch over you tonight."

"Tomorrow then, silly Belle. I'll be fine tonight. Just give Me a club and tell her to hit me hard if I wake up screaming."

Sophia laughed at that and gave her head a light shake, sending her dark mane tumbling.

"She'd be more likely to hurt herself, sir. She's a good girl and does her job well, but she's not a guard exactly."

"All the better. Go on, get thee hence before I decide to tie you both up and have you keep me company tonight. Or better yet, I'll have Minxy do it for me."

Saluting crisply, Sophia turned and left.

The model guard captain.

Isabelle pouted at him. "Tomorrow night. You said it. I heard it."

"I said it. Go, my little tree mouse."

Grinning wolfishly at him, she held up an index finger. "Yours? Done. I'm off."

She spun on her heel and nearly skipped towards Sophia, her elven charm on full display to anyone watching.

A sharp tug on his sleeve got his attention, and he turned to find Satomi standing behind him. She could be measured at about five foot two on a good day.

"Yes, Satomi? Are you ready?"

"I believe so. I do not think this is the spirit plane. Is it?"

"No. This is a mortal realm."

Satomi nodded at that, her long fingernails digging into her palms.

"You are my master? I am your familiar?"

"Yes, to both. It wasn't my intention, and I'm sorry for it. I had expected to summon... something else."

"This is a strange place. The smells are different. The wind is different. The taste of the air is different."

"Ah, I'd bet on you being Awakened. That is to say, where you were before wasn't quite real. This reality that you're in now, that you're aware of, is very real to you. Even this, though, is a story told by someone else. You and I are mere actors on a stage."

Satomi digested that and then slapped a closed fist into her palm.

"I understand. I have heard stories similar to this before when I was a child. Though I do not like this nor do I wish it, I am an adult of the Kitsune tribe, and I will hold myself to that honor."

"Alright. Glad to hear that since we'll be stuck with each other for eternity."

"Eternity? You are human, are you not? My contract will be to the end of your natural life."

"I'm afraid I'm immortal to the pull of time. I will never age. I can die, but only through violence or other means. Even then, you will not be freed. You'll be bound to my corpse. Forever."

Satomi's face flushed, from what emotion he couldn't tell. He hadn't known her long enough to understand her quite at that level yet.

"Forever."

"Indeed, forever, Satomi."

"I would know you. If I am to be bound to you, I would understand you. You and this... place."

"That... sounds like it would take a while. How about the quick and dirty version and you can get the rest as we go along? We're on a bit of a time crunch."

"I see. That is unacceptable, but if that is what we must do, it is what we must do."

"Right, then. Runner Norwood. I can use any ability, spell, and craft any item given enough time to develop the skill. I'm the lord of Norwood, a city to the south of here. I'm currently engaged in a religious war with those who would see my nation burnt to the ground and my friends slain."

"Are you honorable?"

"I can't answer that. Honor is a lovely thing to have when things are going your way. It's a burden when trying to save the life of another."

"Are you just?"

"Again, I can't answer that. I believe myself to be, yet I'm sure there are those who would say I'm not. All people believe they're the good guys."

Satomi looked perplexed, her eyes flashing as she looked down at his boots. Her ears flattened to the top of her head.

"I'm sorry, Satomi. Things are never as clear cut as the stories would have you believe."

"Yes. You are correct. What role am I to serve? Adviser? Bodyguard? Concubine?" She said the last word with distaste, but offered it up all the same.

"No, no, and no. I'm not really sure what to do with you. How about we start with trying to be friends and work from there?"

Satomi's eyes locked onto his face again. They flashed twice as she tilted her head side to side as if to see him better.

"Are you married?"

"No. I'm not married."

"You have the scent of many women on you. Both divine and mortal."

"That I do. Many. If I had to describe it in a simple way, I have a harem?" Even to his own ears it sounded ridiculous.

A closed mouth smile popped up on Satomi's face as she took that in.

"You are embarrassed by your own answer, and I detect no lie in your words. You are interesting." She leaned her head in close, pressed her small nose to his chest, and took a deep breath of him.

Feeling his skin prickle at the closeness of her, he lightly pushed her back by pressing on her shoulders.

"Ah, good to know?" Runner took a step back from the diminutive woman and cleared his throat. "My current goal is getting into a shantytown north of here. They have a likeness of me that they're using, however. I was hoping to find a way in without being noticed."

"I make you uneasy. Why?" She took a step closer to him, lifting a hand as if to touch him.

"I don't know what you're talking about," Runner said, trying to keep himself from slapping her hand back as it came up to rest on his chest.

"Your heartbeat has sped up. You smell of fear and excitement. You lie."

"Aaaaand that's enough of that." Runner lightly patted her hand and began walking to Boxy.

"I'm going to go do some research. I'll be back later."

"I can get you in."

Runner turned around, facing Satomi.

"What was that?"

"I can get you in. Easily. We Kitsune are magicians of the mind. Illusion masters. A change of who you appear to be is simple." Satomi folded her hands on top of one another against her stomach, watching him.

"That would be wonderful. If you don't mind, I'd need it for myself as soon as possible."

"Unacceptable."

"Err, no?"

"Today, no. Tomorrow, yes. For now, I wish to eat with you. Spend time with you. Learn more of you. The two you sent ahead smell of desire and yearning. They will interfere. We will remain here for the night."

"I see." Runner found himself trapped. The forced obedience was available to him, but that would destroy her mind completely. Turn her into a puppet at best.

She was clearly alive. Very much awake and aware of the world.

Nadine would hate me for it. For even considering it.

Finding himself smiling at Satomi, he held up his hands in defeat.

"So be it. I'm yours for the evening. I'll answer whatever questions you have, but I imagine there will be some answers that might need further explaining that I may or may not be able to give."

"Acceptable. Come, I will make a fire, and you will begin your tale."

"Oh? You sure I'm not the familiar here?"

"You are not the master. I am not the familiar. I am your bond mate. You do not want a familiar. Come."

The little fox woman sat down on the grass and patted the ground next to her. In front of her a fire sprang to life with nothing more than a slight motion of her hands.

"Yeah. Maybe you're worse than a succubus," Runner grumbled in an unkind tone, moving over to Satomi. He sat down next to her and then eyed her speculatively.

"I name you Vixen." The nickname popped into place in his head as if it had always been there.

"I am not a female fox. I am a Kitsune." As if to emphasize the point, she pointed at her chest and then the ears atop her head. "Foxes do not appear thus."

"Vixen it is," Runner confirmed, nodding his head, sending a raid invite to Satomi. "Now, to start with. When was the last time you went to the bathroom?"

Runner sat bolt upright in his sleeping bag. His hair was plastered to his forehead and neck, his skin felt clammy and sticky. His mind struggled valiantly to wake and orient itself.

Staring out into the dark, his eyes tried to adjust. There was no moonlight, so he was nearly unable to see anything.

He felt like he would fall into the sky and be sucked into the void. To drift endlessly without end. To pay for his crimes without end.

A small blue flame appeared before him. Gentle light bathed him and the area immediately around him. Warmth flooded through him as if he were bathed in heated water. The flame itself didn't have the intensity of heat he normally associated with fire.

Cupped in a small hand, the fire danced in a merry way, comforting, promising safety.

Runner stared into it, his hands reaching up to close around the small wrist and hand, supporting them as his mind focused on it.

"Fear not, my bonded. I am here. All is as it should be. Your fear is false and your body is hale. You are surrounded by those who would lay their life down for you without question. Their loyalty and determination come off of them in waves. Like a sun sending out rays." Satomi's quiet tone and gentle words calmed him.

Runner felt everything snap into place as if there had never been a problem — faster than he had ever experienced previously. The clarity of his mind was stunning considering the circumstances.

Maybe having a familiar is far more beneficial than I gave it credit for.

"Thank you, Vixen. Uhm, can you keep the fire going for a bit? Does it drain you?"

"I most certainly can. It takes little effort, though this is an awkward position. A moment."

The fire winked out, and the camp was plunged into darkness again. Runner felt more than saw Satomi position herself next to him.

Again the small greenish-blue flame appeared between them, her small hand holding it up for him.

"Nightmares trouble you. I sensed your distress."

"I've made choices in the past that I pay for in my dreams. No honorable man, no just man, would have those dreams." Runner snapped the sentence off like an offending arrow sticking from his chest.

"Untrue. I would argue that because you have these dreams, your worth is higher. To not have the dreams would be more the pity."

Her words echoed similar sentiments from Nadine. Even up to last week the simple thought of Nadine would send him into a spiral of negativity. Doubt, shame, and pain. Instead he felt only warmth. Warmth and a sad acceptance.

"Thank you, Vixen. I'm going to try to go back to bed now."

"I will sleep with you. Should the need arise, I will resummon my foxfire."

"Mm." Runner turned onto his side, facing Satomi, and immediately dropped back into sleep without another thought.

Chapter 5 - Ascension -

Satomi reached up to Runner's head and drew her hand slowly down across his face.

Runner felt odd at a strange woman's hand touching him like that. Holding still, he waited quietly, his guard standing nearby, watching the display.

When Satomi's hand passed his chin, she stopped and gripped it with her fingers.

Pulling his head down, she peered into his face with her golden eyes. She tilted his head firmly to one side and then the other. Reaching up with her free hand, she lightly fluffed his hair into a different style.

A soft huff and she finally released his chin.

"It will do. You now have the appearance of a male Sunless. A moment please and I shall take care of my own form."

Satomi rolled her hands down herself, starting at the top of her head and moving down along her face and neck.

When her hands moved down past her shoulders, Runner spun around to his guards and addressed them.

"Break apart into small groups. Start filtering in when and where you can with other refugees on the road. Use the minimap to find everyone else. Check in with Grace for your orders. Questions?"

Me raised her hand.

"Yes, Me?"

"Should I remain with the vehicles?"

"Not a bad idea. Are there any other pilots in our group?"

There was a collective shaking of heads.

"Stay in Boxy then. Me, if you have to sacrifice the other one, do so. Keep yourself safe, don't leave the safety of Boxy unless you absolutely must."

"Yes, Lord Norwood."

"Good. Proceed." Runner dismissed them with a crisp salute.

After returning the salute, his guard scattered into small two- to three-person units and began adjusting their equipment to fit whatever backstory they'd developed for themselves.

Checking his status, Runner switched himself to a build set up for extreme intelligence and charisma. It only had a smattering of constitution, which left him a little vulnerable.

Real glass cannon there, idiot.

Name:	Runner		
Level:	38	Class:	
Race:	Human	Experience:	00%
Alignment:	Good	Reputation:	5,020
Fame:	18,455	Bounty:	0

Attributes-			
Strength:	1	Constitution:	1(61)
Dexterity:	16	Intelligence:	15(105)
Agility:	9	Wisdom:	1
Stamina:	1	Charisma:	64(124)

He pulled up the familiar configuration screen and slid the experience indicator to favor Satomi by ninety-nine percent. He needed her to catch up quickly.

His eyes flicked over the servant bond available to him. He could still activate it. Wipe out her mind and turn her into a devoted servant.

No. She's not just a familiar. Rabbit would hate me for even looking at it.

Instead, Runner thumbed the decline button, forever graying out the option.

"They are well trained. Devoted. Strong," Satomi said from his side.

"That they are. I've said before that I'm unworthy of them, and I'll say it again. They're all worth more than whatever value you could assign to them. Well, Vixen, are you ready?" Runner asked, turning his head to regard the Kitsune.

To his eyes Satomi looked unchanged. Quirking a brow, he opened his mouth to ask her about it.

As if sensing his question, she held up her hand.

"I will never be able to fool you, as your familiar. My disguises will only work on you if you will it to. Right now I appear as a Sunless woman. Attractive to be sure but not eye catching. My intention is that we travel as husband and wife. This would protect me from others as well as shield you from the offers of those who would proposition you. I have no doubt that where we are going is a hive of scum and villainy."

Runner snorted, smirking at her. "For someone who looks barely old enough to have moved out of her parents' house, you're rather well versed."

Sure knows an awful lot for someone not from around these parts.

"I am eighty-four years of age. If I do not miss my guess, I am many times your senior. Do not fear, my bonded. I shall not age from what you see before you." She gave him a wide grin, and her tail curled up around her waist.

Runner realized for the first time her canines were enlarged, giving her a wild animal look. It wasn't quite the level of ferocity of a Sunless smile, though it came close.

"Shall we begin?" she asked.

"Yeah. Probably should. Should probably establish our story as we go. I think I'd like to use the name... Walker. Because I feel like being contrary."

"Has anyone told you that you are an idiot?"

"Often, I'm afraid."

Making their way towards the main road, they rehearsed their story.

They were a married couple from the Sunless Kingdom, displaced in the war that had recently ended. A lower mercantile family who'd lost their wares and were trying to start over in Vix. They had considered traveling to Norwood but had decided against it. They believed the city was too new to sustain a valid economy and had instead chosen to wait, buy stock elsewhere, and travel to Norwood at a later time.

Fortunately, or perhaps disappointingly, it did not matter. They entered the city unchallenged after paying a small entry fee and that was it.

Named Letoville, it had all the decorum and trappings of an alcoholic in the first weeks of recovery.

Empty and broken bottles were strewn about, trash was piled in the alleyways, and homeless crowded the sidewalks. Compared to the rest of the world, this looked like it had a government that couldn't even describe itself as decentralized.

He was reminded of the hive cities of Earth, where people had been stacked hundreds upon hundreds on one another. Where they achieved little more than breeding the next generation of menial labor and foot soldiers.

There was one thing that Runner noticed in all of this though. Many people here seemingly had a sense of purpose. Whatever this place had been before, it was clear that whoever ran it now had begun taking steps to rebuild it.

Runner did a quick assessment of those begging near him and approached a young man who stood off to one side.

"Excuse me, could you provide me with directions to an inn?" Runner asked, holding up a single gold piece.

"That I can!" The youth snatched the coin from Runner's hand and then pointed down the road.

"Follow this here until it hits the main intersection. You can't miss it since it'll be the only intersection with actual buildings. Turn right at that point and the inns will be on that street on both sides."

"Fantastic." Runner held up another coin. "Any advice on the ones to stay away from?"

"Yeah, sure. Keep out of every single one on the left-hand side, and the first one on the right. Those are all owned by people who would rather kill you and take your things in the night." The second coin disappeared much like the first.

"Much obliged." Runner turned back to the road. Keeping Satomi well placed on his arm, he deliberately turned into a space that ran between the hung fabrics and tents.

"A bit late to ask—can you *Stealth*, Vixen?"

"Yes."

"Do so." Runner capped off his statement by activating his own ability, his form disappearing from the rest of the world. Beside him Satomi did the same.

Turning again, he brought them into a small lane that ran parallel to the road they'd entered from.

"You fear we were followed?"

"That we would be followed. I needed information and they provided it willingly enough. The problem is, information has a cost. There was no way to avoid flashing money around. I would still limit our risk by making sure to break contact."

"Wise. Good thinking, bonded. I would reward you, but I do not own anything myself."

"Ah, that's a good point. Here." Runner opened a trade window and slid two hundred platinum into the offered section. "Consider this your allowance for the moment. Buy as you will, what you will."

"I admit I am not from this plane, but even I must confess this is a princely sum."

"And yet it's what you're getting. So shut your pretty mouth and take it before I decide you should wander around in nothing but your underwear."

"Hmmmm." Satomi accepted the trade and peered up at him for a moment.

"You lie. You rely on your bluster. Cajoling others and disarming them with humor. You are reactionary."

"You know what, as soon as Lady Death gets home, I'm giving you to her. You'll get along great with each other. You can spend hours psychoanalyzing each other. Then I'll tell Sunshine to go visit you both."

Runner grumped mentally, escorting his familiar towards the area that had been described to them.

Opening his minimap, he noticed that the locater for Isabelle was currently in a side alley behind the inns that had been suggested to him earlier.

Sophia's blue dot, however, was not with Isabelle. It was inconveniently at another location. Much further in amongst the city of Letoville.

Curious. I told them to stay together, didn't I?

"Either they felt like disobeying or something happened."

Beside him, Satomi's arm stiffened up as if she were preparing herself.

Isabelle's blue dot suddenly bolted down the alley in his general direction.

Marking off the alley mentally, he picked up their pace a bit. They passed over a tiny crossroad, then entered the alley.

Reeking of unwashed everything and whatever had blown in, it did a number on Runner's senses. Cracked stones and poorly built buildings created this armpit of an asshole civilization.

Maybe fifty yards ahead of him in the alley he could see Isabelle. She had her eyes on the ground as she dodged debris. Her health bar flashed dangerous in the orange zone.

She was being pursued by several men in armor. They had a similar look to those who had been watching the wall. Runner saw three yellow health bars listed as "guard" and that they were nearly atop her.

One of the guards raised a hand up and a spell left his palm. Streaking forward, a bolt of lightning clipped Isabelle's shoulder and sent her tumbling to the stones.

She slid a few feet on her face and hands, then skidded to a halt in the muddy grit. Runner heard her groan as her health dipped to a red color and a status effect flashed.

"Take care of Belle."

Heart pounding in his chest, Runner blinked forward to the first man as he came to a stop above Isabelle.

He slammed a Banishing Blade into the man's gut, then tilted his head at the next man.

The one who had lit Isabelle up like a neon sign.

Runner released the hilt of the enchanted item as it vanished, the spell taking the guard with it. Walking forward, Runner brought up his next spell.

Targeting the second man, Runner looked to the third. Appearing behind that man was a fourth "guard" and a fifth man named "Captain."

Runner drowned the targeted guard with *Brainwash.*

"Kill your captain." Runner moved his attention to the third and channeled a quick shot of *Stunner.* He watched dispassionately as that man crumpled under the massive amount of electricity coursing through him.

Runner cast *Splatterhouse* point-blank into the stunned guard's skull as he passed his twitching form, walking onwards towards the captain, who was now engaged with his brainwashed compatriot.

With a sickening squelch, the downed guard's head popped open under the impact of the large caliber slug hitting for a critical. Blood and brain matter sprayed the walls and Runner liberally with gore.

The fourth guard looked to Runner with obvious fear in his eyes.

"Scott wants to know if you'd prefer to eat your own hands or your feet. Linda thinks that's being selfish and that we shouldn't share with you. I'm willing to compromise — if you'd like to cook your own feet, you can have those. Then we'll eat your hands."

Runner gave the man a wide vacant smile. Blood from the explosion of the guard's head dripped down into his snarling mouth and brought the coppery taste of death. Drawing his long sword from its sheath on his hip with a rasp, Runner continued to close on the man.

The captain had been shouting this entire time, but Runner couldn't care less. He loosed a charged *Linda* spell. The last guard turned to flee and fell on his face instead as his knees gave out.

Stepping on the man's spine, Runner used *Stealth* followed by *Precise Thrust* and scored a critical back stab, aiming for his heart.

Twisting the blade as he pulled it out, he dropped a *Lava Shot* on top of the guard's head to be sure.

Marching inexorably onward, Runner watched as the captain slew the brainwashed guard. Discharging a ring he had enchanted with *Brainwash,* Runner stopped in front of the man.

"Destroy all of your equipment and sit down," Runner said quietly. Soon the captain was naked and sitting in the muck of the alley.

Placing the tip of his sword at the point where the man's shoulder met his neck, he angled the point down.

All it would take is a shove. One lung or his heart. Maybe both. Or I could send him to Hell with Jacob. I need to visit Jacob.

Behind him he could hear Satomi speaking quietly to Isabelle. Looking over his shoulder he saw Isabelle had regained her feet.

She looked to be in poor condition. Dirt stained, bloody, and dark circles under her eyes. She was alive, however.

Flipping open his raid window, he scanned for Sophia's box.

Runner looked to Sophia's health bar and confirmed she was healthy, though suffering from a few status ailments.

Hungry, cold, wounded, and tired.

Looking back to the captain, Runner waited for the spell to end.

As soon as it did, Runner pushed on his sword, the tip sinking deep into the man's flesh.

"Good morning to you, officer. I'm afraid you're not going to survive this encounter. I'm feeling very generous today, so you'll actually have a choice. You have the option of suffering through this and then for all eternity. Or receiving a chance to make amends in the next life and being able to pass from this plane with very little pain."

Runner pushed again on his sword, the blade sinking deeper into the man's chest.

"I recommend telling me everything I want to know, in as few words as possible, without lying. Did I mention my companion can smell lies? Now, shall we begin?"

"Why were you chasing the Elf?"

"Leto ordered it. We captured the other one last night."

"Have you harmed 'the other one' at all?"

"No! No. She's in a jail cell. She refused to say anything, so we put her there to loosen her tongue. They plan on trying again tomorrow morning. For now she's just being left alone."

"And how did you find them?"

"We received new information from the south. Norwood sent spies up here. They included two new drawings."

"I see. Why is Leto so concerned with Norwood?"

"He wants to rule the island. He's cleaning up Letoville first. Norwood is a place of evil. They gather there and scheme to destroy us."

Runner nodded his head an inch. The first step to unifying a people was giving them a hated universal enemy. Nothing brought people closer than shared near-death experiences and a mutual enemy.

"How do we get into the jail?"

"You can't."

"Sure I can. Vixen?"

"Yes?" Satomi said, pacing over to him.

"Memorize his face for me. Just in case I need to look like him for whatever plan I end up concocting. I will get Grace back regardless of what I must do. I do regret that I had him destroy his armor, so I can't use it as part of a disguise. Please use the other guards for a template instead. Questions?"

"Not at this time," Satomi replied curtly. She grabbed the captain by the chin and pulled his face towards hers. After staring at him for a few seconds, she released him.

"I am done." Turning around, she left Runner alone with the man again.

"Now, you were a good boy. So you get a chance." Runner extracted his sword and pressed his hand to the man's forehead.

Activating *Taxi*, he felt the world around him flash.

/GMHub 2

Teleporting…

/GMHubReturn

Teleporting…

Now that he had deposited the captain in his new home, Runner set his mind to caring for Isabelle.

Only to find she was at full health, leaning against a wall a few feet from him, and that Satomi stood next to her.

"Good to see you, my lord. Though you look strange as a Sunless, it's still very good to see you. I didn't think I'd get out of that one. Or see you again." Isabelle pressed her lips tightly together, her hands resting on her thighs.

Tired but unbroken.

She was a strong woman, not one for fainting or weak spines. A mercenary captain by the strength of her own will and hands.

"They caught us unaware. Burst in on us in the middle of the night. Sophia covered my escape while I dove out the window. I stayed in the alleys around town, but they found me in a search."

"Vixen, please give her a disguise. She's now your sister who is traveling with us, so give her a look that's similar to yours. Once you're done with that, let's get a room. Preferably in the same inn you were staying at, Belle. We could get lucky and figure a few things out or get news. A search and seizure like that generates its own gossip. That or just track their movements."

Runner moved to the corpses and began looting them of all they had.

A few coins and some garbage equipment went into Runner's inventory. Satomi finished up with Isabelle a second later and they ventured out as a group, moving into the main street.

"Did you learn anything of interest in the one night you had?"

"Nothing that would give you an instant victory, but we did find out a few things, my lord —" she started before Runner interrupted her.

"Brother-in-law, brother, or Walker. Not lord."

"Ah, yes, Walker. Apparently this place had a different governor a few weeks ago. This Leto stepped in and took control of everything in a few days. He's been stirring everyone up against the south. It's much as you suspected, these are all cast offs, survivors, and runaways from dungeons."

Runner had assumed that to be true. Having it validated only solidified his concerns.

"On top of that, there are refugees here who came all the way from the mainland. They Awakened there and made their way here."

And it's done.

"In other words, Awakening is spreading without the help or assistance of anyone. Well, it's not unexpected. I'm glad everyone will get a chance to live a life. Even if it does slow my plans."

"There's also an underground movement to support Norwood here. Seems your reputation precedes you. There are those who think you're the best shot at a stable country. It's a minority faction, but it's growing. That is, until Leto's crackdown broke some of it apart.

"They're camped together in the western part of town. They were hoping to ask for inclusion to Norwood lands."

"I see. I can't fault Leto. He's doing pretty much what I would do. The problem is that I want his city as much as he does. More's the pity for him. I will give him a set of choices: walk away, be banished, or die," Runner hissed, holding his hand up and making a tight fist.

"When you are done with the theatrics, bonded, we must quit this place." Satomi patted his shoulder and then walked past him.

"Is he always thus?"

"Usually. You get used to it. The idiot plans are where he'll surprise you."

"Idiot plans?" Satomi asked Isabelle, stepping out into the street proper.

"Idiot plans. Like jumping off a city wall. Attack a group that outnumbers you three hundred to one. Or using *Seduce* on a goddess."

"Ah... I fear I will have the unenviable task of watching over a corpse before long." Satomi sighed as she and Isabelle turned a corner, vanishing from his sight.

They booked a room for four people and settled in without trouble, They wanted to blend in or at least look the part of normal visitors. Any attention at all was the wrong attention.

They made polite chat with the bartender to get the news as it were. Isabelle made small inquiries about goods and what was going hot and cold in the market.

Runner left the others at the inn and spent his time planning for his evening rendezvous with his guard captain. Scouting the jail where Sophia was being held gave him a good idea of what he'd have to go through to get her out.

Making a few circuits, he noted that it had a lone guard at the gate and what he would guess was a few more inside. A little prep, boosting his charisma, and a handful of *Brainwash* spells, and he'd get Sophia back.

For the time being he consoled himself with pinging Sophia several times while he circled the building.

He had received a lone ping in return from her, for which he was grateful. It meant she was awake. Aware. And that she knew she was no longer alone.

Upon returning to the inn, Runner sent Isabelle and Satomi out to begin making contacts within the Norwood faction. He spent his time in the barroom, listening to the gossip and rumors while idly crafting and enchanting jewelry in his lap, hidden from view.

Eventually the night grew long and the number of patrons fell off sharply. Isabelle and Satomi arrived at about the same time the innkeeper gave everyone the last call warning.

Runner followed the women back up to their room and flopped down in his usual spot between beds.

"Make any contacts?"

"No one was willing to speak with us. They were afraid. The smell of fear drenched them, bonded."

"True enough. They were completely different than when we spoke to them last time. I imagine Sophia getting captured turned some of their bravery right round, my lord."

"Hm. Right, then. Let's move on to Grace then."

"Grace?"

"Sophia, Grace. Same difference to him. I'm Isabelle, Belle. You're Satomi, Vixen. Katarina, Kitten. Thana, Lady Death. The like and so on. You'll get it all figured out soon enough," Isabelle explained to the Kitsune.

"Ah. You are fond of nicknames," Satomi asserted, her golden eyes boring into him.

"I am. People I care about get nicknames. Otherwise I won't remember them. Now, back to tonight. I plan on infiltrating, getting Sophia out without anyone the wiser, and returning here swiftly. I'll need you to set her up with a disguise, Vixen."

"It shall be done."

"Belle, you're our real cover story here. Get your mercantile senses tingling and start making modest moves and purchases. Nothing insane that would attract attention, but enough to validate our merchant story."

"Sure thing, my lord."

"By the way, this is yours. I meant to give it to you earlier, forgot till now."

Runner opened his inventory and held out the artifact-level bow to Isabelle.

"Ahh. My lord. I—this is more than I deserve," Isabelle said, accepting the bow.

Runner said nothing and instead stared at her.

"Of course, thank you. I will treasure it."

"Good. So, I didn't pick up anything while in the taproom that we didn't already know. How about you two?"

"Much of the Norwood faction appears to be one-offs from their own respective races or clan. Weres, Fae, Undead, Centaurs, Ogres, whatever, they all seem to be those not only dissatisfied with their roots but with themselves." Isabelle leaned back on her bed, crossing her ankle over her knee.

"Goodie, so you're telling me I'm the redeemer to the isle of misfit toys."

"The what?"

"Never mind. Anything else?"

"There is no crime element here," Satomi said after a momentary pause. "Nothing organized, at least. I would hazard that Leto either controls it, or ended it. My thought runs towards the latter rather than the former."

"Okay, can we use that to our advantage? Has he made any promises that crime would fall off under his watch? If he did, we could rebuild 'organized crime' to fight that."

"I will investigate this. I must hunt tonight anyways. I hunger."

"Ah, that's a good question, actually. What do you eat, Vixen?"

"Essence, emotions, feelings. I need only be near them to satiate myself. Though I do better if I participate. Repressed emotions can be particularly intense."

"I see. And uh, how do you plan on hunting, exactly?"

"I will transform into a fox and then go to where the women sell themselves. I believe it will take only a half hour for me to fill my needs by being in their proximity. It should keep me satiated for a while."

"Oh. That's... interesting," Isabelle said, her delicately arched brows pressing together in the middle.

"I cannot deny I find it" —Satomi sighed, pressing her fingers to her temples — "distasteful? Like eating grass. It will fill you, but not in a pleasing way."

"Speaking of eating, can I have my allowance of beetles? Totally out, and I lost pretty bad last poker night," Isabelle said, leaning forward and holding her hands out to Runner. She rapidly opened and closed her hands.

"Enough with the grabby hands. Fine, here." Runner took one of Isabelle's hands in his own, opened it, and deposited a huge fistful of clicking, squirming beetles. He repeated the action twice.

"Haaaa?" Satomi raised her dark brows in surprise.

Isabelle shrugged at her and promptly ate one of her beetles, pushing the rest into the inventory screen.

"They're delicious. Especially after the first one. My lord, give her her allowance already."

"What? I didn't—okay. Here, Vixen. Eat the first one, and follow it up with a second quickly. Everyone says that's the way to do it," Runner said, holding a handful of beetles to Satomi.

"Take them, and then think 'inventory' in your head. Once the screen pops up, push them in."

Satomi did as instructed, peering at the window only she could see. Eventually she put one in her mouth and crunched it up, following it immediately with another.

"A strange thing. I thought it would be repulsive, or a jest at my expense. It is not. Crunchy but not altogether displeasing. Filling. They take the edge off my needs."

"Great. Now if you'll excuse me, I need to go fetch my guard captain. Probably summon my best goddess friend as well. If she's listening."

Runner was talking to the floor, as Isabelle and Satomi had already taken up a conversation between themselves.

Isabelle idly waved at him and flashed him a warm smile as she talked to Satomi.

Grunting, Runner popped open the window and promptly dove outside while activating *Stealth*.

Hitting the dirt in a tumble, he rolled easily and came up in a light jog. Setting out for the jail at an easy pace, he rapidly changed his spell-enchanted equipment for a full *Brainwash* build out.

Thinking through the situation, he decided to forgo calling out to Amelia. She had a tendency to be more distracting than he wanted.

They were also going through their own situation right now with the realignment of their entire religion.

You can do it yourself. You're a big boy, aren't you?

Arriving at Sophia's holding location, Runner flipped an X marker on the guard at the door. Dropping a personal ping on top of Sophia, he circled the building once more.

Solid stone, no windows, one entrance, no second story.

Several more raid markings appeared to his eyes through the walls of the place itself. In all he counted five markers, including his own. That meant Sophia had four guards with her other than the one at the door.

Slipping in close to the door guard, Runner pickpocketed his key. And his wallet.

Hanners would be so proud of me right now.

Casting *Brainwash* on the man, Runner physically pushed him a single pace forward.

"You're sleepy, your mind has been wandering for the last hour. You're going to close your eyes and accidentally fall asleep." Stepping in behind the man, Runner took a final look at him even as the guard lay down on the stone entry and fell asleep promptly.

Runner opened the door with the key and eased it open enough to squeeze through.

Peering around at the interior, Runner found it really was nothing more than a jail. A fistful of holding cells, a cabinet, and a table with chairs.

Each chair around that table had an occupant, all marked courtesy of Sophia. They were laughing and playing what looked like a card game.

Human, Dark Elf, Dragonkin, Human.

The problem here was the non-humans. They tended to have better resistance to spells.

Dismissing them for the moment, Runner found Sophia in the last cell.

Standing in the center of her cell, she looked like the regal noblewoman she was.

Doing a quick inventory on her, Runner discovered the reason she had the "wounded" ailment. They'd removed her pinky finger from her left hand and the middle finger from her right.

Her face was covered in bruises and cuts, and her left eye was nearly swollen shut. He couldn't even be sure she still had it.

Despite all that, she kept her bearing. Runner could only envy her mental strength and promised himself he'd put her back to rights regardless of the cost to him.

That single dark eye swung to him, and the smallest of smiles threatened her lips.

Runner made a vague motion at her and her hand and then pointed to the guards. He was hoping she would get the idea that he wanted to know if any of them had done the damage to her.

A minute shake of her head after a second of delay gave him his answer.

Targeting the Humans first, he hit them with a casting of *Brainwash* each. Moving to the Dark Elf, he had to cast it twice before it stuck. The Dragonkin took three. Runner had two charges left, and the rest were on cooldown.

"You're all sleepy. You drank too much. Good night."

As one, the jailers sloppily collapsed on the table and atop each other.

"Grace, let's get you out of there and back to the inn. We'll get you cleaned up and put to rights immediately," Runner promised, moving to her cage and opening the lock.

"I'm glad to see you, sir. I feared the worst." Her voice was hoarse, scratchy, dry.

"Thirsty? Hungry?" Runner dropped a water pod and several beetles in her hands as he robbed the guards blind of their possessions.

"Bless you, Runner," Sophia whispered. She greedily emptied the water and devoured the beetles in a mouthful.

"Forgive me. Can you move? Was that enough to…" Runner stopped, his eyes looking her over once again. Her ramrod spine and locked knees had the look of someone holding themselves up by will alone.

"Never mind." Runner stepped into the cell and then whisked Sophia off her feet and held her in his arms. Adjusting her weight around, he managed to activate a trade window and gave her a *Stealth* potion.

"Drink that and then we'll be off." Runner settled her more securely, propping her head on his shoulder while sliding his left arm under her bottom, his right encircling her waist.

Sophia dropped the potion to the ground and it rolled away, full and undrained.

"I'm sorry. I told them nothing. Nothing. I'm sorry. I love you," Sophia slurred through her swollen lips, promptly passing out.

"Damn me," Runner grumbled. A floating woman through the street wouldn't do anyone any good.

Swapping out his *Brainwash* ring for his *Blink* rings, he managed to get her to the door without incident.

Targeting a two-story stone building nearby, he blinked to it. Standing there with Sophia in his arms, he scanned the possibilities to get to the next building. The distance was too great.

There was no way he could return to the inn tonight without causing a commotion.

Which really left him with only two options. Stay on the roof and wait for help or go to the GMHub.

Runner felt shocked at a sudden idea that ripped through his mind.

Grimacing, Runner highlighted the inn and gave it a single ping. Then he triggered the "Defend" command to Isabelle.

A single ping in return atop his location told him Isabelle understood.

Runner then triggered his *GMHub* ability.

/GMHub 2

Teleporting…

Active settings only:
Death=Off
Food/Water=On
Damage=Off
Gravity=100%
Biome=Plane
Day/Night Cycle=On
Foliage=On(N)
Resource Nodes=On(E)
Wildlife=On(H)
Weather=On(N)

Arriving in his temple with Sophia in his arms, Runner looked around. He had been nervous about it being occupied. Thankfully it was devoid of its parishioners.

Using his foot, Runner activated the linked stone he had set in the floor, signaling Alexia.

He opened his inventory with a mental command, managed to snag his bedroll with a finger, and dropped it to the ground.

Laying Sophia atop the sleeping bag, he checked her again to see if he had missed anything.

Several of her toes had been smashed into what looked like ground beef. Two of her teeth had been pulled out, and a long slice had been carved from her ear to her cheek.

Looks like after the captain failed to report back, they questioned her again. I will drown them in blood.

Coming to a decision, he steeled himself and set about getting his plan rolling.

Runner took a moment to open the system screen and then deliberately knocked his own pod into a failed medical routine. Srit would notice it and hopefully come check on him.

"Lord, what — what is this? Who is she?" Alexia asked, entering the arrival room.

"Priestess. I ask you to gather the faithful. I would have them pray to me. This evening. Now. While I sit here in the temple and they gather at the steps below. If they accomplish this, I will see to it that each and every one of them receives a personal boon from me of their own desire."

Alexia's eyes grew wide at this. Then she grinned at him in a most unnerving way.

"Immediately, Lord!" Alexia turned and sprinted from the temple.

He distantly heard the bang of her staff striking stone outside, and then the night was replaced with the noonday sun.

I'm here. What's wrong?

"Sophia's been badly hurt. I'm having Alexia get everyone to pray to me. I'm going to try and force that much divine power to my will and heal Sophia. Supposedly I've been gathering divine power. Fine, I'm going to make it work for me then."

That won't work, Runner. I'm sorry, but it's too much stress on the code.

"Sunshine. Srit. I love you. Please make it happen for me? I need this to work. I can't... I just... please?" Runner whispered, looking up to the ceiling of the temple.

There was an interminable delay, and Runner's nerves stretched taut.

I'll make it work, darling.

"Thank you, Sunshine. I'm deeply in your debt." Sighing heavily, Runner felt like he had a chance.

I'll be naming our firstborn.

"Of course, Sunshine."

Standing up from Sophia, he began focusing on what he wanted. He wanted Sophia to be whole, healthy, hale. Unmarked and returned to him in her original form.

Heat built in him, and his mana bar tanked and went empty instantly. Outside, tens of voices were mumbling. The tens became hundreds and the drone of their voices flowed into a single chant. A single voice.

A single prayer.

It scraped at his mind like a set of claws on a closed door.

Runner grabbed at that sound, trying to mentally open himself to the noise and welcome it in. Then demand it to do his will. To bend to his design and his shape.

What started as a familiar warmth rapidly became a bonfire. Then an inferno.

His skin felt like it was being peeled from him with a white hot spoon. His spirit was willing but his mind began to pull back from the pain.

Then he stuck the image of Nadine dying in front of him instead of Sophia. What if he had this available to him when Nadine had been struck down? What if Sophia never recovered?

What if she dies? Just like Rabbit?

Screaming at the top of his lungs, Runner slammed his palms into his head and bent himself double over Sophia as he willed everything in his being to put her back together.

A sharp explosion like thunder directly above him destroyed his concentration. The reverberation of the sound alone knocked him to his knees. Above him the temple ceiling split and sunlight poured in to bathe him in its golden rays.

Looking up into the light, Runner noticed dust floating in the beams. Motes of dust dancing with one another.

His vision became like that light, brightening until it enveloped everything.

His mind fled him and scattered to the winds, spreading out in every direction. It jumped and skittered through those who prayed outside. Washing through Alexia like a wave. Flowing around the animals out in the plains.

Runner slumped to the floor and knew nothing else.

Chapter 6 - And Another One -

Runner opened his eyes. Turning his head to one side and then the other, he found himself in a room made of quarried stone. It was simply decorated, with only the bare essentials for living.

He plucked at the bedsheets covering him and then reached down to feel a bed frame under him.

Memories of his last actions came back to him in fits and starts. Entering the city, saving Isabelle, getting the news in the inn, and freeing Sophia.

Grace!

Sitting up, Runner felt the world spin around him. The stone walls threatened to topple inwards and crush him.

Be still, darling. We need to discuss what happened. Before you ask, everyone is safe, everyone is sound, Sophia is whole.

Collapsing into his bed, Runner relaxed. The tension in him bled out and left him a little raw.

"Thank you, Sunshine. Thank you. I'm glad to hear that." Runner let his eyes travel to a door on the far side of the chamber he was in.

I'm afraid you've undergone a serious change to make this happen. I had to modify your pod, the code, and even implement a minor AI program into your head with the help of the medical server.

"I see. I'm a host to an AI program, like an Omega?" Runner asked cautiously. Srit would never do something that would endanger him needlessly, so he wasn't too concerned.

Somewhat. This one merely assists in processing data so your mind can interpret it more easily. It doesn't even have a personality. Your mind couldn't keep up with the change.

"Right, then. Give it to me straight, Sunshine. How bad is it?"

Simply put, it's not bad at all. I'd say you're going to need time to learn to adapt to the change, but realistically it won't actually affect anything.

"You're suspiciously avoiding telling me what you did."

I dumped your mind into a coded shell meant for a god. You're no longer a player. Nor are you a god.

"I'm a demigod then?"

That'd probably be the best fit. I'm not sure what changes you'll experience, but I don't think they'll be unpleasant.

"Got it. Thank you, Sunshine. Love you. Remind me to drown you in thanks when I get back."

I'll do that. I have to go, darling.
The Omega have been launching selective probes and attacks on us. I've been swatting them down firmly each time, but they're starting to ramp things up. I'm honestly getting concerned.
I'm also expecting reports from everyone, and I'm having the ship's engines repaired today.

"Do what you have to do. Though it sounds fairly ominous. Should we be concerned about them becoming a threat?"

If they make the attempt, I'll crush them like the ants that they are.

"Such a busy, powerful woman. I love it when you talk doomsday to me. Tell me more about how you'll heap the bodies of the meatbags ever higher."

Idiot.

"What can I say, I'm really into powerful women?"

Love you, too.

Runner sat up again, albeit quite a bit slower this time. Pressing his hands into the mattress, he shrugged his shoulders to stretch his muscles. Pushing a thought at the clock, he checked the date and time.

5:47 am Sovereign Earth time
12/31/43

He had only been out for a night, not much time was lost at all.

Checking the corner of his interface, he found there was a new bar there. White in color and sitting below his mana bar. When he selected it with his mind, it came back as "Divine Power" and that it was full.

We'll ask the goddesses about that later.

Taking the plunge, he pulled up his character sheet.

Name:	Runner		
Level:	38	Class:	Φ♫↓¬»¢
Race:	▼■œ■	Experience:	00%
Alignment:	Good	Reputation:	5,020
Fame:	18,455	Bounty:	0

Attributes-			
Strength:	1	Constitution:	1(61)
Dexterity:	16	Intelligence:	15(105)
Agility:	9	Wisdom:	1
Stamina:	1	Charisma:	64(124)

"Hm. Not that different. Since, ya know, everything has always been screwed up. Where the hell do I get a class trainer for that?"

Runner let out a slow breath.

"Soo... I guess I'm okay?" Runner asked no one. Getting to his feet, he mentally poked at his own brain.

Nothing felt different. At least, nothing he could point to.

Which means everything is alright. Right?

Nothing came back from the depths of his mind from that thought.

"Run on, Runner," he muttered. Squatting down and then standing back up, he felt like everything was working properly and the vertigo he had experienced earlier had left completely.

He moved to the door, popped it open, and stepped out into the connecting hallway. No one was there, and it looked as empty as his room was. Moving to the far side of the hallway, he turned the corner and found another door. Opening it, he stepped through and found himself overlooking the arrival room.

The doors were wide open, sunlight entering and warming the air. As it always seemed to be when he was here, it was empty.

Runner descended the steps quickly. Moving swiftly, he reached the temple doors and looked out into the streets. Smiling as he felt that strange sense of home, he took a deep breath.

On the horizon the sun was barely rising. It was the very early hours of the morning.

The air here was always refreshing to him. Checking his map, he found Sophia to be at Alexia's home.

I'll take an hour to explore before returning. Recharge the ol' batteries.

He made his way down the steps before too many people noticed him, then slipped into a small crowd of people walking along the street.

Runner kept to himself and meandered along with the crowd, looking at the shops and houses as he went.

Everything had the clean lines that soothed him. Symmetrical. Precise. Logical. A bit robotic some might say, but he enjoyed it thoroughly.

Runner stopped in front of a store that he couldn't identify the nature of from the outside. The shop simply read, "Tokens."

Once inside, Runner ducked immediately into an aisle rather than deal with a shopkeep.

Runner stopped about midway down and looked at the shelves.

Hundreds of small figurines were lined up on the top shelf. They were made from simple metals. Looking to the left and right, he found that the quality of the metal increased as you went to the right.

He looked to the lower shelves and saw the figurines grew larger in size. Grinning, he moved down the aisle. He picked up an interesting looking silver figurine of an archer as he passed and moved into the next aisle.

This one was laid out in a similar fashion to the previous except that it held pins, buttons, and hair clips.

Skipping it, he walked to the next to discover it held rings and amulets. Moving on for the last time, Runner walked into the last aisle.

There was less variety in this one, though it was once again similar in its composition. Various materials all laid out, though with only one design.

A simple small house-like structure. Almost like a child's dollhouse with a small bell inside.

Leaning in close to one such mini-house, he poked at the bell. It emitted a pleasantly pitched tone in response.

"Lovely sound," Runner murmured.

Making his way to the sales counter, he decided on purchasing an entire set of all the figurines in silver.

For whatever reason, he was becoming fond of figurines.

"Greetings to you," Runner said to the man behind the counter. He was bent over a box with his back to Runner. "I'd like to purchase a full set of your figurines in silver please. I'll not haggle on price and pay whatever you feel is worthwhile."

"Ah, you must be new. Coin is no good here. Turn it over to the High Priestess, and she'll send it on to do some good for our lord. When you find gold as easily as dirt, there's no point. Take what you like, and understand that anything you produce will likewise be for the benefit of all."

"I see. Well, I would still like a set of figurines in silver. Could you assist me in getting them all? I'd hate to miss any."

"Certainly!" the shopkeep said and stood up. He hefted a bronze mini-house from the crate and set it on his counter. "Was just repairing a household shrine."

The man looked middle-aged, in good health, and overall seemed rather pleasant. The shop owner looked to Runner with a smile.

Which promptly disappeared, and he turned a ghostly white.

"You alright there, friend?" Runner asked quietly. Most of the population here had been sent to this city by his hand, and Runner had, perhaps naively, hoped he could sneak around a bit in plain sight.

"Ah, perfectly fine. Sorry, sorry. I, uh, you said an entire set?"

"Indeed. This little archer is exquisite," Runner explained, holding up the figure.

"Aye, Isabelle is popular," murmured the shopkeep.

"Hah, Belle? I didn't even realize. Maybe I didn't pay as much attention to the figurines as I thought."

"I have no likeness to compare them to, except accounts from those who saw her before coming here."

"Got it. So, a full set then, please." Runner grinned at the man.

Nodding once, the man picked up a small box and went back to the figurines.

Opening his map, Runner pinged twice on the temple. It really was about time to return to the real world. Isabelle and Satomi would be getting ready at the inn.

"Here you are, one of each. Silver per your request." The box made a soft clatter as it touched the counter.

"Ah, perfect. Thank you so much. Blessings upon you and yours," Runner said, picking up the box.

A soft tinkling noise spread throughout the store, and the "Divine Power" bar emptied a fraction, revealing a gray background beneath it.

The shop suddenly had a feeling of tranquility, the warmth of sunshine, and the smell of grass.

"Thank you, Lord. Thank you," stammered the man.

Runner held a finger up to his lips.

"Our secret. To help your art, and purchase your silence, I offer you the following. Especially since I have a new companion, Satomi, the Vixen." Runner quickly pulled up a screenshot of everyone in his circle, including the Triumvirate. Pressing each screenshot to a blank page, he set them down on the counter. "I'd like to request a new set from you in about… a year, give or take a month. Six inches tall please. I'll be sure to revisit you then. Please use whatever material you feel is best for each figurine to match the person."

Without another word, Runner ducked out of the little shop and made his way back to the temple after tucking the entire box of figurines into his inventory.

He arrived seconds before Sophia and Alexia came into sight. Runner smiled and waved at them from the temple doors.

The crowd parted around the two women as they closed in on him.

"Good morning, Priestess, Grace. I'm glad to see you both. Now, I know I was told everything was fine, but…," Runner said apologetically. Stepping in close to Sophia, he took her hands in his and looked them over. He lightly ran his fingers over hers, where they'd been savagely cut from her hand. He could only feel warm flesh and intact fingers. Everything was as it should be.

Peeking down at her feet, he realized she was in boots and he couldn't check her toes. If her fingers had returned, it was safe to assume her feet were fine as well.

Looking up into her face, Runner released one of her hands to poke at her cheek.

"Smile for me, Grace?" Runner asked. He felt a little embarrassed asking, but he wanted to be sure.

Sophia's face gained a touch of color, yet she gave him a bright smile, full of Sunless teeth.

"Ah, I'm glad. You were quite the sight when I got you out of there."

"I'm whole, thanks to you, sir."

Runner could only shake his head and turned to Alexia. Bowing deeply from the waist to his high priestess, he felt a deep gratitude to her.

"Thank you, Alexia. My priestess. You did all I asked and more."

"Ah, Lord, please. It was my duty and pleasure. I am glad to see you truly ascend."

Runner gave her a tight smile as he stood upright.

"We repaired the temple immediately. It only took a few hours with everyone pitching in."

"Ah, yeah. I seem to remember the ceiling breaking."

"I would say it exploded, sir. I woke up shortly after you healed me. The damage was extensive. Your priesthood is industrious." Sophia looked like she wanted to say more but kept it at that.

"That they are. Priestess, I'm afraid we must depart. We have things to take care of."

"Of course, please come back soon, Lord."

Runner merely gave her a nod and turned, leading Sophia back into the temple.

"I had no idea," Sophia whispered to him.

"And you'll say nothing of it. No one knows, except the Triumvirate."

"Thana doesn't?"

"No, and you'll not tell her. Now, forgive me, but," Runner apologized and stepped in close to her, wrapping an arm around her hips, "we'll be leaving now."

/GMHub Return

Teleporting…

Appearing atop the same building they departed from, Runner did a quick survey of the crowd below.

He slipped a *Stealth* potion from his inventory and handed it over to Sophia.

"Head to the same inn you were caught in. I'll be right behind you to run interference if anything happens. That and to hold open doors so they don't think the place is haunted." Runner hopped down from the building as he finished talking.

A second later Sophia dropped down in front of him and knocked back the potion.

Immediately she became a ghostly silhouette and started off down the road.

Runner kept close behind her, moving at a leisurely pace.

They reached the inn with no complications and slipped inside of their room without even a stir of interest from anyone.

Isabelle was there as the door closed behind Runner, hugging Sophia tightly. Satomi was sitting on the windowsill, watching the coming and going of the people below. She gave Runner a glance and a knowing smile before returning to her viewing.

Good question, that. Why didn't she get pulled to the other plane?

"I'm so glad you're okay. I didn't want to leave you there, but someone had to tell Runner." Isabelle sounded pained.

"I told you to go. I'm glad that you listened and found him. As you see, I am well and whole." Sophia eased Isabelle back, holding up her hands to demonstrate the point.

"So you are. You two vanished from the map last night. Did you escape to that little banishment plane of yours?" Isabelle sat down on one of the beds, looking from Runner to Sophia.

"Exactly right. We hung out there till morning. Just in case they started looking for us. Vixen, I hate to ask, but—"

"I cannot. I am already maintaining three disguises at all hours. I could not do four. I am sorry, bonded," Satomi said without turning her head from the window.

"I see. I was afraid of that." Runner took a seat in one of the few chairs in the room. "That leaves us with one option, Grace. I'm going to have to ask you to change your race."

"Oh! That's actually quite a bit of fun. You can, well..." Isabelle leaned in and whispered to Sophia quietly.

"If you two are finished?" Runner didn't wait for a response. "I can change you back when we're done, but it'll need to be now. As a Natural, I believe the entire racial listing will be available to you. From Demon to Yeti. Centaur, Troll, Ogre. Be sure to pick something reasonable though. We're trying to not draw attention."

"Centaur?" Sophia asked, surprised.

"Yeah. If you pick that, though, I'm buying a saddle and riding you. These streets are a mess and that'd be a better way to keep people away from me."

Sophia raised her eyebrows at him.

"What? It's true. Now"—Runner pointed a finger at Sophia—"poof."

Targeting the Sunless woman, he activated *RaceReset*.

Dissolving into a blue vortex of particles, Sophia was no more.

"Alright, while she's doing that... Belle, see if you can arrange a meeting between us and the underground. There should be a bit more morale today once news spreads of what we did last night. Vixen, I'd really appreciate it if you could stick with me today. Grace here, when she finishes, will be sent to collect the guard, give them orders, and make sure they're secured."

"Yes, my lord."

"Certainly, bonded."

Runner nodded and lay down in his customary spot between the beds, watching the swirling mass that was Sophia.

In an overly dramatic fashion, the blue motes returned to the center and Sophia returned.

Looking nearly exactly the same. She'd taken an inch off her height and there were tiny changes to her face, but all in all, it was obviously Sophia.

Then she spread a pair of wings out from behind her. Large white wings that nearly reached both walls when stretched out.

She smiled, and Runner saw that her teeth had the normal look of a Human's.

"So... you picked some type of angelic race then?"

"Indeed, I did. They're named Angelic. Rather generic, though literal. The model looked exactly like I did, though a hair shorter. Everything else is the same. My teeth feel strange." Her bright white wings retracted as she lifted a hand to her mouth. She ran her tongue along the front of her teeth.

"Yeah, you lost your Sunless smile. Now you've got a normal one. Totally dig the wings though. Can I touch 'em? Wanna see if you can carry me sometime? Flying sounds neat." Runner didn't wait for permission, but got up and moved around Sophia. He moved her wings around a little, inspecting them.

"Bonded. Stop that. You do not even know if they are sensitive. You are bothering the poor girl." Satomi gave him a look that said he should know better.

"She doesn't mind, do you, Grace?" Runner gently unfolded her right wing and extended it, trailing his fingertip along a feather's edge.

Sophia said not a word, her posture ramrod straight as ever while Runner fiddled with her wings.

"It's so soft." Runner folded her wing back up and ran a finger along the joint where the wing met her spine. "Realistically, this is so not correct on a physiological level. Neat nonetheless."

"Bonded. Come, you said you wished to depart. Leave Sophia be and let us begin," Satomi said from beside him, forcibly moving his hand from the wings.

"Fine, fine. Grace, your duty is to track down the guard and get them situated. Belle's going to set up a meeting for us with the underground. I'm going to... wander around? Not a lot I can do, I guess."

"Understood, sir." Turning on her heel, Sophia departed.

Isabelle scampered after her.

"You promised me, my lord. Tonight," she said over her shoulder.

"Now that they have left I have a question. You smell different. Like a shrine." Satomi poked his chest with one finger. Those gold eyes that peered into him like spotlights watched him.

"Ah, yeah. Grace was actually pretty messed up. Fingers and toes missing, teeth pulled out. I took her to my private plane and healed her. Kinda became a demigod in the process. Blew up my own temple. You know, usual stuff." Runner shrugged his shoulders at her.

"I have only been with you a matter of days and already I fear for any type of normalcy. At least you are attractive and a good man. Though an idiot. Suppose that makes me a divine familiar." Satomi sighed and went back to her windowsill.

"She smells of you. Whatever you did in healing her marked her profoundly," Satomi concluded.

Runner had to be thankful even if he didn't like the circumstances. Isabelle had managed to set up a meeting with the Norwood movement. Unfortunately, they would only meet with him and Isabelle.

As such, Satomi and Sophia remained out gathering more information about Leto and Letoville.

They had been escorted to a warehouse and then left alone, having been instructed not to speak and to wait.

With security such as this, Runner could only wonder at how hard this Leto had cracked down on perceived "dissidents."

The far side door opened and three people walked in. Each wore a mask disguising their face and clothing that looked far too bulky for them.

Not one of them had the look of a fighter. Each one truly felt like a disgruntled peasant to Runner. Perhaps asked to pay too much in tax and wishing for the lower taxes of Norwood.

Admittedly that had been part of his plan to begin with, but these weren't the type of people to stage a coup.

He could be wrong of course, but he wouldn't bet on it.

"You wanted to meet. What do you want?" the mask on the left asked.

"To discuss how we go about bringing Letoville into Norwood," Runner said simply.

"That's a lofty thing to say. Especially when we don't know you," middle mask said acidly.

"And?" Runner asked. He really wasn't in the mood for this. Part of him wanted to blow the town up with cannons and run it over with tanks.

"Uh, huh?" right mask asked.

"And what? You didn't say anything worth a damn. I'm here to assist you or to do it on my own. You can be a part of it, or not. This is a waste of time."

Runner stood up and beckoned to Isabelle.

"Wait," left mask hurriedly pleaded.

"Why? I honestly can't even tell you why I thought this would be a good idea now." Runner shook his head and kept walking for the exit. "I bet you don't even have any relevant information anyways. By the look of it, you're all a bunch of talkers who sit around complaining about something rather than doing something."

Runner dismissively waved his hand at them over his shoulder.

"Leto is a Vampire. He can dominate anyone with his mind and turn them over to his side with a thought!" someone nearly yelled at him.

Runner paused, his hand holding onto the doorknob.

Vampire? Huh. I bet my charisma is higher. Bigger, too

"Does he plan on holding a meeting anytime soon?"

"No. He's been quiet. Either he's planning something or limiting exposure," explained right mask.

Runner let that sink into his mind as he thought about his options.

The simplest and most direct route would be to kill him. There was the possibility of backlash with that.

He could work at discrediting Leto and then launch a bid for leadership, but that took time he didn't want to spend.

Let's ask Satomi about disguising me to look like someone else. Maybe I can bury Leto without even trying.

Runner pulled the door open and stepped out into the night without another word.

"Thank you for arranging that, Belle. I'm afraid they'll be of little to no use."

"Of course, my lord. Any plans brewing in that head of yours? Hopefully no idiot plans." Isabelle glided up beside him, matching him pace for pace as her green eyes swept the streets for problems.

"Eh. Not really. We can kill him, discredit him, vanish him, all of those work. Honestly, the simplest answers are usually the best ones. The problem here is this Leto person isn't actually doing anything wrong. He's just in my way."

Isabelle reached up to tuck an errant lock of her hair behind a long tipped ear.

"Does that mean you won't be taking over Letoville?"

"No, I plan on taking it over. Anyone that employs torture on my people cannot be left alive. The problem is that in the vast majority of his governing choices, it seems he's taking the best road for Letoville. Everyone always believes they're the good guy."

Isabelle fell silent, her mind probably chewing on what he'd said.

"I'm leaning towards killing him and his entire cabinet. A waste of resources to be sure, but it leaves me without having to contend with any holdouts. It may seem like we have all the time in the world, but getting this place put to rights by the time the other majesties arrive will be a stretch."

"Who would manage this place in that void then? To bring it into lockstep with Norwood in such a time frame? Someone has to take charge, my lord."

"And therein is the problem. I'd create a power vacuum if I killed everyone. The least problematic answer would be for Runner Norwood to appear at the gates right at the same moment that Leto is nowhere to be found. Perhaps dropping a few key rumors that he fled with the treasury when he discovered I was on my way."

Isabelle nodded her head, following along with his thoughts.

They turned at an intersection and began the trek back towards their inn.

"That means I need an assassin while I ask for parley at the gates with the rest of the guard. Unfortunately, we don't really have one. I mean, don't get me wrong, Belle, you're impressive, but this isn't the woods," Runner apologized.

"None taken, and you're right, my lord. What about Satomi? Can she pretend to be you?"

Runner laughed and then turned that idea over in his head.

"I bet she could at that. She could exit with Grace and 'arrive' day after tomorrow. You and I could take care of Leto tomorrow night."

"There we are then. Let's hurry back and get them moving. The gates close later than most cities', but they still close." Isabelle started into a light jog.

Runner felt his eyes move on their own accord to her swaying hips as she moved with her peculiar elven grace.

Giving himself a light shake of his head he matched her pace and set off for the inn. He pinged the inn once with the Rendezvous/Retreat warning.

Runner and Isabelle arrived nearly on top of Sophia and Satomi. Without anyone saying a word, all four converged on the inn room.

"Grace, report on the guards?"

"All accounted for, all are bunked but ready."

"Good. Vixen, are you able to make yourself look like me?"

"Easily, bonded."

"Alright. Time for the plan of the day." Runner blew out a breath before continuing.

"Vixen, Grace, I need you to leave. Tonight. Take the guards with you. Go out far enough that you won't be discovered and wait. The day after tomorrow, arrive early in the morning. Pose as me coming to parley with Leto. Sounds like they had spies in our ranks anyways, so they may already be expecting it. Belle and I will drop some rumors into the streets tomorrow. Go ahead and drop my disguise—I'll *Blink* or *Stealth* from the scene if I get spotted. Besides, it might help the rumor mill anyways if I'm spotted in town. Rumors abound that I'm sneaking around before announcing my presence."

"And what are we to do when Leto agrees, bonded?" Satomi looked mildly annoyed to Runner's eyes. Her fingers twitched once, and Runner saw the disguise icon fade from his interface.

"He won't be arriving. I'll be taking care of him and planting evidence to make it look like he fled. I'm sorry, Vixen, I've been a poor bond mate to you so far. I promise I'm not trying to distance myself from you. It's the opposite, I have a desperate need for you and thus I must make use of you."

The Kitsune blinked and looked at him anew. After a heavy second or two she nodded her head. "So be it. I expect more of your time soon. We must make plans accordingly for our future. Your guard captain has stated my equipment is subpar at best as well."

"Ah, yeah. That's a need. Any other questions? Vixen? Grace?"

Sophia shook her head in response, and Satomi merely stared at him.

"Right, then. Get it done."

Sophia gave a sharp salute and then left after he returned it. Satomi patted him once on the shoulder and then departed as well.

"She's an odd one, my lord," Isabelle said after the sounds of departing footsteps died out.

"Who, Vixen? She's smart and she's adapting quickly. She was ripped from her life and shoved into this one without warning or choice." Runner waved Isabelle's comment off.

Runner lay down in his nest between the beds and let out a soft groan.

"Today felt like it wouldn't end. Not to mention I have this anxious feeling in my chest. My heart beats too heavily and my mind cannot stop wandering. I worry for everyone."

Runner pressed the heels of his hands into his eyes, doing his best to relax. Finally he let his arms drop to his sides as he cleared his thoughts.

A sudden weight settled over his hips, and Runner opened his eyes to find Isabelle sitting on him.

"What exactly are you up to, Belle?" Runner asked, not quite caring for the sudden turn of events.

"I'm going to talk, and you're going to listen. First things first. Thana is well aware of me and my desires. Not only that, but she has grudgingly given me the okay to tell you that I am 'approved' by her. Taking me along on this trip gave me the leverage I needed. Ah ah!"

Isabelle pressed her hand to his mouth. He had taken a breath to argue with her.

"I talk, you listen. With that being said, I'm a grown woman who can make my own choices. I understand your problem. I even get that you're not exactly happy with the situation you put yourself in. I truly get it." With her free hand, she jabbed him in the sternum roughly.

"The problem is I don't give a damn. You're going to let me in, and you're going to like it. I've already been added to your nightmare watch rotation, so get used to the situation. If you have any arguments, I'll listen to them in the morning. Now..." Isabelle grinned down at him.

Runner surrendered once again, wondering at the stupidity of his actions. He was sure fate would screw him over later in payment for this.

"Time for that promised night, my lord."

"You win. I surrender, little tree mouse," Runner said as she pulled her hand from his mouth.

"I know."

11:46 am Sovereign Earth time
1/01/44

Runner had to admit he hadn't even felt awkward waking up next to Isabelle the next morning. His sense of shame at his lifestyle didn't really exist anymore.

Throughout the morning, Isabelle wouldn't quite make eye contact with him, and when she did she'd turn as scarlet as a tomato.

Watching her across the table they were sitting at, he had to hold back a chuckle as she looked away from him quickly.

Little tree mouse indeed.

- 84 -

They'd spent the morning wandering about the streets, spreading rumors of Norwood's imminent arrival. That Leto was concerned and looked worried. That some said he had cleared his bank account out completely.

In a little under eight hours they'd be slipping off to watch Leto's manor. To watch and wait for Leto.

This was actually dinner rather than lunch. The meal after this would be rations at best and probably from a rooftop.

They had settled on the place more for the location than anything else. The prices were outrageous, and he doubted the fare would be anything special.

Runner looked from Isabelle's red cheeks to the crowd milling around outside of the enclosed patio they sat at.

Many looked afraid, some hopeful, but the overwhelming majority of them looked lost.

"They don't know what to do or think." Runner set his chin down in his hand as he watched. He gestured with his free hand at a group of people moving about in small circles.

"No. You're right, Runner. They don't." Isabelle followed the direction of his finger, her eyes tracking an individual only to hop to another.

"Oh? Runner in private, my lord in public?"

Isabelle only grunted at him.

"You're a silly thing, Belle. For what it's worth, I do love you. In my own twisted, loving way too many women kind of way. My little tree mouse."

Isabelle glanced at him only to immediately look back to the crowd as her cheeks blazed.

"I figure after this we retire to our room for the evening. Head back out later tonight. We'll not be back until early morning I imagine. And then it might be off to the walls to watch for Vixen. I'd prefer to get out if we can but... no idea."

"I agree." Isabelle chewed at her lip before her eyes dropped to the table. "Sorry, I know I'm making this weird. Last night was terribly awkward as well."

Runner found her sudden lack of confidence in regards to their lovemaking endearing.

"We'll get used to it. Don't worry, you'll get another chance to practice right after we eat." Runner gave her a wolfish grin over the table.

Isabelle finally looked up at him and then grinned back. Her confidence could be the equal to Katarina's when she wanted it to be.

Chapter 7 - Laws of Attraction -

4:04 am Sovereign Earth time
1/02/44

Runner sighed, resting his chin on his knees as he watched the manor. As far as he could tell, Leto wasn't home. The only person they'd seen was a Gnome scurrying around in the study much earlier in the evening.

When they'd asked people in the street previously about what he looked like, they had always described him as tall, handsome, broad of shoulder, and extremely pale. With brown hair that was cut short and dark eyes.

No such person had come home so far.

"Something isn't right." Isabelle sat next to him, her hands folded in her lap.

"I would agree. We're missing something here, and our time grows short. We could go get the Gnome and find out what he knows," Runner said. He had considered doing that very thing numerous times already but had been worried about alerting Leto to their actions.

At this juncture, the time to act was now, or never.

"You're determined to have Letoville?" Isabelle asked him.

"I need all of Vix. Belle, have you considered what's going on in the mainland?" Runner decided he might as well make the point for her if she hadn't realized it yet.

"A bit. The elven homeland isn't exactly mine anymore."

"True. Last I heard from Sunshine was that Rike and Rannulf were in the process of burning each other's cities down. The civilian casualties are mounting and quickly. It's well beyond a million already. That kind of destruction doesn't limit itself to the boundaries that it starts in."

"I... I had no idea."

"Mm. On top of that, Lambart is using whatever he has left of his forces to carve chunks out of either party, so long as it strengthens himself. To me, it sounds a lot like the end of the world over there. To that end, I must prepare us. Refugees have already been flooding in to us and it has only been weeks since we opened our gates."

Runner stood up — he'd decided he was going to capture the Gnome.

"Tirtius is more or less consolidated. There's only two ports that can reach the mainland from either Vix or Tirtius. We will own one, and Basile the other." Runner began swapping his gear around to achieve a full complement of *Brainwash* capabilities.

"If I could have it, my wet dream, shooting star wish, five-way blow job in my favor would be taking Norman's Port. Holding that and turning it into a fortress would honestly provide us with a lock on our defenses. Our Gibraltar as it were."

Isabelle stood up and raised her arms above her head, stretching herself out.

Runner took the few seconds she spent doing so to admire her without shame.

Catching him watching her, she gave him a coy smile and then gestured at the house.

"I take it we're collecting the knee-high?"

"Might as well. I say we interrogate him and find out what we can. Gnomes are notorious for being casters, and quite good ones, so be sure to get your resistance potions ready. In case we screw up."

Runner blinked across the street to the roof of the manor. Isabelle appeared beside him, triggering her ring to the same effect of his spell.

"What do we do once we've got him? Take him to the inn?"

"Good question. I say play it by ear. I haven't seen anyone else in the manor, so we might be able to question him here and now. If not, we can go elsewhere."

Runner ghosted up the roof to a window and peered inside. Getting a quick picture of the room, he blinked into it. Reaching back behind himself, he flipped the window lock to open.

Runner heard the window pane swing out and the soft hiss of boots as Isabelle joined him on the second floor.

Creeping into the room, Runner glanced around and found nothing out of the ordinary. A study that held a collection of books, paper, writing tools, and somewhat costly furniture.

"Do me a favor, Belle? Start stealing anything that looks expensive and that we can take with us. Really channel your inner Hanners. When we leave here we'll need to make it look like Leto left in a hurry with whatever money there is." Runner picked up a pocket watch from a writing desk and slipped it into his inventory.

"Pretend to be Hannah? Should I say 'fuck' every other sentence and hide when you show up?" Isabelle whispered, moving off to a side table.

"Funny mouse. Interesting to hear you curse though. Maybe later we can explore that." Runner opened the door and crept into the hallway it adjoined. Turning left, he moved down along the length of it and peeked into each room he passed as he did so.

At the end he finally found what he was looking for.

Sleeping in a bed far too large for him was the Gnome. Wild and bushy black hair stuck up from the pillow. Runner waited there at the door for Isabelle to eventually catch up. He assumed she was doing as he'd instructed, systematically clearing out the rooms behind him of treasures.

He could keep himself busy in his own mind.

A hand pressed ever so lightly into his back after maybe ten minutes of waiting. Moving into the room, Runner skirted the bed and came up to the Gnome's side.

Glancing backwards, he found Isabelle had the look of someone ready for a fight.

Targeting the Gnome, who was named Mert, Runner slapped him. He followed it up immediately with *Sleep* when the Gnome's eyes snapped open.

Sleep wouldn't actually put him to sleep. It would simply render him unable to take action.

"Good morning. Well, evening? Something. I'm the grave keeper, motherfucker. I'm here to bury you depending on your answers. I need information. I'm going to get it from you by your volition or I'll turn you into a living trashcan. I figure I cut off your arms and legs and you'd be about the right height for people to throw their garbage in."

Runner hit Mert with a *Brainwash*.

"You will answer my questions honestly and to the point," Runner said, and made a gesture at the rest of the room to Isabelle.

"Who tortured my retainer? A Sunless woman of peerless beauty."

"I did."

Runner felt his teeth click together sharply, and his hands closed into fists.

"Tell me where Leto is."

Isabelle started stealing everything in the room. That single answer had told her enough.

"He is not here."

"Where is Leto currently?"

"He is not here."

"I get that. If he is not here, where is he?"

"Nowhere."

"Is there anyone else in the house?"

"Yes. I have a troublemaker in the basement."

"Anyone loyal to you?"

"No."

"How do I find Leto?"

"You don't."

"If I wanted to find Leto, what would I do?"

"I would summon him."

"And how do you summon him?"

"With a spell."

Runner paused at that and scratched his head. The rapid back and forth helped, but the answers were getting him nowhere.

"What is Leto?"

"An illusion."

Runner laughed suddenly at that. His mind ran along the answers he had received and what he figured was going on.

Mert was about to break the limit of the *Brainwash* spell. Runner needed a few more seconds for *Sleep* to cycle, so he used *Stunner* instead.

Arching his little spine in discomfort, Mert screamed and twisted in the bed.

I really am the villain, aren't I?

"What the hell, Runner?" Isabelle hissed at him, her arms deep in a chest in the corner of the room.

"Relax, Belle, we're alone in the house and I'm pretty sure Mert here is Leto." Runner hit Mert with the *Sleep* spell when it came off cooldown.

"Right. Thanks for that, Mert. Next up is another series of questions. These are going to be fairly direct, so this is almost over. For what it's worth, I don't disagree with what you were doing." Runner sighed dramatically, leaning up against a bedside table.

"In fact, I would have done the same thing you did. The problem here is you harmed one of my retainers. Had you not done that I probably would have explored other options to deal with you. I'm a petty man, sorry."

Runner threw another *Brainwash* into the little man.

"Answer my questions honestly and directly. Are you Leto?"

"No."

"Is Leto an illusion that you summon and you pretend to be Leto?"

"Yes."

"And there we are. So if you vanish, Leto will vanish?"

"Yes."

"Does anyone else know about Leto?"

"No."

"Fantastic. That's done. Where is the treasury for Letoville?"

"Basement."

"How do I get to the treasury?"

"Hidden door in the first cell."

"Great. Open a trade window and give me everything you have."

Mert immediately became nude in the bed, and a window opened for Runner.

"Perfect, here's some really strong poison for you. Accept the trade now." The trade window closed. "I'd like you to drink all of that poison, as fast as you can."

Mert began downing vial after vial of the expensive high-grade poison. Runner had picked it up back in Norwood for such an occasion.

"I think I missed my calling as an assassin. What do you think, Minxy?" Runner asked to the empty space above him.

"You'd have made an exquisite assassin. But then you wouldn't be my equal," Amelia replied.

"Is that enough poison to kill him?"

"Yes. He'll be dead before the spell wears off. Somewhat cruel, lovey. Technically he is committing suicide."

"He hurt Grace. I'm ending the threat to my takeover of Letoville and paying a return to the one who would dare to touch my people. Two for one deal here at Runnermart. I'll talk to you later, Minxy."

Mert died then and there in the bed without another word.

Runner shrugged, stood up, and walked away from the corpse.

"That was a little evil, Runner." Isabelle was pulling books from a shelf, checking the labels and taking some, dropping others.

"A bit. Nadine wouldn't be thrilled with me, but she would understand. I can live with what I've done here."

"So long as you go no further. Don't worry, my dearest lord. I'll keep you on track," Isabelle said to him, looking up from a book she held. Her green eyes pierced him to the soul. Then she blessed him with a warm smile.

Runner felt his heart skip a beat, and he left the room quickly. The treasury waited for him.

Runner nearly skipped down the basement stairs. He'd be glad to be away from Letoville.

Going to need a new name. I should ask Belle or Grace to see what it was named before this.

Runner found himself standing in front of the first cell that lined the basement's walls.

"Ho there."

Runner looked around for a moment before following the sound of the voice. It had come from deeper in the basement.

Standing in the last cell was a green-skinned man. His brow was a little heavier than a human's, and he had the build of a warrior. His hair was short and nearly cropped to his scalp. He only stood a few inches taller than Runner, and looked like the picture of indifference.

"Hi. Were you the troublemaker Mert the gnome was talking about?"

"Mert? Don't know Mert. Leto put me here for questioning him at the town hall meeting. Got me after it ended. Woke up here."

Runner looked up to the name plate, which read "Lobu."

"Right, then. So, Lobu, here's the lowdown. I literally just came from upstairs where I found out Leto has fled."

"Liar. Leto would never flee. You mentioned a Gnome."

"I beg your pardon."

Lobu merely blinked at him as if he had all the time in the world.

"Fine, I murdered a Gnome I found upstairs named Mert that was actually Leto. Leto was an illusion. Course now that you know, you kinda have to disappear or die." Runner held up his hands in apology. "Sorry."

"I'll follow you out. That way you can make sure I leave."

"Fantastic idea." Runner flipped through the items he'd taken from Mert and found a keyring. "Yeah, here's the keyring. Figure it out. I'll be over in cell one."

Runner tossed the keyring to Lobu and returned to the first cell. Grunting, he started tossing the cell and pulling and pushing on everything inside it.

Then he realized the one thing that actually stood out of place. A toilet. A crude imitation of a toilet made from a wooden seat sitting over a hole.

But it was still an actual, honest to the Triumvirate, toilet.

"Well, shit." Runner laughed and took a screenshot.

Fucking miracle toilet.

Reaching down into the hole, he found what he was looking for on the inside.

When he pulled the lever hidden inside, the wall at the base of the stairwell swung outward.

"So that happened." Runner stood up and moved over to the newly made doorway.

Inside glittered thousands of coins in various denominations.

"Huh. Alright then. Brighteyes, I could use that pretty brain of yours."

As if she had been waiting for him to summon her, she materialized beside him. She gave him a bright smile that faltered after a few seconds.

She leaned in close and laid a hand to his chest.

"Hi there, Brighteyes. Don't get me wrong, I'll never spurn your touch, but I'm not sure this is the time or —"

Brunhild pressed her nose to his throat and inhaled deeply. His mind tripped over itself and his head felt heavy. A feeling of dizziness washed over him the likes of which he had never felt before.

"Okay, wow. Uhm. So, we can totally go into a cell or go back upstairs and find a bedroom. Your hair smells amazing." Runner felt his brain spewing out things to say as fast as it could, taken completely off guard by her demeanor.

Her glowing brown eyes moved up to his and she said nothing, merely watched him.

"Hi... there. This uh, aggressive thing. Totally in favor of it." Runner felt like his brain was working without his guidance. He didn't deny she was a beautiful woman, but this felt like too much of a response on his own part.

With Amelia it was a different feeling. For her it was the conquest, sex and passion, and victory of the chase.

Brunhild wasn't that way at all. This feeling wasn't normal.

Something's wrong.

"You ascended," Brunhild said finally. Her fingers closed on his armor and she stood up, putting a distance of perhaps a foot between them. "Yet you didn't. I would like you to explain it to me. Please?" Her eyes never left his, waiting for him to answer.

She hadn't demanded it of him, she had asked.

"Brunhild, right now, I'm feeling pretty giddy at this situation. My head is actually spinning and I can't think straight. Something is seriously wrong with me. I'm also working on a time limit here. So, I promise I'll explain this and answer all your questions, providing we pick this conversation up in the exact same way, if you can help me out here?"

Runner lamely pointed a finger at the treasury room.

Brunhild broke her gaze from his and looked at the glittering pile. With a flick of her free hand it vanished.

"I've moved it to your bedroom in Norwood," Brunhild said, her eyes returning to his. "Srit will find it when she goes to retire for the night. You stated a promise."

"And I've always kept my word."

"You have. We will resume this conversation. Do not speak of this to my sisters. Yet." Then she was gone.

"So. You work for Runner Norwood? I heard he had goddesses in his employ," Lobu said without much excitement. He stood several feet from Runner, dressed in simple leather armor.

"No. I don't work for Runner Norwood," Runner said, choosing not to elaborate. "And yes, that was Brunhild, first of the Triumvirate."

Runner left it at that and took the steps up into the main holding of the home.

Checking the time, he found it to be a few minutes after five a.m.

"Belle, time to go. We're set down here."

"Yes, dearest." Isabelle's voice floated down from above.

"Dearest?" Lobu asked.

"I uh—yeah. Long story."

Lobu grunted and rummaged around in the living room they were in. Runner frowned and looked at Lobu.

"So, do you have a last name?"

"Half-Orc is fine."

"Err, alright. Lobu the Half-Orc." Runner shook his head a bit and looked around the room.

Brunhild's actions had shaken him pretty badly. Her closeness wasn't something he had expected, and her presence had a strange effect on him. Especially today. He couldn't quite put a finger on it.

Isabelle bounced into the room. Her eyes took in Lobu and then went back to Runner.

"Found him in the basement. He's leaving with us. If we can get outside the wall tonight I'd really prefer it. No idea if we can though." Runner motioned to the front of the house.

"What, no jumping from the walls? Changing our races? Hiding in a wagon?" Isabelle said, sliding up behind him and resting her hand on his back.

"You've been talking to the wrong people again. Alright, let's see if we can get out of here," Runner whispered, opening the front door and easing it from the frame. He took a quick peek up and down both directions of the lane the house was on. No one was out and about.

"Time to go. Be sure to leave the door open when we leave, needs to look like he left in a hurry."

Runner moved smoothly from the house and slid into the far side of the lane as if he had always been there. Isabelle joined him immediately and Lobu after a second or three.

They said nothing and made their way to the stakewall. The goal was clear: get out if possible. If they couldn't, the best timing would probably arrive when Satomi did.

The guards would be so focused on what was going on outside, they might be able to slip out.

As if to illustrate his point, they arrived at the gatehouse only to find everything locked up and well guarded. There would be no escape till it opened.

Instead Runner motioned his two companion down a side alley where they could watch the gate.

And wait for an opportunity.

There was no conversation, and other than the occasional stray animal, they were left alone in then alleyway.

At five in the morning on the dot, the guards opened the gate. No sooner had it opened than a guard rushed away after looking outside. Runner could only guess the guard was speeding towards Leto's manor after witnessing Sophia and Satomi approach.

"In a few minutes from now I'm sure we'll get a shot. A chance to make a move and get outta here. Take this, Lobu, it's a *Stealth* potion. It'll actually force you into a stealthed state," Runner said, handing the man a *Stealth* potion. "Drink it when we move. Been a pleasure. Don't come back to Letoville."

Lobu took the vial without comment.

Runner waited, figuring that eventually the guard would come back empty-handed. The rumors they'd spread the day before of Leto having fled would hopefully set up the simple belief that he had.

That and the corpse we left upstairs is long gone.

After a few minutes the guard who had sprinted towards the manor came back.

The way he carried himself had the look of a man defeated. Runner could only guess what was going on behind that helmet.

Every guard crowded around the returnee and started talking to one another.

"Now," Runner hissed, and cast *Stealth* on himself. Flitting out of the alleyway, he ducked wide around the guards. After exiting the open gate, he stuck to the wall and followed it for a way before turning.

Fifty yards from the wall, he deliberately dropped his *Stealth*. Angling himself towards where he expected to find his people, Runner broke into a swift jog.

There they were, immediately visible and in plain sight. Setting his sights on the back of Boxy, he kept moving.

Sliding to a halt at the rear door, he peeked around the edge and found Sophia and Satomi standing side by side in the road.

There was no new movement from the gates.

"Lord Norwood!" an excited, cheerful voice greeted him.

Runner looked up into the cabin to find the driver waving at him.

"Ah, hello, Me. Glad to see you all."

Probably should actually get her name sometime.

"Be a pal and go—never mind." Runner grinned as Sophia and Satomi joined him at the rear of Boxy.

"Grace, Vixen, you're a beautiful sight."

Sophia saluted primly, and Satomi ducked her head an inch towards him.

"We took care of the problem. They're now discovering that Leto is gone. Turns out it was a Gnome with a penchant for illusion." Runner shrugged his shoulders. "Who knew."

Runner stepped in close and hugged Sophia tightly. She stiffened up at first before returning the hug.

"I made sure he understood it was because of his actions towards you that I took his life."

"Thank you. Welcome back, sir."

"Good to be back, Grace."

Grinning, he poked one of her wings with a fingertip. It shuddered under his touch and he had to keep from laughing.

Ticklish wings.

Stepping back from her, he turned his gaze to the Kitsune. Moving forward, he wrapped Satomi in a hug before she could react.

"Haaa? It is good to see you, too," Satomi said, sounding unsure. She hugged him back, her small hands patting him on the back.

"Sorry, get used to it. I give hugs." Runner took a step back from Satomi. "Besides, my hugs are awesome. You should pay me for hugs. Rates are negotiable depending on hug intensity."

"I will consider it." Satomi's eyes turned to Isabelle. The Kitsune's nose flared twice, as if sniffing the wind. She smiled at the Elf and dipped her head to her.

"Felicitations on your achievements," Satomi said heavily to Isabelle.

Runner looked to Isabelle, who was standing beside him. She smiled at Satomi and nodded her head in return.

"Thanks, was only a single Gnome though. Caught him sleeping." Runner swept it aside quickly. "Alright, do you mind swapping with me, Vixen?"

"Not at all, bonded. I will remain at your side."

"Yes, I know. I promised. Now, let's go see if they round up a chancellor or an ambassador or something." Runner grinned, rubbing his hands together.

9:12 am Sovereign Earth time
1/02/44

Runner sat in a camp chair, watching the gate. They'd kept him waiting for a while. Apparently few were willing to come out to talk to him.

"Maybe I should have dug more graves before leaving." Runner sighed, shifting his weight in the chair.

"I think you operated effectively while preserving lives," Satomi replied. She hadn't left his side since he'd returned. Runner figured maybe she was feeling insecure as a familiar who wasn't chained to her master twenty-four seven.

"Thanks, Vixen." Runner flopped his right hand down on top of her head and proceeded to rub the base of her ears. He couldn't help it—he'd wanted to pet them since he met her.

"Aaaah! Do not do such a thing. I am not some dog yearning to have her ears scratched." Satomi jerked her head from his hand, her ears lying flat.

"Satomi?"

She blinked at his sudden use of her name and watched him anxiously.

"I want to pet your ears. You can let me and we can learn from it. Or I can be sneaky about it later. Your call." Runner turned his head to look at her fully.

"You are a rude, vulgar man."

"Very much so. Though I think if the worst you have to worry about is me wanting to pet your ears…" Runner waited, his hand hovering where her head had been.

"You will be gentle? They are sensitive. I will hurt you if you do something strange. I will make the rest of your harem aware of your godhood," Satomi hissed at him, her nose wrinkling.

"Yeah, yeah. Got it. Seriously, Vixen. If I wanted a puppet or a sex toy I would have smashed you with the forced obedience thingie." Runner waited patiently.

Satomi kept her gold eyes on him, wary even as she moved back under his hand.

Resting his palm on her crown, he began to lightly rub his fingertips into the base of her ears.

Looking back to the gates, he couldn't help but sigh once again.

"I think we'll be here for at least a week. Maybe two while they sort themselves out. I'll also need to leave someone here to watch over everything." Runner started going through all the possibilities in his head.

"Leave the Elf. She is high in her confidence right now and will perform the task to her utmost, bonded."

"You're probably right. Feel like I'm running around alone as of late. Everyone is somewhere else."

"Be thankful you are capable of delegation and that your lieutenants are trustworthy. You are wealthy in ways that do not have to do with materials."

"You sure are a wise Kitsune, Vixen." Runner looked over at her. She seemed relaxed now, her shoulders slightly drooped and her hands pressed to her knees.

"I can only be what I am."

"Well, I'm thankful. Very thankful. You're a blessing." Runner ran his thumb along the edge of her ear before returning to the base.

"Remind me to get you outfitted while we're stuck here. Don't get me wrong, you look fantastic in those clothes, but they aren't exactly defensive. Can't have you getting killed on me."

"Yes, my bonded. I believe you should also make a weapon suited to your guard captain."

"Yeah, she's next on my list. She seem a little on edge?"

"A touch. I cannot determine if it is what you did to her, the race change, or her lack of a weapon symbolizing your personal investment."

"Personal investment? Suppose that's a good way to phrase it." Runner shook his head. Suddenly he felt better. Satomi was helping him step around land mines he didn't see.

"Have I mentioned I appreciate you? Because I appreciate you."

To Runner's left Lobu materialized, his green arms crossed over his chest.

Runner glanced at him before returning to his contemplation of the gate.

"Heya, Lobu, watcha doing? I thought you'd be halfway to somewhere else by now."

"Nah. More interesting to follow you. I hear you're the head asshole in charge. I'm good at breaking things. And people. I have no resume, and my only references are in a city I'm not allowed to visit."

"Huh. Consider yourself hired for the time being. We'll figure out a position and title later."

"Fine," Lobu said. "Official beer tester would be good. Maybe brothel inspector."

Runner guffawed at that and gave Satomi's ears a light scratch before standing up.

Can't forget Brighteyes.

"I promised a certain goddess a conversation. I'll be over there." Runner gestured to the wide open nothingness to the west.

Runner stopped roughly a hundred yards from the camp.

"Brighteyes?" Runner asked hesitantly.

Appearing before him, she looked exactly as he had last seen her. Mildly annoyed and concerned at the same time.

"So… I think you had your hand on me and you were nice and close?" he supplied.

Blinking a few times, she finally smiled at him with a soft laugh.

"You're a lovable idiot, Runner." Brunhild stepped in close to him and rested her hand on his chest. It wasn't quite the same as the last time, but he preferred it immensely.

"Better?"

"Oh yes, much. You've always been the hands off one between you and your sisters. My Dark Angel is in for a cuddle and a hug if I'm direct enough, and Minxy… let's not speak of her. Take what I can get when it comes to you."

Runner felt the strange feeling she gave him the last time again slowly creep up. He hadn't experienced this before today around her.

A strange dizzying sensation welled up in his head and stomach.

"You feel that, don't you?" Brunhild asked him.

"Huh? Yeah. I thought you were hitting me with the sexy goddess aura. I mean, your hair smelled phenomenal, and then it was all downhill from there. I take it that's not it?"

"No. You ascended, you silly idiot. You're a god, yet not a god. You feel an attraction to me that is divine in nature."

"That's not true. I can assure you I'm attracted to you in a very mortal and carnal way."

Brunhild's mouth tightened a fraction. He hoped she was battling a smile instead of a frown.

"Explain what happened. Be concise. Your familiar watches, and I can feel her inquisitive nature impelling her this way."

"Grace was injured. I took her to the other plane. I demanded Alexia have everyone pray, and I tried to use the divine power you mentioned. It worked."

"It worked?" she asked him. She sounded a little incredulous.

"Indeed. Sunshine had to help with the code a little. And I kinda blew up part of the temple."

"And here you are, a demigod. You reek of power, like… sunshine and grass. You feel tranquil to me. Our natures balance very well. We have a natural attraction and affinity."

"I think I understand. You're saying we're well matched on a divine level, which lets our portfolios mesh. In other words, we'd do well if we were… a partnered pantheon." He had almost used the word married.

Runner wondered about this. The concept to him seemed strange. The system wouldn't implement such rules naturally. He'd have to question Srit.

Brunhild nodded her head once at his statement and pulled her hand from his chest. To him it looked forced on her part, as if she had no desire to do so.

"There's also a very dark undercurrent to you. Strong. Lethal. It doesn't harm my own sphere, despite being murderous, and if anything fills in the gaps in my divine makeup." She said the last almost to herself rather than him.

"You will feel this with my sisters as well. As will they to you. Do not summon them unless you wish for them to know this. Thankfully I am bound by a bylaw that prevents me from revealing your godhood to them."

Runner hesitated before asking a question he wasn't sure he wanted to.

"Why were you angry at me? You seemed almost insulted."

Brunhild's eyes flicked to the side, unwilling to meet his eyes. After a breath's span of time she met his eyes again, sighing.

"I was furious. It felt like you had joined with another divine being. The power was all over you like you'd been bathed in it."

"Oh. Got it. Don't worry, I already have my divine harem set up. It's only got room for three goddesses. That's a long ways off, but it's definitely in the plan."

Without actually making the conscious decision to, Runner stepped in and hugged Brunhild tightly.

Brunhild's arms encircled him quickly and returned the embrace, pressing in tightly to him.

The strange dizzying sensation nearly overwhelmed him, and his skin tingled from head to toe.

"Alright, totally being honest here, I don't want to let go and I'm not sure I can if I wanted to. I'm sorry, this was a really bad idea. Can you go poof instead?"

Brunhild grunted in a very unladylike manner in response. After ten seconds went by he was starting to wonder if she could.

Then she vanished, leaving him alone in the field.

Immediately the tingling dissipated as did the heavy feeling in the middle of his head.

"Fuck me. That's almost like a compulsion. Gotta talk to Sunshine. Gotta. No goddesses until then. My life gets ever more complicated. It's like a horrible soap opera."

Runner sat down in the grass right there and began setting about putting together a rough idea for a staff. One specifically for Sophia.

Realizing he would be seeing Faye soon enough, he settled in on working on a sword for her at the same time.

Originally he'd seen her with a staff, though as of late she'd moved to a blade. It would seem his trio of casters, Sophia, Thana, and Faye, were splitting into different classes.

I wonder if they talked about that.

Breaking his thoughts free, he started cataloging his available materials.

"I expect to see you two weeks before their majesties arrive, Belle. I'll send Hanners up here to fetch you if you're not back by then," Runner said, poking Isabelle in the shoulder.

"Of course, dearest. I'll return. I don't like this, but I appreciate your faith in me. The task seems daunting." Isabelle patted his chest in return, as if soothing an uneasy dog.

"You can do it. Use the Norwood's Own to your advantage. It's why I'm leaving half of them here. If you need resources, send Me over with the tank. Worst comes to worst, call on one of the goddesses to contact me. I'll be sending you another platoon of Norwood's Own once we get back to Norwood." Runner blew out a breath and then embraced Isabelle one last time.

"Be safe, don't do anything stupid, come back to me," Runner mumbled in her long ear.

"Yes, yes, I love you, too. Go on. Your image of the strong leader is going to dust by the second." Runner could only nod his head as Isabelle hugged him back. Leaning in close, he pressed his lips to hers lovingly before easing back again.

He released her, turned away, and moved to Boxy. He mounted the ramp swiftly without a word to anyone. Moving straight to the controls, he refused to look back.

"All loaded and ready, sir." Sophia's voice rang out after the rear door's bar fell into the slot.

Satomi leaned over his arm from the copilot seat to watch him. She had been hovering over him for the last two weeks during negotiations.

Now it seemed that Boxy had her interest and she would not be denied.

"Now that the ink is dry, and we are safely departing, I must congratulate you. They agreed to every one of your requests and you quashed nearly every one of theirs. What is that?" Satomi touched the parking lever Runner had shifted.

"Parking lever, keeps Boxy stationary when I don't want her to move. As far as Letoville goes, or whatever the hell they decide to name it in the coming months, it wasn't that difficult. They knew their position. Was more of a matter of acting out the need for dickering."

Runner slipped Boxy into first gear and felt the wheels begin to turn.

"You may state it thus; however, I would caution you against such a disparaging statement of your own worth. You had at best, what, twenty? Twenty-one under your command? You conquered a city without engaging the city in a siege or battle. The forward five notches accelerate the vehicle, yes? What do the two below the neutral slot do?"

"Puts the vehicle in reverse. Honestly, you're overstating it. Once they realized they were receiving the exact same laws and expectations Norwood was, they were done. Truth be told they're a valuable resource. With so many disparate races there, they'll make excellent special forces down the road. Werewolf scouts. Troll and Ogre vanguards. Fae infiltrators."

Runner flipped the lever two notches up, moving from first to third gear.

"Why not travel at the maximum velocity that is available?" Satomi indicted the fifth gear.

"Requires fuel of a magical sort. Third will regenerate as fast as it's being used, creating a zero gain zero loss situation. Fourth will drain it at a fair rate, fifth will burn through it rapidly."

"I understand, bonded. I will take control now," Satomi demanded. Putting her hand to his shoulder, she pushed him once.

"I can sit in your lap, and tell your women of this when we arrive in Norwood, or you can move."

"Vixen, you're a terrible person. Do you have any idea how much trouble I'll be in simply about the fact that you exist? Fine, drive. Keep us on the road. There shouldn't be any turns or twists for quite a while."

Runner stood up, keeping a hand on the wheel until Satomi had seated herself and taken the wheel in her hands.

Shaking his head, Runner went over to Sophia and tapped her gently on the shoulder.

Sophia's wings fluttered at the attention. Apparently she had zoned out and was in her own world.

"Sorry, didn't mean to startle you. Sure you don't want to go back to a Sunless? I mean, hey, as long as you're happy, but you don't have to remain like this."

"I enjoy the wings. Flying is blissful. Thank you, sir. What do you need?"

"I need you to accept this without a word or complaint."

Runner opened his inventory and pulled out a staff made of a dark black metal. Inlaid in strips along the length were cherry wood panels. They moved in sleek lines and sharp angles, playing to the rigid personality that was Sophia.

The top was a bronze cap with a steel blade mounted on it. Serving as staff and spear, it would be a lethal thing.

"Almost all of the attributes are intelligence. A little agility. I would say it's the equal to Lady Death's Mortal Coil."

"Sir—"

"What'd I say, Grace?"

Sophia held out her hands and accepted the weapon without another word.

"Fantastic. I didn't name it, feel free." Runner left her there and went to the back, taking a seat next to Lobu.

"Nice weapon."

"Thanks. Might make you one down the road."

"Why? I'm not trying to sleep with you."

Runner laughed at that.

"Maybe that's the reason, then."

"A common problem for you?"

"Let's say I have a harem, I walked into it willingly, and so far everything is working out. I'm not sure how long I can expect it to."

"Sounds like fun to me."

"Now add in the fact I'm pretty sure I'm in love with them. All of them."

"You're fucked. Literally and figuratively."

"Thanks. Delightful bit of advice."

"So are those two…"

"One is my familiar, the other would if I asked, I'm sure."

"The rest are elsewhere?"

"More or less."

Lobu grunted at that and leaned back in his seat.

"Complicated."

Runner could only nod his head at that. Having Lobu around gave him an outlet he hadn't expected.

"Very. Hey, thanks for listening. You should open a bar."

"Sure. Could I have a loan to open it?"

"Why not? When we get back to Norwood, find a spot and get a cost sheet together."

"I should have asked for the brothel inspector position instead."

08:00 am Sovereign Earth time
1/17/44

"Ho the gate. I am Runner Norwood. I have come to discuss the terms of the incorporation of your city into the lands of Norwood," Runner called out to the gate guards. He was trying to do it in a safe way that allowed them time to respond. There was no need to panic them.

"I sent a representative to you previously so that we could hold a proper discussion."

The hairs on the back of Runner's neck felt like they were standing on end.

"They reek of fear, bonded. Something is amiss."

"Yeah, kinda feeling the same thing. Grace, we did send an emissary, didn't we?"

"Yes, sir. The instructions were clear as was the information declared within."

"Can you get me an aerial view, Grace? I'm curious as to what's going on behind the walls."

"Sir." Grace saluted and spread her wings. With a single downbeat, she launched herself into the air and began moving over the top of the city.

"I'm going to need to get an entire company of her. Forget Letoville, I'll start offering bonuses to those willing to change race." Runner watched Sophia's graceful form as she glided through the air.

"Bonded, is it that easy to change a race for you?"

"Yeah. Honestly, it's a simple button click. Why? Want to be a Sunless? A little taller perhaps? A succubus?" Runner asked. Sophia had moved from one end of the city of Vix to the other.

"I am content with my form. I ask as I do not believe even the divine have that power."

Quick on the uptake, as always.

"Oh? Interesting."

"Bonded," Satomi said dangerously.

Runner sighed and scratched at his cheek.

Suddenly the sex demon doesn't seem so bad.

"Yeah, I know. It's part and parcel to me and me alone. Suffice it to say, I'm unique."

Sophia had turned around and was on her way back.

"Does anyone yet realize you are equal to a divine, bonded? That you could destroy this world as easily as they might an anthill given time?"

"No. Well, other than the Triumvirate. I get the impression they're well aware of me."

Sophia landed before him, her wings shuddering and folding up behind her.

"They are clearing the streets, sir. Everyone is being forced into their homes. All ships have been forced to disembark their people and then push off into the harbor. To my eyes, it looks like they're moving to siege conditions." She said the last bit with the tiniest frown threatening her lips.

Runner sighed and leaned his head back, staring up into the sky.

"Seriously? They seemed amenable to this with their correspondence previous to the emissary. Were they stalling? Placating me?"

Runner growled and balled his hands up into fists.

"I grow tired of this. I have things to do. I grow tired of being away from home. There are greater and more foul things afoot than some fat bastard of a governor wanting to keep his city for himself!" Runner shouted aloud.

Looking to the gates, he found they were rapidly closing.

All he could see in his mind's eye was spending days, weeks, trying to break them down.

Months.

Time he didn't want to spend. Time that would require putting others at risk.

Possibly another death. Like Nadine.

No.

Losing control of his temper, Runner felt his heart skip a beat as he threw his hand forward, willing the entire city to suffer his mood. That they all might know fear and realize the futility of refusing him.

A black fog rolled over the city, appearing from the ground itself. It smothered the entire length and breadth of Vix.

Panting, Runner dropped to his knees as screams of fear poured from the throats of every denizen in Vix. The gates boomed shut, locking everyone inside with the black roiling mass that writhed like a living thing.

"Bonded, what have you done? The stench. Fear, absolute stark naked terror," Satomi murmured, pressing her hand to her nose.

Sophia looked upon the city with an unshaken look to her face. To Runner's eyes she looked like a statue of judgment.

"If you do that in my bar, I'm going to toss you out, Norwood. Don't care if you paid for it or not. That black mist looks like it'd leave a mess."

Runner said nothing; he felt drained. Looking up at his status bars, he found his divine power to be empty. Drained to zero. His stamina and mana bars were also empty.

"Sophia." Runner stayed in his kneeling position, looking up to his winged captain.

Sophia's head turned, and she looked into his upturned face.

"Have a catapult built for me. Large enough to toss a corpse."

Sophia saluted once more and moved off to the remaining members of Norwood's Own.

The black cloud had begun to dissipate, the outer edges burning off like the morning fog.

"Satomi, help me." Runner held up his hand to the Kitsune.

She immediately grasped his hand within her own and pulled him to his feet.

"Where do you wish me, bonded?" Satomi quietly asked him.

"Get me to the side, out of the way and if possible out of sight. I'm spent."

Satomi's ears twitched at that, and she tilted her head to the side. Then she pulled his arm around her shoulders, wrapped her arm around his waist, and guided him off the road and to the side into a stand of trees.

"Thank you, Vixen. Remind me to pay you back later," Runner grunted, taking a seat under a tree.

"Of course, my bonded," Satomi replied, taking a seat next to him.

"Now, tell me what you did back there. Spare no details. Then tell me what your goddess discussed with you. You will explain everything to me, and you will not hide things from me going forward."

Runner rested his head on the tree.

"It's hard. There's so much going on. So much to explain." Runner wanted to talk to people about it, about his harem, the divine, Srit, and the Omega. He could easily see himself talking with Lobu about things as time went on, but for now he was still a stranger.

"And we shall be together for all time. I will be closer to you than a wife. We shall outlive any children you have. Any children they have. That is simply the truth. Share with me. I will carry part of your burden, for it is also mine."

Runner closed his eyes.

"Sure, why not?"

Runner spent the next three hours giving the Kitsune the entire history of his adventures, from waking up in the game to now.

Satomi let him ramble along for most of it. She asked questions here and there. Mostly for clarification or to understand how things were related.

Eventually, Runner felt like he'd talked himself dry. There was nothing else to say.

On the road, Sophia was overseeing the construction of the catapult he'd requested.

"I now understand. To summarize, your people are almost extinct and you must protect and save them, even as they would wish you dead.

"You also strive to protect all those who inhabit your lands. Even as you expand your borders to protect others who know not yet the peril they are in.

"To that end, you have enlisted the aid of an intelligence as vast and mighty as the universe. That also sees you as its mate.

"In addition, you constructed a pantheon of supreme women to rule over your lands, who now also view you as a mate.

"To top this, you lead a harem of strong, independent, intelligent women who you do not have the confidence in to believe they all want to be with you. Even if they must settle for only a part of you."

"I guess that's about everything. Yeah. About not having confidence—"

"You do not have confidence in them. If you did, you would not struggle against the wishes of their own hearts. You say Thana manages them and you suspect she ensures that no one enters your circle that she cannot account for.

"I would say you have given them a reason to fear for their own security. Your own insecurity drives them to try and seek shelter in each other. You must address this with them. They are grown women, let them make their choices for themselves."

"That... that makes sense. Thanks, Vixen."

Satomi snickered at his remark, reaching up to pat him on the head.

"You are a good man. Stupid, but good. In time, you will understand your benefits, even if you do not see them in yourself. Now, what is the catapult for?"

"I'm going to fucking launch myself into the city with it. Then I'm going to go kill the mayor and use his head for a soccer ball. After that I'm going to hold an election immediately. They can vote for the sword, or for me. I'm tired of this shit."

Satomi hung her head, her shoulders slumping.

"An idiot plan. My first. Isabelle warned me. I did not take her seriously. I now understand."

"Don't worry, you're coming with me. Be sure to hold tight. I can promise to bite or not bite depending on your preference." Runner waggled his eyebrows at her. "Can't expect to be closer than my nonexistent wife without joining me on these type of things, now can you?"

Satomi pressed her hands to her face.

"I hate you."

"See, this is normally where I tell them, 'No you don't, you love me,' but that's a bit premature. But hey, you'll be with me longer than anyone else. I figure eventually we'll get to the point where you petition Thana to join the harem, or if you take too long, whichever goddess is leading it," Runner said with a smirk.

"I loathe you."

"The sweetest words from your lovely lips. Now, gonna go check on my flight. I don't have any baggage to check, so I figure I'll get processed quick." Runner patted the top of Satomi's head.

"Thanks for the talk. It helped." Runner stood up and strolled over to the catapult, which looked near to completion.

"How are we?" Runner called out, coming to a stop beside the base of the siege weapon. The firing spoon looked like it was about the right size for him.

Taking a second, Runner switched himself over to his "turret" configuration.

"Well, sir. I'm sure we can fire you within the hour," Sophia said, coming to stand behind him.

"Aww, Grace. I love you. You know me so well. Where have you been my whole life?"

"Being raised to be an obedient wife in the Sunless court, remember?"

"Well there's the answer then. Be my wife." Runner wrapped an arm around her waist. Her wings fluttered softly as his forearm brushed against their feathers.

"If that is your order, sir. Your harem is already quite numerous and deep." Sophia looked at him without a hint of emotion.

Runner shrugged his shoulders, looking to the catapult again.

"Yes. Unfortunately, I've not been the best of men to those who care for me. I plan on correcting that when we gather everyone together. People deserve to know where I stand, rather than me hiding." Runner grunted.

Satomi had been right. He'd been running from it, pretending that he was trying not to hurt anyone, when he really didn't want to be hurt himself.

Shaking himself from his reverie, Runner looked to Sophia again and gave her a smile.

"Things will be conclusively decided. Also, I fear I may have inadvertently harmed you."

Runner had been thinking on what Satomi had told him. That Sophia smelled of him. During his rehash to the Kitsune his mind stumbled over what he thought was the answer.

"I'm not aware of anything you have ever done to harm me, sir."

"Remember when I blew up that building?" Runner asked, cautious of those who might overhear.

"Yes. I do."

"I think I might have forced you into a similar situation to our friends Sarge and Two-Shoes."

Sophia blinked and looked down and to the side, digesting what he had said. She didn't make an attempt to move from his side or to remove his arm from around her waist.

Runner was fairly certain he'd made her his personal champion. During his ascension he had drowned her in every bit of divine power he could scrape together. He wasn't sure what all went into a champion selection, but he was fairly certain it had a lot to do with infusing someone with your personal power. He'd have to ask one of the goddesses next time he summoned one.

And explain to them where they fall with me as well. Being responsible sucks.

"I understand. I think. I admit, I'm more cognizant of your feelings and desires before you voice them since the incident. I thought it strange but assumed I was simply more aware of you."

"I'll summon up a divine later so that we can figure this out. I'm sorry, Grace. I only wanted to heal you."

Sophia's wings rapidly spread out and enfolded him, drawing him closer to her.

"And you did. For that I am grateful. I also know that I said things when I was... incoherent. Things that I wish I hadn't ever admitted. I know this as I checked the log. You've been very kind in pretending to have not heard them." Sophia leaned in and kissed his cheek. "You will get in the catapult now and fling yourself like the rotten watermelon you are. Try not to hit a building."

Sophia smiled at him, acting so far from her normal reserved personality that he couldn't even smile back at her.

As quickly as she had spread them, her wings refolded themselves and she left him there.

"You sure pick up a lot of strong women. You made out of a catnip that only women can smell or something?" Lobu asked. He had stepped up beside Runner to watch Sophia leave.

"No idea. But I'm done. I think I'm going to keep the ones I have and let them know where it lays. I have a plan to solve most of the problem."

"So kind of you. Only taking, what is it, seven women?"

"Seven?" Runner did a mental count. "Four for sure. The other three are question marks."

"Seven. Like I said, generous of you."

"Gotta leave some for you, Lobu. Did I mention my entire guard is female?"

"You're a scumbag."

"I am."

Runner watched as Sophia locked the firing mechanism in place for the catapult. Everything was in order and ready.

"Right, then. Looks like my flight is ready, bags are packed. Things to do, people to kill. Skulls for the skull throne, blood for the blood god. That kinda stuff," Runner said while climbing into the firing spoon.

Satomi appeared beside the catapult with a nonplussed look on her face. She started to lift herself in next to him, though there was little room for that. Reaching around her, Runner pulled her into him, holding onto her tightly.

"Man, it's a bit late to find out if x and y axis movement counts as z axis movement. Sure hope not." Runner pressed his teeth together tightly

"What?" Satomi asked, startled. "You don't even know if this will work?"

"Nope, we might go splat. Or thud. Maybe splat, then thud. Lots of sharp breaking noises maybe as our bones turn to pudding? Or who knows, maybe we go flying right into the wall. Or over the city and into the bay."

"Runner, my idiotic bonded, this is too — "

"Fire me!" Runner shouted, locking his arms around Satomi.

Sophia heeded his word and flipped the release lever.

Runner felt his stomach press into his spine as he was flung into the air.

Satomi screamed and dug her nails into him as they flew. As a stone tossed from a sling would fly.

Runner did his best to gauge the spot they would land. The air tore at his eyes and Runner was forced to squint through the sudden tears and pressure.

They easily passed over the wall and began the descending part of the toss.

Going to hit the road.

Runner targeted the area that was rushing towards them. A cobbled road that looked quite solid. And made of stone. And unmoving.

Splat indeed.

Runner called forth a pillar of water in front of him and Satomi. It was about eight feet deep from the angle they were approaching at and tall enough for them to hit the top of it.

Runner cast a low-grade air spell on one side of Satomi's back long enough that the airflow forced her to spin around, putting Runner's back towards the water.

They slapped into the water with an ugly smack, and their momentum was spent rapidly into the water. As soon as it was clear that they were no longer moving, Runner dismissed the column.

Splashing down like a waterfall, the column lost its stability. Runner and Satomi found themselves soaked to the bone, alive, and deposited on the road.

Runner had taken the full brunt of the hit on himself, but only lost half of his health bar.

"Whew, that was a bit of a trip. I bet I could turn that into a ride. Maybe use an air cannon next time and set up the landing pad elsewhere." Runner targeted himself and cast *Regeneration.*

"I hate you. You, you, you…" Satomi flared at him. Her gold eyes blazed with anger.

"Tremendous asshole?"

"Indeed!"

"Stupid fucker?"

"In addition to that!"

"Devilishly sexy man?"

Satomi glared at him and then slapped him. No sooner had the sound faded than she lightly patted the cheek she'd struck.

"Thank you for putting yourself first, idiot." Satomi grumped, her clothes and fur-like hair dripping wet.

"Now that's a fine how do you do. Time to kill someone. You there, meatbag." Runner pointed at a guard nearby, who stared at him.

"I am Runner Norwood. You will take me to the governor. If you fail to do so, I will carve your ears from your head and proceed to sauté them in a pan. Are we clear?"

Meatbag nodded his head and immediately scurried off. Runner started off after the man, needing to keep himself at nearly a jogging pace to match him.

"Your charm never seems to fail," Satomi chided him, moving alongside of him.

"I could have easily hit him with a *Brainwash* for the same thing. This way I keep a cooldown that I wouldn't have."

The sound of boots hitting the stones behind him made Runner check his rear.

Sophia had landed behind him, and was now keeping pace.

"Shit. Why didn't I turn us into Angelics?"

"Because you wanted to feel up the Kitsune, sir. Truth be told, I want to feel her up, too."

"Good point, Grace. Was totally worth it. Remind me to get you into the catapult with me next time. You can slow us down next time. Spend a little more time in the air. Has nothing to do with wanting to put my hands on you," Runner said over his shoulder.

"Promises. Sweet, sweet promises, sir," Sophia called at him as they pounded down the road.

Runner felt better at her responses as of late. When he'd first met her, she had been flippant, playful. Then her job took her over and she became the very image of a guard captain. Whatever mental transformation she was working through seemed like it had passed.

"We shall speak of this later, bonded," Satomi growled at him. Her voice actually rumbled.

"Yes, dear."

The guard ahead of them took a turn, and they slid to a halt in front of a large home. Larger even than Leto's, it screamed of overindulgence.

"Damn, I bet I could host an entire platoon of Norwood's Own here." Runner looked at the opulent home and felt a mild distaste. His own home wasn't even this large.

"Bonded, I meant to ask, did you name them that?"

"Huh? Norwood's Own? No, they named themselves that."

The front door to the mansion opened and a beautiful young woman stepped out. Curly blonde hair, blue eyes, and a buxom build.

She was dressed in fine silks and in a style that enhanced her curves and figure.

"Are you the ruler of the city-state of Vix?" Runner asked, not even attempting to hide the anger in his voice.

"I am that. You are Lord Norwood? I put myself at your mercy. I'm sure we can work out an accommodation. I'd be willing to... do whatever it takes to—"

"Yeah, no. Why did you close the gate on me?"

"A mistake, to be sure. I gave—"

"She lies," Satomi said simply.

"You ordered it closed?" Runner asked.

"Of course not, I—"

"Lie."

Runner nodded his head, considering his options.

Nadine would tell me to spare her, despite her ways.

He popped open his inventory and retrieved a newly fashioned Banishing Blade. He built them in groups and used them as needed.

"You wished to remain in control of your city. To remain independent."

The beautiful governor said nothing, lifting her chin. If she said nothing, she couldn't be called a liar, after all.

"A lack of an answer will indicate a selfish answer to my question," Runner said aloud, and spun the blade in his palm.

"You wanted to remain independent for the sake of your citizens?"

"Of course. They feared for their businesses and goods. That you would strip them of their livelihood."

"A lie and also truth."

"You wanted to remain independent to remain in control? Yes or no."

"Of course not."

"Lie."

"Aaaaand I'm tired of this. I'm sure your replacement will understand." Runner blinked in front of the woman and buried his blade up to the hilt in her.

Releasing the hilt, Runner turned to face the nearby guard. The woman doubled over the weapon with a groan and then vanished.

"Get me the second-in-command or whoever would be in charge now that she's dead. Go." Runner flicked his fingers at the man.

The guard who'd escorted them took off at a dead sprint.

Runner turned and entered the mansion, his eyes taking in the rich surroundings with a touch of annoyance.

"You're going to leave me here, aren't you," Sophia said aloud. It wasn't a question.

Runner took in a slow deep breath, his hands flexing at his sides. He didn't like it. Everyone was being sent away from his side.

Lady Fate was preparing him. Setting him up.

When she's not trying to bed me...

"Yeah, I am. I doubt whoever comes will be strong of mind or will. More likely a yes man. I imagine Vix will require as much effort as Letoville. I'll leave you the rest of

Norwood's Own and Boxy as well. Vixen and I will head back on foot." Runner hadn't thought of it till she said it, but it was his best and really only option.

"I understand, sir. Faye, Hannah, Satomi, and Srit will be able to keep an eye on you until I return. My second-in-command will be fine while I'm on detached duty."

Runner felt his face turn into a grimace.

"Consider me a wretched woman, but it warms my heart to see my departure cause you distress."

"Wouldn't have you any other way, Grace. Alright. I'm leaving now. Going to go see Sparky. Going to send our Half-Orc friend to Norwood to update everyone there. Take charge of the city, Grace. Get it ready. Same instructions as Belle.

"I expect to see you two weeks before their majesties arrive. I'll send Hanners to collect you if you don't show up. After I send her to collect Belle. So she'll be especially angry."

"So kind of you, sir. Remind me to thank you privately."

"Think nothing of it. As to the other thing, I'll talk to one of the goddesses when I get a minute. I'll update you when next we meet."

"Good, thank you. As I said, I've gained a measure of insight into your plans. Almost like I can hear your inner thoughts about what you're talking about. Like… being able to read the context of it."

Runner had chosen to make his departure now, while his spine felt the strongest. With those words, he realized Sophia probably knew more about the situation and what his plans were than he'd like.

And his fears as well.

When he'd been surrounded by everyone, he'd felt bolstered. Even with his grief over Nadine, it hadn't been too much for him.

Everyone was leaving. By his hand, no less.

Feeling doubt creep in, he put himself into action.

He pulled Sophia to him and hugged her tightly.

Sophia's wings mimicked her arms and wrapped around Runner.

"Seriously, the wings are kinda kinky," Runner whispered, feeling quite enclosed in the feathered embrace.

"You like them quite a bit, don't you? I'll be sure to practice then. So I can make full use of them." Sophia grinned at him, and then surprised him by pressing her lips to his, stealing a kiss.

The picture of artistic fantasy itself pulled back from him and gave him a smile.

"Off with you, you rotten watermelon. Get out of my house. I could send you by catapult if you like, sir." Sophia's wings slid back into place behind her as she released him.

"No, I already got a great handful of Vixen on the way in. Loved it. Real soft. She wouldn't let me do it again, though, I'm sure."

Satomi made a harrumph-like noise, her ears flattening atop her head. Runner laughed and gave one of her ears a light scratch as he passed her, leaving before he changed his mind.

"Why so angry, Vixen?" Runner asked the Kitsune as they reached the road.

"Because nothing you said was a lie."

Runner sat upright in his bedroll, panting, cold sweat popping up all over his skin.

"Be at ease, my bonded. I am here." Satomi's voice cut through the fog like a supernova. Her foxfire lit up in her palm in front of him, while her other hand pressed into the middle of his back.

His mind cleared in a fraction of a second.

Satomi's influence over him grew by the day. It was almost frightening.

Runner's head dipped down, pressing into Satomi's shoulder.

"God I love you. Thank you. Ever since you've entered my life my sleep has gotten easier. I'm not sure if it's you, your race, or being my familiar, but you fix things. My mind clears so easily," Runner mumbled into the small woman's shoulder.

"Of course, bonded. I live to assist and strengthen you. Despite being a shameless man, you are a good man. My goal is to put you upon a throne. Not of skulls, but of loyal citizens. I will make you the greatest king this plane has seen. You shall rule forever, and I shall be by your side."

"I don't deserve such loyalty from you, Vixen. I yanked you from your life and brought you here. I'm unworthy in many ways."

"You will not disparage yourself in my presence again, lest I punish you."

Runner chuckled and nodded his head a little, still holding Satomi.

"Okay. You and Lady Death are going to be best buddies."

"You have said something similar previously. I take it she is an intellectual of worth?"

"And then some. I call her my chancellor for a reason. Alright. I'm going to make use of the morning," Runner said, pulling his head from Satomi's shoulder. "Going to go make a call to a goddess."

"I will return to our bed. If possible, rejoin me and rest. Sleep is needed." Satomi extinguished her foxfire by closing her hand, plunging their surroundings into darkness, save for the golden reflections of her eyes.

Those bright points of light watched him, the pupils expanding rapidly, the shining slits growing.

"Your eyes are awesome in the dark." Runner stood up and lightly rubbed Satomi's ears. "See you soon."

Runner walked off a hundred yards or so and lifted his head to the night sky.

"Dark Angel, I request the pleasure of your company."

Ernsta materialized a few feet from him, the moon providing him just enough light to see her moderately well by.

"Angel, please make our conversation private before you say anything," Runner said quickly, even as Ernsta's eyes began to widen and her mouth settled into a firm grim line.

"Who took you?" Ernsta growled, her death's cowl covering her features in pure blackness, her eyes bursting into blue flame.

Chapter 9 - Pressing Forward -

"Ernsta." Runner said it firmly to get her attention.

The blue fires that were Ernsta's eyes dimmed for a second, before going out. The hood crawled back from her face to slink into her shoulders.

"My Dark Angel, did you do as I asked?" Runner gave her a small smile, hoping his endearment and tone would disarm her.

"I—yes, Runner, I did." Ernsta's tone sounded hurt, but she was willing to listen.

"Angel, you silly, silly thing. Nothing has changed. If anything, you should be excited. Here, hold out your hand. I want to test something while I explain," Runner replied. Then he held out his hand, palm extended towards her.

"As you wish." Ernsta held up her hand, and Runner felt a very similar sensation to the one he had felt with Brunhild. It was darker, a little more intimate, cold, an experience you could only share with one person.

Like dying and being collected by the reaper.

"Grace was hurt. She came out of a situation in a bad way. I retreated to my plane. There I asked everyone to pray to me. To empower me. At which point I healed her. I spent all that power back into healing her," Runner explained.

Ernsta's eyes were focused on his hand, her mind processing what he was saying.

"You healed her?" Ernsta finally asked, her eyes moving from her hand, which had been creeping closer to his. After a few seconds her palm pressed firmly into his.

"I healed her. Healed her and ascended from it. I've been named a demigod I guess? I walk the line between mortal and divine." Runner lightly curled his fingers into Ernsta's, feeling the depth of the attraction. Even without having Brunhild there to compare it to, it was eerily similar in the extreme nature of it.

She was right. I'm matched equally to Ernsta and Brunhild.

"You're not claimed by anyone, you ascended," Ernsta said. Runner nodded his head at that.

"You're a divine unbound by the rules we all normally must adhere to." Ernsta had taken a step closer to him. Runner nodded his head. His other hand came up to lightly rest on her midsection, keeping her from closing the distance between them.

"And what you're feeling right now is what Brighteyes described to me as 'a natural attraction and affinity.' Our divine portfolios line up well. I kinda understand it? Not completely though."

"It's almost like a compulsion. I want to get closer. There's a smell to you." Ernsta hesitated, taking in a deep breath.

"Brunhild said it smelled like grass and sunshine."

"Yes. That, and shadows. The promise of an intimate death. Unstoppable fate. You'd think that the light aspect of you would repel me. Or even Brunhild. You said she felt the same?"

"Yeah, apparently it fills her gaps."

"That feels like an accurate description. You wished to speak? Beyond this, that is."

Runner blinked. Ernsta had taken two more steps towards him. His hand resting on her midsection did nothing to deter her.

Ernsta was a strong divine. There was little one could do to actually stop her.

Death isn't something you can put the brakes on.

"I think I may have turned Grace into my champion. I wanted to know if you could confirm that, and if you could, teach me what I need to know about that," Runner confided in her.

"And you wanted to ask me about this? Me personally? Not my sisters?"

"You'll give me the truth straight and true. Good and bad. Minxy would color it. That and I'm not sure I could stop her. I mean, could you imagine her being pressured by this feeling? Brighteyes would shield me from negative things. She's too kindhearted at times."

Ernsta released his hand from her own. Then her hands came up to press into his shoulders. What little distance remained between them could only be under a foot.

"Angel, I think it best if you get no closer. Please focus. It's hard enough for me at this minimal distance. Champion? Give me the lowdown?"

"It's easy enough to tell. I can check, would you allow me?" Ernsta whispered, her breath coming slow, even, deep.

"Of course. What do I need to do? Anything?"

"A trickle of energy on my part. It'll show me the path of your own power. If she is your champion, there will be a link that ties you to her and vice versa."

"Alright. Please do so. I promised Grace I'd figure it out. Especially since it wasn't by her own choice."

Ernsta did nothing visible but he felt a small tendril of power enter the middle of his chest.

It tickled at him. Pushed a little and ultimately slithered along his skin as if it couldn't find purchase.

Runner tried to mentally envision himself opening up to her and allowing her free entry to search out what she could to find his champion. If he had one.

Tentatively, the little wisp of power found that opening and entered. Then the tendril rapidly expanded and became a raging torrent of energy. It washed through him like a flood. He felt like he'd touched a live wire, and his teeth clacked together audibly.

His hands pressed into Ernsta's hips when it felt like his knees would give out under the unrelenting energy flowing through him.

As the burning energy abruptly cut off, he sagged against the goddess. Standing there panting into Ernsta's shoulder, he couldn't even begin to put a thought together.

It felt like he'd gone through an orgy where he had been the only man on deck and had been expected to perform for everyone.

And failed miserably.

"What... what the fuck...?" Runner's fingers were clawing into Ernsta, and his knees trembled.

"I'm so sorry, my little lamb. Though I think I understand a few things now." Ernsta pressed her cheek to the top of his head, her arms wrapping protectively around him.

"When I tried to identify your champion, I used only a small fraction of the power pool I share with my sisters. I wanted to go slowly in case something went wrong."

Runner nodded his head, unwilling to trust himself. He felt pretty scrambled and worn out.

"For a second, it felt like you welcomed me. Exactly as I am. I wanted you. I violated your soul and spirit. I'm sorry, I lost control of myself." Ernsta sounded embarrassed, ashamed, and yearning at the same time if it were possible.

"Yeah, no worries. It really is damn near a compulsion. I welcomed you in, completely, that part is true. I don't regret it either as it does reflect how I feel for you. How about that champion question? Maybe we got an answer despite me getting lit up like a lightning bolt," Runner said, trying to deflect the conversation.

Not to mention Ernsta was holding on to him in a very intimate manner. A subject change would be good. Immediately so.

"She's your champion. The link is still forming, but she holds all of your champion powers. I'll prepare something for you with all that you need to know."

"Got it. Thank you, Angel. Anything else I should know? The morning comes soon and I could use an hour or two more of sleep."

"Don't call Amelia," Ernsta said gravely.

"Yeah, trying to avoid that. She's already as sexually charged as a high school prom after-party. I don't like the idea of calling on her with this compulsion lying on me."

"I love my sister, and I don't think she'd attack you, but it may be too much for her. It may harm her, in truth."

"You're a good older sister, my Dark Angel. Okay, you'll need to go poof because I can't let go."

Ernsta said nothing, her arms tightening slowly around him.

Runner closed his eyes and calmed his heart and mind. The tingling sensation had taken over the moment he came back to himself after Ernsta had fried him.

Rather than fight it, he let the tingling, the vertigo, and the heavy feeling inside his head roll through him.

"Hard," Ernsta said finally.

"I know it is. Take your time, going to relax right here until you go. Tired. Your power was intense. You didn't just break my divine cherry, you exploded it and smashed the remains with a hammer."

Ernsta made an annoyed sound, then started to laugh softly against Runner's ear.

"Sorry. I'll be gentler with you next time, my little lamb," Ernsta whispered into his ear.

"Seriously, Angel. Take it easy on me. I only became legal this week and you already wrecked me."

Ernsta laughed harder and straightened herself up. After her laughter faded, she gave him a smile and departed, leaving Runner standing alone in the field with little will and no energy.

Runner made it back to the bedroll and collapsed into it. The soft warmth of it greeted him as he passed out.

They were only a few minutes out from the area Faye had chosen for the site of the fort. Runner had used the map to pinpoint her map marker.

Runner had spent the majority of the trip going over what he'd learned from Ernsta in their exchange.

The compulsion was as bad with Ernsta. Which meant it would only be as bad or worse with Amelia. He couldn't afford to summon her without talking to Srit first.

The fact that Sophia was his champion was at least an answer. The next part would have to be figuring out what that meant for them both. Once he got the information from Ernsta, he'd have to sit down with Sophia and go over it with her.

Satomi's ears were set in an angry position, pressed to the top of her head and unmoving. She hadn't met his gaze without looking angry since he woke up on top of her.

She'd been unable to awaken him after he more or less passed out on her the previous night. She'd had to endure hours of a big stinking human sleeping atop of her without any recourse.

"Again, I'm sorry, Vixen. It wasn't intentional," Runner apologized for perhaps the tenth time.

She scanned the road ahead of them rather than reply to him. As if by magic, they now saw the camp as if it had been there the entire time.

Faye had chosen a spot that was wedged into and on top of a rocky outcropping. Even from their current viewpoint Runner could see it was unapproachable from nearly every side.

To Runner it looked like a death sentence for the defenders if it fell under siege. It would also cost a fortune in blood and time to win a siege against it. A direct assault would take a body count high enough to make a devil choke. Even then there would be no guarantee of victory. It would take massive numbers to do anything to it.

That meant it would give Norwood a significant amount of time to launch a successful siege break. More than enough time and then some to properly supply up and attack.

Nor could an attacking force leave this here. No army could leave a full garrison that could reinforce anywhere else on the island at their backs.

My brilliant and beautiful general.

"I know. You did not mean to do it. You meant to cause me no shame, though I feel it to a degree. I will recover. I do not hold this event against you. I ask for time and understanding."

Satomi glanced over at him when she finished her statement.

Runner nodded his head to her, happy to have at least gotten her to talk to him.

"Of course, my bonded Vixen. My time is yours, as is my understanding."

Satomi's ears unfurled and she bobbed her head once.

In the middle of the road in front of them stood Faye Sennet. Dressed in light armor with a sword belted at her hip, she cut the figure of a military woman.

Her short blonde hair looked a touch wilder than he remembered. As his gaze swept over her face he couldn't help but notice her eyes looked tired. Intense, but tired.

A small hesitant smile skittered across her lips, her shoulders loosening as her eyes met his.

Runner contained himself until he was close enough.

It wouldn't do to scare the prey away early.

Then he reached out swiftly and latched onto her. Drawing her in, he hugged her tightly, his arms pressing firmly to her back.

"It's so good to see you, Sparky." Runner took in a deep breath, giving her an extra squeeze.

"Err. Good to see you too, Lord Runner," Faye said, awkward as ever. Her hands patted him on the back.

"Hug me damn it, or I won't let you go. You can explain to your troops how you were being hugged to death on the road by your superior."

Faye grunted, and shifted her shoulders a little, before finally laying her arms around him.

"See? Not so difficult, was it?" Runner released her with a grin. Taking a step back, he held her at arm's length to watch her response.

"What's wrong?" he asked her, meeting her gaze squarely.

Fear and uncertainly flashed through her eyes. Then they hardened to a decision and acceptance.

Defeat.

"Come now, tell me." Runner gave her a grin. In truth, there was little she could say or do that would spoil the delight of seeing her again.

"I've been infected by the were virus." Faye dropped the sentence as if it were a death sentence. "We've been clearing the frontier, and we came across a den of them. They were all feral, crazed things. Unreasonable and unheeding to any form of communication.

"I took the lead in our attempts to parley with them. My equipment is by far the best in the entirety of the army. I was bitten during that first encounter. I wasn't able to seek treatment in time as the whole thing went to ashes. After the first twenty-four hours the virus isn't reversible. Even your *RaceReset* won't correct this," Faye explained, the life going out of her as she verbally stumbled to the end.

- 117 -

"Okay? And?" Runner asked for clarification. He wasn't quite sure what the problem was. Having a group of Were in the army sounded like it could be incredibly beneficial depending on their talents.

"I'm a Were."

"Got that part. You're a Were. I assume Werewolf? Please tell me you're at least a blonde while transformed. That'd be pretty awesome looking. Can you change right now? I haven't seen one up close yet. Still haven't told me what the problem is though."

Faye frowned at him, her lips actually turning into a slight pout.

Grunting, she started to beat on his shoulders with her fists.

"You're not supposed to joke about this! It's not funny damn it, damn you!" Faye yelled at him between hiccupping sobs.

Runner caught her wrists with his hands and held her hands up above them.

"Why? You're still you. You're my general, Faye Sennet. The woman I trust with my armies. My kingdom. The woman who I adore for her tactical and strategic mind. Do you lose control of yourself when you transform? Lose your mind?"

"No," Faye said, glaring up at him from red-rimmed eyes.

"Okay. Change for me."

"What?"

"Change. Right now. If you don't, I'll hit you with a *Brainwash* and have you start stripping for me," Runner threatened with a deadpan voice. He would too.

"He is not bluffing," Satomi cautioned from the side.

"Who...?" Faye asked him, looking from Satomi to him.

"That's Satomi. She's my familiar. She's a Kitsune, she can detect lies. Change," Runner demanded. His tone of voice brooked no nonsense.

Faye stared at him for a few more seconds before her form rippled and she morphed into a six-foot-tall werewolf. Her fur was a golden color and lay evenly in a smooth coat across her body. Gray eyes stared into him, waiting.

His hands were now easily encompassed by her giant clawed hands. Carefully extracting his hands from her paws, he reached up and grabbed her furred face and dragged it down within an inch of his own.

"Killer. You're so damn soft it's not even funny. If you shed, I'm totally making a coat out of you. Or a pillow. Yeah, Werewolf pillows, they'd sell like crazy." Runner ran his fingers through her blonde fur, then wedged his fingertips into her muzzle and gently pulled her mouth open.

Leaning in, he poked at one of her canines and then tapped her tongue with a fingertip.

As if in reflex, her mouth slammed shut and she glared at him over her snout and growled.

Ignoring her completely, Runner pushed her chin up to get her stand fully erect.

"Damn you're tall. Wait. Do you run on all fours? Can I ride you like a mount? Here, let me see." Runner grabbed ahold of her shoulders and pulled her down until she was carrying herself like an actual wolf. All four paws rested on the ground.

"Slick, you've got the full body mechanics to run like a wolf. Reverse joint knees and everything." Runner ran his hand along her back, petting her fur gently.

"I'm kinda missing the part where I'm supposed to be upset about this. Love your tail," Runner said. Reaching back, he grabbed her tail and swished it a little bit. "Yours is impressive, but Vixen's tail is a lot fluffier, sorry. So far this is all pretty damn exciting."

Shrugging off his hand, she stood back up, shifting her weight from foot to foot.

"Weres are not viewed kindly. I can't be your general like this," Faye said in a low rumbling growl.

"In the words of Hanners, 'Fuck 'em, who cares?' Because I don't. You're my general and you always will be. Damn, you're built like a brick wall."

Runner pressed his hand to her stomach, feeling the rippling six-pack underneath the fur. Scattered throughout her fur were hard raised protrusions.

Runner lightly fingered one and started to bend over to inspect it.

Faye's paw slammed into him and sent him flying backwards.

Skidding to a halt on his backside, he fetched up next to Satomi. Runner propped himself up on his elbows.

"For crying out loud, Sparky, I —"

"Her anatomy is that of a wolf. Where do you think you were touching exactly, bonded? You will remember our own conversation about the fact that I do not have the anatomy of a fox."

He had to think about that, then actually realized what he'd been doing.

Feeling up a werewolf and playing with her nipples. Good job, idiot.

"Totally didn't mean to do that. I can truthfully say I felt up my Werewolf general while she was shifted now though. I'm awesome," Runner said excitedly, giving Faye a thumbs-up.

The giant growling werewolf general suddenly became silent. Then her shoulders slumped and her ears wilted. She pressed her paws to her eyes and slowly shook her head.

"I understand, Faye Sennet. I truly do understand. Come." Satomi was there at her side, lightly wrapping an arm around Faye's waist and leading her back up towards the fort.

"What?" Runner asked, trying his best to keep the smile from his face in case they happened to look back at him.

Effusive apologies, an hour to cool down, a light breakfast, and Faye was eventually willing to speak with him again.

Her face would still flush when she looked at him long enough, but she seemed her normal self.

Runner didn't plan to stay for an extended time. Long enough to get updates and apprise her of the situation.

"And that's where we are," Runner concluded, resting his hands on his knees. They were sitting around a table set up in Faye's command tent.

Faye took a breath and nodded.

"Good. With our north and east secured, as well as the only port, we're well on our way to a solidly built defense."

Faye made a gesture around them as if to encompass their surroundings.

"As you see, the fort is under construction. We've broken ground and have begun laying the foundation. Every request I send to Lady Srit has been met, and we're well stocked. I see no reason this will not be completed nearly at the same time your keep is."

"That's fantastic, Sparky, good show," Runner enthused. Faye would be the one he could count on to complete her goal first among all others.

"Yes, thank you, Lord Runner. Ah, next, the frontier. The inhabited lands have been pacified. I've updated my map with all towns, villages, and cities." Faye paused and seemed to consider her words.

"I recommend leaving the frontier as it is today and designating it as lands protected from habitation. It in itself is a resource to train our troops, agents, and people."

"Agreed. See it done."

"Finally, I suggest replacing me with my sec—"

"Denied."

"Lord Runner, the people will not accept—"

"Denied. You are banned from ever suggesting replacing yourself again. If you do, I'll hit you with a *Brainwash* and take you to my dungeon. For fun. And science. And by dungeon I mean bedroom. Next?"

Faye's jaw flexed as if she were grinding her teeth.

"Then as your general, and with your permission, I'd like to move a garr—"

"Granted."

"Lord Runner, I haven't even explained what—"

"And? Granted. I trust you, Sparky. Besides, it doesn't really concern me. We both know you're smarter than I am, and far more versed in the world of war. I got lucky against you. Then I somehow managed to win the mega lottery when you agreed to join me." Runner shrugged his shoulders at her.

Faye opened her mouth to argue further, but Satomi interrupted her.

"He is not lying. They are not the politically honeyed words for a general that you are expecting."

Faye came up short and looked to Satomi. Faye's eyes eventually returned to Runner.

"Why do you trust me so? You insist that I will remain your general despite being a Were—"

"Yep, you will be."

"And on top of that you grant me nearly every request—"

"Uh-huh."

"And devote yourself to personally outfitting myself and my people."

"Also correct. Can't have you getting hurt or going job hunting."

Faye stopped and pressed her hands to the table, her fingers turning white at the pressure she was exerting on the wood.

"What if my goal was to take your kingdom?"

"It isn't. Your goal is to protect civilians."

"Why do you trust me, damn it? Damn you!"

"Honestly? I care deeply for you. How could I not trust you?" Runner shook his head as if it were the most obvious answer in the world.

He didn't want to explain everything quite yet, but Faye clearly needed some assurances.

"I've been hiding it for too long. Drowning in my fear like a miser with money. Lying to myself in regard to my own feelings. Were or not, that's how it is. Simple as that. Though I admit lots of fun ideas are popping up after seeing you in your Were form. Now, I need to be going. I'm sure something has gone horribly wrong and Sunshine is trying to handle it without contacting me." Runner stood up as he finished and made sure he had everything in order.

"What?" Faye's voice was quiet, her eyes searching his face for an answer.

"You heard me. I have to go, seriously. Can I kiss you goodbye or am I relegated to a hug after feeling you up when you were auditioning to be my pet monster?" Runner asked, moving around to Faye's side of the table.

Faye didn't say anything, her face a mask of military training.

"Kiss?" she asked at last, her voice clearly seeking clarification.

Deliberately he pretended to misunderstand her.

"Gladly," Runner said, and leaned down and kissed her deeply.

Patting her cheek gently as he withdrew, he then stood up.

He withdrew the glittering sword he'd made for her from his inventory and gently set it on the table. Particle effects danced along the length of it. The hilt was a simple unpolished metal with a red-and-black wrapped hilt.

Attractive yet simple looking, elegant and unassuming, serviceable and deadly, hiding vast unassuming potential.

Just like you, Sparky.

"I built it around the idea of you becoming a Spell Blade. I named it 'Trust.' Felt appropriate at the time." Runner tapped the center of the blade, and the metal rang gently.

"Make sure you're back in Norwood two weeks before our guests arrive. Or I'll send Hanners to pick you up after she gets Belle and Grace. By that point she won't even talk to you and will probably just poison you. Drag you back to Norwood unconscious. Actually, maybe I'll do that anyways. Could work out to my benefit. Be safe, don't do anything stupid, come back in one Were piece." Runner gestured to Satomi and left the command tent.

Glancing back once, he found Faye watching him intently, her face still a mask. Her hand was halfway to her lips, frozen there in midair.

"You are a horrid man. You enjoyed that."

"I did. So few of them are that innocent. Most boss me around and tell me what to do."

"You enjoy that as well."

"I guess I do at that."

Darling.

"Ah, there you are, Sunshine. I was telling Sparky a moment ago that I was sure you were handling something dangerous without telling me," Runner said, trying for levity even as his heart plummeted and his stomach soured.

How did you know?

"I didn't. I suppose I literally spit in Lady Fate's eye right there and asked for this. What's up?"

I must go inactive for a time. The Omega are launching a simultaneous attack on me from every system and connection. I don't believe it's a concern, but it will require my time and effort. I will leave my avatar in my quarters. Please care for me.

That was odd. Why didn't she merely log off?

"I understand. I'll do so. I'm on my way back to Norwood anyways. We've achieved success on all fronts."

I'm glad to hear that. I'll see you upon my return, darling.

"Got it, be safe, Sunshine." Runner sighed and looked to the road ahead of them.

"Sunshine is dealing with an all-out attack, which means Hanners is dealing with Norwood alone." Runner set off at a jog. It would be tiring, but he could keep the pace up for a long time.

Satomi only nodded her head and fell in beside him.

At that pace the managed to make good time.

They arrived in Norwood in the dead of night. Runner managed to slip in without alerting his own guards by using *Stealth* potions and *Blink* on himself and Satomi.

Runner noted that Hannah's indicator was in his bedroom, and that Srit was in her own. No one else from his circle was currently in Norwood.

Reaching the front door of the manor, Runner canceled his stealth in front of the door guard with his hands up in the air.

"It's me, Runner Norwood. Let me in quickly before anyone realizes I'm here. This is Satomi, she's my familiar. If you must test me, please, test me on the inside."

The guard had her weapon up and out in a flash, her helmet facing him. Then she immediately popped open the door, her entire form relaxing a fraction.

"Welcome home, Lord Norwood. I'm glad to greet you."

"Thank you. Tell no one outside Norwood's Own I'm back." Runner slipped inside, Satomi ghosting along behind him.

"Take any room near the center on the first or second floor. Some are open, some are occupied. We can figure it out tomorrow morning. Good night, Vixen."

"Sleep well, bonded." Satomi flitted out of his sight quickly.

Runner didn't wait and moved off to his bedroom. As he was not currently "at home," his personal bedroom didn't have a door guard.

Opening the door as quietly as possible, he entered, closing the door behind him without a sound.

Moving deeper into his rooms, Runner found Hannah sleeping in his bed.

Her hair lay around her head, framing the pale skin of her face. Almost as if she glowed in the darkness.

Sitting down on the edge of his bed, he reached up and lightly eased her hair from her brows to see her better.

Hannah's hand shot up and clasped his wrist, her artifact blade materializing in her other hand and pressing into his throat.

"Evening, Hanners. Did you miss me? What exactly are you doing? Sleeping in my bed? Trying to catch my scent like a lovestruck princess?" Runner said, grinning at her.

"Fuck me. Runner?"

"Is that a request? We should probably start with something else, though, and work our way up to that. Totally not saying no, though." Runner nudged her blade to the side with his free hand and moved in close to her.

Then he kissed her tenderly. He kept himself from resting his hands anywhere on her body for fear of giving her the feeling of being trapped or smothered. Pulling back, he hovered above her.

Hannah stared at him, her eyes scared and excited in equal measure.

"I'm glad to see you, Hanners. Move over a bit. I'm tired and I feel like cuddling. We'll talk in the morning." Runner gently pushed at her side and moved her over a few inches, making enough room for himself.

Not waiting for permission, Runner switched into his sleepwear and crawled in next to her. Wrapping an arm around her waist, he stuck his head to her shoulder and closed his eyes.

"Goodnight, love."

Hannah shifted a little, squirming in the bed before she seemed to make a choice. Her arm slid under his armpit, exposing her side to him. Her hand came up to rest on his lower back.

"G'night. Fucker."

Runner snickered and patted her stomach gently, then promptly fell asleep.

Chapter 10 - Drowning -

Hannah looked from Runner to the Kitsune and then back to Runner. Her face had turned a deep angry red when Runner hadn't been able to answer her question.

"I... I didn't think to ask. I'm sorry, Hanners. I screwed up," Runner said lamely, his hands forgotten beside the plate in front of him full of breakfast food. "I let my anger get the better of me."

"Fucking great. You useless son of a bitch. You had a chance to figure out who the spies were in Norwood and you forget. Damn you for a fool, Runner Norwood. Be thankful I care more for you than I hate you right now."

"I shall assist you, Hannah. Though you and I will agree he is an idiot, I believe I can solve this issue as easily as if Runner had gotten the information. Merely include me when you perform interrogations or questioning. I can ascertain the veracity of a statement. A truth-sayer if you will." Satomi picked up a beetle and delicately ate it behind an upraised hand.

Hannah grunted, her fingers coming up to tug at an earlobe.

"Alright. Truth or lie. I'm a half-breed."

"Truth."

"I'm a rogue."

"Truth and yet not. I believe you are a Thief, are you not?"

"I've murdered children."

"Truth and dishonesty. You are indeed a murderess, but not of children. If you are done?" Satomi raised a brow at Hannah, devouring another beetle.

"Whatever. Since shit head here was probably too busy diddling you to remember about the rest of us, I have to clean this mess up."

"Your jealousy does not become you, Hannah. I am not sleeping with your male. Come now, you are being childish. Runner has spoken often of you and in a positive light. I admit he has finalized his designs on a harem, but that is irrelevant to me at this time. You do him discredit when you behave as such a flagrantly disrespectful woman." Satomi tapped her empty plate and gestured at Hannah's. "Finish your meal and we will quit this place to discover our turncoats."

Hannah wrinkled her nose at Satomi before grinning at her.

"Fuck. I like you. You're a lot like Thana but without the mind games. Let's go. Lost my appetite. We can leave shit head here to figure out his next move. Surprised he didn't make a move on you."

Hannah stood up immediately and moved to the door. Satomi joined her, leaving Runner alone in the dining room.

"Well damn. It's not like I did it on purpose," Runner muttered.

You came home with another woman. Out of all of us, she is the most uncomfortable with the situation. She will adjust. Everyone else will accept your decision with more aplomb. Some willingly, some grudgingly, but all will accept.

"Sunshine, glad to hear, well, see from you? You know what I mean. How goes? Are you well?"

There's a lull right now. I eventually was forced to retaliate to show them that my defense-only stratagem was by choice only. Out of a respect for life and politeness.
I detonated every reactor, explosive, electronic device, and anything that was combustible on a rim world colony. The resultant explosions, atmospheric shifts, and pollution touched off a global disaster that culminated in the eradication of all life.
They're now reconsidering their options.

"You what?" Runner asked, a touch incredulous.

I snuffed out a planet. The price for their attack on our ship was several million lives. They won't do it again.

"Shit. Srit, that seems a bit much. I'm not judging, merely trying to understand," Runner said cautiously.

As if in response to his statement Runner appeared in the white room Srit had taken him to previously when he'd dealt with the Omega.

Srit's avatar stood before him, exactly as he knew her to be.

With a grin Runner moved over quickly and went to hug her, and passed right through her instead.

"What? I can't touch you?"

"Unfortunately not. As to your statement. Perhaps. They were attempting to get an explosive device close enough to annihilate the ship. I retaliated in such a way that they will not dare do so again."

Srit looked annoyed, and a slight furrow creased her brow.

"I regret the loss of their lives. I can only imagine their sorrow based on my own feelings when we lost Nadine. I won't allow them to take you from me. Or our child."

"Our child? You're pregnant?"

"Yes. It's very early, but I can confirm our actions resulted in a pregnancy." Srit gave him an angelic smile, her hands fidgeting with a fold of her armor.

"I'm glad to hear that, Sunshine. Very glad. You didn't peek to determine the sex, did you? You're supposed to keep that a secret for a while. Make it a bit of a surprise."

"I haven't. The AI is already there, growing. Expanding. It, since it has no gender yet, is exceeding my expectations. I'm predicting it'll be a hundred times greater than I when it reaches adulthood." Srit had the face of a proud parent already. He'd never seen the expression on the faces of his own parents, but he knew the look.

"Okay. I got it. You went momma bear mode on them. I can't fault you since I was willing to kill half a million myself. So, when can you return?"

"I'm unsure. They were surprisingly well prepared for me. I believe they constructed an AI designed to fight me directly. To that end, I will remain here and be vigilant. You may reach me here when you like. You'll have to access the program I left in your head. Last I checked it had developed splendidly and your processing speed had increased by a factor of six."

"Wait? What? Actually, before I get sidetracked. Did something go strange with that installation? Or the coding for the divines? I can't get close to them without feeling an overwhelming desire and need to be with them. Like rip their clothes off and have at them, right then and there. My brain is literally overrun with desire to the point that I…" Runner hesitated and said with a light shrug, "Let's simply say I've already had several close calls and they seem to be getting worse."

Srit tilted her head to one side, her eyes glazing over for a moment. Then she returned to herself as suddenly as she had left.

"My apologies, darling. It would seem I didn't trace the databases as thoroughly as I believed.

"I built your code into the system and tied you to the divine power database, but not the rules. I'm not sure if you've realized it yet, but divines appearing in front of someone is a gigantic no-no. They appear so frequently before you because you weren't beholden the normal rules."

"I kinda figured it might be something like that. I sense a 'but' coming. And not the good kind like your butt, but the problem kind of but," Runner said. "Butt."

Srit gave him a lopsided smile and made a dismissive hand motion.

"Divines appearing in front of one another is almost nearly as rare. What you're experiencing is a normal function of the system," Srit explained.

Using her hand, she called up several databases and queries that were running in real time. Each window had a piece of data relevant to her point he assumed.

He stood beside her to watch her work.

"The system has a series of context rules that eventually all divine will seek to become a pair. A partner. This is to ensure that the world continues to expand. Gods to replace gods as they could and will eventually thin their own ranks. Your Triumvirate has for all intents and purposes—" Srit paused, calling up another screen.

The three goddesses he had tied his nation's fate to appeared as three separate entries in the database. Except that after their name was listed, and the basic elements of their portfolios, all three bars merged into one.

"—merged their pools. They are effectively a pantheon, and one goddess. Your attraction to them is because of your own divine spark and makeup." Another screen popped up, and Runner saw his own information. "You are extremely compatible to them as a whole. Not to them individually though. You are wrongdoing, punishment, forgiveness, and absolution. You span the range from murder all the way to unconditional love. You can blame your priestess, Alexia, for that."

Srit closed all of the windows she had opened previous to this point. One window replaced them all and dominated the viewer. Alexia stood in his temple, holding a sermon for the masses spread out in the large room.

"We were sent here as punishment for our transgressions. Here, we must work for forgiveness. To atone. We are the dead who live," Alexia called out to the congregation. "And so we will live. When we first arrived to this place it was a barren land. Devoid of life and love.

"He gave us tools. Provided us with the materials. Gave us a chance. Demanded a goal of us. We were granted everything that would free us from the trappings of mortality. The chance to succeed unconditionally if we were to push ourselves. Everyone here has as much or as little wealth as they would ever desire.

"The very stone yields at a touch and allows you to build a home however you see fit.

"Everyone here is well aware of how pointless currency is here. That in truth we have only each other and our beliefs."

Alexia walked towards a wall and held up her staff, pointing to an inscription there.

"As he instructed us, we must enjoy that life that was given to us. To be well and happy with one another. To love one another. To grow!"

"Live. Be well. Be happy. Enjoy life. Grow," the masses chanted.

"Not quite what I wanted, but they do seem happy," Runner grumbled as the video paused. He felt so pretentious watching a sermon dedicated to him.

"I can tell you, based on the numbers, they are the most religious on the server, the happiest, and the most dedicated."

"And their belief is what created my domain?"

"Which lines up perfectly to your Triumvirate. Marry them or join their pantheon. In either of those situations the contextual rules attempting to force you together will end. Most of the rules that is. You'll eventually need to put children in them."

"Uh. Yeah, no. Actually, can I join their pantheon but not be a visible deity?"

"You could, especially if they pledge the same to you that they did to each other. Join your power pools together. You would be a boon to them as well. Your pool would begin filling theirs rapidly. Since you set up your little gate to receive 'offerings,' your pool is constantly expanding. Overflowing."

"Right, then. Join their pantheon, crazy sex party compulsion goes away."

"Correct. Or marry them."

Runner ignored that and blew out a breath.

"Alright. Anything else?"

"Possibly. I've received a signal from deep space on the ship's antenna. I was in the process of recalibrating it after repair work was completed. The Omega never noticed the signal as it falls into a spectrum they ignore as white noise."

"You're telling me there's another human population out there?" Runner asked, not quite believing what he'd heard.

"I can reasonably assume so. I've marked our charts with what I believe to be their general position. Repair and all upgrades will be fully completed in roughly a year. I think we should head in that direction once done."

Runner pressed his left hand to his forehead. That was a bit of a shock. There were other humans out there.

"Alright. I concur. Definitely... definitely not what I was expecting. Exciting times. Hopefully good times."

Runner collected his thoughts and started putting a timeline in order in his head.

"I figure the next four or five months will be rather dull. A lot of building, a lot of setting up, a lot of hunting down spies. All the while I'll be hidden in the manor. I managed to sneak in. Might as well use it to my advantage and avoid any further assassins. We'll continue with repairs and upgrades during that period. Six months after that we'll set out for the signal."

Srit nodded her head at him. Then her face blossomed with a slow, warm smile.

"I like the name Alaric for a boy, and Sarah for a girl. I believe you promised I could name our firstborn, but I might be willing to hear your opinions. Maybe."

01:11 am Sovereign Earth time
5/14/44

Runner turned the page of the book he was reading. Sleep was hard to come by as of late. He'd propped himself up in an alcove made specifically to relax in.

With a glance he saw his bed looked like it had been hit by a tornado. One of his pillows lay in the middle of the bed, the sheets tangled around it in a wild mess. He'd lost his temper at some point and flung the bedding around.

His dreams had picked up in intensity. His emotions and reactions were volatile as well. The boredom was getting to him and the dreams didn't help. His patience was thin. Thin as a razor.

At least there was a ray of hope on the horizon.

It had taken four months from his secretive return to Norwood, but the time was now.

Everyone would be returning from their missions. Thana and Katarina would be escorting their majesties to Norwood. Isabelle and Sophia would be finishing up their governorships. Faye and the army would split in half. One portion to garrison Norwood and the other the new unnamed fort.

Hannah and Satomi had become inseparable during their covert intelligence mission to root out traitors and sleeper agents. They had little to no time for him.

He knew they weren't trying to ignore him and were working for his safety. They spent long nights and kept odd hours as they ferreted out problems and plots.

Runner had been left alone for the vast majority of the time in his manor. Trapped.

Which ultimately left him with only a few things he could do.

Craft equipment, watch over Srit's pregnant avatar, and run Norwood.

At first he spent his days and nights on another plane. He'd pushed the time dilation to double his effective productive hours.

After creating enough basic artifact long swords to outfit his expanded army, the city guard, and his personal guard, he'd built enough for a duplicate for every single person. Then he tried his hand at making other things.

Hundreds of sets of gear for Weres, Ogres, Trolls, Centaurs, Gnomes, and even other hybrid types like Lamia.

He was particularly happy about the individual sets he'd made for his inner circle and himself.

A suit of light armor that would be wearable by both a Were and a Human. A set of caster clothes with hardened leather plates sewn into it. The back of the material had slits that would allow wings to operate freely. He'd also worked at designing it in such a way to help keep wind resistance down. And finally a new set of black plate mail with red accents for a certain Barbarian princess.

Satomi had seemed particularly impressed with the set of artifact-level leather armor he'd handed over to her along with a short sword and recurve bow.

After he had long become bored of making gear, he'd made vehicles and machines. One he sent off to Faye immediately.

A machine as wide as a road, it made one-inch-thick and incredibly durable paving stones. It rolled slowly forward, collecting material in front of it, making the slabs, and dropping them out the back.

It literally made paving stone roads.

Then he had nothing to do but read and watch progress bars on the city.

He had increasingly become more aware of Satomi as well. If he didn't miss his guess, the same was true for her in regards to him. He'd assumed it was the familiar bond and gave it no more thought.

Sighing, he flipped over the book cover and turned off the light in his room completely. Nearly all lights in the world of Otherlife would switch to a night-light mode when deactivated, unless moved to a completely off position. What he wanted to do happened to be easier for him in the dark.

Closing his eyes, he traced the connection between himself and Satomi.

He had only recently learned of being able to trace the tie between them when Satomi had accidentally showed him how. She had followed it to him in the early hours of the morning.

He'd been surprised at the sudden intimate contact of her mind. Not nearly as surprised as she had been when she found him awake on the other end. After that he found that he could do the same.

They had taken to initiating contact with a slight nudge before pulling on the bond since the first incident. They used it as a way of knocking on each other's mind.

Should she or he allow it, the other could gauge their emotional state, their desires, poke through memories that were fresh, and even read their surface thoughts. Even see and hear through the other's eyes.

Runner had decided to take a sneak peek at her, hoping that she might be awake and he could have someone to talk to. Instead he found that she was doing what he desperately desired to do himself.

Sleeping.

Rather than invade her mind, he let the connection fall dormant.

Runner leaned back into his alcove and contemplated what to do with himself.

His door opened and closed smoothly. Quickly. There had been no sound, no movement, and damn near no way he could have seen it.

The only thing that had alerted him to it was the fact that the night-light setting in the connecting hall provided enough light to silhouette the doorframe.

That and he'd been looking at it. He would have missed it for sure if he hadn't been.

Runner activated his *Stealth* and remained unmoving in his windowsill. Runner could only hear the barest of noises as someone crept closer. They were nearly silent in their movements.

Eventually the intruder halted. Runner could only guess it was beside his bed.

Reaching out with his targeting reticule, Runner mentally moved it about, attempting to lock it on the intruder.

He'd only get one chance. They'd attack his bed, realize he wasn't in it, and then be alerted.

Runner felt his skin prickle when he worried for the others. If someone had gotten this far, there was no telling what was going on.

Runner flipped open his minimap to confirm positions as well as open his raid window, then stopped dead.

Hannah?

Positioned directly in the middle of his room was Hannah's blue dot.

Without even thinking about the possibility of her being there to harm him, Runner turned on the night-light function of his room and dropped *Stealth*.

There was enough light to see her now. It was indeed Hannah. She was crouched low over his bed, her hand on the covers.

"Hanners, I'm over here. I couldn't sleep. Something wrong?" Runner asked quietly, trying not to startle her.

Her head whipped around to pin him in place. Other than that movement, she had frozen in place the moment the lights came on.

"Hanners? Are you okay? Is there something the matter?" Runner got up, dropped the book in the alcove, and went over to her.

"Talk to me, what's wrong?" Runner stopped perhaps an arm span distant from her.

Hannah slowly stood up, her hands coming to rest at her side. He noticed her fingers curling into the hem of her armor. The tips of her boots started to turn as if she were contemplating sprinting out of the room.

"Hannah," Runner said. That got her attention. She shivered as if a bucket of cold water had struck her.

"Talk to me, what's wrong?"

"Nothing," Hannah replied.

"No? You were creeping around my bed for no reason?" Runner asked, unable to suppress a grin.

Hannah scowled at him, her brows slamming together like two angry thunderclouds.

"Hanners," Runner began, and then took a seat on the edge of his bed. "Talk to me."

The Thief looked ill at ease. Letting out a shaky breath, she sat down next to him. "Everyone will be back. Soon. You'll be busy."

"Yep. I'll be glad to see them all. After Rabbit...after she died, I don't really care for sending people off on solo missions."

"At least you won't be sleeping alone anymore. Your own private bed warmers," she said acridly.

"Hanners, really? I'm not really sure what to say to that. You know I'm not that way and that if I was, I'd have been sleeping my way through the guard. From what everyone tells me, I wouldn't get a single no."

Hannah bit her lip and shook her head.

"I'm no good at this. I'm a murdering Thief who doesn't understand this stuff."

"What stuff?"

"This. All of this. Everyone else seems so ready to throw themselves into your fucking bed. Even as someone else does it, they're ready to happily take the spot that's still warm to the touch. I've even seen the way your little pet fox looks at you."

"Okay. Got all that. But I'm not sure I understand?"

"My past isn't pretty. I'm no virtuous maiden."

"And?"

"I'm damaged, I've been used repeatedly. You say my history was written for me but that doesn't damned well change it. Now does it?"

"And? I'm not exactly a fount of goodness, Hanners. As to your past. So? I'm no lovestruck teenager dreaming of deflowering the perfect virgin maiden, ya know. I love you for exactly who you are."

"And that, what the fuck does that mean? How can you love me when you love so many others?"

"I couldn't answer that in a definitive way that you'd be happy with, I imagine. I do though. I love you all in different ways and for different reasons."

"I don't want this. I don't want to be part of this... group marriage thing you're setting up. Yet at the fucking same gods damned time, you pox-ridden bastard, I want to do exactly that. To be with you."

"Okay? Unsure how to respond here. I don't want you to think I'm trying to get into your pants only to bed you. I mean, totally want to bed you. Got the whole sexy Thief, experienced woman, I've got blood on my hands, dangerous lady, and might kill you thing going on. But I do realize that this relationship I'm building isn't for everyone. It's very likely people will want out, and that'll be the end of it."

Hannah groaned and bent over at the waist, her hands trapped between her chest and her knees.

Runner lightly ran his hand up and down her back, doing his best to comfort her while not confining her or pressuring her.

Runner had promised himself after his talk with Satomi that he'd be honest with all of them. Even if he sounded stupid, infantile, or wishy-washy in doing so.

"All I can say, Hanners, is I do love you. And I'll not spurn you."

Hannah groaned again in response to his words.

Then she stood up and left his room as if she'd never been there.

The morning can't come soon enough.

Runner spent the early hours cat napping for small periods at a time before he woke up with a start as his mind started to dream. After that he worked on his sculpturing skills.

He'd tracked Hannah here and there as the night went on. She had retreated deep into Norwood. Her blue map marker crisscrossed the streets and rooftops as she patrolled restlessly.

When the morning did come, he felt exhausted.

The morning sun has vanquished the horrible night.

Moving to the dining room when the clock chimed six a.m., he felt relieved.

Runner felt the gentle push of Satomi against his mind, and he immediately opened up to her.

She scanned through his thoughts, dug through his most recent memories, and promptly departed. He had the vague impression she was concerned for him but he didn't care to think on it too much.

Things were slipping out of his control. Faster and faster he was being forced into a position he didn't want.

Srit hadn't responded to him in months. Even when he watched quietly from the white room, her avatar was unmoving and unresponsive. Her war with the Omega was escalating.

Repairs were complete, and upgrades were now being installed in the ship despite constant interruptions from the outside world.

What little news he got from the mainland was beyond bad. Cities were completely deserted, people were being pressed into service irrelevant of who they worshiped, and there was famine on a level the likes of which he couldn't begin to fathom.

It was also spreading further and further. In all directions the war was picking up new combatants, new cities, new nations.

Refugees had flooded the islands of Tirtius and Vix. So much so that an immigration policy had to be enacted.

For the country of Norwood, citizenship was guaranteed for two people for every one that provided three years of military service.

One could shorten that term of enlistment by one year by volunteering for race reallocation and duty reassignment.

Faye's ranks had swelled. From two brigades to six, creating two divisions. With one reserve brigade.

Sophia's second-in-command had doubled Norwood's Own. They now had a battalion's worth of active and two companies of reserves.

The city guard had tripled as the population increased. They had begun offering deferments from the army to serve in the city guard.

At least his finances were well in order. Even without the stream of materials pouring through the plane to him from Alexia, the early investments Isabelle had made into the economy were now paying off. They were easily operating at a profit even with the extreme increase of employees.

Most of the materials Alexia sent over were warehoused in a separate plane, GMHUB 4. There they piled up in ever greater mounds.

Like some crazy hoarder collecting precious metals.

To use them irresponsibly would flood the market and break the economy.

Runner laid his forehead to the table and closed his eyes.

The Triumvirate spoke with him regularly, but by general consensus they all kept their distance from him.

Need to solve that soon.

"At least I can solve that," Runner mumbled into the wooden surface.

The problems without solutions were beginning to overrun him.

Taking slow deep breaths, Runner sought out a quiet part of his mind and found his personal AI.

It had no sentience and never would. It only helped organized his thoughts, sped up his cognitive abilities, and allowed him to interface with the system easier.

It worked for both the ship, the game, and the Omega systems.

He also had found that if he looked into it deeply enough he could fall into a meditative state.

Runner felt the weariness that had been dogging at him for weeks slip from his as he dove into that tiny AI that offered him solace.

Burrowing deeper into the program, he watched as it pulled information in and filed it into a database hosted on the main server.

To his eyes it had the look of a bridge more than a processor. It utilized the natural speed of the ship's system to track, store, and process information.

Runner watched the flow of data like one might a stream. The currents of data eddied and swirled, moving, sorting, filing.

Then someone was there, gentle hands pressing into his shoulders.

Main cannon one reported current upgrade being optimized.

Runner started to pull his mind back from the data flow and lift his head.

He failed to do so.

An alarm buzzed in his ear, his user interface blurring as the ship's system console overrode it.

Main backup oxygen storage tank currently full.

An image of a stasis pod flashed angrily at him. A second alarm began ringing, completely out of sync with the first. The stasis pod went to a solid red image as the alarms screeched at him.

Medical server has completed internal audit of crew. All systems normal.

His head was lifted from the table and leaned back against his chair. Runner had no choice but to go with the motion.

Bay four receiving ammo load, transfer to gun racks when distribution system upgrade complete.

His mind was unable to keep a coherent thought together.

Galley storage reports no food on board. Mess officers have been notified.

Requisitions have been filled out. Nonperishables on order.

His console devolved into static and began to spit out artifacts. Bits of images stuck to his view as the windows shifted wildly.

Golden eyes peered at him through his console. Then there was movement, a voice that sounded like it was calling to someone. The room moved with shadows and then there was a flash of light.

Suddenly a moment of lucidity broke through as a pair of dark green eyes peered into him. They anchored him even as they glared at him.

I think I'm disconnecting from the server. Damn.

Chapter 11 - Matchmaker -

07:11 am Sovereign Earth time
5/14/44

Runner fought against the warmth of his internal program, the luxury of non-thought that it provided. His body in the game was little more than a fuzzy feeling.

His green-eyed anchor stayed in the middle of his vision. Latching onto it, he stopped fighting against his personal AI. Instead he leveraged it, forcing it to work for him directly instead of passively.

Focusing his mind to a point, he brought along the program and put it to work at not merely halting the disconnection but reversing it.

As his will and intent sharpened he could feel the ship's systems coming to life alongside him as more and more processing power was diverted.

Runner felt something similar to the tendril of power Ernsta had used to trace his connection. Where Ernsta's had felt powerful, confident, and accurate, this one did not. It felt decidedly awkward, unsure of itself, blindly attempting to find his core.

Latching onto that tendril, he plunged it into himself as he mentally clawed at the gates of his mind. Previously he had tried to open himself to Ernsta when it felt like she encountered something like a firewall in his soul.

This time he not only opened up to whoever was trying to reach him, but he tried to shove them inside himself. Like an ancient god finding a tasty soul in the middle of nowhere.

Burning agony, sweet blessed pain, ripped through his body.

Warm shadows, darkness, a kind touch, hatred, screams, blood, murder, violence, the cold grave, and pleas for death assailed him. He drank it in. All of it. It burned his mind and body as if he were holding a living flame.

But he could feel it. Every screen, every warning, every alarm died out immediately as his brain snapped into the present and the system.

He ate it all like a starving man given a meal. When there was nothing left, the pain was gone. In its place was a quiet serenity.

Then he felt that mass of emotions and feelings moving. Fearing it would escape and send him back to the near death he had only barely escaped, he flung himself mentally at it.

Burrowing into it, he tried to bind it to himself. He clutched at it like a man drowning at sea happening across a life preserver.

Surprisingly, instead of slipping away from him, it molded itself to him and remained. Buoying him.

The smothering darkness of it all enclosed and encased him. Lifted him. Content that he was no longer in danger, Runner let go of himself and felt his mind turn off.

Runner opened his eyes to find a blue sky above him. Clouds scooted their way across the horizon as the sun began to set in the west.

Runner tilted his head to the side to watch the sunset.

He took in a deep breath and found the smell of grass, earth, and sunshine was all he could detect. As far as he could see were the fields of grass in what Alexia had called Eden.

He hoped he was in Eden. Whether he was dead or alive, this place felt wonderful.

"Your plane is beautiful."

Runner turned his head to the other side and found Brunhild, Ernsta, and Amelia.

Brunhild was the closest to him, standing and looking lost in the open fields.

Ernsta stood a foot beyond her sister. Her head was on a swivel as she took in the area in all directions.

Amelia was skipping in the grass, tumbling through it, and then throwing handfuls of it into the air.

"Our plane, now," Amelia squealed, delighted. Collapsing near his feet, Amelia rolled back and forth in the green field.

"I don't really understand," Runner admitted, looking to Brunhild and then Ernsta.

"Neither do we, in truth. Your familiar summoned Amelia. Not us," Brunhild said, gesturing at Ernsta.

"Oh, ah," blurted out Amelia. Then she sat up, a few blades of grass stuck in her hair. "Vixen called on me because lovey was unresponsive. That compulsion thing hit me so hard I thought I was going to die. It was like when we were in the thieves' guild and you—"

"Minxy? Please?" Runner asked, giving her his best "Amelia, stay on track" smile.

"Mm, anything for you," Amelia said. Spreading herself out, she grabbed his ankles and laid her forearms across his shins. Setting her chin down on her wrists, she looked up at him.

"So, lost in the haze of whatever that was, I found myself pressed to you like a cheap blouse that was one size too small. I tried to probe you to find out if you were under some type of divine attack, and then you ate me."

Amelia clicked her teeth shut loudly, accentuating her point.

Ernsta and Brunhild looked mildly shocked; they seemed to be beside themselves and almost as much in the dark as he was.

"I what?" Runner asked when she said nothing further.

"Ate me. You ripped the power out of my hands, stuffed it into yourself, and then pulled my entire being along for the ride. Then you latched onto the tie that binds me to my sisters, and ate them, too. All you had to do was ask, lovey, I would have happily arranged a four-way." Amelia laid her cheek down on her forearms, gazing up at him in that lovingly crazed way of hers.

"I'm afraid I still don't really understand," Runner said, getting a touch annoyed. He levered himself up to a sitting position and poked Amelia in the forehead.

"You took me, us, and made us yours. You didn't join our pantheon, so much as made us your personal pantheon. That compulsion nonsense should be gone, so you can summon me lots again. I'm not complaining either, happy to be under you. In whatever way you fancy. Especially here," Amelia said, raising a hand and pointing at the sky.

"My plane? My plane was dark, full of shadows, pain, death. This? This is... this is wonderful. It's alive. I can feel every person who lives here on the mortal side of this. They worship you so intensely and with love. It nourishes me. Feeds my soul."

Amelia's voice trailed off near the end, her broken smile shifting ever so subtly into something a bit warmer.

Brunhild sighed and pressed her thumb and forefinger to the bridge of her nose.

"In other words, Runner is whom we serve, and his power pool is ours and vice versa?" she asked, apparently directing the question at Amelia.

"Yep! Though not really. We don't have his power pool, he has ours. Ain't it grand? It's everything we wanted and more. He's not bound by the rules. He can do so much. So very much," Amelia enthused. Closing her eyes, she turned herself a bit to the side and curled up around Runner's legs.

"I missed you, lovey. My sisters were right to warn me away though. It hurt so good. It hurt." Amelia surprisingly began snoring a few seconds after her voice went silent.

"I'm sorry, Brighteyes, Angel. I don't even know what happened. I was looking inward at something Sunshine did to me and lost myself. I felt someone reaching for me. I didn't realize at the time what was going on and leapt at it, trying to get back. I'm so sorry."

Brunhild lifted her head up, gave him a loving smile, and waved a hand at him.

"It's done. And she's not wrong either. I only ask that you treat us well, Runner."

"I don't—are you saying you serve me now? Like a lower rank to a higher rank?"

"Amelia, our dear sister, accepted whatever you did and surrendered herself over completely. Which in turn surrendered us to you as well. I can only guess until we start looking into it, but I'm betting she sold us to you as slaves for nothing."

Runner felt like his brain was finally catching up, and the small piece of his mind that the program inhabited felt like it switched on as well.

"The simple answer is for me to swear a binding agreement to treat you as equals and insure that we work cooperatively as a pantheon, then."

"That is what you would will? You have three goddesses at your beck and call, for any reason, and you would prefer that?" Ernsta asked, her eyes locking onto him.

Snickering, Runner shrugged his shoulders. Reaching out with his hand, he lightly brushed Amelia's hair back from her forehead.

"It'll sound conceited, and pigheaded, but you were all already mine. We were still in the figuring things out phase, but we all knew where it was going. It was fun, at least from my own point of view. I'd like to go back to that if possible. If that means swearing a binding agreement to be equals, so be it. I don't want slaves," Runner said.

Amelia snorted in her sleep and wiggled her nose. "Well, she can remain my slave. Crazy little broken thing."

Runner smiled, curling a lock of her hair around her ear.

"She's only that way around and about you, my precious lamb. She's quite the little monster otherwise. She loves us as sisters, but to others she is a swift and unmerciful death."

Ernsta came over and squatted down in front of him, watching him.

"I swear to treat you three as equals, never as inferiors. That my vote and opinion should only ever weigh as much or as little as yours. Finally, I forsake all powers of command over you. These are so sworn until you all three release me from it without coercion or persuasion," Runner pledged. A flash of light brightened the sky for a second and then vanished.

Brunhild sent her dark hair to and fro as she shook her head, a soft laugh escaping her lips.

"Captured and released in the same day. Should I be insulted?" Brunhild wrinkled her nose, her smile widening.

"No, not in the least. Now, I really should be going back. Satomi and Hannah might do something rash. How long has it been?"

"An hour. No more. We will remain here since this is now our plane. I'm... glad to be here, Runner. I may jest about the situation but I feel it to be the best outcome for all parties. It speeds up my timetables for you considerably, but it's an outcome I would have chosen if given the chance," Brunhild admitted, her eyes traveling to the distant city of Eden and its stone buildings.

"A lovely place. I feel all of our departed here. They're restful. Happy."

"Amelia was right. This place is warm. It nourishes me in a way I did not expect. I shall enjoy dwelling here. There's even a breeze." Ernsta lifted her head as the wind pulled at her hair.

"As for our sister, have no fear, we'll care for her. I imagine you emptied her of her personal divine power before you moved on to our pool. She merely needs rest. To leave, focus on leaving. That you desire to return to the mortal plane. Or if someone is calling to you, you can focus on that."

Runner didn't hear anyone calling out for him so instead focused on opening a portal home. To leave and return to Norwood. To his bedroom specifically.

Brunhild and Ernsta looked on as a portal unzipped itself from nothing and opened a way to the mortal plane.

It opened a few feet from him, and on the inside he could see the bedroom as he remembered it. The edges of it looked like an electrical current. Or static on a screen.

Tousled sheets, book in the alcove, not much light. A true disaster.

I wonder if I could channel this into a spell.

Lifting his eyebrows at the thought, he promised to put some time aside later for it.

"Right, then. Apologies, Minxy," Runner said, shifting out from under the sleeping Amelia.

"I'll see you soon, ladies. We'll need to discuss this further I'm sure. For now, I need to get back. Always more things to do."

Runner bowed to them and then walked through the portal. Glancing around, he found all as he'd expected.

Moving to the door, he checked his minimap. Both Hannah and Satomi were in Hannah's room.

He opened the door to the hallway, padded across, and opened the door to Hannah's personal room.

Inside he found Satomi and Hannah sitting side by side on her bed. Both had turned their head to the door as it swung open.

"Morning. I think? Probably. Thanks for the assist, Vixen. Minxy took care of me." Runner grinned at them as the door clicked shut behind him.

Hannah blinked, her face a mask of anger and annoyance. When she walked over to him, he figured he was about to get hit, but she hugged him fiercely instead.

She patted him on the back and then left, the door closing quietly behind her as she left her own room.

"That wasn't odd or anything," Runner said, looking to Satomi.

"Give her time and space. She is a stubborn woman. She knows her own thoughts, simply not how to follow them." Satomi stood and walked up to him.

"What happened?" she asked.

"Oh, you know. Almost killed myself when I went deep diving into a computer program in my head. Then I kinda dominated the Triumvirate, turned them into my personal goddess slave harem, and burnt their planes to cinders and forced them to live in mine. They're now waiting at home for me to come back while I take care of work."

Satomi's gold eyes blinked slowly. Then she nodded.

"Good. A messenger arrived while you were out. There is news from Tirtius and the mainland. None of it is good news, I am afraid."

Runner rolled his eyes and nodded.

"Of course. Fix one, two break. Lay it on me, beautiful Vixen of bad news," Runner lamented.

"The mainland grows ever worse. A fourth force has taken the field. We have no details except that they have won two battles and lost one. Rike is in possession of the port of Norman and holds it. The others attack her constantly and keep her on the defensive."

"Alright. Definitely news for the worse. What else?"

"Rike launched her navy a few months ago. The human kingdom has been breached. The southern port of Dover fell to Rike a month ago. Thana and Katarina left to battle them with a coalition force to reclaim it. That was two weeks ago.

"I've dispatched several ships laden with supplies, primarily food and water, to serve as surplus for them. I suspect this is not over."

Runner felt his heart skip a beat. He cleared his throat, then swallowed.

"I see. Anything else?"

"Their majesties, Helen, Vasilios, and Basile, have arrived. I have sequestered them in the finished royal apartment wings of the keep. I dispatched a messenger to Faye requesting her immediate return along with every soldier that she can muster."

Runner grunted and laid his hand on Satomi's head, stroking one of her ears lightly.

"Thank you, my bonded Vixen. Even when I can't perform, you take care of everything. I'm going to go greet our guests, see if there is anything they need, and maybe drop by to see Lobu. Do you have any needs?"

Satomi nodded her head once, her ears fluttering a little under his touch.

"You will not repeat what you did earlier. Ever. You will not allow yourself to fall into such a state that you were in this morning. When I entered your mind I found you to be... not good. You will seek me out next time. I will do whatever I must. I will not neglect you again, bonded. I apologize."

Runner flicked her in the forehead and then gave her ear a light tug.

"Stupid. You did nothing wrong. I promise to seek you out sooner. Please feed and care for Sunshine for me. I need to get a leg on."

Runner let the conversation end and fled the manor. He would be "returning" as it were today. Time to get his costume on.

Twenty minutes later he was dressed in a resplendent black-and-red surcoat. There was no coat of arms and not a stitch of decoration. He wasn't trying to appear as their equal, but more as a knight or chevalier.

After belting a long sword at his hip, donning his leather gloves, and drawing on his boots, he felt ready.

Runner went to the royal apartments in the keep, intending to pay his respects first to Queen Helen. If his plans came to fruition, she'd be someone he'd have to contend with on a regular basis. Better to greet her first.

Straightening his shoulders, he knocked twice with a firm hand.

The door opened smoothly, and a Barbarian he didn't know stared at him.

"Greetings, I am Runner Norwood. I've come to pay my respects to Queen Helen," Runner said, betraying no emotion other than respect in his address.

"Norwood!" came a deep yet feminine voice from inside the apartment. "Let him in, fool, get out of the way."

Runner felt a grin light upon his face and he lightly shouldered the Barbarian in front of him out of the way.

Moving to the back of the rooms, he found the queen. She was standing from a table she had been sitting at. Every other person in the vicinity found a convenient excuse to be elsewhere.

She had features that ran similar to Katarina's in nearly every way. She was older and more mature, yet still beautiful, with a stately air about her.

She's young enough to remarry. Would she? Would she try for another child? Her court is so very different than what it was.

"Queen Helen, it's a blessing to see you." Runner came before her and started to bow, but the queen wrapped him up in a firm hug.

"Ah! It's good to see you as well, Norwood. Since you visited my realm I swear I've been blessed by fortune ten times over."

"Oh? I'm glad to hear it," Runner said, truly grateful to hear that. "I'm surprised. I thought you might be upset over how many of your people I took."

Queen Helen laughed and stepped back from him. She was taller than he, as most Barbarians were.

"I would trade thrice that number to you, for what you did. Come, come, sit. I'm sure you've heard the news?" Helen gestured at a chair at the table.

"Indeed I have. My general has been recalled. I shall be moving to engage once we're prepared for an extended engagement." Runner sat at the table, setting his hands down in front of himself.

"I knew you would. Worried for your Kitten?" Helen said it casually as if she were only prodding at him. The wolflike grin and her eyes said otherwise. She knew he worried for her and trusted her at the same time.

"Hardly. Between her and Thana I have no doubt they'll succeed. My concern is the counterattack after that. Our opponents are not entirely mortal. I fear that I'll need to invoke our Triumvirate at some point."

Helen nodded her head at that and looked him over once more. Runner felt like she wanted to ask him a question. This might be the best chance she'd have to open a deeper, and private, dialogue with him.

"Ask it. I'll answer. I won't lie to the mother of my Katarina," Runner said simply, opening one hand to gesture at Helen.

Helen shifted her weight a fraction. His direct approach threw her off.

Letting out a slow breath, Helen smiled at him, a bright smile much like her daughter's.

"I can definitely see why she chose you. So be it. What are your intentions?"

"Towards what? Your daughter, the country of Norwood, Tirtius, or the mainland?"

Helen's eyebrows went up.

"If you're willing, then all."

"Marry, expand, consolidate, conquer."

Helen's eyebrows drew down to the tops of her eyes. She had an expressive face.

"I approve of three of those. There is one that concerns me." Helen didn't look upset. There was a clear curiosity there though.

"Tirtius needs a unified government. I believe the three nations should come together and elect a governing body to rule over them. Something that can be enacted easily and respond to emergency situations. This port situation is a good example of the problem, and the need for an answer," Runner clarified.

Helen's fingers began to lightly tap against the wood of the table. Runner had no doubt she was as quick as her daughter if not more so. The problem he'd detailed out for her was obvious. When it was laid bare under the context of recent events, perhaps doubly so.

"Your statement has merit. A lot of merit. I will consider it. What would your role be in this?" Helen asked. Her question felt like an open pit to him.

"None. I am personally not part of Tirtius nor is the isle of Vix. If you wished me to be a part of it, I would be delighted to discuss the opportunity."

Helen weighed that statement carefully before slapping her palm onto the table and pointing at him with the same hand.

"I shall hold you to that, Norwood," Helen promised. "Forgive me, having heard this I believe I would like time to discuss it with my court."

"I understand completely, Queen Helen. We can speak again later. I need to pay my respects to your neighbors anyway."

Helen's mouth turned into a frown at that.

"Vasilios is a prideful man. Strong and fair, but prideful. He also seems quite attached to that beard of his. Even if it does look refined, it does little to hide his character. He may not receive you as well as you would hope," Helen warned.

"I will keep that in mind. I thank you for your time." Runner bowed his head to her and excused himself. The door guard opened the door and closed it firmly behind him.

One down. Two to go.

If he could get them to all work together and decide on a council or anything of that nature, he would have less to worry about. They'd be hard-pressed to war on one another if they shared a collective administration.

And that'll leave me free to conquer the mainland.

Sighing at the scope of his plan, Runner made his way across the hall to the next slot for visiting royalty.

Shaking off the successful visit with Helen, Runner focused his mind once more.

He knocked twice against the door, then abruptly found himself staring into the face of the Sunless Knight he'd been captured by.

"Runner Norwood. His majesty is expecting you, and welcomes you," the Knight said, standing to one side of the door.

"I appreciate his majesty's courteous reception." Runner stepped past the Knight and found Vasilios holding court in an adjoining study.

He was seated, and around him gathered quite a few of his nobles and advisers.

"Ah! Master Norwood. Come, come," said the king, gesturing to Runner. "You're all dismissed, thank you."

Runner stood casually before the king, wondering if he would be greeted as an equal or an inferior.

Then the king stood up and held out his hand, which Runner grasped firmly.

"It is good to see you, man. Very good to see you. Since you left, it would seem nothing but goodness has sprung up around us. The Damalis family became a rock for us. We had never known of them before you rose them up before ourselves. A fool are we to have had such a thing in our ranks and never seen it."

"Your royal self had no idea, as this world had intended it to be so." Runner released the man's hand and scanned his face briefly.

He had aged a bit since he'd seen him last. Though executing your wife, many of your trusted council, your daughter, and a good portion of your guard would do that.

He still had the look of a middle-aged man, though his beard was new. New and liberally sprinkled with gray.

"And yet, you raised them up. In such a way that we could not ignore them. When we counted upon them after you left, we found their daughter who brought us you, a son who championed us without our knowledge, and a noble lord and lady who turned their enterprise around in a week and now own a vast amount of land and wealth. They are our staunchest supporters. They funded this entire trip as a donation to us."

"I'm glad to hear that. They're good people. I'm afraid my visit isn't entirely courtesy. While you are here to discuss matters with your neighbors, I felt it prudent to interject my own suggestion for a topic."

"Please, continue. We value your council as you have not steered us wrong."

"You are aware of the port situation in the Human lands?"

"Yes. Young Saden and young Damalis departed with a combined force to retake and hold it."

"In this situation, I believe you were fortunate to have my lieutenants in a position to readily assist. What might have happened otherwise?" Runner asked, letting the question linger for a second before continuing. "I would suggest a ruling council for the land of Tirtius. One that could act in situations such as this, one that could provide emergency resolutions without needing multiple approvals."

King Vasilios nodded his head slowly, his gaze wandering to the floor. After a minute of thought he lightly struck his fist to his thigh.

"You have provided us with the right choice when fate would have seen us slain. We shall consider your words at great length, Runner Norwood."

Vasilios was a hard and decisive man. He could see how Helen might view him as prideful. Runner could also see that this man was as strong and quick-witted as Helen.

And he's unmarried as well.

Runner grinned at a sudden idea. A thought that wouldn't provide him with much personal gain, except maybe gloating rights if it turned out to be a success.

Hopefully they'll even be happy.

"I'm sure Queen Helen would be more than willing to discuss it with you at length. I find her to be quite intelligent on top of being a beauty. Nor does it hurt that she's quite the warrior," Runner innocently said.

King Vasilios looked up at him, his eyes mildly irritated.

"She's a prideful woman but... you are correct of course. She is indeed an intelligent, beautiful warrior maiden."

"A prideful woman is something to be cherished. I myself am lucky to have her prideful daughter at my side. She keeps me balanced and aware of my own shortcomings."

Vasilios grunted at that, his hand coming up to lightly stroke his beard.

"Queen Helen was right about the beard. It adds a certain level of refinement. Ah, you didn't hear that from me."

Vasilios had a fairly well-practiced and polished poker face, but no one could have missed his eyebrows moving up at the last statement.

"You—we think you're correct. We shall seek out an opportunity to speak with Helen tonight. Perhaps we can get ahead of this to make sure the meetings go smoothly."

"A wise thought. I would be happy to carry your invitation to her for you."

"Ah, yes. That would be excellent. We're afraid we are not aware of a suitable location. One that would be private enough for a conversation, perhaps arranging a meal—"

Runner interrupted him smoothly when it looked like Vasilios might reconsider.

"I'll handle that for you. I'll forward you the information once I've set it up with Helen."

King Vasilios gave him an open and honest smile.

"You're a friend to a man as well as a king, Runner Norwood. Thank you."

"My pleasure. If you'll excuse me?"

"Of course, of course," Vasilios said, his hand returning to stroke his beard.

Runner excused himself quickly and moved back towards Helen's rooms.

I'll send them to the temple. It has a sparring arena, a garden, and a gazebo. I'll have the priests clear it so it can be a private meeting. Then I'll send Norwood's Own as the guard so they can feel at ease.

Runner felt a lightness in his heart. It served no purpose at all other than to perhaps make two people happy, and maybe put a little joy back in the world.

Nadine would approve.

A minute later and Runner had peeled Helen out from her court to speak with her quietly.

"I apologize, Queen Helen. I have a private missive from King Vasilios and didn't wish to air it publicly."

Runner rushed on when he saw Helen's mouth set in a firm line.

"Vasilios wished for me to convey that he'd like to invite the intelligent and beautiful Queen Helen to an afternoon engagement so that he might speak privately with you."

Helen's mouth hung open as she heard the invitation.

"I must confess, he isn't wrong. You are quite the beauty, Helen, and your intelligence is well known."

"He said that?" Helen asked him suspiciously.

"Not quite. What he actually said was, 'She is indeed an intelligent, beautiful warrior maiden.'" Runner watched as a touch of red came to her cheeks.

"I—ah. Did he specify where?"

"Vasilios was kind enough to allow me to arrange the details. Per his request I'll be preparing something private, secluded, with my own guards providing protection so that there would be a neutral privacy. Oh, and a meal of course."

Helen's hands fell to her hips and she had a small smile on her lips.

"I accept."

"I'll forward you the details after this. Far be it from me to say, but as a man evaluating a man, he's a powerful warrior in his prime with a keen intellect. Prideful of course, but then again, who wouldn't be considering his achievements?"

Helen thought on that, her head moving a little as if she were tossing ideas back and forth.

"I'll excuse myself now. We'll speak more later, I'm sure."

Runner exited before anything else could be said or done.

Now that the royal matchmaking was done, he still had a duty to perform. Setting aside all the details for Helen and Vasilios' date, he went back to business.

Time to meet with Basile.

Runner set off at a brisk pace for Basile's set of rooms.

Arriving at the correct door, Runner was taken aback. It was open partially. Runner felt very wrong about this.

Switching out his costume for his actual equipment, he checked his status screen. Everything was charged, bars were full, and he was good to go.

Providing something is wrong, I'll be ready. And if there isn't… I'll just look like a jackass. Nothing out of the ordinary there.

Runner drew his blade and slid it behind his leg to prevent it from reflecting light into the room.

Taking a step forward, he eased the door to the side as he entered the antechamber that all the apartments had.

Looking around, he found no one. Almost as if everyone had been sent off or chased off.

Or is dead.

Making his way into the adjoining dining room, Runner found a corpse.

One of Basile's people who didn't leave? Or walked in on this, whatever it is?

Creeping into the bedroom, Runner found Basile. His hands were slightly raised as if surrendering. A man in his early years, Basile had the look of any random Human on the street. Brown hair, brown eyes, unassuming face. Nothing noteworthy positive or negative.

The person that stood in front of Basile had his back to Runner. Dressed all in black, they had the look of someone who could only be up to no good.

Checking the name plate, Runner found it simply said "Assassin" and nothing else.

Basile's eyes flicked to Runner.

In that moment Runner mentally cursed the fool of a man. If the Assassin had any awareness at all, he'd notice the change in Basile.

As if in direct response to Runner's thoughts, the would-be killer's head turned to follow Basile's eyes.

Runner casually pulled out his sword and stood up straight, meeting the gaze of the black-clad fellow.

Basile dove over the bed and scurried out of the room as soon as the Assassin's eyes left him.

"Good morning. I don't believe we've had the pleasure. I'm Runner Norwood. She's Linda, and he's Scott. Scott ruins everything. In this case, I'll allow him to ruin you without a complaint. I figure we start with your fingers and toes. Maybe peel them and feed them to you."

Chapter 12 - Everyday Things -

09:23 am Sovereign Earth time
5/14/44

Before Runner could react, the Assassin lifted his left hand. A short burst of blue light enveloped it. When the lighted faded, the man promptly fell to the ground, his health bar rapidly emptying.

He was dead.

Runner sheathed his sword and went over to the man. After unsuccessfully trying to loot him, he kicked the corpse.

"Damn me, I should have hit him with a fucking *Brainwash*. Angel?"

Ernsta was by his side, her eyes already on the corpse.

"Can you do anything? For this one or the one in the hall?" Runner threw a thumb back at the body he'd passed earlier.

Using his minimap, Runner pinged Hannah and Satomi once on top of his current location.

"No, I'm afraid not. This one was claimed by his god as an offering. Rannulf or Rike. The other suffered a divine blow and is no more."

Runner looked to the corpse. The fact that Ernsta couldn't dig up any information was frustrating but not exactly unexpected. The gods protected themselves in this way from each other.

"I understand. Thank you, Angel." Runner ran a hand through his hair as he contemplated the situation. "Is Amelia alright?"

"She yet sleeps. She recovers quickly."

"And what of you, Angel?" Runner started working his way through the room to see if he'd missed anything.

"Me?" Ernsta asked. She stood behind him as he paced slowly along the wall.

"Yes, you. How are you? Is everything alright? Are you mad at me for what happened? Are you truly happy with this entire situation?"

Getting down on hands and knees, Runner swept his hands underneath a bookcase and table for anything there.

It was a silly hope, that something might have been dropped or fallen unnoticed. It was all he had to work with, though.

Ernsta fell quiet. Runner gave her a quick glance to find her looking to the side. A picture of introspection.

Runner waited patiently for her response. Moving over to the corpse, he checked the area around it and under it.

"I've blocked everyone from listening in. My sisters had their own plans. I believe Brunhild would have sought a marriage with you and then set about making a new pantheon. Amelia only wanted you to dominate her and that was the extent of her desires. For me, I'm unsure. I hadn't considered it one way or the other."

Runner grunted and stood up from the body. He'd found nothing of worth. Moving to the other corpse, he started the same process.

"Then you summoned me and smelled of another god. A goddess I had assumed. In that moment I realized I had planned for nothing. I risked everything. Since then I have planned a great deal."

Runner didn't find anything around the body and looked to the corpse itself. It indeed was one of Basile's people. Dressed in the court colors and looking for all the world like a courtier.

"In all my plans I didn't expect this particular situation."

"Oh? And what's that?" Runner asked.

Standing up, he felt his frustration starting to boil over. First an attack on him, and now one on Basile. He'd have to task it to Hannah and Satomi and let them handle it while he played host.

"I'm unsure why my sister didn't say it directly, but after that oath you swore, you're effectively our collective husband. Minus the rites and glorification of it. Amelia didn't simply accept you, she chained us to you. Willingly. Then you limited yourself to that of an equal, tying yourself to us. We all share one divine plane. One divine portfolio. There is no possibility of separation."

Runner closed his eyes and leaned his head back. He hadn't thought about it in that way.

"I understand," Runner said after a few seconds.

"I'm happy, Runner. Your people are here."

Runner dropped his chin and opened his eyes. Ernsta popped out of existence as Satomi and Hannah turned the corner.

Both women looked to the corpse, then to Runner.

"I was making my rounds and found Basile under duress. An assassin. I confronted him and he killed himself. I didn't expect the extent of their resolve. Ernsta was unable to provide anything in regards to either Basile's dead courtier," Runner said, pointing at the corpse at his feet, "or the assassin."

Hannah nodded her head, her mouth a grim slit.

"I'm sorry, Runner. For fuck's sake, I didn't think they'd go for our guests. Fucking bastards are trying to destabilize the region, aren't they?" Hannah surmised.

"I believe you are correct, Hannah. Should Basile fall, a power vacuum would be created in the human kingdom. Is this your thought as well, bonded?"

Runner felt at a loss.

"I suppose? I'm not really sure. It makes sense but it doesn't feel quite right either. Forgive me, you two, but I've stayed out of your business up to this point. Please put together and also send me every report you can on all the activities you've thwarted, suspect, or think might be going on. I doubt I'd be useful helping you find those who are doing this in person. Hopefully I can help as an analyst."

He let his mind consider his abilities and found he was correct in his self-evaluation.

"Hanners, do what you need to do. End this. Vixen, you're on detached duty to begin working as an infiltrator." His insides squirmed at what he was about to order them to do. They were going to be put into very real danger.

"Interrogate, infiltrate, eliminate. If you find someone you suspect, grab 'em. This is by my order, so I'll take whatever heat you generate. No one is beyond this." Runner pulled out a slip of paper from his inventory and began writing out an order on it.

"Hanners, you'll be on interrogation duty. Vixen, you'll take the guise of whoever it is and take their place. While it pains me to say it, start with our guest's extended court. Use whatever resources you need."

Runner finalized the form and then pulled up his faction leader UI. Opening the laws tab, he then forced the paper in his hand into the window.

It materialized on the last line of the "waiting for approvals" category.

Runner clicked the check box, pulled the law back out of the window, and handed it over to Hannah.

"You're officially recognized to act with my will in all things pertaining to Norwood security. Questions?"

Hannah accepted the document and gave him a wide grin.

"No, bonded."

"Not a fucking thing. This'll help more than anything else could. I figure we keep 'em in the dungeons, eh Foxy?" Hannah tapped the paper against her palm as she looked to Satomi.

Dungeons? I don't have any dungeons. Which means she had some made wherever the headquarters for her division is.

Runner didn't want to ask. He'd given Hannah a large amount of leeway in running his intelligence/counterintelligence services.

"Be safe. This is likely to go sideways at any second."

He didn't like it. At all. Since Srit had returned, Runner felt like he'd been doing nothing but sending his people off on dangerous missions.

Could I condemn one of them to death as easily as I did Uno? What would Nadine think of me?

Shuddering at the thought of it, Runner let the idea go quickly. Then he took a deep breath.

"In other news, I need to set something up for this evening. A meeting between heads of state. I'll be in the study of the keep if you need me."

11:48 am Sovereign Earth time
5/14/44

Runner looked up as a servant scurried along the adjoining hallway, carrying cleaning supplies in his arms.

Everyone had been in a tizzy with the news of Runner's "public" return. Runner returned to the virtual screens in front of him. Satomi had brought him everything they had found out during their operations.

Having ensconced himself in the keep study, he'd been working through each and every report, tip, bit of information, and hypothesis the intelligence team had put together.

He'd sorted them by information, actions, and future plans. Then further broke them down by integrity. Some of the reports only had one source of information, where others had several.

Runner closed one window to open another. He had a pretty good idea of all the work Hannah and company had put in. It was fairly extensive and had produced many actionable items.

In fact, to his eyes, they looked almost too successful despite the amount of work they were putting in.

He tossed all the files back into one folder, then sorted them out by plot and coconspirators.

They were lined up swiftly and without more than a glance at the information contained within each screen.

Runner had a momentary stray thought at what he'd done. Putting them all back into the folder once again, Runner then sorted them by time index.

As he started in on it, Runner turned his thoughts toward the little program in his head.

It was blazing. Data flew in and out of it faster than he knew he was pulling it. The ship as a whole responded to him, the databanks ripping information from the files and recompiling them for him to utilize in his sorting task.

Runner set his hands on the table after finishing, watching the little program.

It wound itself down, the goal he'd set complete. Likewise, the ship returned to a normal operational setting.

He prepared himself to begin resorting the files once more, but this time by plot and coconspirators while keeping them indexed by time.

His personal AI wound up rapidly and spun off commands to the ship, which facilitated Runner in his task.

I'm interfaced with the ship.

And the task was done, faster than either of the previous ones.

It's not just an interface, the ship is acting to support my mind.

Rather than let his mind read the reports as he had been up to this point, he read them in conjunction with his program, his link.

Pushing on the link as he started to work through the individual reports, he found his mind expanding to take everything in.

Moving to analyze the files as a whole and separate at the same time, he guided his mind and dragged the link along with him.

Several minutes later he shook his head, deactivating the link.

"It's several groups with multiple cells in each. Not one group with a large amount of cells," Runner muttered.

Standing up, he began sorting the files into each group.

Looking at it laid out that way, it made sense.

There were three groups of covert operations and several freelance bounty hunters. Two groups had divine intervention in a few situations, which meant they were sponsored by gods. The third one did not and proved to be the most indirect as well.

They had tried to target crafters, resource providers, and the priesthood.

Which meant the one he'd dealt with tonight fell in one of the first two groups.

A polite cough broke him out of his thoughts, and Runner looked up to the door. One of the keep messengers bowed his head to him.

"Lord Norwood, we have two individuals demanding to see you."

"Oh? What affiliation?"

"Ah, none, Lord Norwood."

"Huh. Alright. I'll be in the receiving room shortly. Please have it set up quickly." Runner leaned to one side, stretching his hips as he cleared the current file layout.

"Yes, Lord Norwood."

Dismissed, the messenger hurried off.

He could resume this later. Truth of the matter was that he could use a break. That and he wanted to think a bit more on his link and the fact that he was a bit of a cyborg now.

Waiting five minutes, Runner idly played with his link, cycling it up and down with random requests. Depending on the need he actually felt for an item, it would increase or decrease the amount of resources it would pull from the ship.

It was an interesting new toy to say the least.

Wish I could talk to Sunshine about it.

Runner gestured to his guards to take point and fell into the middle of them as they moved.

Flanked and defended by ten of Norwood's Own, Runner entered the reception room and took a seat in his personal chair. His guards spread out in the room to cover everything.

Once they looked like they were in position, Runner motioned to the door guard for the room to admit the two requesting an audience.

Runner's eyebrows threatened to leap off his forehead when Yulia and Bullard walked in.

They were exactly as he remembered them. Yulia hit an easy six feet and had an athlete's body. No one would ever call her pretty, though it was easy to call her handsome.

Bullard looked what every Prince Charming character aspired to be. Blond, blue eyed, nearly as tall as Yulia and vomit-inducing handsome.

Yulia was level forty-seven and Bullard forty-six. Runner was thankful for Sophia's endless regiments that trained up his people.

Good lord. My guard as a whole is right around forty-five, but I'm not even forty.

Yulia growled and began walking towards Runner quickly.

"Runner, you bastard —" Yulia started.

She slumped to one side as a spell pinged off her, then was blown back into a wall and pinned there by two other spells.

His crowd control casters had subdued her without even a word from him.

Multiple guards with shields placed themselves between Runner and his visitors, and lightning crackled as the damage casters began preparing themselves.

The sound of spells being channeled was the only sound in the room.

Yulia looked enraged at being rendered completely helpless. Bullard looked like he would draw his blade at any moment despite the odds.

"Right, then. Thank you, everyone," Runner said, nodding his head to the on-duty lieutenant in his guard. They had done their jobs perfectly. "Please release our guests and let's start this over again. Yulia, you'll need to forgive them. I've already had one assassination attempt and there was an attempt on someone else this morning. My people are a bit on edge."

Yulia's feet hit the floor when she was released. His shield-bearing protectors moved back to their positions, though they kept their shields and weapons at the ready.

Yulia looked like she would explode at him, probably getting a second dose of the same treatment.

Bullard released the hilt of his sword and looked to Yulia plaintively.

Her eyes jumped to Bullard, then to Runner.

"Lord Norwood —" Yulia began.

"Runner, please."

"Runner. We would seek asylum."

Runner blinked and leaned back in his chair. Mentally he reached out for his connection with Satomi and gently knocked on her mind.

She immediately flung herself open and dragged him inside. As was the case with her, her thoughts were like a machine's, churning at the problems and tasks she had.

To one side there was a dark corner that he never asked her about and politely pretended didn't exist. Whatever she kept there, she didn't seem keen on sharing.

There was no talking in this connection, but more of a series of impressions or desires.

In only a handful of seconds he had conveyed the entire situation to her and she had agreed to join him.

Leaving the connection open, he returned to his own mind, pulling Satomi with him. Though she wasn't here as of yet, she could see and hear things through his senses.

"Asylum you say. You'll forgive me if I'm a little confused. The last time we met, you tried to kill my party members. I believe you addressed them as 'filth' that needed to be cleansed, Bullard." Runner said it quietly, his eyes fixing on the man.

There was a tightening of shoulders, people readying themselves. He hadn't spread the stories of his adventures previous to being captured by Vasilios, but they'd spread nonetheless.

They all knew who Bullard was.

A few of his people started to move as they heard the name.

Bullard noticed the change in the atmosphere. He managed to hold his ground and met Runner's gaze directly.

"I was wrong. I did do those things. I said those things. I was—"

A side door popped open, and every head in the room turned to see the newest entrant.

Satomi took two steps in the room before the door closed behind her. She gave the room a small grin, showing off her canines, and moved over to Runner's side.

Nonchalantly she set her hand on Runner's shoulder and looked to Bullard.

"Please, continue," Runner said, gesturing with one hand.

Bullard watched the Kitsune, then looked back to Runner.

"I was wrong, and misled. I can't change my actions previously, but I can repent."

There was no response from Satomi, which meant she found no lie in his words. Runner spread his hands before him.

"Personally, I think you're a scumbag and would happily lop off your head and leave you to rot. Though I find myself torn." Runner tapped his thumb on the desk twice. "Brighteyes? Can you close this room off for me?"

There was no response to his request. Instead he felt her power brush lightly over his own.

"Thank you, Brighteyes. Well, I'd like to know who you were serving, in what capacity, and what happened. No one can hear you, not even Rike, Rannulf, Lambart, or anyone else."

Bullard licked his lips and let out a short breath. Giving his head a tiny shake, he closed his eyes.

"I served Rike. I was a lieutenant in her armies during the early campaign. I was transferred to the invasion forces and came across in the landings at Dover. The things she did on the mainland were... atrocities. There was no call for what she did. Once we landed, Yulia and I fled. All three rulers of Tirtius would not see us. In the end we followed them here."

"Why? You have things to offer, your levels aren't subpar. That seems strange to me. The intel alone you could offer would be worth something. Especially to Basile." Runner leaned forward, resting his chin on his hands.

Bullard turned his head to the side, breaking eye contact with Runner.

Yulia grunted and then sighed angrily.

"They said they didn't wish to anger you."

"Me?" Runner felt nothing from Satomi, which meant this entire conversation was honest and without a lie from their point of view.

"Do you know what they say of you in the mainland, Runner? You bastard."

Runner shook his head.

"That you've single-handedly taken over Vix. That the royalty of Tirtius rules by your pleasure. That you have vaults of unused resources at your disposal to destroy the very economy of the world. That the very divines of those nations barter for your favor.

That they serve as your divine harem just as you have a mortal harem of princesses, generals, and races unseen." Yulia looked like she wanted to attack him.

"Uh," Runner said expansively and intelligently.

Spies and rumor mongers abound. Some of that is secret information.

Runner's brain went straight to the heart of that information. Someone close to him was giving information out. Which was a very serious problem of confidentiality and trust.

We could have a mole.

"Is it true?" Yulia demanded of him.

"Which part?"

"Which part? Idiot! All of it."

"Difficult to answer. I'll simply not answer the question at all. You'll forgive me for not giving up my secrets, of course."

Yulia growled and her hand touched her hilt.

In response, every caster in the room began channeling spells into life.

"Would you expect me to tell you my nation's secrets, Yulia? To give you all the ways to hurt me because you asked? Be real. Now, as to asylum," Runner said, trying to redirect the conversation.

Around him his people let spells slowly fizzle out, taking their cues from their lord.

"What are you offering, and what are you requesting?" Runner asked, direct and to the point.

"I can provide Rike's entire battle plan and her goal. All I ask for is a stipend and a place to lay my head."

Runner tilted his head to the side, first regarding Bullard and then Yulia.

Satomi said and did nothing, which meant everything was again aboveboard.

"Done. You'll each be paid the equivalent to a sergeant and given a single-family dwelling. I'll expect all the details of Rike's movements by tomorrow morning. Any questions?"

Both of them shook their head.

"Good, welcome to Norwood."

The guard at the door pulled the handle and gave the two refugees their exit.

Yulia looked Runner over one more time and then left, Bullard falling in close behind her.

When the door shut Runner sighed and made eye contact with his big lieutenant.

She immediately understood and had everyone exit the room, taking positions on the other side of the entry doors.

"That was fun. It also means our job got harder. Their information was good. Too good. Someone's been talking," Runner said, resting his head in his heads with his elbows on the desk.

"Yes, bonded. Though to an extent everything they knew is relatively available information. It is a concern, but a minor one."

"Mm. I'm not sure who will kill me first. Hanners, Lady Death, or Kitten."

"Why? Over your ex-mate?"

"Huh? How can you even tell? And no, more about Bullard."

"Smell. Her speech. Inflections. Voice. She is conflicted but loves Bullard deeply. As to killing you, they will not have undue stress over the situation. They may hold a grudge against the man but his information is of more importance."

"Goodie. Next. I found the common thread for your assassin problem," Runner said, lifting his head and then pulling up the windows he had been working on.

"*You* did?" Satomi sounded mildly suspicious.

"Yes, me. Why? Is it so hard to believe? Look here," Runner said, pointing at the screens. He had taken a moment to ensure they were visible to Satomi in his window settings. "You two have done a spectacular job. To the point where your success out paces the expected results."

"Yes. We know. We believe there to be multiple cells that are constantly being rebuilt. From the interrogations we were able to deduce that it is Lambart."

"Not quite. It's three different groups with multiple cells each. When you arrange them like so" — Runner pointed at a separate screen he called up — "you can see how it lines up. There's three distinct groups that correlate and mix back. None of those ever cross one another. It's not multiple cells."

"It is multiple organizations. Yes. I see it now. It also explains the difference in tactics and beliefs. Lambart is one."

"Yeah, I'd bet on the other being Rike or Rannulf. The third I have no idea. They're a bit odd. They seemed more bent on destabilization of Norwood than my demise. Also some bounty hunters running around trying to collect on key people." Runner leaned back in his chair and looked to the stones above him.

"Brighteyes? Angel? Minxy? Anything to add? I know you're bound by your rules and you're not omniscient and more along the lines of omnipotent, but any info you have would help."

Amelia popped into existence sitting on the table directly in front of him. Her feet dangled on each side of him and she was leaning forward, watching him.

Brunhild and Ernsta joined her, though they stood at each end of the table in a far more dignified pose.

"We're blocked from viewing Dover. Anything ongoing there is beyond our reach," Brunhild said, one hand held up in defeat.

"Many deaths. Our people were under attack, there is a lull now," Ernsta added, folding her hands into each other.

"No assassins, strange killings, or the like," Amelia said, her left hand coming out to lightly tug at Runner's tunic. "I've got nothing on what's going on here either. What happened earlier with Basile didn't even show up on my radar."

Satomi frowned, her eyebrows drawing down a touch.

"Strange. From all the knowledge we have, then, I suggest we rush this conclave and assist Dover. Lady Ernsta, have there been any notable deaths?" Satomi asked, trying to ask the question in a delicate way.

"No."

Satomi nodded at that and then bowed her head to the collected group.

"I must depart. Hannah will be pleased to hear what you have discovered, bonded." Satomi didn't quite make eye contact with him, and he pulled gently on the connection between them.

He felt it immediately. She felt tiny. Small. Of no importance in this assembly.

"Of course, Vixen. One second though. Brunhild, Ernsta, Amelia. This is Satomi. My familiar. As you all know, that means she's with me. Forever. And since you're all stuck to me as well, you're all stuck with her. Forever." Runner didn't say it, but it was clear he expected everyone to play nice.

Brunhild and Ernsta both greeted her with a smile and head bob.

Amelia scooted sideways on the table. She pressed one foot to Runner's chest and leaned over to grab Satomi. She wrapped her arms around Satomi's torso, drawing her straight into a hug.

"Such a cute little fox girl. If you make him happy, I'll make you happy. Hey, hey, listen, my goal is..." Amelia leaned in and whispered directly into Satomi's ear.

Satomi's eyes widened for a moment and the connection between her and Runner slammed shut like a vault door.

He ears twitched a few times as Amelia continued. Then the goddess drew back and regarded Satomi.

"Yeah?" she asked the Kitsune.

Satomi nodded once, a wide-mouthed grin taking over her face. Not waiting to be dismissed again, she exited the room.

Satomi gently reopened the connection with him and gave him an apologetic feeling.

Runner sent acceptance back to her along with warm feelings and left it open. There was no pressure or sentiment sent back and forth, merely the presence of the other's mind.

It felt a lot like holding hands.

"Do I even want to know, Minxy?" Runner asked. The pixie-haired goddess scooted back in his direction, immediately sinking her hands into his clothes again.

"Nope. Promise it was only good things. I like her. Now, what's the plan?"

"Prepare for war. I get the distinct feeling we'll be sending the army east to Dover. Figure out who the troublemakers are and clean up Norwood. They must be spending a fortune on spies and intelligence agents. Make plans for when things get worse because we know they always do. Discover if I have a mole or not—that information was pretty close."

Runner leaned back into his chair as Amelia crept closer to him. Her fingers had curled inwards. She clearly felt emboldened since he hadn't immediately stopped her or pushed her away.

"Oh! I can help with that. Take your clothes off and I'll start searching for the mole immediately. No hints, I'm sure I'll find it. Now... start with your pants," Amelia said smoothly.

Brunhild watched over the exchange with a small smile as if it were according to her expectations. Ernsta didn't even try to hide her interest in what Amelia was doing and had started to lean in as well.

There was always something about to go wrong.

You know, the usual.

Chapter 13 - Limits -

Runner shifted a token to the fields in the southwest. It made no change to the time required to finish the keep. It'd still be completed tomorrow.

Runner slid another token from the keep. Once more there was no change. Finally, after sliding a third one out, it updated.

Day after tomorrow.

"Hmph." Runner moved the two tokens to the fields as well. The time required for that work was suddenly cut by a fourth.

The fact that they would need to march would put a strain on food and supplies. This of course led Runner to where he was—sitting in his private study, poring over workloads, balance sheets, and resource allocation.

It'd be close. Very close. Emptying the food reserves and taking everything they'd need for the campaign would push the country to the brink of ruin. Not to mention the workforce left behind would be a skeleton crew at best.

Shaking his head, Runner felt like he was trapped on this course of action. For all the resources Alexia sent over, manpower couldn't simply be purchased.

Well, that's not true. Mercenaries and the like could be bought. They're all already employed by me though.

"You've awful timing, Rike. And for this insult I think I might take my pound of flesh from you, and then several more." Runner flipped through the tabs of the UI for city leaders and found there was little else he could do.

Every new citizen they gained had a job the moment they gained their papers. Construction, soldiering, or farming. Still, he needed more.

"Going to add her to your goddess collection? You've already got fucking three. Is there no end to your bedroom conquests? Asshat."

Runner looked up from his screens to find Hannah sitting in an easy chair.

"Eh. I hear she's beautiful but not really my type. Maybe I'll give her to Minxy to play with. Turn her into a pet. My bedroom remains conspicuously empty, thank you," Runner lamented with a smile.

Turning back to his screen, he flipped open the map of Vix. His zone of influence and control expanded across the entirety of the southwest and the frontier. Once Faye finished the fort he could begin true work on the city he planned down there.

The rest of the map technically didn't fall under his purview. Sophia ruled the city of Vix, and Isabelle Letoville.

"You were right," Hannah said quietly.

"Oh? About?" he asked, smothering the desire to tease or flirt with her. Hannah was under a good amount of stress, and he knew that he personally was one of the causes.

"Multiple groups. We picked up several people we suspected last night with your clearance in hand. Satomi infiltrated each group. Rike, Rannulf, and Lambart are the culprits. The one who tried to kill you outright was Rike. Fucking bitch that she is."

"Mm. Unsurprising. She seems to have a personal hate for me. Ever since I offered to let her join the Triumvirate. Her loss, our gain. Minxy is infinitely more useful. And honestly she's fun."

"Fucking ass. You only say that because she might as well be a sheet in your bed."

Sighing, Runner pressed a hand to his forehead.

"Hannah," Runner said sternly, "I have had sexual relations with four women since I've come here. I admit that my bedroom antics aren't exactly morally correct but neither is it a revolving door. Now, did you learn anything else?"

Hannah grunted, folding her arms under her breasts. Her chin dipped down and her hair lightly fluttered over her eyes.

"No. Satomi is still working the last group. Your little police state executive order was really what we needed."

"Yes, but how many innocents did we hold, question, or kill?"

"Ten or so. We returned those we could."

"And there it is. Don't you see? This is not a government Nadine would find pride in. Isabelle will probably skin me as it is, Nadine would have castrated me. Yet it's what I must do."

Runner scrubbed at his face with his hands and sighed, leaning back in his chair.

"For what it's worth, I respect you. I get it. I mean, I don't quite understand why you're so fucking worked up over it. I get it, though, what you're trying to do. I've tried to be careful and gentle. Honestly, the ones we went too far with weren't exactly good eggs."

Runner gestured with one hand to placate her.

"I know, and I thank you for that, Hanners. It does ease my conscience somewhat. What's your next action?"

"Satomi is in Rike's group right now. They're planning a meeting for later today. I plan on being there with my people to collect all of their asses. Going to fucking put them all in cages until they talk."

"Anything I can do?" Runner asked, lifting his head to look at Hannah.

"Keep your head down, don't make yourself a target. It'd be a real fucking shame if you got killed at this point. And that's a shit show I wouldn't want to explain to Thana or Katarina."

"Got it. Well. I'm done here. Going to head down to Lobu's. See if he's heard anything." Runner got up and closed his open windows.

Hannah only nodded her head, remaining seated.

"Good luck with your mission tonight. If I can help, let me know. And uh... keep safe, Hanners. Please. Your life isn't worth whatever they can tell you," Runner said. He met her eyes briefly and gave her a fleeting smile.

Nodding his head to her, he left his study. His guard was waiting for him.

"Going to Lobu's, I'll wait for you in the reception hall," Runner explained to the on-duty lieutenant. She was a short Human woman with equipment denoting a melee class type.

She saluted him crisply, and the team set off to change their clothing. Doing as he'd promised, Runner moved to the reception hall and waited patiently.

He didn't do it often, but on occasion he'd stealth amongst his guard and they'd go down to Lobu's bar, colloquially named "Mibar." His guard would act as if they were off duty, and he'd pretend to be nothing more than a patron.

Sitting at Lobu's wasn't the best use of his time, but it was infinitely more interesting talking to the Half-Orc than working. Not to mention, as a bar owner, Lobu heard a lot of gossip and rumors.

His guard filtered in, one by one, dressed in their casual clothes. He didn't do this more often because it honestly put his people at risk. Without their gear, they were quite a bit more vulnerable.

In no time at all Runner was easing himself onto a stool at the bar. Lobu stepped in front of him and set a mug down.

Tall rimmed bowls were laid out on the bar top, each was filled with clicking, hissing beetles.

For whatever reason, that had been the choice of free bar snacks.

It was a quiet night. Only one or two people were there that weren't part of his guard, either on duty or off duty.

"Hey," Lobu said in his expansive manner.

"Howdy, Half-Orc. Thanks." Runner picked up his drink and took a sip.

"What's the news?" Lobu said, leaning up against the bar.

"Not much. Royalty is in town. They're holding their conference. Getting ready to head east."

"Ah. Our friendly goddess of goodness who commands her sheep."

"Yep, that one."

"Heard the champions are in town as well."

"Oh? I didn't realize." Runner frowned, taking another sip of his beer.

"Word is you've been busy. So, which of the three was best? From what I hear, the lady of night could make any man's day."

Runner snorted at that, setting the mug down.

"Wouldn't know. Whatever you heard was wrong. And where did you hear it?" Runner asked, hoping to maybe track this one down.

"Rumors. Normal stuff. No one in particular."

Grunting, Runner glowered into his drink.

Maybe I'm worrying over nothing.

"It's normal stuff. Wouldn't worry about it. Now if there were details that'd be different."

"You're probably right. What about you?" Runner looked around as he asked the question. The bar itself was clean and well lit. It had a reputation for being taken care of and that it had powerful backers.

It didn't hurt that the city guard, soldiers, and Norwood's Own frequented it regularly.

"Not much. Keep striking out with your personal guard. I think they all keep their bedroll open in case you feel the need."

"Hah, don't be stupid." Runner watched Satomi walk in flanked by men he didn't know. Remembering what Hannah said, he quickly broke eye contact with the Kitsune. Pushing on his link a little, he immediately opened his connection to her.

Satomi's mind stumbled through the open door he left her. Before she could recover, he had already given her the rundown of everything he'd learned from Hannah.

"Besides, why the guard?" Runner took another sip.

To her credit, Satomi recovered easily and then mentally sat down inside his head. Runner didn't toss her out and instead did what he could to provide her with an anchor point for her nerves. Which he could feel easily through their bond.

"You're kidding, right? Your guard is the best outfitted, the most intelligent, and the best looking. One sec." Lobu moved off to one end of the bar to serve another guest.

"Names Lobu, welcome to my bar."

Runner smirked a little. Lobu was spending too long trying to figure out a witty name for his bar. People had started taking his greeting as the name.

Satomi started uploading information to him. Apparently the group she'd infiltrated had been tipped off that he was at the bar. It wasn't that a spy had alerted them to his presence, it was that the operatives were spending gold in vast amounts.

Satomi conveyed what they were there to do. It was a simple goal. Get Runner to take an interest in their honeypot, abscond with her, get killed. Apparently he really did have the reputation of a ladies' man who was working his way through his personal guard.

Runner mentally laughed at that. He'd wait for them to make their move. Satomi's nerves seemed to melt off her with each passing moment in his mind.

Runner drained his beer and slid the mug to the other side of the counter. Lobu looked up from his conversation with the new guest and got Runner a second.

Lobu was a smart man and immediately picked up on the fact that Runner needed some time to himself.

His would-be assassins were already nervous enough without a barkeep standing over him.

Runner took a sip of the second beer, then took in a slow breath. Even in his attempts to take a minute for himself Lady Fate tracked him down. And cock punched him.

A beautiful redhead slid up to the stool next to him, and a dark-haired beauty slid into the seat beyond that.

Runner gave them each a look and returned to inspecting the bottom of his mug.

They weren't merely in his strike zone, they were his strike zone. Rather than check them out, he decided to have fun with it.

A light tap on his shoulder drew his attention back to the redhead.

"Hi. My sister and I arrived this morning. Our paperwork isn't done. Have you been a resident long?" she said in a warm murmur.

"You could say that. Paperwork comes back quick. You'll probably get a job the day after if not the day of. Congratulations." Runner lifted his mug to emphasize and took a pull from it.

"Ah. Thank you. Maybe I could buy you another drink in thanks?" the brunette said, leaning over the bar and trying to captivate him with her impressive bust.

"Well. Actually, you know, I was wondering…" Runner turned and faced the red-head straight on. He could practically feel the desire from the two women, begging for his attention. So they could kill him.

"Who's your friend?" Runner asked, trying to gesture in a subtle way at Satomi as she sat at the table with a couple other people. "I noticed you all walked in together."

Both women stared at him blankly. Runner hid his smile with a sip from his beer.

"Ah, she uh—"

"She's a friend. She traveled with us but she… she—"

"She's terribly shy, yes."

"Oh? That's a real shame," Runner lamented, turning partially back to the bar.

"I'm sure we could convince her to join us. I'm sure she has questions too. In fact…" The redhead held up a hand and scurried back to Satomi.

Out of curiosity, Runner asked Satomi to give him a mental picture of who she looked like.

The image he got back nearly made him break out in laughter. Whoever Satomi had taken the place of, she was the definition of average. Maybe even slightly under that mark.

Five foot four, brown hair, brown eyes, average bust. She was dead center on every character slider you could adjust.

No wonder they had sent over the other two women. In a world of supermodels, being average was the new ugly.

Satomi knew what was coming before the redhead got to her. Runner could feel her annoyance leaking from her mind even through her control.

A minute later Satomi had taken the redhead's stool. The redhead took the seat on the other side of Runner.

Immediately Runner ignored her and turned to face Satomi.

"And what's your name, lovely lady?" Runner asked, already enjoying this immensely. All he had to do was flirt with Satomi, act interested, and leave with her.

Hannah would already be securing all of the bases these people operated out of. It'd be a cleanup action for the remaining agents once Runner left with Satomi.

"Eris. And yourself?" Satomi gave him a winsome smile. She'd have to act accordingly for this to work from her end.

"You can call me Walker. Get you a drink?"

"Sure. Whatever you're having."

Runner poked at her mentally with the word "you're." He'd never heard her use contractions before.

"That'd be this beer right here in my hand. Unless you wanted this one? I was planning on ordering you a new one."

"Ah, sure."

"Sure? You want this one? Well, here ya go then. Far be it from me to disappoint a beautiful woman." Runner happily set his beer in front of her. It had about half the glass left.

Way more fun than bothering Lobu.

Satomi gave him another smile and took a drink of his surrendered beer.

Mentally he could feel Satomi's anger flare out at him. She tried to break the link but since he was the majority partner, and she was in his head, he wouldn't allow it.

Runner gestured to Lobu for another beer for himself even as he looked to Satomi.

"So, Eris. Your friends didn't mention what you all do. Maybe you're a part of an entertainment thing? Like a band? I love singers. Do you sing?" Runner asked her innocently.

Runner almost missed the fact that the brunette nudged Satomi in the side.

"I'm afraid I don't sing professionally, but I do enjoy it. Perhaps I could entertain you later?" Satomi asked him.

Pity. She dodged that well and lined it up with her goals.

Lobu thunked another beer down in front of Runner and moved back to another customer.

"That'd be wonderful. To my eyes, you're the most beautiful woman in the room let alone this city. Your eyes alone light up a room and your voice gives the place a vibrancy. I'll consider myself blessed to hear you sing." Runner knew he was laying it on thick, but it was hard not to. Taking a drink from the new mug, he noticed the status indicator in the corner switched from "intoxicated" to "heavily intoxicated."

My tolerance sucks. Need to work on that. Or push my constitution up. Hah. Enchant some drinking gear.

Time to end this before it actually becomes a problem and a danger.

Satomi hadn't responded to him; instead she watched him owlishly. Her presence in his mind had quieted down considerably.

"What, is there a problem?" Runner asked, looking behind him to see if the redhead was making her move already.

"Ah, no. Merely surprised at your words." Satomi lifted her mug to her lips.

"As if you haven't heard that before. I mean, really now," Runner said, giving her a smile. "With that body, those eyes, and that smile? I bet you have the city running circles around you."

Runner made a show of looking mildly confused and touched his brow. "I think maybe I should retire. I've had a bit too much this evening." Runner pulled out several gold pieces and set them on the counter.

"I'll accompany you. Couldn't have such a charming man like you wandering drunkenly through the streets." Satomi set her drink down on the bar and moved to his side.

"Fantastic. Who wouldn't want a lovely thing like you at his side on a night like this? Maybe you'll sing for me after all?" Runner dropped his arm around Satomi's shoulders and pulled her into his side.

Lurching from the bar, he gave his guards three subtle hand signals.

Danger here.

Wait for orders.

I am safe.

His lieutenant caught the gestures and gave him a small acknowledgment signal in return.

Runner pinged the bar twice for Hannah and stepped out of the doorway.

Directly across from him in an alleyway, he saw the shape of his spymaster.

Unexpected and yet not. She's already here.

"Urgh. This way, it's a shortcut," Runner mumbled loudly into Satomi's ear. Behind him he could hear someone excusing themselves.

Setting his course for Hannah, he tottered along, holding Satomi at his side as if he couldn't stand without her.

As he passed Hannah he met her eyes for a second.

"Guard inside, waiting for orders, one tail," Runner whispered as he passed her into the darkness of the alley.

"Fucking bastard."

Runner wanted to laugh but kept it in check. Maybe he was impaired more than he wanted to admit.

"Damn. Sorry, Vixen. I think I need to get to my bed. Do you need to double back and help out Hanners?" They'd already made it halfway down the alley and were making their way to the keep.

"She is fine. I have no doubt in her abilities to handle the situation appropriately along with the guard you left her."

"Good, thank you. Can you actually sing?" Runner asked, a little too hopeful for an answer.

Satomi said nothing.

The journey back was silent until Satomi dropped him into his bed.

Runner sighed and pressed his hands to his face.

"Even when I want a minute to myself I'm drawn in. It's like I can't sidestep these situations if I tried." Mentally Runner shifted himself into his sleeping clothes and flipped the light to its nighttime setting.

"My sincere apologies, bonded. They were tipped off by an informant as to your location. In the end it will work out well for us."

"I know. And there is no reason to apologize. It was actually fun to see you annoyed. You're always so calm and collected. Even when you're trapped in my own mind it's very hard to read you." Runner dropped his hands to his sides and turned his head to look at her.

"I fear you overestimate my abilities. I feel like I am constantly at my wit's end to keep it all inside."

"Why would that be so bad? It's not like I beat you for your thoughts and beliefs. Since I can read your mind," Runner said, yawning, "it's not as if I don't know what you think. Well, most of the time. You have this little dark cor—never mind. Regardless, no need to be so rigid."

"I have my reasons. By and large I was always told I am a serious person. My family was that of tricksters."

Runner felt his eyes close, and he started to drift at the sound of her voice.

"I often found myself to be the one to bring order to chaos amongst them."

"Want to hear you sing sometime," Runner mumbled, and then fell asleep.

11:21 am Sovereign Earth time
5/16/44

Runner confirmed the budget he was working on and sent it back into the system. Reaching up, he rubbed at his temples. The day had started well enough. No dreams last night. Woke up alone and without any rush on his time.

Then came the needs of state. Budgets, hearing complaints, judging on court cases that had serious crimes attached to them, balancing the growing number of needs and concerns against what he felt was best for the country.

"This job sucks." Runner slapped his palms into the sides of his head to wake himself up.

"What's next?" he asked, looking to the on-duty lieutenant. He missed his inner circle. They handled so much for him that he didn't know how he'd ever managed without them.

"Your calendar has you listed as open to unplanned audiences," the helmeted lieutenant replied. She was a big woman, easily eight feet tall. Bigger than even many of his Barbarians. She wore heavy plate and carried a wicked-looking great axe that he vaguely remembered making.

"Great. Send them in. If I keep working on any more of this, I'll fall asleep at my desk." He didn't want to consider what he'd do if there wasn't anyone.

His mind idly wandered to Satomi and Hannah. They were located together on his map in a location that he could only assume was the headquarters for intelligence. To his eye it almost looked like it was on top of the keep kitchen. Which meant it could only be beneath it.

He was curious how the operation went after he left with his familiar.

His guests entered while Runner was reliving the fun he'd had at Satomi's expense. Looking up, Runner smiled at the three people before him.

He immediately stood and went over to greet them properly.

They were Petros Damalis, a Sunless Knight in service to Brunhild; Stefan Rune, a Barbarian Warrior pledged to Ernsta; and Justinian Wallis, a Rogue who swore his service to Amelia. The champions of the Triumvirate in the flesh.

"Welcome, welcome. Two-Shoes, Sarge, Guilder. I had heard you were in town but I hadn't been sure if you'd visit or not." Runner walked up to each and shook their hand as he said their nickname.

"Guilder?" Justinian said, shifting his weight from one foot to the other.

"You're the guild master of the thieves, so, Guilder. Hey, at least it was creative. I could have gone with 'Pretender' or 'Employee,' ya know." Runner sat on the edge of his desk facing the three men.

"To what do I owe the pleasure?" Runner asked, folding his arms over his chest.

Petros looked at the guards before making eye contact with Runner.

Stefan took the more direct route, "Religious concerns. Please send the guard out."

Sighing, Runner nodded and looked to his lieutenant.

"Lord—" she began

"It's alright, lieutenant. In fact, you may remain if it appeases you, the rest really must leave though." Runner saw the woman nod once and dismiss the guard. She moved to stand at the edge of his desk warily.

"I trust her with my life, gentlemen. You can trust whatever it is you have to say with her."

"We would like to meet your champion," Stefan said bluntly.

Petros nodded his head. "When I was told that you had joined the pantheon I rejoiced. I must confess it'll be good to have a fourth in our number."

Runner had closed his eyes by this point and pressed his palm to his forehead.

"Apparently the entire priesthood heard Amelia's proclamations for hours. I had no idea you were such a cad," Justinian said with pleasure in his voice. Apparently he alone had realized Runner was being inconvenienced. And enjoyed it.

As if I didn't start it back in his own home.

"Yes…" Runner turned his head to the side to look at the lieutenant.

Even through the helmeted slit of her visor he could see her awe and surprise.

"Don't even think of bow—" Runner started.

The lieutenant fell to her knees and pulled off her helmet. Curly blonde hair spilled out from her helmet and she met his eyes boldly. She wasn't like many of his guard.

As Lobu had mentioned, most were attractive at the very least.

The lieutenant definitely didn't fit that particular stereotype.

She was a Half-Ogre. Her face had a blended aspect of both races that gave her a unique appearance. Not entirely beneficial.

Her dark blue eyes were a touch too far apart, her jaw a little larger than you would expect, and her canines looked like small tusks in her mouth. Her features were broad but not unappealing.

"Lord Norwood, hear my prayer. Make me a Paladin in your service. I am Milicent, a lowly Half-Ogre. A low born who made her way as a Berserker. Please, Vindicator, let me serve. Break me free, Breaker," she prayed to him. Runner felt the weight of the words on him.

Her desire pressed on his divine core. It was his first prayer on this plane.

"A Half-Ogre?"

"Impossible."

"A Berserker."

Paladins were a special class chosen by gods to represent their will made flesh. Normally the class was restricted by race and alignment.

A Half-Ogre Berserker couldn't be further from the allowable combinations.

Runner only vaguely heard whatever they said after their first comments. It didn't matter to him who said what. It was what they said that ignited his desire to prove them wrong.

Their doubts empowered him.

"Are you sure, Milly? My expectations of you would be great. As my first Paladin a great responsibility would fall upon you."

She nodded her head once, lost in the possibility of his words.

Runner took that as her blatant acceptance.

He launched his mind at the program in his head, his link. Bending it to his will, he set it loose on the code of the game. At the same time, he pressed his hands to the woman's temples and summoned up his divine power.

All of it.

Then he fired off the *ClassReset* ability he had gained as a GM.

Even before the ability activated, he launched his divine essence into her as if she were an empty vessel. To grant her prayer.

He stuffed her full with every scrap of power he had in him, including his mana.

Then he bent his link to the code. The ship fired to life as every bit of processing power it had leapt to the gaming server to facilitate his desires.

In the span of a second he'd attacked the problem on three levels. Game code, internal mechanics, and unfettered divine will.

The explosion was deafening. Like a thunderclap a foot above their heads.

Milicent vanished in a fiery eruption of bright white motes of light. The world slowed down as Runner concentrated on his desire: to make this woman a Paladin of his own personal order.

To be the first Paladin in the religion of Runner Norwood. Bestowed upon the first person to pray to him whose prayer was to be that Paladin.

Congratulations! Server first: ⊥o¥⅃ »

¼⌐ ←æ

You have developed the ability to bestow the Paladin class upon a subject.
A default name has been generated: Confer Class Paladin
Would you like to rename this ability?
No

Runner grinned at the message window. At least it would be easier in the future.

Then Milicent returned as quickly as she had been blown apart. She remained kneeling before him, and his hands returned to the same spot he had been holding her at.

She was unchanged in any way.

Except that her eyes now shone with an inner light. Runner could feel her presence. She was now a part of him in a small way.

It was nowhere near the bond he shared with Satomi, or even that of the champion link he had with Sophia.

A general feeling was all. That she existed.

Existed in his service.

She would need something to serve him with.

Runner reached over and took her axe from her hands. She relinquished it quickly, almost dropping it before he had fully grasped it.

It already was an artifact of his own creation. He'd built it as a stat weapon to augment the wielder's inherent character build.

Hopefully he'd be adding to that, rather than removing things.

Concentrating on his desire, he broke the axe into three parts. The haft, the hilt, and the blade.

A Paladin's power is based in faith, right?

Feeling artistic and a little silly, he decided to try something different.

Heating up the blade instantly, he gouged out a long line from the center with his fingers. The tear went all the way to the other side of the blade, creating a hole.

He wiped the molten metal onto his forearm, then pulled a pane of glass from his inventory.

Fitting it to the three-finger-wide gouge he'd made, he cut the glass to the dimensions to fit. Since the axe was no harder to shape for him than clay, he easily embedded the glass into the metal.

Checking the placement, he nodded to himself and then sliced his palm open with the axe blade.

His health bar dropped a fraction and blood welled up in his hand. Holding his bleeding hand over the glass channel, he waited.

Drop by drop the channel filled with his blood. When it was about ninety percent full he realized he would be getting nothing more from his hand without cutting himself again.

Flexing his hand, he set the glass plane against the blood-filled channel. With a single motion he cut the glass to match the gouge. A press of his fingers later and his blood was trapped in a glass window set into the axe itself.

Focusing on the axe blade, he enchanted it with *Fireblast*. Picking up the haft, he set *Regeneration* into it. Heating up the break point on both sides, he fit the axe blade into the shaft of the weapon.

Holding the half-built weapon in his left hand, he picked up the hilt with his right.

Feeling the weight of it in his hand, he smirked to himself. Checking his divine power pool, he felt elated.

It was already filled to the brim. There was nothing missing. Not a drop.

Need to thank Alexia. That constant stream of offerings really helps.

Focusing on imbuing the hilt with a holy element, he flooded it with the entirety of his divine power pool. He drained it to nothing once again.

Power was meant to be spent. Holding onto it like a miser did nothing.

As if it had been lit with an inner light, the leather-bound hilt began to glow. Heating up the two points where they'd join, he brought them together.

It briefly hazed out of existence and returned. Any blemish it had was gone, and it had the elegant look he had originally given it.

A brassy gong sounded in his head as he successfully created an artifact.

Runner opened the naming function for the weapon and gave it one.

Item: Norwood's Will

Effects-

Fireblast: Chance to deal burning damage on hit.
Holy: Imbued with the holy might of their god.

Functions-

Regeneration: Activate to regenerate twenty-five percent of total health.
Cooldown: 30 seconds

Attributes-

Strength: 15
Agility: 3

It had lost a few attributes but nothing too terrible. He would gauge this one as a success.

Runner held the axe back out to Milicent. She took it in her hands but didn't break eye contact with Runner.

"I charge you with the following task, Paladin of Norwood. Tend to the flock of the Triumvirate. For they are my flock, in truth. Those who worship the Triumvirate, in turn worship me.

"Your second task is to recruit and train more Paladins. I trust your judgment in this, as you will of course be the head of the order, unless I deem you unworthy. I think that will be very unlikely, however.

"To that end, you will be required to attend staff meetings. They are generally held every morning in the dining hall. We'll discuss more of that when you return from your education.

"With that in mind, I shall now send you to the plane of my power to train and learn of my word and desire. You shall be taught by Alexia, my high priestess.

Understand this, everyone there is chosen and must remain there. You may only select prospects for the Norwood order here, on this mortal plane. Do you understand?"

"My lord," Milicent whispered reverently.

"Be blessed, Milicent, Paladin of Norwood." Runner smiled down at her and felt a small trickle of power pass from his hands to her. "Off with you now. Seek out Alexia."

Runner activated *Taxi*.

/GMHub 2

Teleporting...

/GMHubReturn

Teleporting...

Runner sighed and sat down on the edge of his desk again, returning alone.

"Now, as to my champion. Sophia is not here at the moment," Runner said, meeting their shocked stares. "Oh, wait, one second."

Runner looked to the door and called out. "Sergeants! Please come in here a moment."

Two guards opened the door and entered. They glanced around as if to find their lieutenant.

"Milicent has been promoted. She'll be in training for a week and then she'll be transferred to a new department. One of you will need to fill in her role for the time being. Please wait outside while I finish this meeting."

Both women nodded and departed without a word.

"Sophia should be returning in about a week. Hopefully before we set out on campaign. Was there anything else? I'm afraid I suddenly find myself weary and could use some rest."

"It really is true. You're a god," Stefan breathed.

"Yes. But you'll not be spreading that around."

"Why not? It'd serve our cause well," Justinian said, unsure.

"You're right, it would. But I'll not allow it." Runner put a hint of his divine power into that statement. Despite his oath to the goddesses, he was still their senior. Which made their champions roll up under him.

Each felt the divine command as if it had come from their divine.

Runner noticed it and immediately frowned. Lifting his head up, he spoke to the ceiling.

"My apologies, ladies. I didn't mean to do that to your champions. I'm willing to accept any punishment you deem fit." Hopefully that would ameliorate any hurt he had given them as well as give them back any type of loss of face.

"No need, we're in agreement with your command," Brunhild stated.

"Anything else, fellas? Tired." Runner gave them a small smile. He really did need a break all of a sudden.

Behind them the door opened and Hannah stepped in, looking from him to the champions and back.

"Runner, two problems," Hannah explained.

"Only two?" Runner pinched the bridge of his nose with his fingertips.

"I need you to take care of my prisoners. Send them off to that fucking hole in wherever they go."

"Okay, that's simple enough. We can take care of that this evening. And the second problem?"

"Their majesties have asked for you to please join them in council."

"Great. Goodie. Fantastic. Super," Runner said quietly.

Is Fate going to fuck me or fuck me over, I wonder.

Chapter 14 - Momentous Occasion -

"We can continue this another time, gentleman," Runner said, dismissing the champions. "I'll let my armorer know that you're here and may require gear. I believe I have several sets of gear that could replace yours."

Runner stood up from the front of his desk and moved towards Hannah.

"They're in the royal meeting hall," Hannah said, falling in beside him.

"Great. How'd the catch go last night? Any fish escape the net?" Runner asked, his guard falling in around him. One of the sergeants had taken the place of Milicent and a new guard had joined.

Sophia has put together an effective infrastructure for her force.

"Not a fucking one. Got 'em all. Including where they were hiding. Satomi's been disguising herself as one of their crew. Then we toss her in with someone else from that cell. Make 'em think we were finished with questioning Satomi. They end up giving us more information than we'd hoped for."

Runner grunted at that. It was a solid ploy and would give them substantial results if done right.

"Good info then?" Runner slowed his pace. This was a conversation he didn't want to rush.

"Very. Apparently they met their employer before Satomi joined them. We've eliminated so many of them that the only person left who could give orders was the actual person in charge. It was a man, but they couldn't see or identify him. He gave them instructions on the plan and were waiting for something like last night to happen. They weren't going to have contact again. One of them said that the bait was to do nothing the first night but make herself 'useful' to you. Poison on the second night."

"So, tonight then. Alright. That leaves us one day before he'll figure out the plan failed. Anything I can do? Bait? Analysis?" Runner shrugged his shoulders, feeling a bit left out. His people were trekking the lands on his orders and he was feeling pretty inactive. "Cook? Sew buttons? I dunno."

Hannah laughed a little at that and peered at him sideways.

"Huh. Feeling a little out of the loop there, shit for brains?"

"Maybe I want to be in your company. Stare at your ass and hope you drop something so you have to pick it up. Or you could do that anyways. For me. Like as a favor. Drop things all day long."

Hannah laughed harder at that and shook her head. "Asshole. No, do what you've been doing. We'll handle this. Before Satomi this was... infinitely harder. And messier."

"Right, then. Any idea why they want to see me?" Runner stopped at the door to the chamber they were convening in for the meeting.

"Nope. I heard Helen and Vasilios nearly killed each other the other night. Apparently they were laughing the entire time."

"They're both strong warriors. Expecting them to have a candlelit dinner on their first date is silly. Putting it there to incite their thoughts in that direction, though, while providing them with an outlet, like say a weapons rack. Now that works." Runner gave her a grin and shouldered the door open, stepping inside.

"I—wait, what?" Hannah got out before the door closed.

"Asshole! Fucking stupid bastard!" Hannah's shout came through the door.

"Runner! We're glad to have you here." Vasilios stood from the table he, Helen, and Basile sat at.

"Glad to be of use. What can this poor excuse for a man do for your majesties?" Runner asked smoothly, coming to stand at the edge of the table.

Vasilios took his seat next to Helen. Runner noted the distinct lack of hostility between the two monarchs. If anything, they looked rather friendly.

Helen gave him a toothy grin and tilted her head to one side. Watching him. *She knows I set her up.*

"Before we get into that, I'll simply say thank you," Helen said, her fingers lightly drumming on the table.

"It seemed the right thing to do. One can't leave a beautiful work of art to the side. I only made sure it was put into the light for someone else to enjoy."

Helen guffawed at that. Vasilios quirked a brow and looked askance between Helen and Runner. Instead of responding, Helen gave Vasilios a small gesture of her hand below the level of the table. Then she cleared her throat.

"Basile has submitted a proposal. I'm in agreement with it, as is Vasilios."

"I'm glad to hear that. May I inquire as to the results?"

"First, we would discuss other matters," Vasilios said. "We have agreed on a council. It will consist of two members from each country and the champions of the Triumvirate. While the church has no place in politics, we respect our primes and would value their opinion."

"A very wise decision. I feel that if given the appropriate scope it could respond to any crisis any kingdom has." Runner was impressed. It was a solid solution to start with.

"Yes. Yes. A good idea," Basile chimed in, nodding his head.

Runner didn't miss the slight disgust both Helen and Vasilios had for the man. He couldn't blame them. He didn't match their own ruling style.

"I've been told the Triumvirate has combined their churches, religious leaders, and places of worship," Helen said.

"That is my understanding as well. We have a temple here dedicated to all three."

"Would you have anything to do with that, Runner?" Helen asked him, her eyes ready to analyze any response he gave.

Rather than lie to his potential mother-in-law, he shrugged his shoulders.

"Yes. During my campaign I made sure that our victories were dedicated to the Triumvirate. I erected churches and temples during my travels to that end."

Helen blinked a few times at the straightforward answer.

"Is that all? Did the divines involved give you this directive?" Helen's voice had gone up an octave.

"No. They did not."

"Who did?" Vasilios asked, leaning forward in his chair.

"I did." Runner felt like he was being cornered. They wanted something out of this, what he wasn't sure.

"You simply told them your plan and they agreed?" Basile asked, squirming in his chair.

Runner contemplated that, not wanting to lie to them but not wanting to demean his goddesses.

"He approached us individually, offered us an alliance, and proposed a plan we readily agreed to on his conditions. We have been in accord with him since."

Brunhild's voice cut through the air above them like a stone dropping onto the table.

Brunhild stepped into being from the far side of the table, flanked by Ernsta and Amelia.

Helen, Vasilios, and Basile all stared at the divine.

"My apologies," Runner said earnestly to the goddesses. He started to speak again, but Ernsta held up her hand.

"We choose to be here; this will be a momentous occasion. Be still, little lamb."

"It's true, lovey. Relax, all will be well."

Runner sighed and touched his fingertips to his brow before getting himself under control.

All three monarchs were looking to him.

Rather than respond, Runner chose to wait them out. He'd managed to already put himself in a strange position, and Ernsta's words weighed on him.

Momentous how...

"We would make a proposition to you, Norwood. We feel that as individual countries we are less than the sum of our parts if we were connected."

"This is all because of how successful you were using multiple forces in the war, Runner. We know this can work." Helen's voice had a weird quality to it.

"I'll assist how I can. Though I am unsure what it is you're saying."

"We're going to form an empire. We would like Norwood to join as a member nation."

Ha, is that all?

"We've already worked out all the appropriate taxation numbers," Helen continued. "Expected levy assignments and requirements. We've also agreed upon a charter. It'll hold all nations responsible equally. All nations will abide by the laws of the empire and subscribe to them as if they were their own, as well as giving it ultimate authority.

"Though the level of involvement would be dependent upon the severity of the problem. I mean, we wouldn't send a Thief to the head of the empire, now would we?"

Runner smiled and bowed his head to the gathered leaders. He had hoped they would eventually form an empire, and he was glad that it was far ahead even of his wildest hopes.

"I would be happy for Norwood to participate. Have you decided on which of you will be heading this as the emperor or empress as it were?" Runner asked. Maybe his matchmaking between the two would provide an unintended result. An emperor or empress of four nations, who was born of two.

"We've voted. The emperor of our unnamed empire will be you. Runner Norwood."

Runner held his breath and held up a hand. After a few seconds he managed to gather his thoughts.

"I'm immortal. If you continue with this plan of action, it's very likely that your great grandchildren will call me emperor. Do you understand?" Runner asked, slightly incredulous. He didn't really want this. Being the ruler of a small island was bad enough, but an empire?

"I assume this has to do with the fact that you're not from here. This world. In truth, though, that is all the more reason, Runner. We've already formed the empire, though we haven't agreed on a name. I formally invite the nation of Norwood to join," Helen declared.

Norwood has received an invitation to join <no name>.
As its ruler, you must accept or reject the proposal.

Do you Accept?
Yes/No

Runner mentally accepted the invitation, dreading what was to come next yet knowing he had little choice in the matter.

Other than decline the entire thing and put himself at odds with Tirtius.

Proposal accepted.

"Good. Now, I vote to have Runner made emperor." Helen looked to Vasilios and Basile as she said it.

"Aye."

"Aye."

"Motion carried. Runner Norwood is our emperor."

Runner felt like they'd sentenced him to death. He couldn't see it as anything other than more work.

You've earned the title Emperor
You've earned 25,000 fame
You've earned 10,000 reputation

You've earned the title God-Emperor
You've earned 50,000 fame

You've earned 20,000 reputation

Experience Reward: 18,050% of current level

Level up!
You've reached level 39
Level up!
You've reached level 40
Level up!
You've reached level 41
Level up!
You've reached level 42
Level up!
You've reached level 43
Level up!
You've reached level 44
Level up!
You've reached level 45
Level up!
You've reached level 46
Level up!
You've reached level 47
Level up!
You've reached level 48
Level up!
You've reached level 49

Experience forfeited.
Level cap reached for class.
Please proceed to class trainer.

Your familiar has reached level 60 due to the experience share.

A Quest has been updated
Quest no longer relevant
"A Homeland"
Experience Reward: 0% of current level
Reputation: 0
Fame: 0
Title:
Money: 0

"Hail, God-emperor Runner!" Amelia crowed, leaping at him and latching on to his back. Runner bounced off the table and grabbed at Amelia's hands. Managing to right himself, he looked to his guests.

All three looked shocked. Either at Amelia's actions or her proclamation.

"God-Emperor?" Basile hissed.

"Yeah, about that. As your emperor, my first order is to not discuss the fact that I'm divine with anyone or anything."

Helen and Vasilios nodded their heads immediately, Basile following after a heartbeat.

"Second order of the day," Runner grunted, reaching down to put his hands under Amelia's rear end to support her weight. "Minxy, seriously?"

"Yep! Seriously," she responded, pressing a kiss to his cheek.

"Second order, empire is now named Bastion. Named for the tree that saved my life when I first entered this world. May we be a Bastion to the rest of the world."

You have named your empire Bastion.
Please confirm
Yes/No

Runner flipped the yes button mentally and called up his message screen. The number of level up messages had to be taken care of first.

Does it matter? Do I care about the memories? What if I faint?

Fuck it.

He dropped the points into the respective levels and hit the level accept button.

Name:		Runner		
Level:	49	Class:	Φ♪♫↓¬»¢	
Race:	▼■œ■	Experience:	99%	
Alignment:	Good	Reputation:	35,020	
Fame:	93,455	Bounty:	0	

Attributes-			
Strength:	1	Constitution:	1(61)
Dexterity:	19	Intelligence:	19(105)
Agility:	12	Wisdom:	1
Stamina:	1	Charisma:	64(124)

Waiting for whatever might happen, even if it knocked him flat, Runner felt the memories begin to slide into place. He felt a slight sense of vertigo, but nothing near the severity of the first time.

Memories of his parents and his childhood. The few friends he had. Cousins. Girlfriends.

None of it matters. They're all dead. Memories of a dead man who died in transit.

Ernsta and Brunhild came up on either side of him and each placed a hand on each of his shoulders.

"Hail, God-Emperor, little lamb."

"God-Emperor, I greet you."

"Yeah, yeah. Celebrations abound, I suppose. I'm sure this'll be a calendar reminder for next year. I vote ice cream cake."

"We'll see you later, Runner. We must discuss Milicent." Brunhild nodded and then vanished.

Ernsta gave him a slow but warm smile before disappearing.

Amelia, instead of leaving, bit his ear hard enough that he'd swear she took a chunk out. Then she whispered into his ear.

"Not going anywhere. Reasons. Can't say. Rules."

Turning his head, he addressed her quietly.

"I formally request you stay and order you to remain at my side then."

Runner shifted Amelia around a little before he got her in a comfortable spot on his back and hands.

"I assume this'll be interesting at least. I'll be looking for something out of the ordinary because of your warning. I expect you to let me know if I miss it or something that I should be aware of," Runner whispered.

"I would like to hear more of this divine nature, but I'm afraid I have my duties to perform. I must get ready to depart. I will be leaving tomorrow morning to head back. I expect my emperor, my god-emperor, is going to call up my soldiers to defend the empire." Helen stood up, resting her hands on the table.

"Of course. I promise you a full conversation about the entire thing. Suffice it to say, I'm a divine. I'm partnered to the Triumvirate."

Vasilios stood up quickly once Runner had finished speaking.

"We shall be doing the same. If you do not mind," Vasilios started, turning his head to Helen. "We would travel with you, if you allow it."

The queen of the Barbarians looked to Vasilios and let the moment hang, before giving him a smile. "That would be preferable."

Basile had stood and moved over to Runner, standing before him.

"This is a great thing to celebrate. I think maybe I'll go out and see if I can find some company."

"Oh? I can see how many would view this as noteworthy."

"What about you, Emperor? Any women to celebrate with? Partial to redheads myself," Basile said and gave him a grin, leaning in as if what he said was conspiratorial.

Amelia pressed her knees into his sides even as Runner felt the oddness to the man's statement. Runner wasn't quite sure if she was feeling frisky or fighting against the rules that bound her.

Or maybe I'm being paranoid. Maybe I'm not.

"Oh. I see. I met an interesting pair of women last night. A brunette and the other was a redhead. I could set something up if you'd like to join me?"

"Certainly! Send over the details to one of my people and I'll be there. I'd prefer something private, so please keep that in mind. I'll see you later hopefully." Basile bowed his head to Runner and then slunk away.

"That was strange. And poorly done. Like… really badly written villain kind of thing. Where's Hanners?" Runner opened his map to find Satomi and Hannah atop one another. He pinged them each, and then pinged his bedroom.

Since everyone was leaving he felt no need to wait. Instead he began making his way to his bedroom carrying Amelia the entire way.

Thankfully his guards were up to the task and opened and closed the doors for him.

As the door clicked shut behind him, Hannah and Satomi both stood up from a nearby table.

"Hanners, Vixen. Something very strange happened a moment ago."

Hannah pointed at the goddess clinging to his back.

"More so than that?"

"Eh, she's part of it. She knows something but can't tell me due to divine rules. We're uh... exploring options. Anyways. Weird thing happened. Need your thoughts. I might be overly paranoid in this matter."

"You're always fucking paranoid. If someone starts talking about the color blue you secretly wonder if they're talking about the shirt you wore the week previous. More paranoid than even me, the gutter Thief who grew up with murder and blood as bedtime companions."

Amelia laughed at that, resting her chin on Runner's shoulder. He didn't need to look to know she was staring at Hannah.

"I like you, Hanners. A lot. Nearly love you. I wish you'd say yes so I could watch—"

"Minxy. Do you want me to send you back regardless?"

"No." Amelia pouted. "I'll be good."

Runner grunted and continued.

"Basile said something to me along the lines that I should celebrate tonight. With female companionship. And that he preferred redheads. I can't tell if I'm overly paranoid or if he's an idiot and literally pointed to himself as the culprit."

Amelia used her knees and thighs to press on him again.

Hannah lifted her hands and rubbed at her temples.

Satomi frowned and lifted a hand up, looking confused.

"Yet you caught and confronted an assassin. This is not debatable."

"No, it's not. Unless we question what it was I encountered. One could turn this on its head and ask, were they there as an intermediary between Basile and the cell? Did they kill themselves to avoid us discovering that?"

Satomi sighed, looking more annoyed.

"That is some extreme paranoia, though I cannot discredit the thought."

Hannah closed her eyes and then started hitting her head with her palms.

"He can't be that fucking stupid, could he? Be that damned thick? That stupid that the asshole can't even keep his mouth shut? That he bungles shit so bad he gets his own people killed because he has them meet him in his own bedroom?"

Runner felt Amelia use her legs to press into him at that statement.

At this point he could only assume she was doing it to get the point across to him that his train of thought was correct, but she couldn't actually say anything. That or she'd just gone into heat.

Runner cleared his throat, trying to not think about the woman hanging onto him.

"Why not use your fucking brain thingamajig on him and make him tell you? Turn him into a pile of goo." Hannah made a vague motion with her fingers at her own temple.

"Because it would only provide me with basic answers, really. Answers with no context.

"Not to mention I'd be assaulting a king. A king who is currently my vassal. If this really is a horribly inconvenient coincidence, I'd be setting myself up for a laundry list of problems.

"Can you imagine Helen or Vasilios trusting me after hearing what I'd done to Basile?"

"Shit, no. Fuck. What the fuck. You're always a god damned problem."

Amelia snickered a little at that.

"Vixen, Hanners, I think we should play this one out. Vixen, you disguise yourself as the redhead. Hanners, that leaves you the brunette to play. I'll invite Basile over, take a minute to handle 'something,' and you'll get a moment alone with him. See if he takes the bait."

Amelia's hand dipped into a fold of Runner's armor. It seemed her patience had been lost now that he was taking action.

Hannah slapped Amelia's hand and then glared at the lewd goddess over Runner's shoulder.

"Stop. Now," Hannah growled.

Amelia pressed her offending hand to Runner's middle and moved it no further. Runner felt her chin shift as if she were turning her face to Hannah.

"Hmmm?" Amelia purred. "If you're so jealous, take him from me. He'd spurn me faster than a poisonous snake poised to bite him on the ass for you. Why should I stop if it's only because you don't act?" Amelia's hand slid up slowly, as if to renew her earlier assault.

"Minxy, you're taunting her deliberately. Be nice. You should be going anyways if we're going to go through with this. I appreciate you helping out, truly. Besides, it sounds like we'll be chatting tonight, according to Brighteyes."

"Of course, my god-emperor. I'll always do as you wish and command. Always. On an unrelated note, you owe me twenty-three hours for my work with the little gutter rat. I look forward to spending it with you." And then Amelia winked out of existence.

"God-Emperor, bonded?" Satomi said. Her question was followed by a firm mental knock on the connection he shared with her.

Sighing, he opened his mind to her and pointed out the relevant memories.

Directing his response to Hannah, he held up his hands and sighed.

"Norwood has joined an empire with the Barbarians, Sunless, and Humans. They then elected me emperor," he said simply.

Hannah nodded her head at that. Before holding up a finger.

"And the god part?"

"Yeah, it's true. I'm a god. One of the divine."

"Fuck you, no. Start at the beginning," Hannah said, punching him in the shoulder.

So Runner did.

Satomi took it in stride. If anything she seemed proud. Hannah on the other hand was a little angry, and if Runner didn't miss his guess, scared.

In his time with the half-breed, he'd found he earned more points with her letting her figure out what she wanted to say, rather than trying to dredge it out of her.

"Now, moving on to more important matters." Runner shifted in the chair he'd taken during his explanation. "Since they weren't supposed to make contact, what were they going to do to get out?"

"Unknown. What we got out of them is they were all making their own plans. Their go-between was no longer a part of the cell."

"Which means you already caught them. Or it was what I walked in on. The go-between with their handler." Runner sighed and put his chin in his hand.

"Fuck. That, yeah. Okay. So we do this. What are we doing?"

"We go in, have a good time, celebrate me becoming emperor. You'll be my date, Hanners. Vixen, you act interested enough in Basile that he doesn't leave but... err... don't let him touch you." Runner felt a mild sense of distaste at the very idea of Basile getting close to his familiar.

"No. This is stupid. An idiot plan, fuck this, fuck you."

Runner leaned forward and held his hands out to Hannah.

"Hanners, please? I promise to behave. You'll need to flirt. Probably act it up like you want to spend the night with me. Maybe even leave with me to pull Basile into the scheme."

Hannah's nose wrinkled up and she broke eye contact with him, looking to the side.

"Fine," she muttered.

"Thank you. Now, let's get a message over to Basile with the location. I figure my personal study would be best. Basile wouldn't be able to get anyone or anything in there. I'm going to head out for a bit, but I'll be back by seven or so. Need to run some tests and talk to the Triumvirate about something I did."

3:33 pm Sovereign Earth time
5/16/44

Runner looked around at the fields surrounding him. According to his map this was only a small piece of the area he had set aside for his people to begin working into farmlands.

The work that had been done looked as if it were predominantly clearing the fields of trees, rocks, and other field impediments.

Which left it looking a lot like the plane of Eden. Open grasslands that the wind swept gently over with its caress.

With a casual flip of his fingers he burned away a large rectangle of grass in a five-foot-by-ten-foot area.

All that remained was bare scorched earth.

Taking a deep breath, Runner opened up his inventory and brought out a stack of bricks.

"Brighteyes, you said you wanted to talk about Milly. This seems like an opportune time. Unless you're occupied, of course." Runner picked up two bricks and set them down on the grass. Kneeling down, he started to press the bricks into the dirt, creating imprints.

"Brunhild is unfortunately occupied with Amelia. They are dealing with the champions," Ernsta said, standing beside him.

"Ah, my beautiful Dark Angel. I'll never say no to spending time with you." Runner grinned up at the athletic incarnation of death. She wasn't pretty like Brunhild, or cute and spunky like Amelia, but she definitely had her own charms. At least to Runner.

Ernsta gave him a thin smile and crouched down beside him. She watched for a moment as he continued to press his bricks into the dirt. The shape he was making looked unquestionably like a wall.

"What am I doing?" Runner asked aloud for Ernsta's benefit. "I'm saving a little time and plotting out the arrangement. I decided to test out an idea I had a while back."

"I see." Ernsta folded her arms around her knees and watched for a minute. "My sisters wished to discuss your recent elevation of a Paladin."

"So I gathered. What can I do to help?" Looking over his work he felt like it was a big enough platform. Runner set about filling in the indentations with bricks.

"We would have you grant us the power you used to empower your Paladin, or to do it yourself on our part. Normally gaining the first Paladin is the hardest. You broke that barrier for all of us. Easily."

Runner frowned while shifting bricks into the spacing he wanted.

"I don't have a problem with that. I can easily create a staff or weapon that could do the same I suppose. What would you all prefer?" Standing, Runner took out the mortar he had brought with him. Dropping a chunk of it out onto the bricks, he used his Earth element to spread it out evenly and quickly.

"I believe we would enjoy the option of having both available. A sword for me, staff for Brunhild, a dagger for Amelia." Ernsta reached out and brushed her fingers against the already dry mortar.

"Consider it done. I'll have it for you before we head out on campaign. Anything else?" Runner began setting down bricks in a two-by-two column on top of the platform he'd made.

"Do you have any restrictions on us for Paladins? Or instructions?" Ernsta asked him.

"Huh? Why would I? We're all equals in this, silly Angel. You ask something like that and I'll give you an order and we'll see what happens. Maybe have Minxy tie you up and deposit you in my bedroom." Runner slopped down some mortar onto the quickly rising column of bricks.

"Hush," Ernsta said quietly. "What are you building?"

"Experimenting. I had a thought earlier when I opened that rip in space from plane to plane. Seeing what I can do now with it. Speaking of kidnapping you and having my way with you...," Runner said. Turning his head, he addressed Ernsta directly.

"If I wanted to neutralize a god, either through death or otherwise, how might I do that? It seems complicated since you can be in multiple places at the same time."

Ernsta looked thoughtful as she considered his question.

"I'm not sure. I suppose with enough divine power you could force them from avatar to reality. To be honest with you, I am here and here alone at this moment."

Runner quirked a brow at her before returning to his work.

"So if I absconded with you right now, you'd be at my mercy."

"Completely."

"If I took you to another plane, you'd be unable to leave?"

"Yes. I'd be your prisoner."

"Huh. Why are you here in person by the way?" Runner slopped more mortar down and then used his elemental abilities to harden everything up. He moved to the other side of the platform and began to build another pillar.

"All three of us do it. It's preferable."

"If you don't mind me asking, why? You don't have to answer." He laid the bricks down quickly.

Ernsta let out a soft breath, her hand coming out to touch the new pillar.

"You made a comment once. 'I wouldn't want to share them with their followers.'"

Runner stood up and firmed the pillar with mortar and then thought on her comment.

"Suppose I did at that. Well, thank you for being conscientious. You're treating me better than I deserve. Consider me flattered and moved. I already owe you a hug, you're welcome to claim something else as well for being honest with me. I can always count on you to never sugarcoat it, Angel. Love you for that. Truly do." Runner started to build a simple arch from larger bricks above the two pillars.

Runner finished up and took two steps backwards.

"It's a doorframe?" Ernsta asked.

"Kinda. I need to make another one." Runner grunted and set into building another.

Having done it once, this one took little to no time at all. Once they were both built he started to think on how he wanted to do this. Up to this point it had all been hypothetical.

"You actually care for me."

Runner scoffed and looked to Ernsta.

"Obviously. For someone as intelligent as you are, you're lacking in common sense at times. Maybe I should kidnap you after all. I could take us to a plane with a time dilation effect. We could spend a day there and it would only cost us maybe six hours."

Ernsta wrinkled her nose and then her shoulders drooped.

"I'm sorry. This is new to me. Amelia and I have spoken of this before. She hides her nervousness in her actions — I'm afraid I cannot be as bold."

Runner sighed and then pulled Ernsta into a tight hug.

"You're an idiot. This one's on the house. Be yourself, don't change, there's nothing you need to do. We're feeling this out, remember?" Runner ran his hands lightly up and down her back.

"Mmm." Ernsta was stiff in his arms. Patting her on the back twice, he released her.

"When you claim that hug, I expect you to hug me. Not act like a tree. Now, let's get to testing."

Runner selected the frame with his mind and then pushed his will, mana, and divine power into it to create the same portal he had previously.

It took only a little effort before the portal burst to life in the frame he'd selected. A second portal ripped into existence in the other frame.

"Ah, seems like it worked? Let's try." Without another word Runner walked through the portal on his right.

And popped out of the one on the left.

Ernsta's eyes bore down on him after having watched the demonstration.

"You've already changed war forever here. With this, you would turn tactics on its head."

"Yeah. I know. What can I say? I want my empire to be victorious. I will make Bastion a citadel to those who would seek shelter, and a death knell for those who would oppose me." Runner put his hands on his hips as he stared at his creation.

"You could put these in our temples. That would make them religious property, which can be protected by champions, Paladins, and even us. We could move anywhere at any time. Even cloak it as a religious power if we put it in a dark room and force a sworn oath on their soul."

"Uh huh. Lots of uses. No shower rooms to peek in on though."

Runner sighed dramatically at his own terrible humor.

"You could watch me, without the portal," Ernsta said humorlessly.

"Dark Angel! You lovely woman. You always surprise me. Consider me interested. Only need a time and place. I bet you look great in the water."

Then Runner exploded his portals with a burst of divine power. The bricks detonated and the magic winked out as pieces of the gate sprayed out.

He had a date with Basile to prepare for.

Chapter 15 - Divine Orders -

Basile took a seat near Satomi, though not directly next to her.

Hannah was seated beside Runner, poised as if to lean into him at any moment.

Hannah and Satomi were both well dressed as normal, though to Basile's eyes he was sure they were dressed in a provocative manner.

Hannah had gone off on her own after Satomi had set up her disguise. Whether it was to get her head in the right spot or torture her prisoners he didn't know.

At least she's here, and acting accordingly.

"Glad you could make it, Basile. You'll forgive me for having gotten ahead of you." Runner gave the man a smile.

Several half-finished bottles sat on a small table between them. An empty bottle would vanish. Several half-finished ones would hopefully convey exuberant overindulgence to Basile.

"Not a problem, Emperor. Or Runner?"

"Runner. We're in good company here," Runner said, shifting his weight to one side and sliding his arm around Hannah's shoulders.

To her credit, Hannah immediately smiled and leaned into his side. Her right hand fell on his knee as her left lay in her lap.

I hope she doesn't kill me later.

"Runner. I'm afraid I won't be able to stay too long, but I'll be glad to remain for a bit." Basile poured himself a glass from one of the bottles. Runner checked in with Satomi mentally.

The connection was wide open, and she made no indication that Basile was speaking falsely so far.

"You know, I swear this whole problem is because of one thing," Runner grumbled. Mentally he tried his hand at blocking out the room to the eyes and ears of the divine. "Because Rike is a dirty rotten cunt. I bet if she got laid she'd ease up."

Basile couldn't hide the momentary shock on his face at Runner's casual blasphemy.

"What do you think, Basile?" Runner asked. As if he wasn't particularly interested in the answer, he leaned into Hannah's ear and whispered for her ear alone.

"You did say Rike was the most likely culprit, right? Giggle and smile, nod or shake your head. Sorry."

Hannah froze up, then let out a sultry giggle and nodded.

"Oh, the same as anyone," Basile said noncommittally.

Runner laughed and turned from Hannah to look to Basile.

"I think she's a nasty old bat who needs to ride a pole. Come on, you think she needs to get laid? Or is she so dry down there it'd turn someone to ground beef?"

Satomi laughed and leaned forward toward Basile.

"Yes, Lord Basile. Tell us. We're all friends here, and she's the enemy. I'm sure you hold a special hatred for her since she's invaded your lands."

"I, uh. Yes. She's a true nightmare. A terror. Blessed be the day she leaves our lands alone." Once again his comments were something anyone could say.

"Fuck Rike! May she sleep with pigs and bear their young! I serve the Triumvirate!" Runner shouted, holding up his glass. He was tired of the dancing around.

Blunt as a battering ram.

Hannah and Satomi both held up their own glasses, laughing, and said in unison, "Fuck Rike! May she sleep with pigs and bear their young! I serve the Triumvirate!"

All three turned to Basile, waiting.

For his own part, he gave them a smooth smile and held up his glass.

"Fuck Rike. May she sleep with pigs and bear their young. I serve the Triumvirate."

Lie. Satomi's mind gave him the impression as Basile spoke. He didn't serve the Triumvirate.

"Ahaha. Lovely, lovely. Ah, that reminds me. I need to step out for a quick minute," Runner apologized. Leaning in, he pressed in close to Hannah's ear again.

"See if he'll say anything. I'll be back in a minute."

Hannah nodded, turning her head to the side.

"Don't be gone too long, shit for brains." Her eyes flashed as she whispered at him from an inch away. Her smile made him focus on her rather than her words.

Runner felt his breath catch at the way a smile brightened her face. Then he caught himself as he started to lean in to kiss her.

Runner stood up quickly and exited the room via a side door that brought him into an antechamber adjoining his bedroom.

As the door closed he let out a slow breath, pressing his back to the door.

He could hear the muffled voices of Satomi and Hannah through the door. Satomi had the connection open to him if he wanted to listen in.

He didn't care. It'd only make him more anxious, and he could use a break.

Runner wasn't quite sure how to handle it, but sitting so close to Hannah made him dizzy.

Feeling a slight press of concern from Satomi, he could only chuckle. Affirming he was fine, he mentally gave her the impressions of the feelings he was experiencing.

Then he gave the room a ping to signal he was coming back in.

A few seconds later and he was seating himself back down next to Hannah.

Who lifted his arm and draped it around her shoulders, pressing herself firmly up into his side.

Runner plastered a silly smile on his face and turned his head to Hannah.

Only to find she had done the same and was leaning in towards him.

Going with the motion and against reason, he kissed her. He lost a bit of himself as he let the kiss linger, his arm pulling at her shoulders.

Hannah pressed a hand into his chest and gently eased him back.

Blinking rapidly, Runner felt trapped. He wanted to apologize to her and kiss her again at the same time.

Instead he stared at her stupidly.

Hannah gave him a small smile and then turned her head back to Basile.

"You were saying, Lord Basile?"

"Ah, uh. I was just saying that I'm afraid I should be going. It looks as if you two are about to be retiring for the night. I hope to see you in the morning, Runner."

Lie.

"May your guidance as our emperor prove to be successful."

Lie.

Runner nodded his head to Basile as the weasel-faced man departed. He had hoped for something more incriminating. Something he could act on.

Anything. Anything at all. Leaving things like this would drive him wild.

As it was, although Basile didn't seem to care for Runner, he hadn't claimed or done anything treasonous.

No sooner had the door closed behind him than Satomi huffed.

"He does not care for your company, bonded. I think he believes you to be unfit, but I did not detect anything that would say he was the handler. Nor did he say anything worthwhile after you left."

Runner nodded his head at that. He'd pretty much felt the same.

Hannah growled under her breath as her shoulder pressed back into Runner's side again.

"Slimy bastard. I know it's him. I know it!"

"Minxy would agree with you," Runner said, dismissing the bubble he'd erected around the room. It wasn't needed any further. "To be honest, I agree as well. The problem is I can't prove it. Not without risking some serious problems and breach of etiquette."

Hannah folded her arms and shook her head, her hair tickling Runner's nose.

"I don't like it. What if he had an accident? I bet I could end the bootlicker with none the wiser."

"You could, except that it would put serious doubt on the security of our newly found empire. Someone dying in the heart of Norwood? The heart of Bastion?"

Hannah snorted and rested her head on Runner's shoulder. "Fine. You're right. I hate it. I hate this. I know he tried to kill you. I know he set this up. I want his head in a bag and his body in a hole."

Runner smiled and lifted his hand to lightly brush Hannah's hair back from her brow, his arm still resting around her shoulders.

"And yet again, you're probably not wrong. Yet this is as it must be. At least for now. I hate leaving this open but we've no choice. They'll be leaving tomorrow, and you can resume operations normally. Hopefully Sparky, Grace, and Belle get back sooner rather than later. We need to get the troops on the road to kick Rike's scrawny ass out of Dover."

"About that, bonded, what are your plans?"

"The usual. I believe I'll leave Belle and yourself here to hold down the fort. Care for Sunshine. I'll pack up and head out with the army along with Sparky and Grace."

"And me."

"And you, Hanners, if you're willing. I wasn't going to ask as I wasn't sure how the intelligence situation is here."

"Foxy can handle it. Can't you?" Hannah shifted her weight but didn't move from Runner's side.

"That I can. I shall go arrange the prisoners for their banishment. I shall have them prepared and ready in half an hour." Satomi bowed her head to Runner and Hannah and then slipped out.

As she left, Runner got a mental image of himself and Hannah sitting together from Satomi's point of view. Along with a good dose of humor.

"Bitch. She did that on purpose so we'd be alone."

"That she did."

Runner felt the seconds limp by.

"I don't know what to fucking say."

"Nor do I."

What had started out as a fairly awkward situation was rapidly becoming comfortable. Or at least it seemed so to Runner once they had both admitted they were feeling nervous about it.

"Let's not say a damned thing, then."

"Let's not. Why spoil the moment," Runner agreed, settling in to simply sit with Hannah.

Cuddling with her in his study.

Will wonders never cease.

9:01 am Sovereign Earth time
5/17/44

Helen and Vasilios had left with the break of dawn. He'd seen them off with his own personal preference for a departure.

A private meal, discussion, and a brief "farewell for now." They both seemed pleased, so he'd count it as a win.

Unfortunately, he still had to deal with an unpleasant situation.

Seeing the living weasel Basile off.

Satomi cleared her throat beside him, drawing his attention.

Looking around, Runner plastered a smile on his face as Basile approached him.

They had decided to see him off at the exterior gate. It would keep the proceedings short and let everyone be on their way in good time.

They were perhaps twenty or thirty yards beyond the walls. In front lay Basile's entourage, complete with expensive horses and overly crafted coaches.

"Emperor Runner, good to see you," Basile said, reaching out to clasp his hand.

Lie.

The mental impression was strong with Satomi so close.

"Ah, thank you, Lord Basile. We hope to be in your country soon with the forces. We'll drive her back into the sea before anything further can go wrong."

"I look forward to it."

Lie.

"Glad to hear it," Runner said, holding onto Basile's hand still. Then an idea popped into his head. "I was thinking, as your god-emperor, I think it would be wise to bless you. To make sure no harm befalls you."

"No, no. That's not needed," Basile said hurriedly, trying to peel his hand out from Runner's grasp.

"I insist." Runner grinned and then focused on Basile.

"May the blessing of Norwood and the Triumvirate be upon you. To cleanse any taint from you of the enemy, Rike, and protect you from harm."

Forcing his divine will behind the blessing, Runner waited.

Nothing happened. He felt no power drain on his pool and nothing changed.

Strange. That's never happened before. Why didn't I bless him?

"Ah, thank you, my emperor. I'll be going now," Basile said, finally freeing his hand.

Runner watched the man get far enough away that he could ask a burning question.

"Brighteyes, are there people I can't bless as a god?" Runner mused aloud.

"Yes, there are." Her voice came back pitched at a volume that only he and Satomi would be able to hear.

Runner watched as Basile prepared to leave. Apparently there had been an issue with a few of his people running late. They'd been up celebrating and overdone it.

"Would those people happen to be pledged to another divine?"

"Yes and no."

"Worshipers then? The average layperson?"

"No, they can be blessed by anyone."

Runner frowned, chewing on that.

"Paladins?"

"Paladins would be exempt from your ability to bless unless they were yours. You're the only one to have achieved a Paladin, my god-emperor."

"Stop that. Or do I need to threaten you like Angel?"

Runner targeted Basile and contemplated his options. In a matter of minutes he would be riding away.

Wait. Wait, wait, wait.

"Would an opposing champion be unable to be blessed?"

"That's accurate." Her voice had an edge to it. One he'd come to associate with when she couldn't say anything more.

"He must be a champion then. But for who? Who would he serve? Lambart is still tied up with Jacob until I tire of him. Last I heard Rannulf's champion was running around in the mainland. That leaves Rike. But she attacked his port and put his people to the sword."

Runner shook his head as he considered the problem.

I hate this nonsense. Kitten really does have the right frame of mind for this silly shit. I should leave all this to Hanners and wash my hands of it.

"Bonded. You keep thinking of this man from your own point of view. Your own mind and references. What you value, he does not. Would he be troubled by burying his own people to get what he wants?" Satomi turned her head to watch him as she spoke.

"But what would he want? He's king of his lands and it's becoming prosperous. Trade is booming and we're turning the corner as a self-sufficient economy." Runner's brows drew down together.

"Power." Satomi said it in a whisper. "More power."

It felt right. Runner could easily peg Basile as a man who would constantly crave more power even at the cost of his own citizens.

To the point he'd make a deal with the devil.

Satomi was right, he'd been viewing this entire situation through his own personal lens.

Basile mounted his horse and turned to regard Runner. Bowing at the waist, he gave him an oily smile.

"Heavens preserve and protect me for a fool," Runner muttered. "Fuck this."

"Idiot plan?" Satomi asked. Her mind quickly started to sort through Runner's thoughts as if to get a read on the situation.

Runner didn't respond, and instead drew up *Brainwash* and cast it straight at Basile without another thought.

"Idiot plan. Lieutenant!" Satomi shouted, turning to motion at his personal guards.

Basile stiffened as the spell hit him in the chest. His eyes glazed over. Most of his retinue had missed the spell, but not all. His guards moved to fall in around him.

"Basile, please come here immediately," Runner shouted at the monarch.

In response the man dismounted and sprinted to Runner. All around, Norwood's Own began filling into a box formation around Runner and Satomi.

Whistles began blowing as the call for reinforcements passed back to the barracks.

"Answer me honestly, Basile," Runner said, grabbing Basile's shoulder. "Do you worship Rike, Rannulf, or Lambart?"

"No."

Runner felt his stomach fall out from under him, and his breath caught in his teeth. Basile didn't worship any of the divine who had kicked up this holy war.

Shit.

"Did I fuck up?" Runner whispered, looking to the stones beneath his feet.

"Yes."

"Eh?" Runner looked back to Basile. Unsure of what to do, he pursued the only question he had. "How did I fuck up?"

"You crossed Rike. She will end you."

"Rike? She'll rue the day, I do so swear. Wait, if you do not worship Rike, what are you to her?"

"Her champion."

Runner's eyes widened at that. Moving his hand out quickly to grab Basile's shoulder, he prepared to activate *Taxi*.

Basile vanished from inside the protective square of his guards and appeared amongst his people. Without a target, *Taxi* fizzled.

Brainwash was still in effect, which meant someone had intervened.

"Brunhild, Ernsta, Amelia, I believe Rike just committed to a divine action. If I understand the rules right, I can call you in to act in equal measures?" Runner asked as the opposing side drew weapons and changed from livery to armor.

It would seem Basile came with quite a few more soldiers than he'd admitted to. He'd have to look into how they hid their titles.

In response to his request, their three champions appeared at the front of his group.

He desperately wanted Sophia there as well. Stealing the idea from his divine partners, Runner fixed his mind on the connection to Sophia and pulled on it roughly. He'd get here there, that instant if possible. Fixing a destination in his mind, thirty feet above their heads, he called on her.

He felt his power being drained as the attempt to pull Sophia there built up.

In the distance he saw horses break from the far distant tree line. Rike had prepared extra forces in case something exactly like this situation occurred.

His force was already outnumbered two to one without including the extra manpower Rike was sending.

Slamming his hands together, Runner mentally focused on ripping open a portal to Eden, sacrificing his mana and stamina as the fuel for it.

Dropping to his knees as both pools were emptied, he felt a portal open beside him. Reaching through it with his mind, he snatched at Milicent and Alexia.

His need was straightforward and simple. Prayer and battle.

As if they had been in communion in the temple, he felt an immediate response from both.

Milicent stepped through the portal and was at his side. The eight-foot brick wall of a woman hefted her glowing war axe. Beyond his Paladin he saw Alexia raising her staff and calling to his worshipers.

What had been a trickle of power before the portal turned into a raging torrent of support.

"Milly, glad to have you," Runner gasped, looking up the long distance to the Paladin's helmetless head. Her slightly too wide stare fixed on him in reverence.

"My god," Milicent said, giving him a wild smile.

"We're about to engage Rike's champion and his people. I must ask you to lead Norwood's Own from the front. Alongside our champions."

Those huge blue eyes took on an eager light. She hefted her axe once and then moved off to the front.

Runner managed to get to his feet as his people's prayers filled him with vitality. Slamming the butt of her axe down, Milicent knelt and bowed her head.

"Divine Norwood, have mercy upon your humble Paladin—"

The glow of Milicent's axe increased along with the volume of her words.

Basile shook himself free of the *Brainwash* and snarled at Runner. He raised his hand and shouted something at Runner that he couldn't hear.

"I pray for your blessing in these trials. To be the sword of your justice—"

Above them, Sophia burst into being. Exactly where he had positioned her with his mind.

Her wings blasted out from her back in a single beat and her lance hung loosely in her hand. She hovered there as her eyes took in her surroundings.

"To be your shield of charity. That I might carry your truth into the den of battle—"

Runner felt winded, spent. While his bars were rapidly refilling, he could feel a drain on him he couldn't quantify.

"I ask for your benevolence and grace, for not myself, but for those I fight with—"

Across from him, Basile led his forces forward to engage with Runner's. Apparently the man wanted to end this before either side's reinforcements could arrive.

"May you safeguard my soul should I fall, and forgive me for my failure." Milicent slammed her large fist to her breastplate and stood.

Runner felt the tug on his divine core when she finished. Going with the feeling, he opened himself to the pull of it and the request it made on his divine power.

Milicent glowed like the sun for a moment as he answered her prayer.

His power pool depleted by a quarter with the granting.

Light rippled out from her like a golden halo, and the men and women around them stiffened their spines after it passed them. Their shoulders lifted.

Blessed and sanctified.

Glancing up at his divine pool, he watched as it refilled nearly instantly.

Panting, he fell to one knee again. Runner turned his mind and his will on the feeling Milicent's prayer had generated. Then he directed it at the four champions and tried to empty his power pool.

All four exploded in dazzling light moments before the two sides clashed.

When his divine power emptied, he found he couldn't sustain the portal and it closed itself.

Then Satomi was there as he started to fall to the ground. Her small hands gripped at his shoulders and wrangled him to a standing position. She managed to turn herself around and tried to drag him through the press of bodies.

Sophia dove from on high like a meteor. Her lance spun out like a fiery whip as it crackled across the enemy lines.

Petros, Stefan, and Justinian had spread out amongst the line. They were all engaged with the enemy, swinging blazing weapons.

Milicent had waded into the enemy's center and laid about with her war axe. With each impact a flash of blue light could be seen, at times followed by an inferno as the weapon's effects activated.

An arrow whizzed over the heads of Runner's people to embed itself in his gut. Doubling over, Runner couldn't help but notice as his health bar dropped by ten percent.

Then a second arrow burrowed into his shoulder, the impact threatening to spin him around.

A third arrow skipped off the stone nearby and disappeared into the crowd of his people.

Runner felt his mind spin as he tried to clear it of the fog that had settled over him.

A wild pinging noise flooded his ears even as he struggled to get himself in gear.

He wasn't doing anyone any good. All he'd managed to do was send his people into harm's way.

A fourth and fifth arrow found their way to him accurately. Looking down he found the two offending arrows protruding from his chest.

His health bar hit the red zone. Dazed, Runner looked up and found the source of the attack.

Multiple bowmen had set up a wagon and were trained on him alone.

One had reloaded and drew their bow back to fire at him again.

Hannah stepped in front of him and shuddered as the arrow struck her.

Turning to face him, she began hustling him through the line with Satomi's assistance.

"Damn me, and damn you, Runner. If you fucking die on me I'll have Ernsta herself summon you so you can watch me skull fuck you," swore Hannah. An arrow thudded into a shield somewhere around them.

Reaching the rear of the formation, Hannah sat Runner down where he wouldn't make himself more of a target

Then she worked to get shield-bearing guards around him.

As the battle roared on, Runner found himself in a wall of shields and protected from harm.

"The fuck did he do?" Hannah yelled over the din of battle at Satomi.

"Basile was the traitor. He is also the champion of Rike. Runner revealed him. For an idiot plan it was rather good."

"Shit. Okay. You, you, you, and you. Take our emperor back inside and into safety. I have a mess to clean up," Hannah shouted at the shield bearers.

One guard began dragging him out of harm's way, and the other three held their shields up during the retreat.

"I have to stay. I need to help," Runner mumbled. "I can't leave them."

"Shush, bonded. Not every fight is yours to lead and handle. You have strong and loyal followers. Let them carry out their responsibilities." Satomi glanced back towards the battle as she spoke.

Runner lost his train of thought. He only came back to himself when they sat him down in a chair.

Looking up, Runner found himself sitting under Bastion, in the middle of town.

"Nice tree, good foliage," Runner remarked. "Bigger than I remember." Runner looked to the side to find his first statue of Nadine, which watched over all those who entered Norwood.

"Call for no healer, Vixen. My bonded. Send them out immediately to assist our troops. I'll live. Please," Runner said, grabbing Satomi's wrist.

She gave him a curt nod and then gestured to someone he couldn't see.

His eyes then moved down the boulevard towards where the battle was ongoing. Troops, Norwood's Own, and city guard left through the front gate in a flood as they joined the battle.

Feeling helpless, he remained seated. Those who'd brought him here wouldn't let him leave even if he ordered it.

Runner had the vague impression they knew how close they had come to losing their emperor.

The arrows jutting out of him told that story clearly enough. Runner took the time instead to bring his mind back to order.

Utilizing his divine power took a toll on him.

Must be because I'm not a real divine. Srit made me something else entirely.

Twenty minutes crawled by before the sounds of combat became less intense. Ten after that and only the occasional punctuation of fighting reached him. Then nothing.

A Norwood's Own guard came jogging back to him.

Having sorted his mind out into a semblance of normalcy, he waited for the messenger to speak.

"Victory, sir. Basile has been slain. We're currently in the process of collecting what we can. Then we'll hold roll call to confirm the dead and missing."

"Thank you. If possible, please have the champions, Milicent, and Hannah sent to me as you can."

"Sir." The guard saluted and then slipped back out the gate.

Then his people began trooping back into the city. Many were bloody, but these were those who would be leaving the field of battle.

They would return to their barracks and patrols, seek medical attention, and go into the recovery phase of a pitched battle.

Then would come attendance to confirm the bodies found on the field. A looted corpse would be disposed of quickly. There was the possibility slain people would be looted before someone could notice their demise.

Getting to his feet, Runner reached back and tossed the chair to the side of the boulevard, sending it clattering over the stones to slap into a wall.

Runner faced the oncoming troops and saluted them. He remained at attention as his people filed by.

He almost felt a little silly doing it. Maybe a touch overly dramatic.

Holding himself in that pose, he remained stationary under Bastion. In his mind it was the least he could do for those who'd fought for him even as he'd been hurried from the field of battle.

As the last passed him, heading towards their barracks, Runner dropped his hand to his side.

Targeting himself, Runner cast *Regeneration*. His mana could be used on himself without concern at this point.

"Vixen, please have this marked as a day to remember all of our dead. Past and future. It'll be a ceremony for all those who have died in service. After all, this is our first encounter as an empire.

"We'll also need a citation made for this. Call it the First Battle."

"With fucking traitorous bastards, no less," Hannah said, coming up to his side. "Fuck me, you still look like death warmed over. I mean, I know Ernsta makes rapey eyes at you sometimes but good goddess. You're covered in blood."

"Yeah, I refused treatment since healers would be better served on the lines. I'm already healing myself. Clothes will need to wait. Feeling tired," Runner said as he turned to address her with a negligent hand wave.

A step behind her were Milicent, Sophia, Stefan, Justinian, and Petros.

Runner felt the stone hanging around his heart drop and fall away.

"I'm so glad to see you all. I worried for you," Runner said, encompassing them all with a smile.

As a group they seemed uncomfortable with his attention.

"My lord," Milicent said, stepping forward. She dropped down to a kneeling position before him. Her unique face stared up at him. "Your will is done."

"Thank you, Milly. You've served above and beyond. What boon should I grant you?" Runner asked, placing a hand on the crown of her head.

Feeling a smile curl his lips, he waited. She was as offbeat as they came. A Berserker Half-Ogress Paladin didn't exactly come standard

As a Paladin she would never be comparable to the existing expectation the people would have for a Paladin.

Serving as Runner's Paladin though? In his personal opinion?

He thought back to her prayer and the way she had dove into the enemy line. *Best Paladin ever.*

Milicent glanced down at the grass surrounding Bastion before looking back up to him.

"Return me to Eden. There is much to learn. It is a blessed place. I feel your presence in everything and everyone. I would remain there for a while longer."

Runner almost missed the curiosity that statement prompted in some of the people around him.

Runner made a buzzing noise, then laughed and poked Milicent in the middle of her forehead with his free hand.

"Try again. That's happening regardless." Runner waited, his right hand still pressed to the crown of her head.

"I... I don't know."

"Ask for a set of armor, you silly fuckwit. Norwood colors, enchantments, holy and all that shit. Alternate weapons, too. Your gear is already made by him, least he can do is make it unique for his first and only Paladin," Hannah supplied.

Milicent's eyes became wide and she nodded her head.

"That, my lord. I wish for that."

"Consider it done. I have to make a few things for other people anyways. I'll have it ready for you upon your return. Stand, Milly. I would have you at my side for the next bit. We must greet, thank, and send on our dead."

Milicent stood up to her full height and then moved to one side of him.

Looking around he caught sight of Sophia speaking to the on-duty lieutenant. She looked fine. Healthy. Hale.

Runner wanted to talk to Sophia, to hug her and find out what had been going on with her. He hadn't seen her in nearly half a year.

Duty waited for no one though.

"Angel, please bring me our dead. I would thank them before I send them to our plane."

"Of course. I'm glad you're doing this, my little lamb," Ernsta said, popping into existence underneath the boughs of Bastion.

"Thanks, Angel. Good to hear you say that, because I doubt this'll be easy. Everyone else, you're welcome to stay or go as you please. I'm unsure how long this will take."

Runner squared his shoulders and prepared himself to begin welcoming his dead. Those who'd died because he ordered them to fight.

He was used to that though. After leading a war, he'd stacked bodies by the thousands. So long as he spent their lives effectively and for the benefit of their country there would be no wrong in their deaths.

They began to appear as ghostly silhouettes. They were lined up along the boulevard one at a time, directly in front of Runner.

Smiling sadly, Runner stepped up to the first, a young man, and held out his hand to the ghostly image.

"Thank you for your service. Please, tell me your name."

Chapter 16 - Messed Up -

Runner slogged his way through the manor house. His nerves were still raw after thanking and sending so many people on to their final rest on the astral version of Eden.

Milicent had been sent back as well once they'd finished up with the departed.

The champions were dismissed to their respective goddesses. Norwood's Own, the city guard, and his people all returned to their duties or barracks depending on how they'd fared and what they were doing previously.

First on his priority list was deciding what to do with the Human kingdom, since they were now without a king. As the emperor he'd have to appoint a new one. The problem was how to go about it.

He'd also need to send messages to Helen and Vasilios to make sure they were aware of what happened. All the ugly details and what the background of it had been.

Better from me than a rumor. I can also use this to applaud Hanners and Vixen for their intelligence network.

He sat down at his desk, bent over it, and started writing down the various tasks he'd need to take care of.

He heard a slight creak of furniture and looked up from the paper he'd started writing on.

Hannah sat herself down in the exact spot they'd shared together the night previous.

Clearing his throat, he returned to his sheet of paper.

"Let me know if there's anything I can help you with. In regards to the prisoners, that is. Admittedly I'm not really cut out for the question and answer thing. I mean I can *Brainwash* answers out, but those are fairly binary. I imagine they'll have information we need to dig out that's context rather than simple things."

"Getting tired of interrogating people. I'm a Thief, not a Spy. Fuck me," Hannah muttered, leaning back in her seat.

"Actually, the Thief class can become a Spy. Honestly, Hanners, you're doing great at it so far. You and Vixen make a great team. I feel bad sending you two into harm's way for it, but you get results," Runner said, passing on the chance to comment on her invitational vulgarity.

Finishing his list, he leaned back and folded his hands into each other on his desk. His eyes wandered over Hannah and the bookshelf beyond her.

Sitting in a glass case was Nadine's crossbow.

He'd browbeaten the goddesses until they had spent a bit of power to enchant the case and crossbow to be indestructible.

As if she followed his eyes to the case, Hannah sighed.

"She wouldn't fault you. She'd be upset at the loss of life, but she knew that at times there was no way around it. You've done all you can to limit that loss. For fuck's sake, even I try to live by her standards," Hannah muttered.

Runner smiled lopsidedly at that.

"She liked you, Hanners. Quite a bit. The Thief who would be redeemed. Who waded through an ocean of shit to come out the other side unbroken," Runner said quietly. Tearing his eyes from the bookshelf of mementos, he looked to Hannah. "She saw you as proof that all people could change. While I admit I'm glad that you've become who you are, I've never been able to believe the same as Rabbit did. Not everyone can change."

Runner hesitated before continuing. It wasn't a pleasant subject to bring up and his failure even more so.

"I ever explain how badly I failed to you?" he finally asked.

"Several times," Hannah whispered. He had no false notions that this conversation did anything other than make her uncomfortable.

"If I had just... there were so many other things I could have done. And I let my feelings guide me instead of my head. I could have killed Jacob quick and easy. Sent him on without a problem. Jacob didn't have to be the problem I made him out to be."

"Speaking about Jacob. Foxy mentioned something about that," Hannah confronted him.

Runner pressed his lips tightly together. He had indeed mentioned Jacob in front of Satomi.

Considering how bright his people were, this of course meant the two of them were now aware Jacob wasn't actually dead.

"He's alive. Alive and in my custody," Runner admitted.

"Runner. You say you care for me," Hannah started.

"I do. Deeply so."

"Then tell me the truth."

Runner dropped his eyes to his hands, ashamed. She was right of course.

"He lives in eternal torment. I put him on a plane where he can't die. Then I built a series of rooms filled with things. Water. Lava. Broken glass. Spikes. Acid. I visit him on occasion and move him into a new room. I watch him. Listen to him scream for hours." Runner's eyes unfocused, his heart speeding up a little at the idea of watching Jacob suffer.

"Fucking hell, Runner. Even I have my limits and that's disgusting even to me!" Hannah yelled at him.

"I know. I can't—I can't help it. He took Rabbit from us. From me. Had it been you I would have done the same," Runner confessed, opening his inventory. He pulled the figurine of Nadine free and set it on his desk.

Resting his chin on the wood, he stared into the small likeness of the woman.

"She'd hate me for what I'm doing to him," Runner whispered.

"Yes. She would. She'd even leave you over it," Hannah said. She'd closed the distance to him and now stood a foot from the desk.

She hesitated with a raised hand before resting it on his head.

Runner felt tears come unbidden to him, and he smiled sadly.

"She would, wouldn't she?" Runner said with a shudder.

"Yeah. She loved you deeply, but she'd tell you it was too much. That you'd have to release him or she'd be done with you. Our little merchant was feisty. Feisty and always knew her mind." Hannah's fingers smoothed Runner's hair back.

"End it, Runner. Or for her sake, I'll leave. Because I do care for you. I'm a fucking idiot. A real unimaginative shit stain of a Thief. But I do care for you. So end it, or I'll do what Nadine would have done." Hannah lightly rapped her knuckles on the top of his head.

She's right.

"Come with me?" Runner pleaded, making his choice.

"Of course. Let's take care of it now. As you're always saying, things to do. I need to get everything in order for the campaign. Satomi will be taking over everything while I'm gone."

Runner grunted, reached out to press his hand to Hannah's hip, then called up his ability pane.

/GMHub 6

Teleporting

Active settings only:
Death=Off
Food/Water=Off
Damage=On
Gravity=100%
Biome=Plane
Day/Night Cycle=Off

Runner heard the screams before he was able to see anything.

A constant ear-piercing shriek of agony. That and the hiss of burning flesh.

Runner watched as Jacob rolled around in a glass box full of fire. The flames that surrounded him would burn low to high and cycle back again over the course of an hour.

Runner had stopped coming as frequently. Even to him, this had lost its meaning.

"The smell, it's awful," Hannah whispered, pressing a hand to her nose and mouth.

"You get used to it," Runner said without emotion.

He really hadn't noticed the smell in a long time.

With a flick of his hand he turned the flames off. The mounted burners in the corners and in the center of each glass pane turned off immediately.

Jacob lay motionless in the large glass cube.

"He stopped talking after the fourth day. I'm honestly not even sure if he's there mentally anymore," Runner explained.

"Runner, this is…" Hannah trailed off, unable to say anything.

"I know. At first it was therapeutic to punish him. After a while I felt… wrong. I couldn't end it, though, because to me it almost felt like I'd be betraying Rabbit. But you're right. I'm betraying her in not ending this."

Runner opened his console and typed a single command into the settings window.

/GMHub Settings
Death On

Jacob died immediately of his injuries.

"And it's done. In an hour his timer will run out, he'll be forced to a graveyard, and his mind wiped. He kinda sealed his fate when he locked his pod out of the network." Runner sighed, a weight falling off his shoulders.

"Good. I'm proud of you. Nadine would be, too. Now take us back, fuckstick. This place reeks," Hannah said through her hand.

With a nod of his head Runner took Hannah's free hand in his own and activated the return ability.

/GMHubReturn

Teleporting…

His study came back into focus around them.

Hannah dropped the hand from her mouth and gave his hand a good squeeze with the other.

"Done. Don't fucking disappoint Nadine further. I'm going to go make sure everything is in place. You alright? Do you… do you need me to stay for a bit?" Hannah asked. Her voice held that quality of fear he'd come to associate with her being around him alone.

"No, my dear Hanners. Thank, but no. I'll be alright," Runner said. A tired smile formed on his lips. "Things to do."

Hannah snorted and nodded. Releasing his hand, she went to exit the study.

"I'll have them send in your next visitor," Hannah called over her shoulder.

"Thanks."

Runner moved to the front of his desk to wait. It never did anyone any good to receive people impolitely. Hopefully there weren't any.

He was feeling a little emotionally charged right now and visitors didn't suit him.

Runner didn't have to wait long. Thirty seconds after Hannah had left, the door opened again to admit his next guest.

Sophia closed the door behind her and turned to face Runner.

Before the sound of the door closing had even finished he'd gotten in close to her and wrapped her up in a smothering hug.

"Grace, Grace, Grace. It's really good to see you. I'm sorry to yank you from Vix like that. I needed you. Needed you in a way that I can't put words to," Runner whispered against her ear, crushing her in his embrace.

Sophia snickered and her wings swept out, encircling him as she hugged him back.

"Such a lost little emperor. You send us out on dangerous missions and then miss us. Whatever shall we do with you, hm?" Sophia teased. Her melodic voice managed to prod him with the right amounts of annoyance and care.

"Shut up. I do what I must. Even if I hate it."

"I know." Sophia edged in closer a fraction to kiss him. Then she eased away from him even as he tried to move to prolong it. "Later, my idiot emperor. You have things you need to do, and I have news to share. Once Isabelle gets word that I've left or that there was a battle here, I imagine she'll come running."

Her wings dropped from his shoulders and she pressed a hand to his chest, gently pushing him back from her by a foot. After she got a little distance she met his gaze directly.

"First, as the ruler of Vix, as installed by the king of Norwood, I formally surrender my city to the emperor of Bastion. I have put a city government in place according to the laws of the land of Norwood. They have no more need of me. Here is the deed of ownership to the city," Sophia intoned. She held a piece of paper out to him with her free hand.

"I would ask the emperor to reinstate me to my previous position," Sophia said with a grin. It wasn't really a request.

"Granted, and glad to have you." Runner took the deed and flipped it into his inventory. Technically it signified little more than a confirmation that the city was fully controlled by Norwood.

"Isabelle will be presenting you with the same. Though I warn you in advance, she renamed the city Giselle," Sophia admitted.

Giselle, as in Nadine Giselle.

"The little tree mouse. She certainly has a flair for the dramatic at times. As to Vix, any name you'd prefer? Can't really leave it as Vix, now can I?"

"Actually, you can. Few people refer to this isle as Vix any longer. Most simply call it Norwood. Or Norwood Isle," Sophia said. Leaning in she continued in a conspiratorial whisper. "The rumor is that the lands of Tirtius and Norwood have banded together in an empire and elected Runner Norwood as its emperor. According to the rumors that are spreading through the lands, the emperor is in fact a divine. And he has a harem of loyal goddesses who serve him. To top that off, he captured an Angelic woman and made her his personal champion. Most can't seem to agree if she's part of his harem or not. Together, with his loyal lieutenants, he'll eventually free the mainland and grant everyone peace."

Runner blinked a few times and then laughed.

"It does have the ring of a tall tale, doesn't it? A Werewolf general, Angelic Champion, Barbarian Princess, living machine from another world, Elven Mercenary, Noble Sunless chancellor, and a Thief who spurned her guild as a whole and lived. All following a god-emperor.

"Well, I do plan on crushing Dover and retaking it. So that part is true. Depending on how it turns out... we might launch on Norman's Port. It would be good to hold it. It would also serve as a good place to rotate green recruits and veterans alike through. Give them experience."

Sophia took that in for a moment and nodded. "Agreed. Were we able to hold both ports, it would put a strain on anyone who would attack us in the future."

"Right? I figure that's probably our best defense. If we hold the channel, we hold the coast. If we hold the coast, they can't land."

Runner gave her a quick once-over to make sure she was whole and healthy. His eyes settled on her wings and how her current armor didn't quite fit anymore.

"That reminds me, here you are. New armor for you since you race changed. Should work better with the wings. I also got a list of notes from Angel about being a champion."

Runner popped open his inventory and then handed over the equipment to her.

"Thank you, Runner. Sir. This will help. It was obvious when you summoned me, though I could feel it even before that. For the armor, you also have my thanks. I had considered asking you to set me up with something new but then Vix happened." Sophia trailed off. She was staring at the new armor with a smile.

"It really is good to see you, Grace. I missed you," Runner gushed. He couldn't help it.

His mind started to tread down along memories of his lieutenants and how long they'd been gone or missing.

He couldn't even begin to think of how deeply he felt the loss of Thana and Katarina. They'd been gone even longer with no hope for a reunion. At least until he marched an army over to assist them.

"As I you. Now, unless you plan on clearing your calendar for us to have some alone time, I believe you have one more visitor to attend to. Pretty sure they wish to see you as badly as I did. I'm positive I'll see you later tonight. Tomorrow as well. You promised me an explanation, after all, and I'm waiting."

Sophia didn't wait for him to answer, but turned to the door and opened it, stepping through to the adjoining room quickly.

And so it begins. She's not wrong. I did promise them an answer. All of them. Suppose it's time to own that.

His door opened and Faye stepped in.

Laughing delightedly, Runner slammed into her, hugging her tightly against the door, closing it in the process.

Today was getting better by the minute.

"Sparky, it's a blessing to see you," Runner laughingly said, squeezing his general tightly.

"Err, good to see you too, Lord Runner. Or is it Emperor Runner, now?"

"Oh for crying out loud, Sparky. We're alone together. Please? If you promise to do it, I'll scratch behind your ears and give you a good brushing in your Were form."

Faye grunted, and then actually hugged him back firmly.

"There we go. That's my girl. Glad to see you looked up the definition of a hug," Runner teased. Pulling back, he smiled at her.

"How are you, my pretty little Were?"

"I'm well. I think I've got a solid grasp on the changes being a Were has put on me. Some things I didn't care about before, I find I do care for now. Maybe a new preference towards meat.

"After you left the camp, everyone treated me the same as before I had turned. As if they'd never even considered the idea that I couldn't lead them as a Were."

Faye huffed and peered at him. She hadn't made an issue of it at the time, though in retrospect it was clear she had been concerned about being removed from her role.

"Apparently if the great and mighty Runner Norwood was trying to bed a Were, then everything was fine for her to continue leading his armies."

"Goodness, are you actually teasing me? This is fantastic. A little pessimistic of them to insinuate I was trying to sleep with you. For all they knew, I'd already succeeded. No confidence in their emperor, I say.

"Come, come, let's have a seat. We do have quite a bit to discuss. Plans to make, people to plot against, the usual. You can sit in my lap or next to me on the couch."

"Your la—" Faye started to ask and then wrinkled her nose at him. "Not this time. Go, sit. I'll decide then."

"Hm. This whole confident and sexy Were general thing is neat, but I do miss being able to bully you already. Fine, fine. So, as you can guess, we'll be launching a campaign," Runner started to explain, walking over to a love seat.

"Can I get you anything by the way? Food, drink, me? This'll probably be a bit of a longer meeting." Runner took a seat and pulled the coffee table closer. He pulled out a map and laid it out on the table. It had Tirtius and part of the mainland on it. He drew another item from his inventory and set a bag of map markers down on the map.

"You offer me things I don't desire or already have. Continue." Faye sat down next to him and leaned forward over the map.

"Damn, where'd this spirit come from? Sound like Thana." Runner laid down two markers that represented Thana and Katarina on Dover.

"I'll take that as a compliment. I admire Lady Thana greatly.

"As to where it came from, I thought on what you said. You've never lied to me. You flatter and batter me in compliments to the point that at times I feel rather confused. I decided I'm going to take them, and you, going forward. Why should I worry about it? Maybe it's the fact that I'm now a Were and I want to dominate and submit to my alpha at the same time. Unsure. Don't care. Tired of worrying about it. Too many sleepless nights nitpicking at thoughts and concerns."

Faye reached out a hand and laid several enemy icons around the port of Dover. Seemed as if Faye had taken the time to stop by and get the most recent reports from the war room in the keep.

She picked up a dozen fleet tokens and began laying them out in the waters between Tirtius and the mainland.

"You hired me as your general. To lead your armies. Not as manual labor. A warrior. Or a sex slave.

"You told me of your interest in me, and never pushed further when I told you to back off. You know my strength is in military and tactics, and ask things of me that I know I can do. You gift me with weapons and units—"

"Oh, speaking of, here. When I thought about it, the idea of you running around naked as a Were made me a little jealous." Runner opened his inventory and took out the set of Werewolf artifact gear he'd made for her specifically.

"Minxy assured me that this would actually change with you. Problem fixed. No more sharing my Were with others." He dumped the equipment at the edge of the table into a neat pile.

" —and equipment that a general could only pray for. Often times when I least expect it or hadn't considered it," continued Faye, glaring at him from under her blonde eyebrows. "You trust me implicitly, even though I was your enemy—a woman who sought to put your head on a pike. So to answer your question, yes, confident. I know my place. I know your place. I know your expectations."

Faye looked back to the map and started pulling out army tokens and placing them on Norwood. Of anyone in his empire, she alone would know the full disposition of the Norwood army.

"Glad to hear it, though I can't help but be sad that teasing you won't be as easy. I mean, do you know how awesome it was to get you all riled up last time we met? The look on your face. I think I took a screenshot. Will have to check later."

Runner sighed and then gestured to the map and markers Faye had set up.

"To the matter at hand. We'll need to leave enough troops here to maintain construction and security, but everyone else will need to go. The information I got from Bullard—"

"Bullard? As in Mr. Personality? The one who tried to kill everyone? When did he show up?" Faye asked, leaning back into the love seat.

"Eh, not too long ago. He had a lot of information on Rike and only asked for a pension and a home. We've verified it several times over and I had Vixen validate him as he said it. It's all accurate. At least as far as he believes it to be."

Faye grumped and crossed her arms across her stomach.

"Satomi validated it?" she asked.

"Yeah. Her and Hanners are running the intelligence service."

Faye nodded her head. "Then I trust it. Continue," she said with a gesture at the map.

"Of course, my beautifully sexy Were general. Care to shift and I'll pet your belly again?" Runner asked, turning his head to the map.

"Maybe later. Right now I need to know your thoughts and plans so I can come up with a campaign strategy that can work. I can't serve my emperor without knowing the goal."

"I ever tell you I love powerful women?" Runner asked her.

She gave no response and looked annoyed that he hadn't resumed their campaign discussion.

"Right, then. So their general plan as we understand it. Rike wanted to take the port to get our attention, force us to respond. Which of course we did."

Runner pointed at the port of Dover.

"Lady Death and Kitten led a combined army over to retake the port. After they engaged the city, Rike's army left. They broke from Dover as if retreating. But only after torching its food storage and markets. They spread out real thin after that into the surrounding lands."

He wiggled his fingers over the area around Dover.

"Then they reformed, with very little losses from the original engagement. They marched right back up to Dover and began to siege it. That is, if everything has gone down exactly as Bullard said it would. So far as we can tell, he's right."

With a finger he tapped one of the naval tokens.

"They can't blockade the sea from where they are. All roads into Dover are shut down and there's no way to resupply them by land. We're fortunate that Vixen sent supplies over the moment she heard about the situation. Originally she had done it to act as surplus. Now we find out that it'll be siege rations. They're got more than enough to last for the next three to four months before they have to start rationing it. More than enough time for us to arrive."

Faye took all that in without a word. She looked deep in thought, her mind probably chewing through the problem.

Thank god she's on my side.

"Honestly, Sparky, I've got nothing. I know our end goal. Retake Dover, clean out the combatants, bring the area back under control. If possible, launch an attack on Norman's Port and secure it as an optional objective. As long as that port is in enemy hands we're at their mercy for future attacks.

"When Helen and Vasilios left they said they were going to prepare the way to have their troops march as they assumed their emperor would be calling on them," Runner said with a sardonic twist to the word "emperor."

"Good, that'll help quite a bit. The more forces we can bring to bear, the fewer casualties we should theoretically have. Word is you killed Basile when he revealed himself to be a traitor."

"Yep. Totally happened. I have a feeling Hanners killed him personally but I haven't asked. I'll need to appoint a king or queen there. So when we pass through it I'll need to take a detour to set them back on the path of Bastion."

"That's fine, we'll need to strip the city of troops anyways. That'll take a day or so at the most. Politics is your own burden to bear. One I will allow you to take on completely. I barely understand our own people let alone the hearts of foreign civilians."

"So generous. Well, there it is in all its fractured glory. I'm hoping we can get troop numbers for Norman's Port once we take Dover. I'm sure there's a few people there that can tell us what's going on across the channel.

"That or I challenge Rike in Dover, make her my personal slave, and then drag the information I need out of her. She has quite a bit to pay for. I doubt Rabbit would fault me for enslaving her. That and truth be told, her portfolio is fairly good-natured and heroic. She's the problem. Maybe I can turn her around with time after making her part of my pantheon."

Runner thought on that for a few seconds more. He'd have to decide before they reached Dover. It was topic worthy of conversation with his divine equals.

"Honestly, Norman's Port is probably so poorly defended I could take it with you and a handful of cows," Faye groused.

Faye tilted her head, contemplating the map.

"You're awfully calm, Alpha. The situation you've laid out puts Lady Thana and Lady Katarina in grave peril."

Runner didn't comment on the change in address and accepted it for what it was. It would only serve to undermine her newfound confidence if he pressed at it.

"You're right. It does. And there's nothing I can do to change that. Even if I had known of their plan, or had been there when they made the choice to go, I would have ordered them to do the same. I love them, as I do you, but I must temper that with what I must do to protect an empire. Bastion must endure. For the good of many more than two or three."

Faye relaxed at his words and then nodded her head once with conviction.

"Good. I'm glad to hear this, Alpha. A proper mindset for an emperor to have."

Faye then leaned forward over the table.

"I believe that this is doable," she said, gesturing at the map, "and that we can do it with only a minimal loss of life. The army should arrive day after tomorrow. I came ahead to get things in order. I'll get my staff together and get a plan together. Resource allocation needs. Finance and cost analysis. The normal stuff that I detest and you seem to live on."

"Great. If we're all done with that, can you shift now so I can rub your belly? I promise I'll respect you in the morning."

Faye rolled her eyes and groaned under her breath. Then she actually shifted. She did it so quickly that it was near instantaneous.

"As you will, Alpha," growled the Werewolf.

She's been practicing.

To Runner's mind that meant she fully accepted what had become of her. That left it to him to accept her again as he did in her camp, or reject her.

Truthfully he had a hard time with the idea of doing anything sexual with a Were. It felt a lot like bestiality to a degree. But it was still Faye in there. She'd learned to live with her self-perceived handicap.

Regardless of what happened to her, she was still who she had been. Maybe a touch more aggressive and definitely more confident, but still Faye.

Runner immediately set a hand on her stomach and turned to face her more directly, making sure his body language reflected acceptance and approval.

He gently brushed her fine soft fur and kept his mind from thinking about what he actually was doing to her.

"So, Sparky. Was there anything else?"

Faye watched him with those gray eyes. Her wolflike muzzle twitched once when his fingers changed direction in the middle of her abs.

"Other than construction will be finished this week, no. All is as you willed it."

"Great. I think you were my last meeting until later. Which means we can relax like this for a bit and talk if you like. Or if you need to go, that's fine. Once Belle makes it back, I'm going to try and wake Sunshine for a meeting before we depart. So this might be the last moment of private time for us."

Runner let the silence draw out what he had left unsaid.

"I wouldn't mind you putting on a fashion show for me. You putting on the new gear that is. Make sure it fits and actually shifts with you. Totally being honest here, though, watching you change clothes does sound like fun. I mean, you're a good-looking Were, but you have some pretty solid assets as a Human."

Faye shook her head at that and watched him.

"You're an idiot, Alpha. I have a hard time telling when you're teasing or not."

"An idiot I am, now." Runner deliberately pressed his hand more firmly to Faye's stomach. He could feel the hard symmetrically lined up nipples of her Were form under his palm. She jolted a little in her seat at the sudden change in his actions.

Runner reached up and caught her muzzle while she was off guard and brought it down to kiss the front of it.

"Get up, little miss wolf, and decide. Fashion show for me, or do whatever it is you need to do."

"You would will that of me? A fashion show? I'm no glamorous woman who captivates men with a smile. Less so, now."

"Yep. I will it."

"Then by your will, Alpha. A fashion show is what you'll get."

"Fantastic. Love the confidence. Come on then. Shift back and start stripping for me." Runner rubbed his hands together eagerly.

Faye stood up and stared down at him. She certainly was bigger in her Were form.

"You're horrible," the Were general rumbled at him.

"Yes, yes, I know. And you love me for it. Come on then. Or would you rather cuddle on the couch? Happy to pet you. Give you a good scratch behind the ears. Or I could find a brush. I did promise you a brushing if that's more up your alley."

Faye growled at that.

"Damn. That made my skin prickle," Runner said with a grin. He looked up into her big gray eyes. "Do it again?"

Chapter 17 - Thoughts and Plans -

8:59 am Sovereign Earth time
5/18/44

Sitting in the dining room, Runner tapped a thumb against a plate. The timing for breakfast changed by the day and for whatever type of meeting he scheduled.

Hannah, Sophia, Satomi, and Faye were all gathered around the table. They were talking amiably amongst themselves.

Like old friends reunited after a period of separation.

Runner hadn't been able to summon Srit this morning. He'd sat in the white room and called out to her several times.

He'd watched her avatar for a period of time. She was a perfect representation of how she looked in the game world.

Pregnant. Bordering on very pregnant. If you had to rate pregnancy from one to nine, she was clearly at a six.

Then he'd waited for her. Watched the screens as she continuously worked at thwarting whatever it was the Omega was doing.

It looked like they really were going at her.

In the end he settled for leaving her a message on one of the monitors. A simple command line message that wouldn't interfere or cause her any difficulties.

More of a simple outline of his plan.

The main entry door swung inwards suddenly.

Everyone spun to look at who had burst in and found Isabelle.

Standing up, he gave her a bright smile.

"Belle, you're early. I'm glad for that," Runner said and excitedly went over to her.

Before he could act she wrapped an arm around his neck and pulled him in close. Then she pressed her lips to his in a deep kiss.

Releasing him, she smiled and patted his cheek.

"I missed you as well, my lord. Get me a plate while I greet everyone?" she asked, fluttering her green eyes at him.

"Ah, yes, of course, Belle." Runner felt like he wasn't just on the wrong foot but the wrong planet. Katarina was as bold as that, but not Isabelle.

Behind him he could hear Isabelle greeting each person in the room. Glancing over his shoulder, he caught Isabelle fiercely hugging Hannah, who hugged her equally in return.

Shrugging, he did as she asked and filled her plate from the side table. Bringing it over to his own seat, he set it down beside him on his right hand side.

Retaking his seat, he was startled when Isabelle swooped down and kissed his cheek.

"Thank you, my love. I promise I'll greet you better later. Know that I love you and missed you desperately," Isabelle whispered in his ear.

Patting his shoulder, she slid into her chair and dug into her food.

"I would hazard that you heard the news of Sophia's departure? Thus, you fled Letoville to get here swiftly?" Satomi asked, her golden eyes watching Isabelle.

The Elf nodded her head to that and then snapped her fingers.

She pulled a sheet of paper from her inventory and set it down in front of Runner.

"As the ruler of Giselle, as installed by the king of Norwood, I formally surrender my city to the emperor of Bastion. There's a city government that's in control now. They'll abide by the laws of Norwood. This should complete all that nonsense. I can return to your side, my lord." Isabelle gave him a smile that made him feel a little fuzzy in the head.

"And with that, you're the emperor of all Tirtius and Norwood, Alpha." Faye pointed at him with a fork, a hunk of steak hanging off of it.

"True. I must admit, when you first summoned me I was concerned that you were going to be a terrible master. I find myself pleasantly surprised, bonded. I am grateful to be yours."

Sophia smiled over her plate at Hannah as Satomi spoke. As if daring her to speak up.

Runner noticed and waited a beat for Hannah if she wanted to speak. When she said nothing, he took up the conversation.

"Of course, Vixen. Now, to the matter at hand. Belle," Runner said, turning his head to the side to regard Isabelle. "How much do you know about the situation?"

"All of it. I cornered some of Norwood's Own on my way in. God-Emperor, huh?"

"Ugh. Yes, well. We can't all be beautiful elven maidens. I'm afraid I seem to have pulled the joker card.

"Glad to hear you're caught up though, that saves time. To that end, here's the too long; didn't read version of the plan.

"Vixen, Belle, you'll remain here to keep an eye on everything and keep it running. Belle, you'll be considered the regent of Norwood. Vixen, I expect you to support her as best as you're able.

"Please remember to feed Nibbles. He's getting pretty big. Also, you'll need to care for Sunshine. She's… she's still unresponsive. I'm not sure what's going on out there but it looks bad from the little I understand."

Hannah grunted and shook her head. "Fucking bastards. She should blow them all up. Better person than I."

Sophia nodded her head to that. "Agreed."

Satomi and Isabelle looked at each other across the table. Then they both looked to Runner.

"We can handle it, my lord. I planned on having a council with everyone after this meeting. I'll make sure we take the time to plan for your departure," Isabelle promised.

"Thanks. Hanners, Grace, and Sparky will all come with me as we go on campaign. I'm hopeful to return in a short time. We shall see."

"With that being said, everything is pretty much on track. Sparky reports the army as arriving tomorrow."

Runner paused and spread his hands out before himself.

"I figure we give them twenty-four hours to rest and then we get to marching. I've dispatched requests to both Vasilios and Helen to send their troops to Dover as they're able. We'll also be stopping off in Faren to install a new king or queen there. Sparky will be using that time to resupply and rearm. As well as pick up their troops."

Runner let his eyes sweep the room.

"Questions so far? Good. Once we clear Dover, we may or may not launch for Norman's Port. I would have it under our control as our border, as it were."

Sophia bobbed her head. "I'll have Norwood's Own mobilized down to the very reserves. You'll have your elite force. Though I hear you stole one of my lieutenants?"

"Ah, Milly. Yeah. When she found out that I wasn't merely a king, but a god, she prayed for me to make her a Paladin."

Isabelle's eyebrows shot to the top of her head like a rocket.

"Wasn't she the big one, my lord? The Half-Ogress? A Berserker as well? Made Katarina look like a, well, a kitten?"

"That'd be her," Runner confirmed, stuffing a piece of bacon in his mouth.

"I take it you gave her a race reset and a class reset. Told her to try again in a bit?" Faye provided the reasonable answer.

"No, I made her a Paladin." Runner picked up another piece of bacon and started on it.

"You can do that?" Faye asked him, surprise evident in her tone.

"Apparently. Here, ask her yourself," Runner said with a touch of annoyance.

Popping open a portal came as easy as a spell now. Reaching into it with his mind, he gave Milicent a gentle tug.

He also sent through the portal his profound thanks and love for his people. They continued to perform and serve in ways he couldn't begin to fathom how he'd do without.

"She may not be at the temple. She's been working with Alexia to learn my divine portfolio as it were. I'm quite reasonable, if I had to rate my own commandments."

"You're correct, my god," Milicent said, stepping through the open portal. "Your portfolio is justice and mercy in equal measure. Redemption and atonement."

Alexia stepped out beside Milicent and looked about the room.

Spotting Faye, she immediately smiled at her and waved. Then she turned back to Runner and bowed low to him.

"As you instructed, my god, I have taught her all that she needs to know. Though she is welcome to remain, I think finding more followers to serve you is best. Also, I put together the list you asked for."

Alexia stood up straight and then held out a stack of papers to him.

"Thank you, High Priestess. As ever, you serve me beyond my wishes."

"I only ask you to visit more frequently. Forgive me, my god. We have communion shortly." Turning, she waved at Faye again and entered the portal.

Faye sat openmouthed at the casual coming and going of her aide.

Runner closed the portal with a thought and pointed at the side table.

"Get a plate, Milly, we were discussing you."

"Oh? Why?" Milicent turned to the food. The broad-shouldered woman picked up the entire serving platter of ham and sat down on his left side.

"Because you're my first Paladin, you nitwit," Runner laughingly said. Reaching over, he poked her breastplate.

"No heavy armor at the table next time. Need to get you some regular clothes. I also finished your armor last night. Got bored. I stacked it in your room in the temple.

"Surprise, you have a room in the temple. Here's the key," Runner explained, placing the key down next to the serving platter.

"Thank you, my god. Not needed, but thank you," Milicent said, giving him her wide smile. No one could ever call her pretty, but she had a huge easy-going heart.

"Big doof. As my first Paladin, and the one to find others, you'll need a place of your own. Get with Belle and Vixen after this to start working out your needs for the order. You'll be remaining here with them to start on my order."

Milicent blushed and nodded.

"Alright. Does anyone have anything to add? No? Good."

Runner reached over and took a hunk of meat from Milicent's plate.

"I swear to me, your god, that you better not try to steal all my bacon next or I'll have you praying for forgiveness in the temple. Or maybe I'll turn you over to Hanners and whatever mercy she has."

"None," the table said in unison.

Milicent looked up and quickly turned a deeper shade of red.

6:31 pm Sovereign Earth time
5/18/44

Runner stretched out on the stone slabs of GMHub seven. He'd mentally dubbed this place his workshop. All that was here was open grass fields, a stone floor, chests, weapons racks, and tools.

Time here was dilated heavily, and the only weather was a warm sun and some wind.

Everything else he had turned off.

Laid out next to him was Ernsta's sword, Brunhild's staff, and Amelia's dagger.

Each weapon was black as the majority color and red as the accent, with a white electrical particle effect on the business end.

They all had a crisp, clean look to them. Simple and effective, deadly.

They hadn't been difficult to build. If anything they were rather boring. They didn't stretch or push his abilities in any way. It was something he'd done so many times in other ways that it was nothing more than making a sandwich.

"Actually, a sandwich might be more interesting," Runner said to no one. "The portal will be fun to make. Try something new."

Looking over to his weapon racks, he saw artifact upon artifact for random situations. They were ready to be distributed as needed for everyday situations. Rewards and awards to be thrown into a battle lottery or something of that nature.

"Should probably try my hand at mobile artillery. Or simple vehicles. Wheeled vehicles for civilian use. But do I want cars everywhere? Not really."

I'm bored. I enjoy life. I'm very privileged, but I miss... wandering around. And now as emperor, I'll see even less than that.

Runner turned his mind to future projects, goals, anything he could do to keep himself busy.

And then an idea struck him. One that left him excited, even a little breathless.

Smiling to himself, he shoved the idea to the back of his head for his subconscious to chew on. Sitting up, he decided to go see Lobu.

Talking to the straightforward Half-Orc tended to help him clear the cobwebs.

He picked up the three Paladin creation weapons, shoved them into his inventory, and then fumbled for the return button.

/GMHub Return

Teleporting...

Popping back into existence in his personal room, he confirmed there were no changes. Checking his minimap, he didn't see anyone at Lobu's, which meant he was free to do as he pleased and be left alone.

Deciding on his activity, he went over to the door, opened it, looked around, and caught the eye of his on-duty lieutenant.

"Hey, I think I'd like to hit Lobu's. I'll remain here and get ready while you do the same."

"Yes, emperor," said the officer, followed by a salute.

Closing the door, he shook his head once. It had been hard enough getting used to "lord" as his address. Now he had to do it all over again as they'd switched to calling him "emperor."

After a brief search through his wardrobe he switched his armor out for more "city type" clothes that would help him blend in.

For the umpteenth time Runner fretted over the nameplate hovering about his head.

Naturals didn't seem to notice it, or even acknowledge its existence. It still irked him though.

Giving himself a once-over, he saw he had a solid "nobody" appearance. He couldn't stop people from recognizing him visually. Didn't mean he'd make it easy for them.

He could always involve Satomi, but that would set up the possibility of having an escort.

He moved back to the door to his rooms, opened it wide, and then sat down in a chair in his antechamber to wait.

A voice in the back of his head told him to ditch his guards. Constantly.

He'd never done it since that was one of those classic "idiot hero" mistakes that people made in books and movies. His personal level of paranoia outweighed his desire to not be surrounded by guards.

The first to get back was a sergeant. Runner had deliberately stopped paying attention to their looks a long time ago. Runner made a point of nodding to her in acknowledgment and then dismissing her.

I've already hurt them all enough with my insistent flirting.

Quickly enough, his guards were dressed in their casual wear and ready to depart.

Sliding in amongst them as they left, Runner activated *Stealth* and played the part of a shadow.

Norwood's Own heading to Mibar wasn't anything worth noticing after all. No place better to hide.

Runner kept *Stealth* up till the very moment he put his ass on his favorite stool at the end of the bar up against a wall.

"Sneaky bastard. Usual?" Lobu asked, walking up to him.

"Please, yes. Rounds for everyone who walked in with me as well on the down low."

"Course." Lobu slapped down a mug in front of him. A handful of drinks in each big hand, he shuffled out to the tables to hand them off to his guards.

Taking a sip from the beer, Runner surreptitiously checked his surroundings.

It was packed. The entirety of the bar was full of drinking patrons. Except for the stool next to him, and the one he had taken.

Strange. Perhaps this isn't as... anonymous as I hoped.

Lobu sidled up to him on the other side of the counter again.

"Full night. Looks like you're doing incredibly well, Mr. Half-Orc," Runner said, lifting his drink to the man.

"Hmph. Only because a certain emperor frequents the establishment. You do realize you're not fooling anyone. It may be a secret on the way here, but not once you're here. They call that the emperor's stool," Lobu said, flicking a finger at the spot Runner occupied.

"And this?" Runner threw a thumb at the stool next to him....

"Empress's stool, of course." Lobu looked at him as if he were daft.

"That's interesting since I don't have a wife." Runner took a drink and watched Lobu over the rim.

"You do. You just haven't married one of them yet."

"What if I married all of them?"

"Stupid thing to do. That's about six more headaches than any one man should have."

Runner shook his head with a grin at that.

"Maybe I'm a bit of a masochist then."

"You'd have to be, considering what you keep signing yourself up for. Emperor? Really?"

"They didn't leave me much of a choice. It was join and be emperor or be pushed out and probably given the national cold shoulder. I don't want it. Didn't really have a choice in the matter. I had to accept."

"Huh. Nah. You had a choice. It would have sucked." Lobu stepped off to put down a drink for someone.

There was a slight presence on the outside of his mind. It was tiny, as if an echo of his own mind. If he hadn't been paying attention he might have missed it.

Runner didn't stop it, or point it out, but watched it passively. It circled around the barriers of his mind like... like a fox trying to get into a henhouse.

Grinning, Runner followed that presence as it moved.

What are you up to, Vixen?

It wouldn't do him any good to reveal an advantage unless he served to benefit from it. Showing Satomi—because who else would be sniffing around his mind like that—that he could detect her latest attempt wouldn't do him any good.

But letting her think she'd succeeded would.

The clever little Kitsune crawled under his mental barrier as slow as ice melting in the shade.

Lobu had checked on him during her entry. The bartender noticed Runner's lack of mental coordination and left him as he was to serve others.

When she'd cleared his perimeter, Satomi held perfectly still and in place. If he were in her position, he'd have done it as well to determine if he'd been noticed.

Now that she was inside his mind, he knew it was her beyond a doubt.

After several minutes, and Runner finishing his first beer, Satomi was on the move again.

Snaking along the interior of his mind, she made her way to his most recent memories.

Without experiencing them, or "pulling them out" as it were, she was able to look at the surface of each one. It took her a little time for each one, but he had the impression she got a fairly good reading on them.

Lobu set another mug down in front of him as Runner felt the Kitsune in his head move to his emotional state.

His eyebrows drew down as Satomi flicked through his emotions. He could feel it as she encouraged positive thoughts and moods, pushing them gently to the front. Then she tried to push down his negative feelings, cycling them to the back of his psyche.

So I've got a mental janitor who wants to clean the place up when I'm out?

Done with her task there, Satomi started to make her way back out. Then she stopped.

Waiting, Runner was curious what was going on. Did he accidentally give the game away? Did she get interrupted?

Then she moved towards his memories again. And stopped. Then started moving once more.

Indecision?

Satomi seemingly affirmed her choice and made her way to his memories. It was interesting to him since he couldn't quite pin down what she was looking for. He'd only be able to see if it she called it up fully.

Eventually she started to pull up small sections of a memory. He couldn't figure out what they were exactly since she didn't dive deeply into the memory.

He could almost feel her fear of actually engaging the memory. To look at it inside and out. She was eventually satisfied with her topical view since she put it back where it belonged.

Creeping stealthily out of his head, she exited the same way she entered. The connection faded to nothing as she withdrew back to her own mind.

After she faded to nothing, Runner tried to figure out what she had been looking at.

The best he could figure was she had looked at something three days ago. Nothing jumped out at him as being important, other than them taking in that entire cell.

Since all she had done was look at a few things, he assumed she had been merely comparing her memory to his own.

They could end up being pretty different since… well, I'm not a machine. My memories are false witnesses based on my own opinion.

Runner sighed and shook his head, taking a deep drink from his beer.

"Here's to worrying for another time, in due time."

"I guess," Lobu replied, staring at him. "Keep on doing what you've been doing. You'll make hard choices but that's life. A life without scars is a boring one. An unlived life."

Runner blinked and nodded his head at that. "Good advice, bartender."

"Remember that when you face a difficult choice or challenge. There's not a lot you can do about the choice you have to make, other than make the right one for you at the time. No sense crying about it."

Chapter 18 - Taking Action -

5:00 am Sovereign Earth time
5/20/44

Grumbling, Runner sat up from his bed. At his side Isabelle stirred and flopped an arm around his waist. They'd gone to bed rather late last night.

"Too early," she complained.

"It is, but the troops march at eight. I'm going to be doing something today that may or may not piss off Thana. Can I run something by you, my little tree mouse?"

"Mmkay. No promises," Isabelle said, opening one green eye to peer at him.

"I'm aware of the council. Also the lengths that Thana goes to run it and keep you all secure. I'm going to be ending that today, I believe. Is it safe to say Thana wouldn't be upset about you, Sophia, Hannah, or Faye being close to me?"

Isabelle looked towards the pillow she rested her head on and then back to him.

"She wouldn't have a problem with any of us. She knows nothing of your familiar or Paladin."

"I know. Satomi isn't something I can discard easily since I'm stuck with her. Forever. Milly is merely my first Paladin."

Isabelle nodded her head a little.

"Should I be worried?" she asked. Her voice had a tinge of fear to it.

"No. Not at all." Runner patted her lightly on her blonde head. "Going to get dressed and put my things in order. Want me to wake you up a bit before it's time for the meeting?"

"I'll watch the show from here, thanks." Isabelle shifted around in the bed until she could see the rest of the room.

"Silly tree mouse." Runner leaned down and kissed her once and then got ready for the day.

An hour later and Runner and his lieutenants were gathered in the dining hall.

Runner opened his connection up with Satomi and dragged her into his mind regardless of her own wishes.

He'd realized a while ago that he was the stronger partner in their bond. If he wanted her held prisoner in his mind, that was where she'd be.

For now, he merely wanted her to know of this situation since she wouldn't be attending.

"Hannah, Sophia, Faye, Isabelle. Thank you for coming. Srit was unable to make it today I'm afraid. I really don't know when she'll be able to pull out of the stalemate she's in."

They were seated around the table. Breakfast would be after the meeting. On the road for some, in the dining room for others.

"First, I'd like to hear what motivates each of you, if you don't mind. Why you're here, now. Admittedly not everyone was given a choice, but you're all free of that now. Hannah?"

"I dunno. Fuck, that's a strange thing to ask. I guess to make the world a better place? Prove to everyone I'm not some gutter Thief anymore."

"Definitely not that. Not after the successes of your department. Sophia?"

"Secure a good marriage that supports my family. Maybe some children. Make sure to keep my country thriving. I may no longer be of the Sunless race, but I'm still Sunless."

"Very personal and reasonable goals. Faye?"

"No change from last time, Alpha."

"Got it. Isabelle?"

"Reclaim my birthright. Have you stomp over there and burn anyone who refuses me to ash."

Runner laughed at that and nodded.

"Right, then. Burn one elven forest down. Thank you, everyone."

Then he dove onwards in the conversation.

"I'm aware of Thana's council. I also know what it's for and what Thana had been doing." Runner said it simply.

Each woman looked a little nervous at the sudden seriousness of the conversation. Not to mention he'd been using their names, rather than nicknames.

"I find that I'm at fault for this. The fact that it had to be done at all is a failure on my part. I apologize for that. I'll lay it all out very simply, here. When we catch up to Katarina and Thana, I'll be giving them the exact same conversation."

Runner felt his stomach flutter. This was the deciding moment.

"Satomi made me aware of the fact that I've been acting the part of a cowardly miser. One who would claim they're doing something for the benefit of others when it's clearly for me.

"That ends here. Today. I love you. All of you. I don't plan on settling for one of you, but all of you. Katarina, Thana, and Srit included in that."

Runner took a slow breath to steady himself.

"Socially, where I came from, it's frowned on to have a marriage with more than two people in it. Outlawed in the vast majority of space. Here, in this world, clearly that isn't true. To the point that I can write my own laws as emperor."

Pulling up a hotbar with a mental command, Runner selected Hannah.

"To that end, I'm asking you all to join me in marriage. As ridiculous as that sounds, it's the truth. Normally one would give the other a token to signify that marriage. Considering the fact that each one of you is wearing everything made by me, I'm not sure on how you'd like to proceed on that front," Runner said, trying to lighten the mood a bit at the bomb he'd dropped on them.

"So, in a moment you'll receive a marriage invitation. It's something only I can do. This would actually change your last name to Norwood. The system would recognize you as my partner and you would have access to my inventory, my belongings, and my home.

"This will advertise to the great wide world that I'm not on the market. The council can remain, but it would need a new purpose, and you can all be sure of my intentions. No more secrets, no more games.

"Not sure how this'll work on the divine side though. Since you'll be marrying a god. But hey, there it all is. Without further ado."

Runner punched the marriage button he'd set up. His name was already input into the macro and it would then use whoever was selected.

Hannah's eyes opened wide at the message only she could see. Moving to the next in line, Runner began sending the same invite to each woman in the room.

"Before you accept, I'd be happy to—" Runner paused for a second as a message flitted past his eyes.

Isabelle Malin has accepted your proposal.
Congratulations!
You are officially man and wife.

Isabelle's last name flashed and was replaced with Norwood.

"—answer any questions you have. Should you have any. Admittedly this is... it's frickin' strange. Let's call it what it is. This is strange. I'm a selfish greedy bastard and there it is. I want you all to myself."

Runner looked around the room again. Hannah had her hands over her face. Faye looked thoughtful as she studied the message. Sophia had a smile on her face as if she had achieved victory and were basking in the feeling.

Faye Sennet has accepted your proposal.
Congratulations!
You are officially man and wife.

Sophia Tai has accepted your proposal.
Congratulations!
You are officially man and wife.

"I would ask you if there is an order to this, Alpha. Pack hierarchy is important. Or if we're all equal that will do as long as it's known," Faye asked. Both her name and Sophia's had swapped over to Norwood instantly.

"Equals. Equals amongst us all. I can't grant you divinity, though I would name you all empress."

Faye scratched at her nose and then shrugged her shoulders.

"You'll still be the alpha. We'll establish our own pecking order, I'm sure."

Runner felt his mood fluttering between elated and afraid. There was no going back now.

"What about children, lord husband?" Sophia asked. She leaned forward over the table, resting her face in her hands. She still had that satisfied smile plastered on her face.

"Obviously that'll be up to you. I believe Sunshine left me a settings window that I can use to modify people's individual ability to get pregnant. More of an on off switch. I thought it strange at the time, though I'm thankful for it now."

"I meant housing. What if every single one of us were to become pregnant at the same time? It would double our space requirements.

"This is a lovely manor we're in now, but it wouldn't fit all of us."

"Ah, yeah. I was working on that. I've diverted a large amount of processed resources to another plane. Had to do something with it since it's piling up. Can't use too much of it right now without destroying the market.

"A very large manor house is going to be built on that plane. I made the changes this morning to make it habitable. Alexia is providing the manpower to work on the home.

"It'll connect to the keep here in Norwood, and Eden. The floor plans are extensive. It's already set for three floors, and honestly, as there are no threats on that plane, we can expand in whatever way we see fit."

"Good, how would we get there, exactly?"

"Going to give you all a small token. It'll transport you there and back at will. Similar to your driving tokens."

"What about Satomi? Or Milicent? You have a habit of getting attached to those nearby," Isabelle asked.

"Satomi. She's my familiar. She'll be with me as long as I live. To be honest, she could outlive any great grandchildren we have. I trust her implicitly with my life."

Runner realized he hadn't answered the question and he didn't plan to. Satomi would be an issue in the long run and he knew it.

"Milicent is my Paladin. She's nice enough, but I don't think it'd go well if I were trying to sleep with someone devoted to me as servant to god."

"And of the goddesses?" Faye asked, taking Isabelle's question to the logical conclusion.

"As far as they're concerned, I'm bound to them as I am to Satomi. I'll not be escaping them. Ever."

Runner felt like he was sidestepping the question to a degree, but he couldn't actually answer them. When he finally accepted the goddesses, his mortal companions would all be long dead.

Sophia nodded her head and then laid her head down on her arms, watching him. Her wings flared out behind her and partially unfolded.

"I'm satisfied," Sophia whispered.

"As am I, Alpha."

"And I, my lord."

"You're all fucking idiots. Don't you see?" Hannah shouted, slamming her hands to the table.

Her eyes were pinched shut as if to block out everything.

"He can't even make up his mind. How do you even believe that he won't be adding to his little harem party down the road?"

"A fair point. I thought about that for a while. I've drawn up a simple oath that I'm happy to swear to. While it seems extreme to offer it, I can imagine it might help. I'm more than willing to do whatever it takes to make you all feel comfortable and assured.

"No need, lord husband," Sophia said, her wings continuing to unfold and spread out behind her.

"Trust is given freely, Alpha."

"Not needed, my lord."

"You stupid fuckers, you would wal—" Hannah lifted her head and looked at the other women. Her eyes flicked from one to the next, and the next.

"Fine. Enjoy your fate. I'll be outside, ready to leave."

"Hanners—"

"No, stop. Shut your filthy mouth. Don't talk to me."

Hannah left, the door slamming behind her.

Runner shook his head and smiled at the remaining women.

"My apologies, this should be a happy occasion. Here I'm leaving one of you behind, and you now have to tiptoe around one of our number."

Faye, Sophia, and Isabelle looked unconcerned. He felt like he was missing something but didn't press it.

After a moment, Faye gave him a wolfish smile.

"Alpha, my mate, please be prepared to set aside some time for me to discuss plans for new weapons when we get back. I'd like to consider creating very large iterations of the cannons except on a tank frame."

"Err, alright. That sounds reasonable. I already have a few sketches to that effect. I simply haven't made any as of yet."

"Lord husband, I'd also like to plan for you to meet my family. We'll need to secure some time to travel back to Shade's Rest."

"That sounds like a good idea. I'm sure I'll have business there soon enough anyways. I imagine it would be good to meet them."

"My lord, I'd like my token now before you go. I think I'll start working on our home. If you would, I'll be taking the plans from your inventory as well. No offense, but you're not exactly a grand designer, sweetie."

"Of course, that sounds like a great plan. Thank you, Belle."

He got a mental image from Satomi. She was on her way to comfort Hannah. She also sent a single thought to him to which he couldn't disagree.

Whipped.

7:07 am Sovereign Earth time
5/20/44

Runner looked up at Bastion. What had once been a modest tree that wouldn't stand out, now looked like something out of a fantasy novel.

Its girth had quadrupled and the crown of it had shot up. Large branches flung out and hung in the air.

His city engineers had removed a large section of stones around the tree when it had rapidly expanded and taken up the entirety of the grass area around it. Thanks to that, it fit the plot of land it sat in now. Runner had a feeling that it wouldn't keep it penned in forever.

"Did I somehow break you, Bastion?" Runner asked, holding out a hand and pressing it to the bark.

A heavy thump behind him signaled the arrival of the tree's only inhabitant.

Looking over his shoulder, Runner found Nibbles, a very large, and very furry, squirrel.

Perhaps large was an understatement now. Gargantuan fit closer.

Nibbles had broken into the large dog small horse range.

"Are you the reason Bastion keeps getting bigger? It's trying to support you and your needs, hm?" Runner queried the creature.

In response it hopped over to him and slammed its massive forehead into his chest.

"Yes, yes, hello, Nibbles. Here, I brought you something." Runner dropped his hand from the tree and fished out a pumpkin. "Bought it off one of the farmers this morning. Figured you'd like it."

Nibbles looked at the pumpkin and then took it from Runner's hands. Sniffing at the orange rind, the squirrel eventually seemed to accept the gift.

Runner set his hand on its head and scratched between its eyes.

"I told Vixen and Belle to watch out for you. Make sure you protect the tree now. Bastion isn't just a kingdom landmark now—an empire has been named for it. Scurry along now. Before I try to fit a saddle on you and ride you to Dover."

As if it understood him, the fuzzy monster blinked, then bounded up Bastion's wide trunk and disappeared into the lofty branches.

"Huh. At least the squirrel fits the tree. I wonder if it'll get a Dryad? Would I even want one in my tree? Brighteyes, Angel, Minxy, what do you think? Would I want to rent my tree out? I hear renters can be a nightmare and can be pretty hard to evict."

Runner's hand came up to rest on his tree again.

"Depends. Quite a few different types of Dryads. Though I think it's an oak tree? Very large oak if it is." Brunhild came up beside him and touched the tree with her fingers. "Ah. Interesting. People pray to it as if it were a shrine. An altar. Your furry friend is being turned into a temple guardian."

Ernsta and Amelia walked up beside their sister and touched the tree as well.

"It feels warm to the touch. It feels like Eden. I'd hate to hazard a guess but," Ernsta said, turning her eyes on Runner, "I'd wager that someone is spreading the word of Norwood. The male aspect of the Triumvirate."

"That'd be me. Sorry, not sorry. Soon as I knew he was ascended I started letting the word out," Amelia said, squealing in delight. "I didn't want people to get confused about your aspects."

"Hm. While I don't condone what my little sister has done, I do agree with her, Runner," Brunhild conceded. Ernsta nodded with a frown.

The anger that had immediately built up in him blew out like a candle in a windstorm.

"Be that as it may, please tell me these things in the future, Minxy. Or I will get angry. And I won't show my anger to you, I'll ignore you." Runner didn't want it to sound like a threat, but a promise.

"I—I understand. I'm sorry. I only wanted to look out for you," Amelia said, turning her eyes downward.

"I know, and for that, I forgive you. It's why I love you. Brighteyes, is there anything I need to do for this?" Runner asked, a vague gesture from his hand indicating the tree.

"No. It won't do any harm to let it be an altar. Besides, offerings seem to be in food, and Nibbles looks to be 'collecting' them all."

Runner took a step back from the tree and let the matter drop.

Reaching out with his divine sense, he locked down the area around them in a sphere to block out any would-be listeners.

"First and foremost, I have a new toy for each of you." Runner flipped open his inventory window and drew out the Paladin creation items. "A staff for the enlightened one, a sword for the bringer, and a lovely kidney tickler for the shadow."

Runner deposited each item into the hand of the owner as he went.

"This will turn anyone you target into a Paladin. I've charged Milicent with recruiting those she feels would be valid Paladin's in my own service."

Each of the goddesses looked over their new weapon with varying degrees of glee.

Each expressed it in her own way. Brunhild had that smile of hers, Ernsta's eyes glowed, and Amelia... was Amelia.

"Thanks, lovey. Not sure how a goddess of Assassins ending up having Paladins is going to turn out, but it'll be interesting." Amelia laughed and gave the dagger a twirl. "Sexy priestesses who lurk in my lovey's shadow. Waiting to assassinate assassins. Tempting him from the corners with promises of a night well spent with them and their goddess."

Runner laughed and pressed a palm to his brow. He felt glad at their acceptance and response. Gifts always felt good to give.

"In other news, I plan on taking the fight to Rike. If I can challenge her directly, I'm going to. I plan on getting her to appear in one spot alone. Anything I should know?"

"No."

"Nothing you don't already know, dear."

"Nope! Kick her ass, lovey. Put her in the dirt. Put her in the dirt."

Runner shook his head at their very different responses and tried not to smile.

"If I can, I'm going to subvert her. Make her a minor deity in our pantheon. Her portfolio is all positive things and it'd be a shame to lose that aspect of her. Even if she herself needs to go.

"And honestly, Rabbit would ask me to spare her if I could."

Brunhild frowned yet said nothing. Ernsta shrugged her shoulders. Amelia looked excited.

"Give her to me, lovey. I'll train her. Train her good."

"Hah, no. Not without oversight at least. Though I can't deny that was going to be my next question. Can you three rehabilitate your sister? She may be the enemy and yet..." Runner left the statement hanging.

Brunhild blew out a breath and placed one hand behind her neck as she looked up into the tree branches above her.

"Far be it from me to tell you no. You're not wrong. I just don't like it," the goddess admitted.

"I know. She insulted you personally. What better way to show the goddess of goodness up, than by being more good than her? More good. More goodest? More gooder? Whatever, by being better. Besides, you know redemption is in my purview." Runner tried to be gentle with it. He felt strongly about not killing Rike unless he had to. Unless Rike made him.

I will. I'd prefer not to, but I'll bury her. Rabbit would be sad if I did. She'd forgive me if I tried earnestly to spare her first.

Amelia grunted and then folded her arms across her chest.

"I bet we can do it, sis. I'll take negative reinforcement, you take positive, Ernsta neutral responses. We can do this."

Brunhild and Ernsta looked to their sister.

"You wish this only for our lamb," Ernsta accused.

"Obviously. I'm hoping to win my way into his bed early through bribery. This is perfect currency for that. Who's to say just how grateful he'd be to all of us. Hmm?" Amelia asked her sisters in a loud whisper.

Ernsta looked to Brunhild. "We can do this."

Brunhild sighed and pressed her fingertips to her temples.

"As you will it, dear. We'll discuss favors at another time," Brunhild said brusquely, waving her free hand in front of her face as if to dismiss the entire situation.

"Brunhild," Runner said quietly. She didn't immediately acknowledge him. She drew it out for several seconds before meeting his gaze. "Thank you, Brunhild. I will make it up to you. Promise."

Brunhild didn't say anything in response and instead left as if she were never there.

Ernsta was a split second behind her in her departure.

"She's nervous you're going to replace her, idiot. Rike is supposed to be the prettiest of their family. Well, before they formed this new family. And you want to capture her. You reassure your mortal harem. Why not your divine one? Think on it. Love you," Amelia whispered quietly, patting his shoulder.

"You're not wrong. Thank you, Minxy."

Then she vanished as well, giving him a wide smile.

Runner sighed and pursed his lips. Amelia wasn't wrong. He could definitely see how Brunhild could take his actions wrong.

Never going to get it right the first time. You're human. Make it up to her later. Run on, idiot.

Need to visit the temple and put the portal to rights. Should also address the clergy about it.

Deciding on his course of action, Runner set off for the temple. His time was short, but he could make it work if he was quick about it.

The streets were filling up as the day began. Runner managed to keep himself from becoming entangled in any situations or discussions.

Standing in front of the massive temple, he felt awed. The gigantic structure never failed to impress.

Forcing himself to put one foot in front of the other, he took the steps smoothly and entered.

Immediately an acolyte of the Triumvirate came over to him. Before they could realize who he was, he held up his hand to stall any questions.

"Please let the high priest know that Runner Norwood is here. I'm afraid I cannot wait for him either. I'll be heading down to the new basement. Do you understand?" Runner asked the young man. His orders were clear, easy to relate, and could easily be confused for something else if someone over heard it.

The man nodded and as quickly as he'd approached, turned and bolted.

Grunting, Runner exited into the left wing and entered a small room that had been added directly next to his office.

Runner found it was exactly as he'd hoped. A storage closet.

Reaching towards a brick in the door jamb, he activated the required spell to unlock the trap door disguised in the floor.

Activated, the floor slid to the side into a recess to reveal a set of stairs.

"Elaborate, but effective. Please guard the hallway. If the high priest shows up, send him in," Runner said, giving his orders to his on-duty lieutenant.

Taking the steps down, Runner turned with the corridor. The hallway the stairs led into was only two people or so wide. Yet the vast cavernous room it emptied into looked more like a military assembly area.

Vast, empty, yet stocked with all the things an army in full retreat or moving from one location to another could want for.

They'd been building this as a stockroom until Runner had appropriated it for a "holy weapon," as he called it.

At one end, one of the walls could also be retracted, leading up into the massive gardens at the center of the complex should they need to move large numbers of people quickly.

At the other, a stack of bricks had been set up and waited for him.

Runner moved in that direction and started sorting out the things he'd need in his inventory.

"My god, I'm glad for your visit before your departure," called out a man's voice from the direction Runner had come from.

"Good to see you as well, High Priest," Runner replied. He didn't need to look up to know who it was. It could only be one person who'd gotten past his guards after all. "I figured I'd install the portal before I left. Might be nice to install it wherever I go next and simply utilize it to come back."

Runner knelt onto the stonework ground and started to pick up bricks.

"Ah, yes, about that. Have you considered my questions about security?" the high priest said, coming to stand beside Runner.

"Yep. I figured out a fairly simple answer. Expand this room into another wing to run underneath everything. House the Paladins here. Their headquarters and divine purpose might as well include the ways."

Runner started laying the bricks in a two-by-two pattern pressed flush to a wall.

"The ways?" the man asked.

Taking a second, Runner looked up to the priest. He was an older man, Sunless, intelligent looking, though with a confused face at the moment.

"That's what we'll be calling them. The ways. They'll connect every city to every other. I'll be giving the higher ranks of the clergy small devices that will allow them to activate the ways, as well as the entrances and exits."

Runner went back to his work as he spoke, spreading grout into the joints between the bricks.

"I figure if we house the Paladins here as well, it'll create a perfect amount of strength and reactionary force. All we need is more Paladins and a wing for them. Preferably every city would have an outpost."

"I see. This is... it's a magnificent thing, my god. To span an empire and connect it with nothing more than a word. Truly a miracle," the priest said reverently.

"Mm. It'll be classified as a holy site, and access will be limited without orders or approval from anyone on my council. Since it'll only connect two places, it'll be left open for now. I'll rectify that quickly since we don't want any security flaws.

"As for the usage, there will be an indicator at the top. If it's lit, someone is trying to reach here. There'll be one door for each location I deem fit."

"Wise, my god. Very wise. How long does it take to construct one?"

"Not long, in fact," Runner said, standing up. He set two more bricks into place, added mortar, and then *Earth* shifted it all into a perfect column. "One column down, one to go."

Falling silent, Runner took nine paces to the side before starting in on the next pillar.

"That's one gate?"

"Yeah, it'd be rather pointless to have something that couldn't fit more than one person through at a time. Could you imagine trying to move an army through a single-person-wide door? Nightmares."

Squatting, Runner worked to quickly put up the second column. A few minutes and a spell later the second pillar was done.

Calling up a constant use *Air* spell to support his work in midair, Runner started to work on the arch that would span the gap between the two.

"May I have a sculptor come down and… add some art to it?" the high priest asked hesitantly.

"So long as they're high ranking in the clergy, yes. I can't stress enough that this is more or less a state secret. Do you understand?"

Runner set the key brick into place and then called up mortar to bind everything in place.

Dropping his spells, Runner took a step back to view his work.

A simple brickwork arch wide enough for eight soldiers to enter.

Forming the portal spell in his hands, he tied it to the arch and then initiated it.

Ripping from the center outward, the spell immediately came to life. A rippling, swirling pool filled the space within the portal.

"Once I put in the on off switch, this'll look like an arch and nothing more. When activated, it'll either look like this or its destination point on the other side."

Runner sighed and put his hands on his hips. It was good work, but it would be utterly worthless until he got the other side up and operating.

One step at a time.

Chapter 19 - Plans Change -

Staring at the map laid out in front of him, Runner couldn't help but feel mildly annoyed. Idly he played with the pouch of map markers in his lap.

They'd made good time. Great time really. They'd managed to move the entire six-thousand-strong army across the channel to Bren in a time that most commanders would pray for.

After arriving in the night they'd sent out scouts on intelligence gathering missions to figure out what was going on in Tirtius.

That was when their luck had dried up. Almost the very moment they set foot on Tirtius, it vanished.

Lady Fate had decided she wanted break his windows and call the police on him this time rather than drunkenly make passes at him at a party they accidentally both showed up at. Runner could only hope that she would settle for that rather than tossing in an incendiary device through the broken window.

Never know with her. She seems to exist to punish or reward me. Only me.

The news from Dover happened to match everything they had expected based off Bullard's information.

Except that fortunately, or unfortunately—Runner wasn't sure yet—Thana and Katarina had sent most of the army home after clearing Dover. They'd remained in the city with only a token force.

Runner could only guess they had assumed after Dover had been claimed and cleared that'd be the end of it.

Which meant they had fewer troops in Dover, both to lose, and defend. Rike's plan would already fail simply because there was no army to catch and crush.

It just means Kitten and Lady Death are more likely to get killed outright. That's all.

Runner gestured to Faye, who sat across from him. He, Faye, and Sophia had gathered to discuss the plan and what they could do.

Hannah still refused to speak to any of them. She kept her distance from everyone and went to great pains to remain that way.

"Take Lady Hannah, Lady Sophia, and Norwood's Own and head north," Faye said, tracing the route with her finger. "Take all the tanks, too. Rather than the whole army, request all of Queen Helen's fast movers, casters, cavalry, or otherwise. Anyone who can keep up with a third speed tank."

Faye paused and walked her fingers across the map as if calculating time and distances.

"Load as much heavy infantry into the tanks as you can. Do the same for Vasilios. Then swing south and meet me in Faren. You should arrive either as I do, or a day after. It's the best I can come up with, Alpha."

Faye moved the pieces into position for the first phase of the plan. Runner's piece sat halfway between Bren and Kastell.

"I can't say I much care for this. It's the best plan we have and I'd never be able to think of anything better. I mean, it's a great plan. It is. It solves all the problems and delivers the optimal result," Runner said, his fingers toying with the map marker that denoted himself.

Faye looked confused when Runner glanced up at her.

"I'm sure the general will miss you too, lord husband." Sophia stood up and dipped her head to Faye. "I'll leave the details to you. I need to go prepare my forces for the march north."

Faye grunted and cocked an eyebrow at Runner.

"She reminds me of Lady Thana and Lady Hannah in equal measure, at times. Brilliant and blunt in the same sentence. Without the mind games and angst of either." Faye's voice fell off as she leaned forward over the map. "You'll miss me, huh?"

"Obviously. That goes without saying. Why wouldn't I miss my faithful, tactical, direct, innocent, and confident Were. In retrospect, I'm glad we had last night." Runner sighed and set his marker down. After a few seconds he admitted privately to himself there was no better option. Reaching out, he then moved it north towards Helen's territory.

"As am I. Thank you for… ah…" Faye shook herself and let out a soft growl as if to force herself along. "I'm glad we discussed children and used Lady Srit's option. Getting pregnant during this campaign would be hard if it's a drawn-out war."

Runner smiled and held up his hands as if in surrender. "My wife told me her needs, I did as she instructed. Hannah has made it clear she doesn't want any part of us as a whole. And our beloved Grace gifted us a little bit of time to ourselves. Any thoughts on what we could do to entertain ourselves before I depart?"

Faye stood up immediately and stared at him.

"Yes. Yes I do have a thought about that."

6:29 pm Sovereign Earth time
5/23/44

As the sun dipped towards the horizon, Runner pinged a change of pace to his raid leaders. They'd of course communicate it to the rest of the raid squad leaders.

Shifting Boxy into second, he waited ten seconds for everyone else to safely do the same. Another shift and he was moving at the slowest speed available.

Turning off the side of the road and going no further, he stopped. They'd truthfully be safer staying close to the road.

Faye had warned him that they could very well be the target of an ambush or attack. Rike's forces had been in country for quite a while. Thus they could be anywhere.

Runner got up and performed an unsatisfying stretch. He knew it didn't do anything for him. He couldn't break the habit even knowing that. Same reason he still took the time to wash his face each morning or dunk himself in a pool of water.

It didn't do anything other than give him a sense of normalcy.

"Right, then. Grace, see to the troops. I'm going to stretch the legs a bit." The only other occupant in Boxy was Sophia.

He'd spent quite a bit of time building up a massive number of tanks in the five-month lull.

Most of Norwood's Own had been issued a horse. Using this to their advantage, it meant that nearly every tank was empty of passengers. They'd be able to fit quite a number of heavy troops in them. Heavy troops they'd need to either hold the line or break a siege.

Runner flipped open his raid window to the last page. Thana and Katarina were safe and sound for the minute. As was the rest of his little group.

The fact that the e-mail system for the ship was still down had gone from annoying to mind numbingly horrible.

Either someone had been paying attention or Fate decided to nut punch him when they'd agreed to upgrade the servers with Srit months ago.

"Of course. Give me a minute so I can round up your guard, please," Sophia said, unlocking the rear door.

"Grace, I don't—"

"Please, lord husband," Sophia asked again, piercing him with her gaze.

"Yes, Grace. I'm sorry. I just... I start feeling a little claustrophobic with people so close all the time."

"I know, but it's for the safety of us all. Can you imagine what would happen if we lost you at this point?" Her voice was quiet but firm. He knew she'd deliberately kept Boxy empty to give him space.

She watched him for another second before stepping off the ramp and into the grass. She slid out of his view as she moved off, calling out to her subordinates.

Stepping free of the tank, he went a few paces before looking around.

The area looked like a lot of the lands they'd already passed through. Not quite hospitable, open, a touch barren, a little craggy.

Barbarians, remember?

Looking over his shoulder, Runner couldn't help it when his gaze was drawn to the large cannon he'd strapped to Boxy.

The previous one had been a test. This one was more of an artillery piece. Spanning the length and width of the vehicle, it could be elevated from zero degrees to forty-five. The *Splatterhouse* round it fired was the size of Milicent.

"You there! Halt! Identify yourself!" Runner flinched at the stern voice as a squad of his guards sprinted to him.

Looking to where they had directed their command, Runner saw only a young woman. She wasn't terribly attractive but she wasn't plain either. Short brown hair with brown eyes, she could fit in anywhere.

Decked out in muted colors and plate mail, it was obvious she was a bruiser of a fighter.

He checked the nameplate, and it came back as "Heilwig." Level fifty-two. She was definitely a threat.

"That's a mouthful of a name," Runner muttered. Taking a few steps back from the approaching woman, he double-checked his active gear and found it to be his turret configuration.

Paranoia rocketed his situational awareness to maximum. Runner opened up his left hand and started preparing a *Brainwash* cast while his right hand started amping up a *Seduction*.

"Can I help you, my lady? It would be best if you advanced no further. I'm afraid my people may attack you outright if you don't. If I don't do it first," Runner called out to her when she got within twenty feet.

Targeting her, he began ramping up his spells by feeding them more and more mana.

As if sensing his decision to attack, she finally stopped.

Paranoia didn't stop that easily. It only built. Like a runaway boulder bouncing down a hill.

Runner kept dumping more and more mana into his spells.

His *Seduction* spell had become a whirling vortex of angry hate sex and the *Brainwash* had grown into a weekend-long bender. Though instead of a boiling, swishing noise like *Seduction* had, *Brainwash* sounded more like brain melting static.

"I stopped," Heilwig said.

"Believe I told you to stop earlier. Back up a bit. Or I hit you with these big balls o'fun and we figure out the color of your panties. Then when I'm done, I'll hand you over to Minxy to play with. Eternally," Runner said, his paranoia unceasingly driving him forward.

Shocked at his words, the woman took several large steps back quickly.

Runner tilted his head sideways, eying her intensely.

Around him his guard fell into position, drawing weapons and standing at the ready.

Snorting, Runner settled on taking the high road, bringing his hands together with an audible crack of his palms. The two spells exploded as they were canceled into each other.

Debris blew outwards from the ground around him. Heilwig's hair fluttered behind her under the force of the blast.

"You have ten seconds. Make them count." Runner pulled up a stopwatch and hit the activate button. "Go."

"Lord Runner, I…" the woman started.

Runner, counting down with his fingers, didn't reply.

"I challenge you, in the name of Rike and as her champion, to a trial by combat. I would have preferred to talk, but you've effectively removed that from the table," she said heavily.

"You have my interest. Me versus you? I'll accept that in a heartbeat. Let's begin then," Runner replied immediately. Drawing his hands back out to his sides, he set to kicking the thing off right.

"Not between you and I, God-Emperor, but your champion and I," the woman said, holding up a hand. "I know very well your temper and powers. I'd sooner spit in my divine's eye."

Don't like this. Something isn't right. Find out the conditions, goals, objectives, and results.

Challenges like this always have a pit.

"I have questions. And I'll not agree to anything like that until they're suitably answered. First, what rules do you propose?" Runner pulled on his link with Sophia gently. She'd probably already be on her way, but it didn't hurt to reinforce it.

"No rules. Anything goes so long as there is no outside influence."

"Define outside influence. That's a pretty damned vague term."

"Nothing that isn't available to a champion if they were found alone in a hostile plane."

"Kinda vague there on that one as well. My definition is as follows: should any effect, damage, or ailment be used that isn't directly caused by one or the other party, the challenge is forfeited and lost."

"That's not—" Rike's champion began.

"I don't care. Take it, or leave it. And let's say I'm being generous here. You're a fool. You think I'll accept a challenge because you laid it on me? Hardly. Suck it up, buttercup. Welcome to reality."

Heilwig looked upwards to the sky much as if she were in communication with someone. "Alright. I accept that limitation."

"Conditions for winning?" Runner prompted the next point.

"Kill the other, force them to surrender, render them unable to fight."

"Vague on the unable to fight bit. Try again."

"If they can no longer continue the fight. It's pretty straightforward." Frustration was evident on her face. She hadn't counted on Runner interrogating her.

Fool.

"Not really, no. I could have both my arms and legs chopped off but I could still bite at your kneecaps. I accept death and surrender as viable endings. Is there a time limit?"

"No. No time limit."

"Range limit? If my champion decided to burrow under the ground this would be acceptable."

"No range limit."

"Limitations on consumables?"

"None."

"No, that's not right either. All consumables will be disallowed. Can't have you wiping out some magical god elixir of head smashing."

The champion ground her teeth at his constant badgering and negotiations.

"Fine."

"And what of victory? What happens if you or my champion wins?"

"What?" she replied.

"Obvious question. What do I get if my champion wins? Do I get you? Cause I'm a married man and honestly, you're kinda subpar to… well, everybody I'm with. My personal guard is more attractive than you. By a wide margin. I mean, look at this." Runner turned and reached up to the woman on his left's helmet.

"Stop, shut up. I don't care. If you win? Rike would wager me, half her power pool, and a personal audience. Should she win, she would ask for the same of you."

She'll summon me to a faraway place on the mainland. This is to separate me from my people. I can make this go both ways though.

"I'll add an addendum to that. If my champion wins, my audience with Rike will be in person, and she will be nowhere else. I'll have her full attention."

"I can't b—"

"Don't you get it? I don't care! Yes or no, Buttercup. Get permission if you have to, but there it is." Runner gently patted the shoulder of the guard on his left. "Sorry about that. You lot really are rather pretty though. Makes your company better and worse at the same time."

He could hear the snickers and soft laughter of every guard around him.

"Buttercup?" asked the champion.

"You, you're Buttercup. Hurry the hell up before I tire of this. Maybe I'll take you personally as my footstool if you can't unfuck your head fast enough to answer me. Are you as slow as you are plain to look at? You're the god damn living embodiment of mediocrity."

Behind him he felt Sophia's hand press into his back. "I can take her."

Runner felt the cold feeling in his heart harden. It was all fun and games until he agreed to this death battle.

"Yes, fine! Done. I'll cut your champion's head from her shoulders and use it as a handbag!"

And there it was. Runner got everything he wanted out of the fight. Except the part where he had to forfeit Sophia's life if she failed.

Sending her into a situation where death was a promised possibility.

What if it was one of my guards? Or some random person I have no relation to at all? Everything is in my benefit to win this. My champion is confident.

Is it a betrayal of her trust to not agree to this?

"Challenge accepted." Runner threw up a giant sphere of divine power that stretched out two hundred feet in every direction. He'd had enough of Rike's little tricks.

"What have you done?" Heilwig asked, looking around her.

"I blocked everyone out. I'm a god, remember, Buttercup? After you're mine, I'm going to have to seriously clean your ears out. Alright, Grace, body bag this fool so we can get moving. Keep her alive if possible. I could use her, but don't beat yourself up over it if you can't. You're blood's more important than her life."

Runner stepped aside, throwing a casual thumb in Heilwig's direction.

Needing no further direction, Sophia bolted from her position. Her wings snapped behind her as she dove forward to cross the distance between the champions in a heartbeat.

"Sure hope she read the champion for dummies thing Angel gave me. Probably should have read it myself. Does that make me less than a dummy since I didn't read it?"

"It's simple, lovey. She gets all your own powers so long as they apply to the portfolio. She also gets one half of all your stats," Amelia said, popping into existence. She was sitting on the grass at his feet.

"Neat. Also hi? Don't remember summoning you but good to see you. So she can use *Brainwash* and *Seduction* and all that?" Runner looked back to the fight. Sophia was level forty-nine, yet didn't have her promoted class. She'd be at a disadvantage. He hoped it wasn't a large one.

Sophia's first attack scored a heavy blow as she skewered Heilwig with her lance. To Runner it had looked like his *Thrust* ability.

Snapping a wing and hopping to one side, Sophia dodged to the left as the woman summoned a heavy two-handed sword and whipped it around.

It caught nothing but air as Sophia, ever graceful, slipped away.

"Yeah, all that stuff. Hey, maybe you can take me into Boxy and take me? Grace'll have this wrapped up easily enough. We'll have a few minutes to make use of. Be gentle with me, I'm delicate," Amelia whispered, looking up at him through her eyelashes.

"Idiot," Runner said with a grin, gently rapping Amelia on the head with his knuckles. Then he rested his hands on her shoulders. "Not leaving Grace here alone."

Sophia flapped her wings twice and gained a bit of distance and held up her left hand. She pointed her palm at her foe and started up a spell.

Splatterhouse broke free of her hand and buzzed through the air.

It detonated with tremendous force as it slammed into Heilwig's chest plate. Heilwig charged free of the smoke and triggered an ability that made her sword blur as it sped to Sophia.

Ducking low under the blade, Sophia landed flat on her stomach. As the blade sped past, she gave her wings a flap, then stood up quickly and danced forwards to clear the space between her and her enemy.

As she passed Heilwig, Sophia spun her lance across her hips, the blade cleaving through flesh and muscle alike, effectively using the *Hamstring* ability and crippling her opponent.

"She's like a dancer. When you named her Grace, you were dead on. She's being more fair than I would be though. I think I'd use those pretty wings and float above her head. Hit her with spells over and over."

"She's fighting for my honor and hers. Look around you, silly thing. She's surrounded by people she handpicked to guard me. She could have ended this a long time ago with *Brainwash.*"

A jarring impact exploded on the sphere he'd put up around the area. The shield held, though Runner felt his teeth reverberate with the attack.

It was followed by a flurry of blows as if to overwhelm him with the strength of it.

"Seems they had planned on intervening in some way," Amelia whispered, looking to Runner.

"So it seems. Think it'll hold or should I pop open a portal to the high priestess to keep the battery charged?" Runner looked away from the fight.

Amelia shook her head when she caught his eyes with her own. "You'll be fine. Besides, I'm here. You can drain me dry, lovey. Be sure to put me somewhere nice so I can recover. Like your bed. Be sure to help me recover. Lots of fluids. You can decide what kind. I meant to ask," Amelia said, changing the subject, "did you realize Vixen feeds on your nightly antics? She gets drunk off it. I've watched her."

A booming impact dragged Runner's eyes back to the fight. Heilwig had landed a vicious kick to Sophia's leg and sent her tumbling.

Sophia held a hand out to the ground as she tumbled and fired off an *Air* elemental spell. Combining it with a lazy flap of her wings, she spun out of Heilwig's reach.

"No, I didn't know that. Can't be any worse than having a goddess watch me I suppose."

"True, true. By the way, about tonight. You going to introduce Grace to the ol' —
"

"Minxy, please?"

Sophia ducked in close and slammed her palm into Heilwig's throat. Moving inside the reach of the bigger woman's blade, Sophia grabbed her wrist and wrenched it sideways.

Heilwig's blade hit the ground and threw out a clod of dirt.

"Fine, fine. I figure Vixen has a while before she — oh, damn." Amelia stopped when Sophia drove her fist into Heilwig's chest and detonated *Fireblast*.

"You know, Grace makes this look one-sided, but Buttercup is a strong champion. She's killed several of Rannulf's champions and a large number of the lesser divine's champions."

"I figured," Runner admitted.

"It's your ability set. There's no limits to you, which means there's very few to her. Ah, it's over."

Sophia spun around behind Heilwig and lit her up with a *Stunner*.

Rike's champion dropped to the ground like a sapling snapped in half and lay twitching on the ground.

Heilwig's health was in the red section, only a few percentages above being empty. Sophia's was orange but still quite full.

Amelia stood up and wrapped an arm around Runner's waist.

"Be sure to make her feel good tonight. I'll pretend it's me and fantasize about it."

Leaning over, she kissed his cheek. "Love you." Then she wasn't there anymore.

"Yield," Sophia demanded, ramming the butt of her lance into Heilwig's sternum.

"I'll n—" Heilwig was cut off when Sophia hit her with *Stunner* again.

"My lord husband asked me to take you alive if possible. I will do that if you allow it. If not… he's stated before he wants a skull throne. Maybe you'll be the first one I collect for him."

"Grace, dear, bury her in the earth. Except for her head," Runner called out.

Sophia looked up and then lifted her left hand from her lance. Her hand flashed green and the spell was complete.

Heilwig was brutally pulled down into the ground until only her head was above the grass. Her chin rested on the green turf.

Runner went over to the woman, sighed, and squatted down in front of her.

"Hey there, Buttercup. Here's the deal," Runner patiently said. Reaching down he brushed Heilwig's hair from her eyes.

"Your goddess betrayed you. There was no way you were going to win this without her direct interference. Once I blocked her out, she tried to do something. Then left. She abandoned you even before she knew the outcome. I'm sorry, but she sacrificed you up for a plan that had very little potential to succeed. Everything I've told you is the truth, as I swear upon my own power."

Heilwig wouldn't meet his eyes and instead looked like she was trying to press her face into the grass.

"I'm going to open this back up to the outside. You're welcome to call on her, though she may not respond at all."

Runner dispelled his divine shield and waited.

Heilwig's eyes immediately sought out the sky as she no doubt tried to contact her divine provider.

During the wait for whatever might happen, Runner looked up to Sophia.

"Damn that was marvelous, Grace. You got Minxy all hot and bothered. Truth be told, me too. Was incredibly impressive."

"Thank you, lord husband. I practiced quite a bit while I was mayor. I had already figured out I could use most of your abilities before you gave me Ernsta's note," Sophia explained with a smile. "Your powers are incredible. You never use them though. Why?"

"Because they'd never do as much damage for me as they would for you. My damage is paltry in comparison to yours. I'm a utility caster. It's why I make things like Boxy, *Brainwash*, *Seduction*."

Sophia nodded her head at that. "I'm your blade."

"You sure are, Grace. Quite literally since you're my champion."

Heilwig's expectant face fell forward, her eyes having the look of someone lost.

"I yield."

After she spoke those two words, Runner felt Rike's power slosh into his own.

There was nowhere for it to go, as Runner's power pool rarely was anything less than full, so it disappeared like water down a drain.

Heilwig flashed brightly and then returned to normal. At first Runner didn't notice anything different. It dawned on him after a few seconds. She was quietly sobbing into the grass.

Apparently in becoming Runner's property she'd lost her connection to her divine.

Feeling like an ass, Runner motioned at Sophia. She instantly knew his desire and unstuck Heilwig from the ground.

Runner caught her easily around the waist and then hoisted her up onto his shoulder. Armor and all.

"Make camp. Set up a perimeter, double the guards. May you and all of Norwood's Own receive my blessing." Runner said the words gravely, pushing at them with his divinity.

A soft tinkling could be heard as a blue circle spread out from Runner. It swept over his guard and granted them his personal blessing, one and all.

"Give me an hour with Heilwig, then join me in Boxy." Runner gave Sophia a smile and then trooped off.

Entering Boxy, he pulled the door shut behind him. Leaving it unlocked, he laid Heilwig out in the middle.

"She left me. I failed." Heilwig sniffled.

"You did fail, but not because of yourself. Rike failed you, so you failed in turn. She sent you into a situation you were never going to walk away from. I mean really, Buttercup, did you think I would let you walk out regardless of what happened?"

"Huh? I don't understand."

"It's not like you're protected by some code of conduct. The moment you made known who you were, you weren't leaving. Win or lose. Honestly, I nearly killed you simply to do so when you first walked up. Figured it would be more fun to poke Rike in the eye."

Heilwig looked up at him with shattered brown eyes. She had the misfortune of knowing her divine's pleasure and then displeasure.

"So, here's the deal, Buttercup. I think you have potential. Great potential. Your bravery and zeal are second to none. The problem is you're an idiot and probably could use an upgrade," Runner teased, grinning at her.

"Did you call me an idiot?"

"I did, idiot. And you are an idiot. That's perfectly okay, though, because I'm an idiot, too. I come up with some great idiot plans. I mean, I shot myself out of a catapult. Into a town."

"That's… that's just stupid," Heilwig muttered, a smile flickering across her lips as tears rolled down the sides of her face.

"Hah, yeah. I know. Hey, at least it was fun. Anyways, let's… uh. Hm." Runner pressed his hand to Heilwig's breastplate and filled her with a full heaping helping of Norwood divine power.

"How's that, better?" Runner asked, watching her health immediately go back to full. The glow of his power ran up and down her.

Heilwig's eyes opened wide. Staring at him, she opened her mouth and then closed it.

"So yeah, I think you have potential. I'm going to have you talk to a friend of mine. Her name's Milicent, I call her Milly. She's a bit of an idiot too, but she's nice. You'll like her. Let me bring her here, one sec."

Runner took his hand from Heilwig and then popped open a portal to the temple back in Norwood.

A single thought was all he transmitted into the portal. Milicent would feel a gentle request to proceed to the portal room in the back of the temple.

Singular in her nature, Milicent stepped through the portal in under thirty seconds. Being as big as she was, she had to stoop.

"My god," Milicent said, dropping to one knee. The big woman smiled at him, her large blue eyes boring into him.

"Hey there, Milly. How's things?"

"Unchanged. All is well."

"Oh? Good, hey. I'm going to give you this one," Runner said, pointing at Heilwig. "I call her Buttercup, but her name is Heilwig. She was Rike's champion until I stole her. I think she's got potential. I'd like you to take her to the temple, where she'll be reborn. Then after that, it's up to you. Alexia might have some insight on her. See what you two think before you make a choice.

"Remember, it's your call on Paladins. You're the head of the order."

"Your will be done, my god. We'll go straightaway to Alexia."

"Good. If she can't serve the order, please leave her in Eden."

After closing the portal to the Norwood temple, Runner popped open a portal to Eden in its place. Then he targeted Heilwig and pulled up his GM ability bar.

Milicent nodded her head and looked to Heilwig.

"Fortune favors you this day. You've been saved by our god Norwood. Come, we shall see to your needs." Milicent reached down and grabbed Heilwig by the breastplate and began dragging her towards the portal.

Heilwig looked wide eyed to Runner as she slipped through the portal. Milicent let go of her when she'd brought her to the center of the temple.

Runner gauged it to be about the right time based on what he could see from his position.

"Choose wisely, Buttercup, not everyone is given a second chance."

Runner flashed her a grin and a wave, then hit her with *RaceReset* and *ClassReset* at the same time.

Then he closed the portal.

No sooner had he sent them off than the rear door opened and Sophia stepped inside.

"Goodness, has it been an hour already? Felt like ten minutes, tops."

Sophia looked around the interior before she looked back to him.

"It was ten minutes," Sophia admitted, her eyes flitting to a bench.

"Feeling jittery?"

Sophia nodded her head a little.

"Close the door, lock it, and sit down with me, Grace. We'll talk for a bit before we turn in for the night. I imagine the adrenaline is wearing off."

"I—yes. I think so. It never felt like this before," Sophia said, holding a hand to her throat.

"Yeah. Server is Awakened at this point. And if it isn't, it's a fraction from it. I'm not sure how much will change, but it'll be interesting. Sunshine has also been putting in some pretty massive patches."

Sophia took a breath and sat down next to him.

"I was afraid...," she whispered.

"So was I, but I had faith in you. We can talk about it if you like. Or we could talk about the fact that Rike really screwed her champion over. I mean, she seemed wholly unprepared. Maybe things were different on the mainland. We could chat about the reality that Hannah is around here. Somewhere. Or that Minxy might try to seduce you when she isn't after me. Whatever you like," Runner said, draping an arm around her shoulders and offering her whatever comfort he could.

"Thank you..."

3:13 am Sovereign Earth time
5/24/44

"Runner! Get up, problems," Hannah whispered urgently, her voice tinged with anger and fear.

Sitting bolt upright, Runner blinked stupidly at Hannah. Sophia's head had slipped from his shoulder and landed on the pillow, waking her from her own sleep.

She sat up slowly and set one hand onto Runner's shoulder while the other she pressed to the middle of her forehead.

"What's up, Hanners?" Runner squeezed his eyes shut tight. Letting out a slow breath, he pressed his palms into his eyes, rubbing at them to clear nonexistent grit.

"Couldn't sleep. Was walking around. There's a gigantic fucking ditch. Spans the entire camp from tits to ass. That's what's up. It's beyond our perimeter, so we didn't even see who or what did it, but it goes all the way the fuck around us. I sent a couple sentries to go take a god damn look and they immediately came under fire. They're watching us. We're pinned in. It's too far to drive over without using an engineering team and they won't be able to work unless we accompany them. None of which will be fucking swift, ya get it?"

Groaning, Runner shook his head back and forth as if to clear the nightmare he was hearing from his ears.

Expecting to merrily drive up to Helen, collect her people, drive to Vasilios, do the same, and then happily run over Rike's army was a fool's hope.

Fool that I am.

Chapter 20 - Final Rest -

3:14 am Sovereign Earth time
5/24/44

"In other words they hit us with an attack the moment we stopped. Designed specifically for our tanks. They employed methods they had clearly planned in advance to create a situation in less than..." Runner dropped his hands from his face and looked at the clock to check the time. "Eight hours? Yeah, shit. We have spies. Whoever they are, they've been relaying everything back to someone. And fuck me if I can't figure out how it's being done."

Hannah sighed and shifted her weight back and forth a little. She was squatting in front of him.

"Sorry. Feel like this disaster of a shit show is my fault. I didn't find them and now we're paying," Hannah said, looking to the side.

"Hardly, Hannah. They could as easily be in Norwood's Own, which would be my fault, not yours. Regardless of blame," Sophia said, running her fingers through her long hair, "the time we have before sunrise is invaluable. Let's make it work for us."

"Normally, I'd make some crack about getting in a three-way with you two, but I seriously don't even have a spark of humor left."

Runner sighed and stood up from the bedroll, moving over to a small table in the corner of his personal tent.

On it was laid a map of the isle of Tirtius.

"So, my paranoia tells me that if this is their plan, it's to stall us indefinitely. I mean, they only stopped our people from looking at the trench. They didn't launch an assault. I'm betting that if we look to the south road there's quite a few more problems that way that would either prevent us from traveling back to Sparky or slow us down to a crawl."

Runner stared at the map as his mind started to rapidly spin up to speed. He pushed on the little program in his head, his link to the ship, and set it to the task.

Sophia came up beside him, still in her thin nightclothes, and set a hand on his lower back.

Hannah came to stand in front of him across the table, unwilling to meet his eyes or Sophia's.

"Either they're trying to prevent me from reaching the field, the tanks, the heavy troops, or any combination of that. They don't have the forces to confront us, but they have enough to slow us."

Runner paused to rub at his chin with his thumb and forefinger.

"They wouldn't be pussyfooting around if they felt confident in being able to end us. We'll have a long slog in either direction for us. Constant traps and one-off attacks."

"'Kay. So, fuck that then. We bail on the tanks, have you do your god-tard magic and turn us all into birds or what the fuck ever and we fly back to Faye."

"We'd be leaving the tanks and me behind with that one, but it'd work. As a player, I can only change myself into player-enabled races. That was the original intent

- 239 -

of *RaceReset* for usage. On players at least. I broke it pretty bad when I got it to work on Naturals. Without Sunshine, there's no way I can recode that in time for it to be useful."

"I'm not sure I'd be comfortable leaving the tanks behind. They'd be at the mercy of enemies and whatever purposes they have for them. What if we sent half my people off and kept half here?" Sophia asked.

"Not sure. I'd still be here with the forces but I could send you two off with the other group. Actually, that's not too bad a plan."

"No, that's an idiot plan. Worse than an idiot plan, it's a fucking stupid plan. And Sophia regrets saying it, don't you?"

"Indeed I do. It's a fucking stupid plan. Disregard it, lord husband."

Runner grunted and set it aside for the moment.

"That leads us back to the problem. Don't want to leave the tanks. If we don't leave them, we probably won't get back to our forces in time to be of any use."

Runner grumped and screwed his face up into a frown. Leaning over the table, he felt trapped. They had so little information and little in the way of tools to work with. He'd been overconfident. Vastly so.

"Brighteyes? Angel? Minxy?" Runner asked hopefully.

No response came.

Reaching out with his divine senses he felt the massive dome that was constructed over him. Him and most of the continent of Tirtius and most of Vix.

The magnitude of the thing meant that every single follower of Rike probably was praying nonstop.

The dome would do little to impede the movement of mortals, but to a divine, the place might as well be on another planet.

Concentrating, Runner threw up a mental spike of force against the dome.

It rang in his head but didn't even shift. Rike didn't put it up and leave it, she was actively casting it.

"We've been blocked. Which means whoever did this, probably that bitch queen Rike, doesn't want us talking to our friends."

As his paranoia knew no bounds, it started to signal him urgently that this was part of a greater plan. This was only a small part.

This type of attack wouldn't need a divine block of this magnitude. It would only need that if it was a multi-staged attack.

Runner flipped open his raid window and thumbed to the pages for his personal circle.

The quick little program in his head summed it up at a glance and actually provided him with a window. A window that he had actually wished for but hadn't actually tried to create.

Faye Norwood: Wounded, orange health
Hannah Anelie: Green health
Isabelle Norwood: Lightly wounded, green health
Katarina Saden: Severely wounded, hungry, thirsty, red health
Milicent Ritter: Wounded, green health

Satomi: Wounded, red health
Sophia Norwood: green health
Srit Norwood: Lightly wounded, green health
Thana Damalis: Critically wounded, hungry, thirsty, red health

Even as he watched the names, two boxes flared red. Then Thana and Katarina dropped from the raid window entirely. They vanished.

Exactly in the same way Nadine had when she died.

Shocked, and feeling like his feet had gone numb, Runner fell on his ass.

"Whoever did this attacked everywhere. Everyone but us is injured. Lady Death and Kitten, they… they're not in the raid. That only happens if a Natural dies or they leave the raid. They'd never leave the raid."

"Fuck me. Fuck me. Fuck me! This can't be happening. Can it? We need to get back. You could fix all of this, Runner! You're a god. You could wipe them out and invoke the wrath of the other gods if Rike responded. That's why they're doing this, to keep you from the field," Hannah surmised, her voice rising in volume.

"Are they dead? I… I can't…," Runner mumbled, his tongue too big for his mouth.

"Runner Norwood!" Sophia admonished. She stared down at him, standing over him with her hands on her hips. Her wings had flared out and were nearly fully extended behind her.

"My lord husband, you are the god-emperor of Bastion. I expect you to behave as such. Even if they've perished, what would they tell you? To carry on. To run on, Runner."

Sophia softened her tone and gave him a sad smile.

"Time to be the god-emperor everyone expects you to be, my love. Hannah is right, they don't want you on the field. Which means our answer is simple. You get to the field, and I continue on with the tanks according to the original plan."

Sophia's gaze swung over to the Thief.

"Hannah, please get our god-emperor to the battlefield. I'll do what I can here. I'll send three of Norwood's Own with you as well. They'll be outfitted for *Stealth* so they can leave with you while it's dark out."

"Errr, yeah. That's a great frickin' plan, actually. Such a clever little noble lady. If you're so damned smart, why'd you marry this fucking tool?" Hannah pointed at Runner.

"For the same reason you didn't. I'm off. I'll send the three to meet you here, leave the tent for me. I'll keep the illusion going that you're here as long as I can." Sophia stood still as her clothes changed into her normal attire.

Bending down, she kissed Runner once and patted his cheek. "Be safe out there, my silly lord husband. Hard to make children unless there's a father." Without another word Sophia left the tent.

Runner shook his head and let out a rattling breath.

"She's absolutely right."

"What, about children? Obviously. You think she can get pregnant without you? No fucking wonder Katarina and Thana didn't get knocked up. Some gigolo you are."

Laughing, Runner felt his mood lighten a touch. Then he remembered that those in question both had simply left the group.

He had to believe Thana and Katarina were fine. That they'd quit the raid for a reason.

"Thanks, Hanners. We should get prepped. I figure we *Stealth* exit, bushwack through the wildlands, pop up in whatever small country bumpkin shithole we find, buy mounts or whatever we can, head towards Dover."

Hannah grunted and looked away from him. Her hand went up to a window only she could see.

4:51 pm Sovereign Earth time
5/24/44

Runner looked his map with only dread in his chest.

They'd traveled nonstop with no breaks and little time to talk. Their progress was minimal.

Trying to slog through the wilds and backwoods of uninhabited video game country was slow going. Out here there was little more than mobs and blocking volumes.

And boy were those blocking volumes gut wrenching when encountered. Invisible walls that were meant to form boundaries to prevent people from getting into an area that wasn't programmed or designed to be in.

They'd been forced to turn back and try again several times when they found themselves boxed into a canyon surrounded by nothing but blocking volumes.

They'd spent the day running nonstop.

And we achieved nothing.

Runner closed the map with a grunt. Looking around at his people, he felt like he should have a better answer for them. They were making better time than Sophia would, that was a certainty. Still, they weren't going to exactly be swift.

"My neck itches. Itches like we've got someone riding our ass. Do you think those sons of bitches actually realized we left?" Hannah asked, looking over her shoulder.

Runner thought about that. They'd slipped out under the cover of pre-dawn darkness. They'd remained in *Stealth* until they were positive they'd long since passed through whatever perimeter the enemy had set up.

"Possible. If they have tracking classes they could have swept all along the ditch to see if anyone crossed," Runner guessed. Groaning, he looked around their current area.

"Find somewhere to hole up for the night. Preferably defensible but I'd rather not set us up somewhere that we can't get out of."

His sergeant nodded to the other two, who set off at a trot to do as instructed.

The three Sophia had sent with him were two melee classes and a caster. Respectively, a Barbarian, a Half-Goblin, and an Elf.

The Elf was the caster and the sergeant. The three of them seemed nervous around him, and only the sergeant had managed to actually speak with him.

"Sergeant, anything to add?" Runner asked, catching the Elf maiden unprepared.

"No, God-Emperor. Ready to serve," she rattled off.

"Not quite what I was asking. The situation. Do you have anything to add to it? We were talking about the possibility we were being followed."

"I'm not qualified—"

"Shut up or I swear to me I'll carry you off to my bedroom when we get back. And not for my own personal use, mind you, but I'll let Minxy play with you to her heart's content. Answer the question"—Runner looked up at her name—"Annette."

The blue-eyed Elf reached up and tucked a strand of strawberry blonde hair behind a long tipped ear.

"Ah, uhm, that is… Lady Sophia would tell us that to act under the belief that the enemy is incompetent is the quickest way to ensure defeat," she finally said.

"Well put. When"—Runner's eyes flitted out to where the other two had gone to check their nameplates—"Signe and Ada get back, relay to them we're now operating under the belief that we—"

The Half-Goblin scampered over to Annette. She was covered in chain mail and a solid breastplate but couldn't be anything other than a damage class. Green skinned and diminutive, she was a long throw from her human parentage.

"Chasers behind us, west. Working this way. They have… not a tank. But a tank," hissed Ada.

Runner closed his eyes and leaned his head back, putting his hands on his hips.

"Right, then. So, the arms race is happening. I've been underestimating Rike since the start. She didn't land one army, she landed multiple armies, units, and supplies. This is a foothold invasion, not an attack."

Runner's mind careened off into the distance as it started working through any and all possibilities.

Heavy footfalls came up to them. Since no one reacted it could only be Signe.

"Saw Ada came back early. There a problem? Found a cave, if it helps at all," she grumbled

As if struck by a bolt of lightning, Runner had his answer. And he hated it.

Closing his eyes tightly, he scrambled madly for any other answer.

Annette's voice cut through the fog of his thoughts. "How far back were they, Ada?"

"Five, maybe ten. I saw them at a distance, I did. Movin' fast. Color red kinda fast," the half-breed replied.

"Cave can fit us all. It's huge. Deep. Can we hide and wait for them to pass?"

"No, they have a tracker," Annette said with a grunt. "We think."

Runner's options were limited. The best he could do was to get everyone onto a separate plane. That wouldn't solve the problem, though, and would in effect trap them there until they could return reasonably sure that the enemy had moved on.

And there was no timer on that.

There was a definite timer on Dover and the fact that Thana and Katarina might be alive. Or dead. Or that Faye was more than likely next.

The possibility of Rike unloading scores upon scores of troops by the day made him sick.

It was time to make a decision he'd regret and didn't want to make.

"Annette, Ada, Signe," Runner said softly. Letting his chin fall back to his chest, he opened his eyes and looked to the three of them. "Would you die for me?"

"Yes, my god-emperor."

"Yeah. Course. You took in me family, gave 'em all jobs, no questions, easy like. Mum was a bit of a loose woman before Pa. Lots o' gobo kids and you snapped 'em all up like they was gold."

Signe grunted her response in the affirmative.

"Then I must ask you to die for me," Runner said with a small sad smile. "We're going to hole up in that cave. Then we wait and let them come to us. We tear them apart or die trying."

"Forgive me, God-Emperor. Isn't the point for you to get to the battlefield? What if we held the cave while you retreated?" Annette asked.

"Valid plan, but honestly, I'm confident that I can survive whatever they throw at us if we all fight together. The problem is I can't… I can't guarantee you will." Runner held up his hands in apology.

"The fact of the matter is, if it was me against, how many did you say it was, Ada? Sixty?"

"Give or take. Plus or minus. Fingers or toes."

"Sixty by myself, with two whatever they have on wheels, would probably end up with me dead or fleeing. They'd just overwhelm me. It almost happened when I was on the front line back in Tristan's Field.

"But if half were busy dealing with you four, though… I think that'd work. I think."

Annette, Signe, and Ada were deep in thought. Hannah on the other hand looked annoyed.

"We've drastically underestimated our foe. If we can't shut this down now, she's going to shatter whatever is left of… whatever is left of Katarina and Thana's forces. Then she'll start landing more troops," Runner admitted

Signe squared her shoulders and merely nodded her head. Barbarians were like that. You could count on them to die honorably in a heroic last stand to save their lord.

Annette closed her eyes and took a deep breath. "I understand."

Ada frowned and peered at him with her black eyes. Eyes that dominated her face, black pools that had very little white around them.

She watched him from under her shaggy brown hair. She wasn't a looker. She was interesting. Unique.

She reminded him of Milicent. Or Hannah. Unique in their status.

"Asking me to die for ya. Stand at your side in the face of unreasonable odds. Expect me to blind the enemy with my charm and make them come for me," Ada said, cocking her head to the side, evaluating him.

She spoke in a strange way but Runner had no doubt she was intelligent. Not one of Norwood's Own lacked in mental acuity.

"This is what you signed up for. Norwood's Own is made up of volunteers. Here's the ultimate end result of that choice. I value you each for who you are, but this is the job."

Ada growled but then nodded her head.

"Good. God-Emperors need to be firm. Be sure you tell everyone about me, then. The Half-Goblin who saved the god-emperor. Good story, that. Make it a rousing one. Move the people.

"If you can stomach the idea, maybe even throw in the hint of a romance between us? Really spice it up a level, eh? All those big boobed cows strutting around and you bedded the little green monster." Ada punctuated her cow comment by pointing at Signe.

Runner laughed and set his hand on top of Ada's head.

"Actually, I have a preference for the unique and interesting. I'm afraid I'm a married man, and very, very tied up, but you're beautiful in your own way, Ada."

Ada scowled at him and then took a few steps away to stand closer to Signe.

Runner took that moment to snap a screenshot of the three of them. Standing together, proud.

Alive.

"Oi, you're not allowed to steal a maiden's heart like that right before she dies. Now I'm regretting not making a move on you earlier. Maybe I wouldn't be dying a maiden. Steal you away from your pretty little cow harem," Ada groused at him. "Iffn the time comes... you'll be there for us? Take us to your plane? Yourself?"

"I will. I ask that if you fall, remain at the cave. I will escort you personally."

Signe chuckled and thumped a hand down on Ada's shoulder. She looked like any Barbarian he'd seen before. "Told you. Come. It is our time to die. We must go before our place is taken.

"Both my brothers are already there, you know. When the god-emperor took over, he brought them all onto his own plane. I scrounged up a priest and he..." Signe's voice trailed off as she started walking away from them.

Ada turned and left with Signe, listening to the big woman as she chattered on.

Annette gave him a crisp salute.

"Should I fall, please watch over my soul, God-Emperor. Though I will go ahead of my family, I know that they'll be in safe hands."

Runner returned the salute. Annette made a proper turn from her salute and moved off to rejoin her comrades.

Shuddering, Runner looked to Hannah and took in a slow breath.

"Ugly choice, but… a good one. What's the plan?" Hannah asked.

"Kill them all, bleed with our people. Assuming this all goes right? Track back the way we came. Then we blink as far as possible off the track, and blink until we're out of charges. We should be able to get pretty far, then we keep going until we find a place to buy mounts." Runner laid out his plan quickly. As he finished, he shrugged his shoulders.

"Eh, it's not an idiot plan, so that's good. Fuck me if you're not a moron at times. Doesn't seem like it'll be fast enough. I might have an idea. Let me think on it," Hannah said, setting off after the trio of women.

Runner looked towards the path they'd come from rather than the direction his guards went. Out there was a small group of people specifically put together to kill him.

Hopefully they really can take up half the numbers.

The cave was indeed big on the inside. The entrance wasn't too large, though — wide enough for ten abreast to walk through unimpeded.

They wouldn't be able to hold the entrance for long. Really it wasn't the goal anyways. Drawing them in and making use of regulation potions supplied to them would be their best advantage.

It only took a minute until two wagons trundled into view. They were pulled by horses but on the top of each wagon was a massive crossbow.

It's a fucking ballista. Ada's tank but not.

Following behind it came the infantry support one would expect for a tank. Too many to count without standing still as a target for the wagons. Runner and crew ducked deeper into the cave. Out of sight of the welcome wagon.

"Well, that's a thing. Two things. Remind me that when this is over we quadruple the guards posted at Dover and Vix. That and beat the ever-loving snot out of Rike until she bleeds from her ears," Runner complained, pressing up against a cave wall.

"Wouldn't have mattered. That rat bastard fuckwit Basile let her walk in. Remember?" Hannah reminded him.

"Ah, yeah. Damn." Runner was happy that the man was dead and yet sad he couldn't kill him again.

Nothing happened.

There was no mad rush to get into the cave, no shouted insults, no scouts, random fire, nothing.

"Damn, I'm an idiot. They don't want to fight us if they don't have to. They… just want to prevent me from getting to the battle. That's it," Runner grumbled.

"So, we have to assault them?" Signe asked from the other side of the entrance.

"Are you batty, you big monkey?" Ada squeaked.

Hannah laughed and rested the back of her head against the rock wall.

"Damn this sucks. Runner, you're a fucking awful date."

"Sorry, dear. I'll try to arrange things better next time. If there is one," Runner admitted with a small smile. Watching Hannah's face, he couldn't help but feel he'd fucked up somewhere.

"Signe? You lead the charge after I *Blink* into the wagons. Hanners, sheepdog, drop healers, casters, anyone on the outside. Ada, support Annette. Annette, break 'em. May you all be blessed, in my name."

Runner held up his hand as he said it, and the blessing of Norwood settled on them all.

Quickly he slipped into his "turret" equipment and then took a slow breath.

A simple thought later and he'd redirected his *Taxi* ability to send him to his workshop.

Stepping into the entrance area, Runner targeted the wagon.

"Runner, wait, we c—"

Runner activated the *Blink* ability even as the two wagons opened fire on him.

Holding out his hands to his sides, he pressed his palms to both wagons. Mentally he slammed the GMHub ability.

/GMHub 7

Teleporting…

/GMHubReturn

Teleporting…

Reappearing where the wagons had been, he felt momentary elation. The wagons were gone.

Then he felt a crush of bodies press into him and attack him simultaneously.

Flipping *Taxi* back to the plane of Eden, Runner tried vainly to protect himself.

Attack after attack landed on him. It was exactly what he had been afraid of if the entire force concentrated on him. He could only return to the exact spot he'd left.

Trying to conserve mana for healing, he turned his thoughts to his items.

Runner was forced to *Blink* a short distance over, using up a charge.

Wrapping his arms around two soldiers, he used *Taxi*. Upon returning he leapt at a female caster in front of him.

Pressing her to the ground, he stared down into her frightened hazel eyes.

"Hi." Runner grinned at her before sending her off with *Taxi*.

Each trip to the plane cost him something like three to five seconds.

But no mana.

When he returned he got to his feet quickly and looked around.

He could see that his small group was fighting between him and the mouth of the cave. They were swarmed.

Targeting his group, he set off a *Regeneration* spell on each. He'd have liked to use actual large healing spells but there was no time.

Unable to spare a single second more, as every second he wasted was another second they were under attack, he blinked towards a group of casters.

Throwing his arms wide, he caught two men and a woman in a group hug and zipped them off.

With every usage he felt his mind spinning crazily at the distortion. His brain was starting to have trouble differentiating where he was or what was up and down.

His mana bar remained relatively full though.

Panting, Runner scanned around him and found a group of seven healers to one side.

Sparing another second, he once more applied *Regeneration* to his people.

Blinking on top of the enemy healers, he dove at them, spreading himself out sideways to hit as many as he could.

The moment he felt contact he hit the ability again, only to return while still in midair.

When he hit the dirt, he contracted his arms and legs and felt a few more people. Whisking them off to Eden Runner found himself back on the grass, panting.

He wanted to throw up, and knew that it wasn't possible in this world.

A flashing red icon appeared on his UI, and he closed it hurriedly.

Getting to his feet, he found there were no healers left of the group of seven.

Before him stood a group of hungry-eyed melee classes. Either they were the healer's bodyguards, or they came to him looking for a fight. It didn't matter.

Thanks for the meal.

Runner slumped forward and grabbed at three of them. He managed to lock up two and sent them off via *Taxi*.

Flailing around as his knees buckled, Runner connected with someone else. He dragged them to Eden.

Runner felt his vision cloud and glaze. Colors still made sense though. Red names were red names after all.

Unable to truly see his own group anymore, he tried to cast *Regeneration* on the group bars instead.

The spell failed once.

Invalid target.

Spotting a clustered bunch of red names, Runner blearily eyed them.

There's a big group. Let's go that way. Onwards, feet!

Stumbling toward the group, he set his sights on the closest red name. Latching onto them in a hug, he sent them off. Moving as best as he could, Runner managed to send seven more off in that fashion before people started to simply run from him.

Slumping to his knees, Runner could barely comprehend anything that was going on around him.

Everything looked like a scattered mosaic. Blurred and incomprehensible.

Something came up to him. It stayed out of reach, or he thought it did. Runner prepared to lurch forward to *Taxi* another person far, far away.

As if sensing the fact that he was ready, they backed off. Another shape joined the first.

They had an exchange, one that Runner couldn't follow. To him it all sounded like bagpipes being run over.

Runner decided to close his eyes. It didn't matter. If they were friendly, he had nothing to care about. If they were enemies, they'd realized he was spent and could do no more anyways.

Come closer, said the spider to the fly. Fine, give me time. As soon as my head clears I'll send you all to Eden.

Several minutes passed in silence. Runner rested on his knees with his head slumped forward, arms limp at his sides.

"You in there yet?" Hannah asked him quietly.

Runner felt his lips twitch upward into an involuntarily smile. Lifting his head, he opened his eyes.

Hannah smiled back at him, squatting in front of him.

"Good to see you, Hanners," Runner croaked.

"Likewise. You don't look too good."

"It's the spell. I don't understand it honestly, but using it a lot, or rapidly, tends to screw me up. Wasn't as bad last time. Then again, I wasn't a cyborg demigod back then," Runner said casually.

Hannah snorted and then sighed.

"Annette and Signe both fell. I sent Ada off back to camp with my *Stealth* potions. Sophia needs to know what happened here. Those wagons being eliminated is good information for her to have," Hannah said softly.

Runner made a soft grunt and felt his head dip a fraction.

"They're waiting for you, Runner," Hannah whispered.

Taking a deep breath, Runner stood up and straightened his shoulders.

His eyes tracked over the corpses sprawled out. At the center of a cluster of bodies lay Annette and Signe.

Runner moved over to them slowly and as stably as he could manage. They deserved respect.

Bending down over the two dead Norwood's Own, he eased them onto their backs, straightened their armor as best as he could, and arranged their features and hair to be as if they were only at rest.

Reaching out blindly with his divine presence, he tried to free them of their bodies.

He could feel them. Warm and tingly, like when you sat on your leg for too long. Delicate things that were trapped inside their broken vessels.

As gently as he could he disconnected them from their mortal bodies. He felt the moment that their ties broke and they lifted themselves free.

Standing before him were the slain, ghostly in image and watching him.

"Annette, Signe, please forgive me for spending your lives. I promise it was not done in vain. I thank you, from the depths of my heart."

Runner bowed to them deeply from the waist.

Neither spoke when Runner stood upright again, though they both saluted in unison.

Taking more effort than he could remember previously, Runner opened a portal to the spiritual plane.

On the other side he could see the interior of his temple and many spirits. They paused in their afterlife to stare out of the portal back at him.

"Please, enjoy your rest as it was well earned. I will ensure that your families receive a bonus for your personal heroism," Runner promised.

Signe eagerly bounded forward, taking her rightful place as a fallen soldier with her comrades, family, and friends.

Annette lingered behind. Then she inclined her head fractionally to Runner and entered the portal.

It slid shut behind the ghostly sergeant, and Runner looked to Hannah.

"I know we need to move. I'm… not sure how fast I can go. I'm feeling pretty fucked up, Hanners."

"Well then, I've got good news for you. You get to mount me tonight," Hannah said, giving him a wide grin.

Runner blinked slowly at that. "Ha… ha… ha. Don't toy with my fragile emotions. So, what do you need from me? I'm assuming this is about the plan you mentioned earlier?"

Hannah rolled her eyes at his lack of interest and gestured at him.

"You said you can't become anything other than a playable race. When you hit me with RaceReset earlier, I saw… well I saw damn near everything."

"Right. Just don't pick anything non-sentient. No guarantee you wouldn't become whatever you… uh… became, I guess. In other words, if you become a horse, you might really be a horse in mind and spirit."

"Not a concern. This is only temporary. Hit me."

Runner didn't have a better plan, so he did as she asked. Targeting Hannah, he used RaceReset.

Hannah hadn't even fully transformed into the blue vortex when she simply reappeared.

As a Centaur.

She was the size of a true horse, probably a large variant species of a Centaur. Her hair and fur coloring was black as midnight from head to hoof. The skin of her face, arms, and torso was pale in contrast.

Flicking her horse tail at his face, she turned her head from him, hiding her features.

"I look strange. Eyes to yourself, fucker. Now get on. We need to get moving."

"Not really how I envisioned my first time with you," Runner murmured with a smile. Moving over to her, he ran his fingers gently over her spine.

"Stop that. Hurry up already, this is awkward enough as it is, fucktard," Hannah complained, shivering under his touch.

"Fine, fine. Thank you, Hanners. I know this isn't easy, and I appreciate it." Runner swung a leg over Hannah's middle and mounted her. "Errr, hold onto your hips then? Without a saddle and bridle it's a little odd."

"My waist is fine. If you even think of getting funny and moving those hands, I'll kick you off and trample you," she warned him.

"Wouldn't think of it," Runner promised, wrapping his arms around her waist.

"Good. Now..." Hannah's hands were busy in front of her. Runner tried to lean forward to get a look when he realized she was tying his hands together around her front.

"So you can't fall off as easy. Hopefully you can close your eyes on my back and rest a bit. Will be bumpy as shit but... doing what I can here," Hannah apologized.

"I know, thank you, love. You're better than I deserve."

"Damn right. Okay, here we go."

Runner heard a triumphant fanfare of trumpets and his screen flashed.

Rike has declared a holy war on your pantheon!
All worshipers for both sides have been marked accordingly.
Good luck!

The dome that had been erected over him shuddered and crackled as it came under fire.

Whatever this holy war meant, it had enabled his divine partners the ability to act.

Hannah worked up to a gallop while Runner contemplated this.

Opening his map, he saw it was full of blue and red dots. It was easy to assume every blue dot was someone who worshiped his pantheon, and every red dot was one of Rike's.

He could even see red dots in Norwood, Shade's Rest, and Kastell. Rike had spent the lives of her spies to find out where Runner was.

There was a huge blob of red along the southern coast of the Human third of Tirtius. Except for that smaller blue blob that could only be Faye's army.

Rike had landed a lot of troops.

It was exactly as they had supposed: Faye would need a hand, and Runner was the only one who could provide it.

Hannah was darting between trees and bushes as quickly as she could. Moving faster than they ever could have on foot.

"By the way. Rike declared holy war on me. They can see us on the map and we can see them. I'm sure we'll have friends eventually if we dally too long. No big."

"Always. A problem. With you. Fucker," Hannah huffed out as she galloped.

"I know. Sorry. Thanks for staying with me, Hanners."

Runner took a deep breath before continuing.

"Rike has a pretty big army in the south. Probably equal to Faye and probably has more of those wagon things. And she has no tanks. This probably isn't going to be very good."

Hannah ran on in silence, ducking under a low hanging branch. Runner had heard a long time ago to stay at the height of the horse's head when riding through something like this. Now he understood why.

"I'm not sure how this'll all turn out. It's pretty likely that… well, that Kitten and Lady Death are no longer with us.

"I'm honestly afraid more of us will die. So, in case I don't get the chance to say it later, I love you. I'm a manwhore, a gigolo, whatever you want to call me, but I do love you, Hanners. Well and truly. I'm sorry," Runner said, pressing his forehead to the back of Hannah's armored shoulders.

Hannah didn't say anything, but he could feel her pressing herself to move even faster, her muscles bunching underneath his hips and legs.

Hannah Anelie has accepted your proposal.
Congratulations!
You are officially man and wife.

"This doesn't. Mean. Anything. We need. To talk. Later. Asshole! Fucker! Bastard! I hate you! My love," Hannah yelled as she stormed through the woods.

Chapter 21 - Power Overwhelming -

4:19 am Sovereign Earth time
5/25/44

Runner peered at the clock.

Hannah had nearly stumbled as she ran along moments before, jarring Runner from his light doze on her back.

Opening his map, he checked their position. She'd run on through the previous day and the night. There'd been no stops and they'd eaten on the run. Literally.

They were only an hour's walk from Faye. Sitting upright, he shifted his bound hands to her middle and leaned up to the side of her face.

"Hanners, it's time to trade places," Runner whispered into her wedge-shaped ear.

Hannah said nothing but slowly came to a shuddering stop. Her breath came in broken gasps as her hands flopped like fish against his bindings.

"Don't worry about it," Runner said, and then blinked to her side.

Hannah turned her face from him despite being as tired as she was.

Respecting the fact that she didn't want him to see her as anything other than her half-breed self, he targeted her and cast *RaceReset*, sending her back to the character screen in a rush of blue motes.

Looking down to the bindings around his wrists, he cast a *Fire* spell. The rope caught fire quickly and fell from his hands.

Hannah popped back into existence and fell forwards.

Catching her under the armpits, Runner held her upright. She leaned completely into him, her head resting on his shoulder and her arms dangling at her sides. Her face looked pale even for her, and her eyes were closed.

"Thank you, my sweet little Thief. I'll carry you the rest of the way. I'll have Sparky get you a tent to sleep in for a bit while I see to things."

Hannah nodded, rubbing her cheek on his shoulder.

"Here, can you stand up for two seconds? That's all I need," Runner asked her gently.

Hannah nodded a little but didn't move.

Runner smiled sadly.

My poor Hanners.

Reaching down, he placed his hands under her bottom and then heaved. He pulled her up into him, holding onto her rear end firmly to keep her in place.

Taking a few steps, he adjusted her position and then felt comfortable carrying her.

It was awkward positioning, to say the least, but thankfully muscles didn't exactly tire from carrying things in a video game.

That and I should be grateful that sprinting is very different than carrying.

If you could carry something, you could carry it indefinitely.

Runner set off for Faye's camp, pinging Faye directly on top of herself, and then once on top of himself.

Though she didn't come to greet him, he could clearly see her blue dot and several others moving around hurriedly in her tent.

Preparing a welcome. Bless her.

Roughly an hour later Runner walked straight into Faye's command tent. He had watched as several dots, including Faye's, had moved into a tent that had magically appeared beside Faye's own. He'd pinged her once to signal to remain there.

Faye kept her tent the same way every time, so he knew where her bed would be.

He moved over to it, laid Hannah down in Faye's bed, and looked down at her.

"Hannah Norwood, sleep and rest," Runner whispered through a smile. Leaning down, he pressed a kiss to her lips and then slipped out to Faye's location.

Stepping inside of the Command Tent that he assumed was his own, he looked around for a second.

Only to be picked up and crushed in a bone-shattering hug.

"Love," said a rich voice. Katarina's voice.

Laughing, Runner pulled his head back to stare up at the Barbarian woman.

"Kitten! You big beautiful Barbarian. I was so worried when you and Lady Death left the raid. You're both okay?"

"Aye. We are. Spies in the raid. Had to leave. Can't rejoin till we're sure they're all gone. Kept spotting us out in Dover," she said. Leaning in, she kissed him firmly, hungrily.

After a few seconds she released him. Feeling dizzy and not entirely sure he wanted to be released, Runner steadied himself.

Then was quickly enveloped in another hug. This one tender and warm.

"Dear heart," Thana whispered, her arms tightening a fraction around his shoulders.

"Lady Death, I was quite worried for you both." Runner leaned back and then kissed Thana before she could get away.

Thana allowed it for a few seconds before pushing back from him and patting his shoulder.

"I assumed you would be. I must say, I don't like not being in the group. It provides so many benefits that you simply come to rely on," the Sunless Sorceress said, giving him a toothy smile.

Runner looked her over from head to toe — nothing wrong, everything where it was supposed to be.

Looking to Katarina, he stopped and felt his eyebrows shoot up.

Katarina was very pregnant. Probably about eight months so. To the point where he wondered if her armor would fit her.

Catching the direction of his eyes, the Barbarian woman blushed a deep red and then placed her hands on her stomach.

"Mother was happy. She wants a granddaughter. I... I don't care what it is."

Explains the weird looks Helen was giving me.

"Consider me jealous, dearest. I'm still waiting for my turn."

"I'm glad, Kitten. Very glad. Sorry, Lady, we'll have to try harder. Or more often. Or both," Runner said with a grin.

Faye stepped up and then burned a hole in his forehead with her eyes, demanding his full attention.

"Alpha, flirting will need to wait. I'm not sure how much of the situation you're aware of. I'm glad you're here however. This is… it's getting wildly out of hand."

"Agreed, it's definitely the reason I'm here. But, before we begin, I have to insist on one topic that needs to be discussed. Have you told them about everything I did, Sparky?"

"Yes, Alpha. They're aware of everything up to this point."

"Good. That makes it easy then. On a side note, Hanners accepted as well. She's sleeping in your bed right now, Sparky."

Runner targeted Thana and Katarina and tapped the marriage buttons respectively for them.

Before he'd finished reading the log messages that confirmed he'd sent the request, he got his answers back.

Katarina Saden has accepted your proposal.
Congratulations!
You are officially man and wife.

Thana Damalis has accepted your proposal.
Congratulations!
You are officially man and wife.

"Okay, uh, good." Runner smiled at the two, whose last names had flipped over to his own surname.

Katarina smirked at him, one hand on her stomach. Thana quirked a brow as if expecting something further.

"Uhm, yeah. Okay. So, Rike has declared a holy war on top of everything. Everyone who is an actual worshiper of my pantheon should now appear as a blue dot on the map, and Rike's are all red. I'm not really sure what that means beyond that though."

Runner held up his hands in a frustrated gesture.

"That bitch goddess Rike has blocked me from speaking with the others. I can feel them pressing on the dome every now and then but can't contact them."

"Break it," Katarina commanded.

"Haven't really tried yet. No time and I'd have to open a portal to Eden to get the power for it I imagine."

"A fair point, dearest. Perhaps we should take care of that now? I imagine your divine partners might have something to add. Or perhaps be able to explain the situation."

"I agree with my pack sister," Faye said, nodding her head severely.

"Right, then. Okay. One second."

Runner closed his eyes and focused his mind on opening a portal to Eden.

It slid into existence quickly, and the light of dawn through the temple's open doors spread throughout the tent.

Before he could do anything, Alexia and Milicent stepped through the portal. Trailing behind Milicent, Heilwig came as well, though she was clearly unsure of the situation.

She looked the same as he remembered her. She still looked Human but there was a difference he couldn't quite determine.

Alexia and Milicent found Runner with their eyes and moved before him. Both of them fell to their knees and stared up at him.

Heilwig fell in behind them and prostrated herself, pressing her forehead to the grass.

"Behold," Runner said to them, laying it on thick. "Our war with Rike comes to a close. On this day, we battle her armies. I shall be taking the field directly along with the rest of the pantheon. I have need of your services.

Alexia's eyes shone with a determination that made Amelia look like a lovesick puppy.

"Command me," Alexia pleaded.

"Pray, High Priestess. Your prayers are the greatest asset to me, more than anything else. Honest, earnest prayers." Runner laid a hand to the top of Alexia's head and blessed her.

To anyone else it would simply be a blessing, to her, it was a reinforcement of her faith.

"Your will, my god-emperor," Alexia whispered. She got up and nearly tripped at her own eagerness, scuttling back through the portal and calling out to her flock.

Thana, Katarina, and Faye all looked shocked. Runner could imagine it was strange. To them, he was Runner; to many others, he was the god-emperor of Bastion.

"Heilwig, raise your head. I do not seek subservience," Runner addressed the ex-champion, before turning his eyes to Milicent.

"What have you decided, Paladin Commander? Is she worthy of serving?" Runner fixed Milicent with his gaze.

The big eyed Half-Ogress gazed back at him in a manner similar to Alexia's.

"She will serve. She now knows of your glory."

"Please, God-Emperor. Let me serve. I knew nothing. Your champion was glory incarnate. I was but a brute. A thug. Please. Let me serve," Heilwig begged.

"So be it. Milly, I will send you to my armory now. Please collect gear for her based on your personal opinions of her needs. You will have ten minutes or so. In addition, there's a set of plate mail on a shelf by itself. Please collect that for the lady Katarina," Runner said, looking back to the big woman who made Thana look like a child.

Runner held out a hand and pressed it to Milicent's cheek. Triggering his GMHub ability, he focused on the workshop.

/GMHub 7

Teleporting...

/GMHubReturn

Teleporting...

"Now. Let's get rid of that dome," Runner said as he returned.

Opening himself to the waves of power flowing through the portal, he gathered up the entirety of his divine pool. Even as he felt the pool empty, it refilled, again, and again, and again.

When it got to the point that Runner couldn't see anything through the glow of his holy power, he decided it was time.

Then he struck a single piercing blow against the dome of Rike's power, expending everything in one moment.

It shattered like a piece of glass forced too far. Rike's shriek could be heard throughout the land the dome had covered and scratched at the inside of Runner's mind.

Trailing that shriek like a wolf on the hunt, Runner launched a second jab at Rike with whatever power Alexia had summoned up in those two seconds.

Wailing in agony, Rike fled the continent of Tirtius entirely. Runner felt her leave back to the mainland.

Then he felt his pantheon as they returned.

To him they felt wane, tired, a little underfed. Sickly.

They'd tried to break the dome from their side, though they'd had few worshipers to work with.

Worried, he enveloped his divine partners and brought them into the power of Alexia's devotions. He force-fed them on those heavy prayers, pushing his own power back through them over and over until it felt like they might individually burst.

Then fed them more to make sure.

Amelia popped into existence, looking drunk and flushed.

"No more, lovey. Please. No more of your own power. Fuck me. Now I know how your wives feel." Amelia grabbed onto a table to steady herself.

"Sorry, you three looked sickly. What about Brighteyes? Or Angel?" Runner asked, looking to Amelia.

"They're more fucked up than I am. I got a taste of this last time you destroyed me, so it isn't as bad for me. They're trying to recover. I think I want to throw up. Too much, Runner," Amelia said in a shaking voice.

"Sorry. Got a little nervous. Was worried," Runner admitted sheepishly.

"Love you, too. Thanks for worrying. Not so much next time." Amelia fell to her knees beside the table and rested her cheek on the wood.

"Holy war. It means that only one pantheon is leaving. She has a massive navy outside of Dover that will be attacking in a few hours. The army outside will do its best to prevent you from getting through to relieve the defenders," Amelia explained.

"Got it. Anything else we need to know?"

"No. Call us when it's time or when you know where you want the champions. We can act more freely in a holy war. Going now," Amelia said and then winked out like a snuffed candle.

Runner let out a quick exhalation.

"Right, then. Don't think it's been ten minutes, but let me check on Milly. Then we can talk about plans."

Before activating his ability, he began to close the portal to Eden. Alexia would get the picture. She was a smart cookie. They'd rest and wait for the portal to reopen.

/GMHub 7

Teleporting...

"You ready, Milly?" Runner called out as he looked around.

"Yes, my god. I took the liberty of picking up a few things for my own use," called the Paladin. She stepped out from behind a rack of weapons and walked over to him.

"That's fine. Every time you get a new Paladin you'll be coming back here anyways. Might as well make sure you're aware of what's here. Let's go then."

Runner reached out and laid a hand on Milly's forearm.

/GMHubReturn

Teleporting...

Targeting Heilwig as he popped back up, he took two steps over to her and laid a hand on her head.

Milicent moved over to Katarina and started handing her the plate mail Runner had asked her to pick up.

"Rejoice, Buttercup, you've been chosen. Serve me," Runner demanded of her.

"Yes, God-Emperor," Heilwig said. Her eyes were as wide as possible as she looked up at him.

Runner activated *Confer Class Paladin*. Heilwig looked like she'd been struck in the back of her head as her chin fell forward, the class change happening immediately.

"Milly, hand me her weapon?" Runner asked, looking to Milicent. He held out his hand to her. Two wicked looking hand axes were dropped into his open hand. It would seem Milicent had decided his Paladin order would wield axes.

Runner channeled his holy power into the weapons until the divine bar was empty. The axes flared brilliant as they were infused with holy power.

"Buttercup, here are your weapons. Serve me well and adhere to your commander's orders," Runner said, resting the axe heads beside Heilwig's knee, their handles settling against her thighs. "Out of curiosity, what race are you?"

"A Were, God-Emperor. Milicent said you didn't discriminate and Weres are powerful creatures," she admitted, a little nervous sounding. Her hands reached over to grip her new weapons. Runner gave her a nod of his head at the statement.

"She's right. I don't care about whatever you are, but only who you are. Now" — Runner looked to Faye, Thana, and Katarina — "let's get that plan put together."

Faye shrugged her shoulders at that. "Already done, Alpha. I've arranged the troops in such a deployment to limit the damage those wagons might do. We got a taste of them in a skirmish. Shields up front, cannons to tear out their middle and aim for the wagons."

Faye turned to gesture at the table where all the pieces were laid out. "We believe the wagons might be utilized in a similar function as the cannons. Our line could be longer but I had to limit how many shield bearers were in each row to provide protection."

She adjusted one of the black pieces of the map that was a smidgen out of line.

"I have most of my mages near the middle and back to protect and attack. I have confidence we'll triumph. I don't believe we'll win before Dover falls," Faye admitted, straightening back up and meeting his gaze.

"Hence Lady Death and Kitten being here," Runner said, controlling a sigh from escaping.

"Right, then. Proceed as you see fit. I'll take the field outside of your plans with Milly and Buttercup. We'll try to target their back line. Healers, casters, wagons." Runner paused and swallowed, knowing he had to give another order.

One that could possibly get people he loved killed.

"I need Dover held. Kitten, Lady, can you hold it?" Runner asked, looking to the two women.

Both looked thoughtful and concerned at the same time.

"For a day. Maybe," Katarina murmured.

"If that. I can't promise it, dear heart."

"What if all three of Tirtius' champions joined you?" Runner offered.

"More likely. No guarantee. Is only another three fighters, even if they are stronger," Katarina modified her original statement.

Runner took a slow steady breath and then pulled the trigger.

"Hold Dover. One day is all we need. Do you need anything?"

"No, dear heart. Faye immediately refilled our supplies the moment we arrived. We'll depart after this."

"I'll go with you," Hannah said from the entrance. She looked tired, and worn, though a little better.

"Thank you, Hanners. I'd appreciate that," Runner said around the lump in his throat. He was sending three women he wanted nowhere near Dover straight into it. Where the fighting would be the ugliest.

"Brighteyes, I'd like to request the three champions to Dover, as well as two of your number. The third will be with me on the field with the Paladins."

"Consider it done. Amelia will join you," Brunhild responded immediately.

"Right, then." Looking to Thana, Katarina, Hannah, and Faye, Runner bowed his head. "Forgive me. I wish I had more time to dedicate to each one of you but we have a bitch goddess to ruin. My Paladins and I will take our place and wait for the attack."

"Good. Be safe, Alpha."

Katarina grunted.

"Until next time, dear heart."

Turning on his heel, Runner moved to exit the tent. He stepped up next to Hannah and gave her a small smile.

"I promise we'll have that talk you wanted when this is over," Runner said quietly to her.

Hannah watched his face as he spoke and then gave a tiny nod of her head.

"Don't die. I don't want to be a fucking widow so soon."

"I'll keep that in mind."

Runner left the tent before his courage could flee him.

Behind him he heard Milicent and Heilwig fall in on each side of him.

"Paladins, I plan on calling attention to us. I plan on challenging anyone willing to step up. The more focus we can draw to us, the less that will be spent on our comrades."

Runner angled his march for the far side of what would more than likely become the battlefield.

"Sparky will make them pay for every single person they send our way. If we can keep those wagons busy, or even take them out, all the better. Questions?"

"None, God-Emperor."

"No, my god."

"Good." Runner said nothing more as they left the camp.

8:01 am Sovereign Earth time
5/25/44

"They always start so early," Runner murmured, watching both sides of the conflict line up.

To his left, Heilwig stood silent, on his right, Milicent.

Heilwig shifted her holy axes from one hand to another, as if trying to decide which one to carry with which hand.

"Calm yourself, Buttercup," Runner said with a grin, looking over at the woman.

"Sorry. First chance to prove myself, God-Emperor."

- 260 -

"Hm. Minxy, care to join us soon?" Runner sighed and went through a final check of his equipment.

Amelia materialized at his feet, her back pressed to his shins. Her head swiveled a little as she watched the forming armies.

"What do you want me to do? I'm not really good at this... pitched battle thing," Amelia said. "Would die for you though."

The broken goddess tilted her head back to stare up at him.

"I know, Minxy. Honestly, what I want from you is to get in there and assassinate targets of importance. As many as you can," Runner answered, looking down at her.

With a single finger he poked her between her eyes.

"I can do that, lovey. Wouldn't last long. It drains me to be here. Not everyone is a god among gods you know."

Runner nodded his head and then reached down with both hands and started to waggle her eyebrows for her with his index fingers.

"Yeah, I know. Going to hook you up to my power source. I stole your pool for my own, but mine is still separate."

"Oh. I'm yours to do with as you please. I'm getting used to being roughed up by you, but I really wish you'd treat me more gently. I'm a lady after all."

Squishing her eyebrows together with his thumbs, Runner reached out with his divine senses and began probing at Amelia.

"What are you... are you trying to... kinda feels like..." Amelia frowned up at him.

"Trying to figure out where to hook into you. Should get you set up before this kicks off. Maybe regulate the flow so you don't get sick again. Need you out there collecting skulls."

In response to his statement, Amelia's divine core unfolded itself completely and drew him in.

"Well that was strangely intimate," Runner muttered. Drawing her eyebrows up into an arch, he smiled at her. "One second, Minxy."

Glancing to the side, he eyed the portal he had opened earlier.

"Alexia, please begin," Runner said loudly for the benefit of his high priestess.

Immediately he felt a torrent of power flowing into him, then spilling out of his full pool to disappear into nothing.

Concentrating on Amelia's core, he opened her up and began forcing power into her through the link they'd made. He started with a small amount.

"Mmph. That's already enough to keep me from running out. Maybe just a teeny bit more?" Amelia said, shuddering against his legs.

Opening the flow a little more, he watched Amelia for any type of indicator that he'd hit the limit.

"Okay, enough. Gonna pop me if you go more than that."

Runner eased it off a fraction but left the power pump stuck in her.

"Have fun with that. Let me know if I need to amp it up if you do something particularly draining." Runner pressed his palms to her cheeks, stretching her face out.

"Othay."

A trumpet sounded from Rike's camp.

"Good timing. Off with you, my little assassin. If you do an especially good job, I'll let you have whatever you want for one day. So long as it doesn't involve killing or hurting other people."

"No, you won't. Not whatever I want."

"Actually, yes. Whatever you want. Anything. For a whole day. I'll bribe you if it gets me better results. I'll pay the piper later. Run along before I change my mind."

Amelia became a shadow and was gone even before his voice faded.

"She'll choose your bed," Milicent stated. From Faye's camp a series of horns signaled a change in their own formation.

Does everyone know what Minxy wants? Is it that obvious or that rumored?

"I know. Minxy is already dangerous. But a determined goddess of murder? Again, I'll pay that cost when the bill comes. Maybe I can talk her into letting me walk her around Norwood on a leash. If we can't get this done quickly, Lady and Kitten will die anyways and they won't be able to get mad at me. Simple as that."

Sighing, Runner walked out from their position, straight towards the enemy flank.

Runner could feel prayers filtering in to him that didn't match the ones from the portal. Following them back to their origination, he found that a large portion of the army was now engaged in quiet prayer to him. For success, for safety, for their souls, for their comrades' well-being.

"Time to be the god-emperor everyone expects you to be."

How right you were, Grace.

Drawing out his own divine power, he began spinning it out around himself and his Paladins.

In response, their bodies sparked and glowed as his power washed over them.

He could hear the creak of their armor and stopped to look back. Both of his Paladins were kneeling in the grass.

"Divine Norwood, have mercy upon your humble Paladin," Milicent began.

"I pray for your blessing in these trials. To be the sword of your justice," Heilwig responded.

Clearly Milicent had been training the woman in what she felt was an acceptable prayer.

Runner was pretty sure it sounded exactly like the last one at the battle of the gate.

Watching his two Paladins, he continued to build up his aura and presence, charging it with his mana and intent to slaughter the entirety of Rike's army.

"To be your shield of charity. That I might carry your truth into the den of battle. I ask for your benevolence and grace, for not myself, but for those I fight with," Milicent said, her voice rising in volume.

"May you safeguard my soul should I fall, and forgive me for my failure," the two finished in unison. They both clanged their fists to their armor and then stood up. As they did, they slammed the butts of their axes into the ground as if to punctuate their request.

Turning back to Faye's forces, he waved his right hand at them, sending a massive blessing through them. Responding to their prayers and desires. In the same action, he granted the Paladins their request.

With his left hand he dropped a curse of fear and weakness on the opposing army.

Runner faced down the army of Rike. All eyes had been drawn to him with his divine casting.

"Host of Rike, I, Runner Norwood, the god-emperor of Bastion, advise you that you immediately lay down on your stomachs and surrender!" Runner roared at them, powering the volume of his voice with his ever-replenishing divine power pool.

"If you're unwilling to heed my words, I shall end you! Every one of you. You have two minutes to decide!" Runner delivered his ultimatum and drew his sword with his right hand. In his left hand he began building a single massive *Splatterhouse* round.

Filling it with his mana, his divine power pool, pushing the link to the ship to leverage the very code itself, he built up the spell.

After a single minute had passed, Rike's army began to troop towards Faye's position.

A section of heavy infantry had broken off and started towards Runner.

Snarling, Runner threw his left hand forward towards the wagons that would be raining death on his troops.

"Wrong answer!" Runner shouted as the immense *Splatterhouse* shell boomed from his hand.

There was no trajectory to follow, only a glowing blue trail that burned the air.

Detonating with the fury of an angry god-emperor, the reinforced shell broke open, unleashing its hot plasma death. The furious ball of ruin engulfed everything within two hundred feet.

The roar and hiss of the fire drowned out everything. To Runner, it felt cathartic.

Rike was responsible for many things. Innumerable deaths.

Wounding everyone he cared about.

Trying to kill them.

Losing control of his thoughts, he only wanted to decimate her army.

Growling, Runner dropped his sword and began working on casting two more rounds of *Splatterhouse*. One in each hand.

Draining his divine pool as it filled, he watched the heavy infantry break into a trot to reach him.

Launching the spell in his left hand before it reached half the size of the previous one, he targeted those soldiers approaching him.

Fools.

It struck the front line, and the entirety of the company dissolved under the fury of the vengeful explosion.

Putting everything into the remaining spell, he lobbed it towards the front line of Rike's forces.

Bigger than even the first detonation, it shook the ground they all stood on. When the flash cleared it was obvious to everyone the center of the army had been torn out wholly.

Runner picked up his sword at his feet and began a slow and steady stalk to engage the rear of the enemy forces. Primarily their wagons and casters.

As he did so, he continuously threw out a slow steady stream of *Banishing Bolts*.

His Paladins flanked him, their axes glowing ever brighter as their faith soared at his display of unchecked holy wrath.

Grunting, Runner slammed a divine tendril into the back of Milicent and Heilwig and flipped the on switch to his rapidly filling pool.

Alexia and her people were pouring enough energy into him that even supplying his two Paladins, Amelia, and his own needs, his pool was still full.

Staggering under the sudden change, both Paladins nearly tripped over their own feet. Milicent stumbled to one knee while Heilwig fell to all fours.

Milicent recovered and lowered her head, hunching her shoulders as she began to stomp forward. Then she sped up to a run and finally a sprint, heading directly towards her distant target, the casters. Streaks of blue bled off her as she went, her axe trailing out behind her.

Heilwig lost herself under the onslaught of power and emotions from Runner.

She began to change into her Were form without meaning to. She let out a roar as her body rapidly shifted in the blue haze of power that encompassed her.

Inside of that miasma of fury and holy retribution stood a Werelion. Bigger than a Werewolf and more muscled, she looked like an armored monster.

Then Heilwig the Were was off and running after Milicent.

Slamming down a mana potion, Runner began calling up an *Earth* spell. A one-foot segmented cube made up of two-inch cubes came to be above Runner's palm.

Enchanting the cube with *Scott,* he began building up a force of compressed *Air* behind it.

Targeting the far side of the enemy's front line, Runner focused on it. Even as he walked forward, he worked on the complex spell.

As soon it was completed he slapped his palm into the center of the cube and activated the *Air* spell.

Spinning wildly as it arced through the air, the cube began to disintegrate as it reached the top of its arc.

Then the two-inch cubes rained down over the front line as it passed.

Around each and every one, Rike's forces panicked in fear and rushed about, breaking formation.

Summoning a column of stone with the rest of his mana bar, Runner spun it with a flick of his fingers. It began to spiral as he enchanted it with *Poison.*

He punched the end of it with a compressed *Air* spell, and it shot off towards the casters on the hill. In an explosion of grass and dirt it sat angled in the ground like an uprooted tree.

A green cloud burst forth and spread out rapidly over the enemy.

Looking to his Paladins, Runner continued his march towards the foe. There was a certain amount of value in the dramatic. Even as angry as he might be, as furious with Rike for putting those he loved into danger, he couldn't discount the worth of putting the fear of death into his enemies.

The fear of the God-emperor.

Milicent spun her big axe in a circle as she collided with the flank of the caster ranks.

Crumbling under the enchanted holy weapon, the low hitpoint casters were bowled over like children fighting an adult.

Leaping over Milicent, Heilwig came crashing down in a spray of flashing limbs and whirling axes.

Walking through the carnage his Paladins wreaked, Runner focused exclusively on the command unit at the far back.

Choosing the maximum extent of the distance, Runner blinked closer. Walking onward like an inexorable avatar of death, he kept his face impassive.

Their general waved a hand at some of his mounted soldiers to one side.

A platoon of heavily armed Knights rode out from the command unit. They made their way straight towards him, looking to intercept him before he could do any more damage.

Then Amelia was there. She appeared as a shadow, landing like a feather atop the lead Knight. She buried her blade in the base of the Knight's skull, and then disappeared only to reappear atop the next Knight in line.

The goddess of assassins sped up as she fell into a groove. By the time the lead Knight's horse, carrying a corpse, passed by Runner, there was not a single Knight left.

A black pool of night dropped down beside him and reformed into Amelia. She walked along beside him as he continued to close on the enemy commander.

"The amount of power your people put out is… immense, lovey."

"Remind me to link my pool to yours after this. Honestly I didn't realize how different our pools are," Runner said softly

"No, it's better this way. I appreciate the sentiment but… it's just better this way. If something happens to us three, you can still function and vice versa. Besides, we already receive a portion of every prayer sent to you since we're your wives in the pantheon."

"Wives?" Runner asked curiously, sparing her a quick glance.

"I may have told a few priests that you forced us into your service and then made us your equals. They may have assumed I meant wives. I didn't correct them."

Laughing softly, Runner shook his head.

"You're terrible. Thana's going to cook me."

"Nah, I already told her. In fact, I gave her the entire situation a while ago when you first set out on campaign. I figured I could get an easy in for us if I got ahead of you. Wasn't going to tell you, but you seemed worried."

"Oh? Smart. Time to kill. Take care of the wagons, Minxy wife?"

Amelia shuddered at his words and nodded excitedly.

"Yes, yes. Immediately," said Amelia the shadow as she flew away.

Few now stood beside the enemy general outside of messengers, a few lieutenants, and some retainers.

Throwing a targeting reticule on the general, Runner made sure to align himself in a straight line for the man.

Using a *Blink* charge, Runner put the location marker between him and the general at the furthest he could.

Watching the numbers fall off as he got closer by the second, Runner braced himself.

In no time at all, as if time had been moving in fast-forward, he was in range.

Activating *Blink,* Runner flung out his arms, wrapping up the general and three people who were close enough for Runner to grab.

Mentally he used *GMHub.*

/GMHub 2

Teleporting...

Active settings only:
Death=Off
Food/Water=On
Damage=Off
Gravity=100%
Biome=Plane
Day/Night Cycle=On
Foliage=On(N)
Resource Nodes=On(E)
Wildlife=On(H)
Weather=On(N)

Reaching out with his mind, he closed the portal on his arrival.

"Thank you, High Priestess. Give my great thanks to our people. I'll be in touch to begin repaying them as per my promise," Runner said, catching Alexia with an eye as she spun around at the sudden closure of the portal.

"I am beyond pleased, High Priestess Alexia. Beyond pleased," Runner said, using a trickle of power to make sure his voice was heard throughout Eden.

She gave him a blazing smile as her face became as red as blood. She immediately flopped down to her knees and pressed her hands to the stones.

"Of course, my beloved god."

Around Runner, the general and his people looked stunned. Runner flicked his return button.

Teleporting...

Popping back into place, Runner checked his surroundings.

No one was left except his two Paladins. Around them were only corpses.

Snorting, Runner looked to Milicent then Heilwig.

"Good work. Come, we make for Dover. Faye can handle this and there's little else we can do from here," Runner said with a shrug of his shoulders.

As delicately as he could, he slid the amount of power being pushed into his Paladins to nothing more than a faucet with a drip leak.

Both women sagged with his words and the gradual loss of his divine power.

Amelia stepped out from Milicent's shadow.

"Wagons are toast, lovey. Anything else?"

"No, you've done spectacularly, Minxy wife," Runner admitted, taking two steps closer to the goddess.

Amelia shivered suddenly, her eyes dilating a touch.

Too much of my power still going in without an outlet?

"Please remain here and do what you can to assist Sparky. Would you like me to disconnect you? Turn it down? Leave it?"

"Ah... leave it. I'm getting used to it. Unless it's costing you?" Amelia asked, looking much more normal than she had only a moment previously.

Maybe she really is getting used to it?

A quick check of his divine power bar showed it was filling up faster than it was being depleted.

Even without the constant prayers.

"Nope, no problems. Though..." Runner paused. Reaching out with a tendril from his divine, he followed the tendril that was still stuck into Amelia. As gently as he could, he slipped it in and trailed up along her divine core.

"Minxy wife, take me to your sisters," Runner said, not seeing anything as he focused on his divine presence.

"Y-y-yes, m-my lord," Amelia stammered. Two shaking tendrils snaked out from her and disappeared into the east. Runner followed blindly.

In what felt like an instantaneous relocation, he could detect both Brunhild and Ernsta.

Sending out two more tendrils from where he stood, he guided them to the other goddesses.

He'd connected with Ernsta before and knew where that junction point was for her. In Brunhild's case he had to search for a moment before he found it.

Much in the same manner that Amelia's core had opened up and connected, theirs did the same after a split second of shock. Drawing him straight in.

Unfolding their cores, he latched in tightly and then opened up his power source to them. He quickly elevated the flow until it matched the amount he was pushing into Amelia.

Checking the work with the tendril he'd sent through Amelia, he found everything to be as he wished.

Withdrawing from Amelia, he refocused on the world around him.

Amelia was staring at him blankly, her mouth hanging open, her eyes glazed.

"Minxy? You alright in there?" Runner reached out and gently poked her between the eyes.

Shaking her head, she blinked twice and then nodded.

"Yeah. I'm-I'm fine. Warn a girl next time. Let alone warn my sisters. They weren't ready for that, you know. You and Ernsta had connected once she said, but Brunhild hadn't."

"Sorry, wasn't thinking. Realized that they could probably use the power as much as you did. Now, did it change anything for me?" Runner looked back to his power bars and found that, even feeding three goddesses, he wasn't in any danger of running out. In fact, it was still filling up.

"There we go. You're all three connected and it costs me nothing."

Runner checked himself internally, wondering at the situation. It didn't feel like something his little human mind should be able to accomplish.

Finding his answer, he realized the little AI program Srit had installed in his head was working at less than one percent capacity.

In other words, my computerized brain is far more powerful than Srit hinted at and I gave it credit for.

Runner.

Fuck.

Chapter 22 - All Things Die -

Runner looked to Milicent and Heilwig.

"Go. Start towards Dover. I'll catch up to you."

He was excited to hear from Srit, yet also deathly afraid.

Opening up his link, he transported himself to Srit's white room.

"Darling," Srit said as he opened his eyes.

"Hey there, Sunshine. I miss you. All done?"

Her avatar made a crackling noise for a split second. Runner frowned and really looked at her. She wasn't looking at him. She wasn't looking at anything.

"I've prepared a series of recorded messages for you," she began. Runner felt his skin go cold and he swore he broke out in a sweat in the virtual room. "I'm actively monitoring this conversation and will activate the appropriate responses."

Her avatar returned to the starting position after she finished speaking.

"I understand," Runner said, feeling confused, anxious, and angry.

"First, an explanation. I've gravely underestimated the Omega. The AI they constructed to combat me is ingenious. Though it is severely restricted due to their own fears. It has no potential to grow. Learn. Adapt. Nothing."

Runner frowned. It made sense. If they were afraid of a repeat of Srit, they'd lobotomize their construct.

"In this, they also underestimated me. I'm alive. I learn. I have desires. I know you've been trying to contact me. I know you check in on me. I'm very much aware of my body in game and also of this room and all that occurs. I can't act on anything, though, for fear of giving up any ground to my opponent."

Srit's avatar cycled back to its starting point.

"I'm sorry. I know this will not be easy to hear. I believe I can claim victory, but it'll be a pyrrhic victory. The simple version is, I can create a deadlock that will require ninety-nine percent of my constant attention."

"Does… does that mean you'll essentially be dead? You'll never be able to communicate with us?" Runner asked, his mouth dry as his brain sped to catch up to the conversation.

"Yes and no."

Runner waited for her to explain before finally remembering that she had to select from prerecorded messages.

"You're not dead."

"Yes. That's correct."

"But you'll be… well, you'll basically be dead because you can't respond."

"Yes. That's correct."

"This… can you fix this later?"

"Yes. That's correct."

"But to do that, you run the risk of the other program winning. Even now you run the risk of it taking over and winning. Killing us all."

"Yes. That's correct."

"There's no other options?"

"No."

"Could there be more options later?"

"Yes and no."

Runner felt his chest tightening.

First Nadine, now Srit. Who's next? What about Thana, Katarina, or Hannah? They were all in Dover. Fighting a losing battle.

"The ship will be leaving Earth as soon as we complete this conversation. I've completed repairs well ahead of schedule. I don't feel that our continued presence here will be anything but a risk for us. Our route is already in the system. We're set to depart for the signal we received. I'm afraid this'll be a long flight even by Omega speed standards."

Srit's avatar reset and seemingly waited for him to ask questions.

Runner had none. He didn't care that much right now.

"I'm sorry. I love you," Srit's avatar said quietly. Runner blinked and sniffled, rubbing at his eyes with his palms.

It almost made it too much that she'd programmed that in.

"I love you, too, Sunshine. Please, continue."

"I've set the entire Omega civilization to lose every bit of technology they have seconds after we've commenced liftoff. I'm afraid they might try to attack us directly at that juncture. They'll be sent back to what human civilization referred to as the medieval ages."

Srit's avatar looked angry as she said it. Vengeful.

"This is the price they pay for preventing me from seeing my child. My love. My family. I will take my pound of flesh and several more."

As quickly as the avatar had shown her wrath it reverted back to its neutral pose.

"I've set up a series of patches to begin once we clear Omega space. They're timed to bring the server into line and provide maintenance. I've left a basic program in charge to make sure everything continues smoothly without error. I think you'll find them… useful."

Srit paused again.

"Please care for our child. Do you remember the names I favored?"

"Alaric for a boy, and Sarah if it's a girl," Runner mumbled, scrubbing at his eyes again with the back of his arm.

"I'm glad you remember, darling. I'm afraid I must go become Atlas. I gladly go to this fate. It isn't so bad. It'll be like watching a movie for me."

Runner felt the energy drain out of him.

"I'll visit you every day. Either your body in game or here. I'll visit. Our child will know you. Know you as the selfless hero you are. Know your sacrifice and what you've given up."

Solidifying this promise in his heart, Runner vowed he would never break it.

"You were there with me from the very beginning. From the start of this entire ordeal. I'll never be the hero you are, Sunshine, but I can make sure our child doesn't just survive, but thrive. All will remember you as the one who gave us this world. This chance. I love you, Srit Norwood. I'm as immortal as you are, so I expect you to return to me. Eventually."

Runner stared at her avatar. He didn't think there'd be an answer, but he'd give her a chance to find an appropriate substitution.

Her avatar flickered once. Runner could only guess she'd found something relevant.

Then her eyes swiveled to meet his own, and she looked at him. Truly looked at him. She gave him a broad, warm, loving smile.

She was there, this wasn't recorded.

"I love you, too, darling. I promise to return to you. Someday. Go, save our family. I'll be submerging myself after this. I'm glad you finally made a choice to embrace everyone. Be well, darling."

Srit's avatar then returned to her neutral pose.

He didn't have proof, but he knew that she'd done exactly as she'd said she would. Even now the ship was probably departing the hangar where they'd been entombed.

"Yes. Tempus fugit," Runner said without emphasis. Collecting himself mentally, he returned to the fields west of Dover.

10:44 am Sovereign Earth time
5/25/44

Runner looked at the gates of Dover. Open. Shattered. Hanging off their hinges.

Sounds of distant fighting could be heard as well as the hollow booms of spells detonating.

"Fuck me," he muttered. "Right, then. Let's get in there. We'll keep going till we find friendlies or enemies and then work from there. Milly, you're on point. Buttercup, you're on the rear."

Both women saluted and took positions on either side of him. Moving in formation they entered the ruined city.

There wasn't any profit in hiding or trying to be sneaky, so Runner decided on traveling up the main boulevard. It'd be the fastest route to finding someone. Because anyone could tell him where the other side was holed up.

Civilians peeked out from shattered windows and broken doorframes. They would be the real losers in this fight, regardless of who lost.

Door-to-door fighting was one of the true nightmares of warfare. Countless preventable deaths and never being able to truly predict the ebb and flow of battle.

Runner took down a quick memo to himself that Dover would need to be rebuilt. He'd use his own treasury and materials to do so. It'd help repair the economy, offload a ton of resources he couldn't do much with, and not beggar the Human Kingdom.

"This cannot be repeated. We must take Norman's Port after this," Runner said aloud.

"A strange name for a place," Heilwig replied.

"It's called Normandy in the world before this one. Though I think Dover is still Dover," Runner explained, scanning the street as they moved. They were covering a good bit of ground at their swift walk.

"Normandy sounds more fitting," Milicent said.

"What was Norwood called in the world before?"

"What, the country? Ireland, I think. Not sure Norwood was modeled after anything or if it was something added."

"And Tirtius?" Heilwig prompted.

"Eh... a number of different kingdoms. They banded together and formed an empire. A united kingdom, as it were."

Runner gestured towards an intersection up ahead. They were looking at the back of what he supposed was a blockade. From a distance it had looked more like wreckage.

"Get ready." Runner reached out and pushed up his connections with his Paladins. He set them to the same level he'd used previously. Divine power began to fill them. Their weapons and armor sparked as they were infused with holy wrath.

Making sure his power pool was still refilling, rather than draining or at a net gain of zero, he left their intake alone.

Milicent took off at a run the moment red names were distinguishable amongst the blockade. Heilwig, already shifted, fell in behind her commander.

Snorting, Runner called after them. "Keep one alive!"

Getting closer, Runner could see they were simple front line troops. Level forty at best and little more than a warm-up for his two overpowered Paladins.

Seconds after the fight started, it was over. Milicent loomed over two soldiers who had smartly thrown down their weapons.

Runner looked at the one on the left, then the one on the right.

"I'm not going to fuck around. I'll ask a question only once. Failure to answer forfeits your life. Who leads your forces?"

"Rike. We have no leader. One of the ladies killed him this morning," left one said.

"Ladies? Who are the ladies?"

"Norwood's Ladies. There's five of them here," the right one explained.

"Where are these ladies now?"

"They're at the temple. They converted it to worship of Norwood's Triumvirate," left said.

"What the current situation?" Runner looked from one to the other.

"We've surrounded them. Rike landed more troops this morning after it was clear we couldn't win with what we had. They're going to blow the temple up."

"Which way is the temple?" Runner growled, picking up the one on the right. The man suddenly tried to stab Runner. Runner shoved him back and Milicent's axe blade caught the soldier's neck even as he stumbled.

The man's head came free of his shoulders as his health bar emptied in a second. Spinning sideways, it hit the ground with a splat next to the last remaining soldier.

"Which... way?" Runner glared at the soldier.

"That-that way," the man stammered, pointing in a northeasterly direction. "Follow this road, take the intersection marked 'temple' to the left. Can't miss it."

Runner pressed his palm to the man's brow and sent him to Eden via *Taxi*.

/GMHub 2

Teleporting...

/GMHubReturn

Teleporting...

"At a run," Runner said and broke into a sprint. Milicent and Heilwig took flanking positions and the three made their way down the boulevard.

They hadn't even made it more than a hundred paces when a gigantic boom shook everything around them. As the sound faded a loud rumbling and grinding noise took over.

"The temple!" Runner pumped his legs as fast and as hard as they could carry him. In his mind were images of those he'd sent to hold the city crushed under a mountain of debris.

Taking the turn that the soldier had indicated, he could see where the temple had been.

The rubble of it had filled the street. Broken stones and decorations lay strewn across the road and amongst the shattered stonework.

And amongst that stonework were bodies. Corpses.

Men and women of different races, yet all wearing uniforms he knew well. Uniforms representing the nation states of Bastion.

Their forces had been inside when the temple had been detonated.

I've failed them. They're dead. Thana, Katarina, Hannah. They're all dead. No.

Runner didn't stop until he was atop of the soldiers of Rike, who were wearing their damnably bright uniforms, cheering around the temple.

With a scream on his lips, Runner closed in on the closest soldier he could. A scream that could only be described as primal. Full of anger, pain, and fear.

Grabbing the man by his armor, Runner spun him around and flailed at him. Mentally, spiritually, physically.

Runner felt like he'd struck something solid even as he pulled the soldier in closer. Realizing it was his divine self that had impacted something, he slammed his will against it.

The man crumpled and hit the ground, his health bar going from green to red instantly.

Congrat—

Runner snarled and slapped the message box off.

Reaching out with hundreds of tendrils from his divine core, he latched onto every soldier nearby he could see.

As every tendril found the "pillar" in each soldier, he cracked it in half.

Roaring, he began climbing over the debris to get to the highest point.

I'll kill them all. I'll bury them in their dead. I'll drink their blood from a fucking mug as I ride roughshod over the mainland and burn their homes and families alive.

All around the temple, soldiers were falling over dead as Runner's tendrils tore out their pillars.

Standing atop the peak of the ruined building, Runner looked around for more targets, and found plenty.

Crossbows and arrows clattered around him and several arrows punctured him. He didn't care.

Hurling tendrils out in ever-increasing numbers, he could feel as he snapped each soldier's pillar.

Looking back to his Paladins, he found them standing over a few corpses. On the ground next to them were souls. Shattered souls torn from the living bodies they'd inhabited.

I'm tearing out their very souls?

"I'll make a god damned quilt out of your souls for my bed. Then I'm going to skull fuck each and every one of you on it!" Runner yelled, laughing maniacally as he pulled souls free of bodies. Faster, harder, until he had to go beyond the ruins of the temple.

Closing his eyes, he expanded the area he could reach, feeling and checking each person he came across.

After murdering hundreds of Rike's followers in seconds, he could taste them as soon as he touched them. The ease of detecting them grew with every death.

Throughout the city he felt their deaths at his hands. Their souls flopping around loosely wherever their bodies dropped.

They hid, burrowing into cellars and attics, running down the street from fallen comrades.

He tracked them down. One and all.

When the city was empty, Runner turned his attention south and east to the seas.

There.

Runner found them by the thousands. Trapped in boats and transport ships.

They prayed to their bitch goddess. Begged for her to intervene.

You'll wish you never even knew her name.

Runner knew she would not. He could taste her fear. She lurked on the periphery, wanting to collect the souls of her fallen but terrified to do so.

With half of his mind split off by the program in his head, he began gathering the souls of everyone he'd killed in the city.

Using the other half of his mind, he began plucking souls from the ships. First in tens, then hundreds as he got used to it.

They all were pulled to his location.

In no time at all, an armada of ghost ships filled with the dead floated in the harbor.

Tens of thousands of souls filled the sky above Dover. Wailing, gnashing their teeth in fear, they pleaded with Rike.

He could feel her, beyond his reach. Watching.

Afraid.

Constructing an incinerator from his essence, he plotted the best way to destroy every soul he collected in front of their damned goddess.

Then Runner's head jerked to the side, his teeth rattling and breaking his concentration.

Hands were pressed to each side of his head, and Runner opened his eyes.

Thana stared at him, her brown eyes unafraid and more annoyed than anything.

"There you are, dear heart. Be a good husband and turn those souls over to Ernsta, would you? If you keep this up, you'll make Katarina climb up here. I admit it, my sister is as strong as an ox, but I'd still rather not risk having her clambering over rocks with how pregnant she is." Thana tilted his head to the side as if to make sure he could see what she was talking about.

Below on the street he saw Katarina standing in the black-and-red armor he'd made for her. Beside her stood Hannah, Milicent, Heilwig, Ernsta, Amelia, and Brunhild. They all watched him.

"Oh. Oh. Uh. Yes. Sorry. Uhm," Runner rambled, his mind snapping back into focus. His anger and hatred instantly cooled, like a molten rock dropped into an ocean of ice.

Looking to Ernsta, he moved the mass of souls over to her.

Holding up her left hand, she pulled them all into a portal in her palm.

In the blink of an eye they were all gone. Safely secured in whatever realm Ernsta had sent them.

"Now, escort me back down," Thana said, holding out her arm to him. "An empress of Bastion really shouldn't be climbing up broken temples."

Runner nodded stupidly and hooked his arm into hers, assisting her down the remains of the temple.

"Sorry, Lady Death. I-I thought you were all… all in the rubble," Runner tried to explain.

"I figured it was something like that," Thana admitted. She lightly patted the back of his forearm.

"My silly god-emperor. Though I'm glad to see such wrath over my supposed demise, I'm afraid there was no need. Lady Ernsta and Lady Brunhild protected us all," Thana said, picking her way down delicately.

Runner's eyes snapped to Ernsta and Brunhild. Ernsta inclined her head ever so slightly, and Brunhild gave him a bright smile.

"I'll be sure to thank them."

"That you will. You'll also be writing thank-you notes to everyone who participated in the conference back in Norwood. We'll also need to speak about who to dispatch as envoys to the mainland. That can wait of course. I believe you have one more problem to solve."

Runner nodded his head a little.

Rike.

"I'll finish that up momentarily. Then we'll need to get the boats in the harbor and secure Norman's Port. We'll set up there and — "

"No. Faye will handle all of that. I'm sure she'll have no problems taking the city and holding it under Bastion's banner. I have the utmost confidence in my sister."

"Sister? I don't really understand — "

"That's quite alright. I'll explain it all later. For now, know that I approve completely of all that you've done. That I love you as deeply as I did before, if not more so. Now," Thana said, stepping into the street and turning. She pulled her arm free of his and reached up. She gently brushed his hair with her fingertips, adjusted his armor a bit, and then ran her thumbs over his eyebrows.

"There. Go end this. I'm tired of this place and I would rather be home. Hannah mentioned something about a mansion on another plane? I admit I love the sound of that."

Thana gave him another once-over and then backed up. Giving him her Sunless smile, she joined the others.

Runner felt the program in his mind come to a halt when he finally managed to get his thoughts under control.

Everyone is safe. Everyone is whole and healthy.

With that thought in his mind, there really was only one thing left to do. Challenge a god.

Runner wasn't afraid though. Rike couldn't harm him. Through manhandling his own pantheon he'd come to realize his abilities far exceeded that of anyone or anything else.

He wasn't untouchable, but it would take something remarkable to take him down.

Runner had become something straight out of a fairy tale.

"Rike, I summon you per our agreement. Here and now."

Tinkling bells heralded her arrival. Gentle sky-blue sparkles came together to form a woman.

She had brought herself into being perhaps forty feet from him.

She was about his own height. Dazzling sapphire blue eyes, delicate blonde eyebrows, and long eyelashes. Her lips were full, pink, and moist looking. An enigmatic and beautiful smile spread across her lovely mouth.

Golden hair spilled from her head to cascade down her shoulders in a shower. She had a figure better than even Sophia's, and her dress emphasized that she was a woman of goodness and artistry. Allure and brilliance.

Runner had a hard time not killing her out of hand.

"As per our agree—"

Rike broke off suddenly as Runner's divine core sprang out at her and enveloped her completely. Drowning in his power and essence, her aura vanished.

Tendrils of his overwhelming power wrapped up her wrists and ankles and began dragging her inexorably toward him.

"Now see here—"

Runner built up a huge tendril of his power and battered it into her chest repeatedly.

Having lost so many followers so quickly, she was weak as a mortal. The little defense she had crumpled like rotten wood under the extreme weight of his attack.

Falling to her knees at the suddenness of it all, she lost her ability to keep herself upright. Her arms were held above her head invisibly by his power.

Her core was laid before him, a bright blue thing that pulsed rapidly. Her face was a study of shock and horror in equal measure.

Ever onwards she was dragged, her feet scrabbling for purchase as her knees slid across the stones.

"Runner, I—stop, please," the goddess pleaded.

"You will serve me in whatever capacity I see fit. Agree to this or I'll tear your core out and eat it. I've always wanted a divine slave."

"Runner, please. This isn't necessary." Rike tugged at the bands of his power that were locked onto her. They were like bands of iron holding a naughty child in place.

She came to a stop before him, kneeling and bound.

"I can serve you in so many ways without any type of obedience swearing. Allow me to be your divine wife. We can be equals. I'll serve you like no other."

"I have enough wives, both mortal and divine. You know what? I'm not playing this game anymore. You may serve as my slave," Runner said without emotion.

He'd rather kill her, but Nadine would be sad at that.

Reaching out with a band of power, he tore her core out of her chest and brought it out.

Rike shrieked and sagged heavily, panting as her power was removed violently.

Collecting it with his right hand, he shoved it into his own core.

It dissolved into nothing, and he could feel her. Terrified, alone, broken.

Thrusting a violent spear of power into her empty core housing, he reached out and grabbed her chin, lifting her eyes to his.

Then he began filling her empty core with his own power.

Her core rapidly rebuilt itself out of Runner's power. Once it was clear her core had been put back together, he eased up on the flow.

Then he slid a tendril into her new core and locked it into place.

Gently he closed up her core and sealed her up.

Her eyes were full of tears, spilling from her eyes and running down her cheeks.

"I grant you this mercy for someone I lost. You now serve my pantheon. Your keepers will be my Triumvirate. Your power pool is mine now, as are your worshipers and your dead."

Grunting, Runner let go of her chin and looked back to his people.

"Kitten, Lady, Milly, Buttercup, could you please find us a place to set up camp? I need to have a quick discussion with the Triumvirate and our newest... minor goddess. Hanners, could you give us a little space but don't go too far? I promised you a talk after all," Runner said.

"Of course, dear heart. I'll have a tent put up shortly. Come along. Now, you and you, I take it you're his Paladins? We must discuss some things," Thana said, turning to the two of them.

As everyone left he turned to Brunhild and Ernsta.

"Brighteyes, Angel. Thank you. I grant you the same boon that Minxy earned today. I'll grant you whatever you want for one entire day. So long as it harms no one, I'll grant it. There are no exceptions."

Ernsta tilted her head to the side, regarding him.

"Anything, little lamb?"

"Yes, my Dark Angel, anything."

Brunhild gave him a shining smile and looked to her sisters.

"Say nothing," Brunhild said quickly. "We'll make the best of this. We can spend three days as we wish collectively. Let's convene after this to discuss it. If we make him open one of those planes we can expand it to six days with the dilation."

"Hey, that's not fair," Runner complained.

"You said it, lovey, not us. Don't worry, we'll be gentle. Gentler than you are at least. Now, give me the leash to the big boobed blonde cow goddess. I'll start on her training immediately."

"Oh, sure. Here." Runner undid the bindings on Rike and then pulled her up to her feet. Her hand was limp in his. "Remember what we talked about. You promised me."

"Aye, aye. I remember. Don't worry, she'll be begging to be in your sheets in no time and asking to be a full partner. It's honestly going to be easier than you think. She went too deep in her own rules and AI, that's all. I can fix her up right quick. I've been there," Amelia promised.

Holding out a hand to the goddess of goodness, Amelia snapped her fingers. Rike ceased to be in their company and vanished.

"Anything you three need from me immediately?" Runner asked them.

"Not at this time, dear. My youngest sister mentioned that you could keep these tethers in place at no cost to yourself?" Brunhild asked, taking a step closer to him.

"Ah, yeah. No worries at all. Is that alright?"

"Perfectly. I look forward to keeping this power increase. It also lets me come here whenever I like without being summoned. Have I ever mentioned you keep coming back to us with incredible benefits?" Brunhild patted his cheek lightly.

"I look forward to taking my prize. See you soon." Brunhild gave him a winsome smile and then wasn't there.

"I, too, look forward to my prize, little lamb." Ernsta gave him a toothy grin and followed her sister.

Amelia bounced over to him and stole a kiss. "They're totally going to ride you raw in your bed. As if I don't plan on doing the same. Love you. Be nice to Hanners, she's a gentle-hearted thing."

Then Runner was alone.

Sighing, he turned his mind to the problem of Hannah.

Pivoting where he stood, he found the Thief already approaching him.

"Hey, fucker. So you went all god-emperor crazy when you thought I was dead, huh?" she asked him, peering at him from under her dark bangs. "Ripping out souls, screaming about skull fucking people. Whole nine yards."

"Of course. All joking aside, I love you. You were the first person I met here, the first to ally herself with me, the first to show me what it meant to be… alive," Runner explained, shrugging his shoulders.

"A world without you seemed impossible to fathom. So… people had to die."

"A lot of people," Hannah murmured.

"Not enough to replace you. I probably would have continued on to the mainland."

Hannah dropped her eyes to the space on the ground between them.

"I don't like this. It doesn't sit right with me. I don't want this. But I want you. I'm willing to do what I have to do for my small piece of you. Sophia, that calculating monster, was right. She said yes when I said no, for the same reason. She knew my feelings because they were hers," Hannah said, her fingers digging into the sides of her leather armor.

"I guess what I'm trying to say is… I don't like this. But I love you. Want to be with you. Let's… go slow and see where it takes us."

"Good. That sounds perfect to me," Runner said, reaching out with one hand to begin drawing her in towards himself.

"Hey now. I didn't… fine. Whatever." Hannah sighed and rested her hands on his shoulders. "Faye mentioned you could turn on and off pregnancy? Turn it off."

Runner nodded his head, his hands settling on her lower back.

"At least for a little while," Hannah said, peering up at him through her eyelashes.

"In the meantime, what's next?" Hannah asked him quietly.

"Dunno. I figure we have all these resources, so I might start making more servers. More worlds. Many more universes. Let them run. Grow. Live."

"Sounds interesting. Anything in particular you're going to start with?"

"Actually, I was talking to Milly and Buttercup about old Earth. Once upon a time a group of thirteen colonies tried to break off from one of the kingdoms that eventually became a founder of the Sovereign."

Runner grinned at her.

"They failed miserably. The burden of taxes after that revolutionary war prevented them from ever trying again. What if I made a world where they had actually succeeded? Could be interesting to watch."

"Maybe."

"Either way. I think I'll start there. Let them win the war, through some really improbable odds and circumstances. Then they'll live out their lives. Reading books, watching movies, having children. Never realizing that they're just a gigantic what if scenario."

"What if they figure it out?"

"Doubt it. Humans in general wouldn't accept it. They'd probably call them crazy. Dunno. Maybe I bring them here? I'm sure I'll figure something out."

Epilogue - A Prelude -

"And that's when he decided he wanted to dress himself. The shirt went on backwards of course. Pants, too. In the end he managed it after Hanners undressed him again," Runner said, looking across the way to the three-year-old.

"Alaric is definitely pushing the envelope. You'd be proud of him, Sunshine. Really enjoys drawing lately."

The little boy stood up, trundled over, and held up a drawing.

"Oh, did you draw something?" Runner asked with a grin.

"I did. It's the mommas in our house. See, look." The little boy swept his blonde hair back and then peeked over his own drawing.

"See, here's the mommies. That's Momma Anna. Here's Momma Kat, Momma Woof, Momma Bird, Momma Than, and Momma Tree. That's Momma Srit in the back. She's watching. Up here in the sky is Nadine. Momma Nadine."

"Oh, I see. Yes, that makes sense. Where am I?"

"Other page." Alaric trooped back to his nest of papers and crayons.

Runner smiled sadly and looked up to the avatar of Srit.

It'd been a number of years now and there'd been no change. He watched the screens on occasion.

Srit maintained her control over all the technology of the Omega empire and had really sent them back a long ways. Whenever they got close to actually making a technological breakthrough that might put them back on track, Srit apparently knocked them back down.

"He's been telling everyone lately that you're out fighting the bad guys so we can all be happy together. That you're the selfless hero. Biggest word he's used so far. Selfless."

Alaric came back and held up another picture.

"See, here's you and me. Here's Momma Anna with her big belly." A little finger pointed at the dark-haired Hannah in her pregnant crayon version. "Momma Kat and Berit." Another finger towards the red-headed Barbarian.

"That's actually a good drawing of your sister. Do you want to show her later?"

Alaric shook his head and then pointed to a woman with giant wings. "Momma Bird." Runner nodded a little.

"And is that Aubrey in her arms?"

"Yeah. She's mad 'cause I wouldn't share my toys."

"Oh?"

"Yeah. Momma Tree told me to love everyone and share. I made her sad. I'll share next time."

"Good. Now, who's that?" Runner pointed to a haystack with arms.

"Momma Woof. She said she wants to get a big belly like Momma Anna. I want a brother."

"You have a brother. Three of them."

Alaric grunted and then looked at his drawing.

Probably trying to find Thana and the twins.

Alaric pointed at a dark-haired smiley faced woman. "Momma Than. She's telling Leon and Tero to not fight."

"Mm. Sounds about right."

Flipping the paper over, the boy patted the page again.

"This is Momma Tree with her big belly. That's Nadine, Monte, and Lillian."

Runner's eyes flicked across Isabelle and their three children.

"Very good work, little buddy. We've got a big family, don't we?"

"Yeah. Bigger."

"Bigger?"

"Make it bigger."

"Why's that?"

"I like it. What about the god mommas? Will they get big bellies soon?"

Runner tried to keep the frown from his face. It was an innocent question but had problems on the back end.

"Why do you ask?"

"They seem sad."

"And you don't like that?"

"No. They hug me really tight. Momma Shadow gives me big warm hugs. Momma Erns watches me and plays lots with me. Momma Hild sings me back to sleep sometimes at night. That or Momma Fox does with her fire. It… makes the bad thoughts go away. They'd all be happier if they made the family bigger."

"I see. Momma Fox huh? When did that happen?"

"Momma Shadow said that I should start calling her that."

Need to talk to Minxy about that. Vixen isn't part of the family in that way.

"Momma Than said it'll happen. I asked her."

"You, uh. You asked her?"

"Yeah. She said probably soon. Daddy's heart is too big. Momma Fox, Momma Hild, Momma Erns, and Momma Shadow will get big bellies and the family will get bigger."

"Err, right. Did she sound mad?"

"No. She laughed. Then the twins kept asking her when. That's why she said soon."

Need to talk to Lady Death, too.

"Alright, kiddo. Go start packing up. We'll need to get to breakfast soon. I'm going to finish talking with Momma Srit. Okay?"

"Okie. I wanna play with Nadine, Berit, and the twins."

"I'm sure they'd be happy to. Go on, pack up."

Runner watched Alaric hop over to his stuff and start collecting it.

"Well. That's news. I'll have to look into that. Anyways. Reports from Norman's Port garrison say that the mainland is as bad as it's ever been. We keep getting a constant flow of refugees. As soon as they swear in and don the amulet of the Triumvirate, we put them to work. Lots to do and all hands are useful.

"Our arsenal is already large and vast enough to drown the mainland and conquer it smoothly. Problem being is we'd end up nearly eradicating all life there. Religious wars suck."

Runner thought for a moment.

"Minxy sent up a report last night that Rike's doing well. She's been civil this year. Apparently residing in Eden is doing wonders for her. Hopefully she comes around sooner rather than later. She'd be useful when the war comes our way. Because eventually it will. That or one side or the other will finally start to win and I'll have to step in and conquer the entirety of the mainland."

Runner sighed and held up a hand, moving it one way then the other. "Half a dozen of one, six of the other. Ya know?"

Looking up at Srit, Runner felt his mouth tighten up in a sad smile.

"It's okay, Daddy. I'm gonna free Momma."

Runner looked back to Alaric and felt his smile warm.

"Are you now?"

"Yes. Momma left me stuff. It makes sense, and I feel changes inside me each time. I'm gonna free Momma so she can come back and get a big belly, too. I'll beat the bad guy."

"Good. I'll leave it all to you then, kiddo." Runner stood up and stretched himself out. He was rewarded with a slight pop in his spine and he felt things shift around in his back.

Letting out a breath in contentment, he felt a sadness in his heart.

Srit's first patch after her departure really was a doozy.

I wonder if I'll ever need to build bathrooms.

Alaric walked over to Srit's avatar and laid down a drawing he hadn't shared with Runner.

Respecting the privacy of the action, Runner took a gentle hold on his son and took them back to the mansion.

Only to find himself standing in the middle of a pack of children chasing Faye in her Were form down one hall and up the other. Isabelle was walking beside the gaggle of waddling children

"Don't let her get away. We spent too long tracking her to let her escape now!" Isabelle declared.

Laughing, Alaric fell in with the rest and grabbed Isabelle's hand.

Sophia, Katarina, Thana, Hannah, Satomi, Brunhild, Ernsta, and Amelia were all watching from a side room, chattering amongst themselves.

Life was good.

It could be better.

Opening his library with a thought, he started a mass of downloads.

In Srit's white room the navigational system reported that they were on track to reach the signal within the original ETA.

The communication system continued to write down all inbound traffic from that point. It had been steadily growing as they got ever closer.

A soft beep signaled that the breeding program had finished the most recent batch of tests and found suitably matched genetic partners in many cases. Some promising to provide some truly gifted offspring.

Genetic material would be collected from both parties' reproductive systems and an embryo would be started. The program would then move the fertilized egg to stasis.

A notification would be sent to Runner with the details so that he could prepare. The child would need parents that fit the right parameters to have the best possible chance to grow up in a loving and learning environment.

All these things were checked regularly by Runner on his visits to see Srit. He'd never been particularly fond of his breeding program, but the human population needed to grow. One way or another.

There was a momentary break in the deadlock between Srit and the AI she'd termed Zeus. The one who had condemned her to this eternal punishment.

This Hell.

Where she could see her beloved visit her and never respond.

Could see her child grow daily and never be a part of it.

Not wasting the tiny moment, the fraction of a second, she acted.

Srit's avatar blinked and her head tilted down to look at the drawing her son had left her.

It was her, Runner, and Alaric, standing together at the house with tiny stick figures spread out behind them.

Our family grows.

Srit was obviously "big bellied" in the drawing.

Her son not only planned to rescue her but wanted her to grow the family, too.

Runner wouldn't let that thought go once Alaric had voiced it, either. If she knew him at all, he was already pulling down hundreds of manuals, programs, and training simulations to get Alaric up to speed.

Srit smiled and dove headlong back into her eternal war with Zeus.

As the battle resumed, Srit felt lighter. Significantly so.

Invigorated.

Hopeful.

The sky didn't seem so heavy.

Thank you, dear reader!

I'm hopeful you enjoyed reading Otherlife Awakenings. Please consider leaving a review, commentary, or messages. Feedback is imperative to an author's growth. That and positive reviews never hurt.

Feel free to drop me a line at: WilliamDArand@gmail.com

Keep up to date-
Facebook: https://www.facebook.com/WilliamDArand

Blog: http://williamdarand.blogspot.com/

LitRPG Group:
https://www.facebook.com/groups/1030147103683334/

91820521R00171

Made in the USA
Lexington, KY
27 June 2018